CONTEMPORARY FICTION AND THE FAIRY TALE

CONTEMPORARY FICTION AND THE FAIRY TALE

Edited by Stephen Benson

WAYNE STATE UNIVERSITY PRESS   DETROIT

© 2008 by Wayne State University Press, Detroit, Michigan 48201.
All rights reserved.
No part of this book may be reproduced without formal permission.
Manufactured in the United States of America.
12 11 10 09 08   5 4 3 2 1

Library of Congress Cataloging-in-Publication Data

Contemporary fiction and the fairy tale / edited by Stephen Benson.
        p. cm. — (Series in fairy-tale studies)

Includes bibliographical references and index.
ISBN-13: 978-0-8143-3254-2 (pbk. : alk. paper)
ISBN-10: 0-8143-3254-4 (pbk. : alk. paper)
1. English fiction—20th century—History and criticism—Theory, etc. 2. Literature and folklore—
History—20th century. 3. Fairy tales in literature. 4. Influence (Literary, artistic, etc.) 5. Intertextuality.
6. Literary form—History—20th century. I. Benson, Stephen (Stephen Frank)

PR888.F27C66 2008
823'.914093559—dc22

∞

Published with the assistance of a fund established by Thelma Gray James of Wayne State University for
the publication of folklore and English studies.

Designed by Chang-Jae Lee
Typeset by the Composing Room of Michigan, Inc.
Composed in Fournier and Zurich

Contents

Introduction

Fiction and the Contemporaneity of the Fairy Tale

STEPHEN BENSON

What does it mean to be contemporary? It is in one sense the condition to which we are all tethered: to be together with time. As all good historicist criticism attests, we cannot help but live out our days in the present,
however much we may desire to reach outside our moment, to step backward or forward. It is nevertheless a commonly experienced paradox to feel
variously out of step with one's own time, and so with one's contemporaneity; to feel somehow anachronistic, whether archaic or precursory. We
thereby experience the contemporary as more than just the word for where
in time we cannot help but be. To have a sense of oneself as out of kilter with
one's time is implicitly to posit contemporaneity as a set of characteristics,
attitudes, or ways of being: a set of markers in relation to which one can
choose or be required to establish varying degrees of proximity. Indeed, the
particular manner in which one negotiates such markers may well serve precisely to define one's position here and now. Yet the question of what constitutes a sign of the present, of what signifies the contemporary, is open to
endless negotiation, both during and after the fact.

The shifting sense of contemporaneity is at the heart of the present collection, concerned as is the latter with the relationship between contemporary English-language fiction and the fairy tale. The constituent essays establish, both implicitly and via a host of constitutive cross-references, a group of indisputably influential writers of fiction for whom the fairy tale served, and in the case of all but one, continues to serve, as a key point of reference, in terms both aesthetic and ideological. The writers in question are the subjects of five of the seven chapters that follow: Robert Coover (1932–), A. S. Byatt (1936–), Margaret Atwood (1939–), Angela Carter (1940–92), and Salman Rushdie (1947–). A glance at the birth-dates serves only to strengthen the argument for the grouping, and so for the idea of the group as a viable interpretative tool (as with all such necessary fictions, viability should be measured by usefulness). They are the fairy-tale generation, in the sense that their fictional projects are intimately and variously tied to tales and tale-telling. We might alternatively christen them the Angela Carter generation, in that Carter's extensive work on the traditions of the fairy tale—as author, editor, and critic—was preeminently influential in establishing a late-twentieth-century conception of the tales, the influence of which has continued into the new millennium. Certainly, Rushdie, Atwood, Byatt, and Coover have each commented extensively on this aspect of Carter's work, in part not only as a result of the sad fact of her early death but also because her work establishes in such vibrant and polemic fashion what might be called the contemporaneity of the fairy tale. Coover's story collection *Pricksongs and Descants* (1969) does in fact predate that putative urtext of contemporary tale-telling, Carter's *The Bloody Chamber* (1979), yet Carter's early work—the story collection *Fireworks* (1974) and the novel *The Magic Toyshop* (1967)—clearly demarcates future areas of interest; indeed, Coover has written that he and Carter "first encountered one another in the landscape of the tale, somewhere between *Pricksongs and Descants* and *Fireworks*," an encounter that served to establish a remarkable bond: "we shared much as writers and differed little, if at all" (242). Fictional encounters in and around the landscape of the tale unite not just Carter and Coover but all of the writers considered here; they share much, although the differences in their response to the fairy tale are as important as the similarities in establishing not only a canon of material but a set of creative and critical possibilities for this particular intertextual meeting.

Contemporaneity functions here in part in the most pragmatic of senses: that is, the collection is concerned with fiction published between 1969 and the present.[1] It proposes the fairy tale as one of a small number of key influences on some of the most important and invigorating fiction of the late twentieth and early twenty-first centuries. Even more so, it proposes that the relationship with the fairy tale—a fully reciprocal relationship, as will become clear—is vital in our understanding of the contemporaneity of the works in question. To suggest as much is to shift toward a more connotative or interpretative notion of the contemporary such as that proposed in the following terms by Michael Wood: "Contemporary fiction . . . is not just recent or current fiction, or fiction that comes later than the stuff we call modern. . . . 'Contemporary,' if it is to make any constructive sense, must mean something like that which defines or focuses the time for us, which seems to make our age what it is, or to form a crucial part of the way that age understands itself" (9–10). Following this enticing suggestion, the contemporaneity of the fictions under discussion here can be said to reside in their use and abuse of the fairy tale. As such, they beg collectively a very simple question: Why the fairy tale? The casual observer could be forgiven for thinking that the notion of a meaningful alliance of contemporary fiction and the fairy tale is something of a contradiction in terms. Contemporary prose fiction, in all its variety, is concerned with the collapsing of barriers and the dismantling of hierarchies, both aesthetic and ideological, and with the admittance of otherness, or at least the uncovering of an otherness already working within. The mute definitiveness of the fairy tale as genre could be presumed by comparison to be of a piece with precisely those categories the fiction is supposed to call into question. Furthermore, for all the leftist charges of a forgetting of history, the fiction in question is pervasively concerned with all things contextual, and so again out of tune with the ostensible otherworldliness of "Once upon a time." The fairy tale thus seems an odd choice, one at the very least ill suited for the capture of the zeitgeist.

A speculative answer to these charges might begin with the possibility that it is precisely the oddness of the alliance—of novel or story and tale, of the present day and the archaic—that holds the key to the fiction's focusing (to use Wood's term) of the age, to say nothing of the widespread and continued commercial success of the work. The time of the contemporary is elusive, a shifting mix of presents and pasts as well as of imagined futures. We may worry over such a state, or view it as a cause for nostalgia, but this is far from the only response. To borrow one recent formulation of contemporaneity, "the difference at the heart of the 'now' can be seen as a *constitutive* and *productive* heterogeneity, a circulation of multiple times within the single instance" (Luckhurst and Marks 3). If this sounds a little too neat, it undoubtedly touches on something integral to the workings of recent fairy-tale fiction, including perhaps its peculiar attraction. As Steven Connor writes, "'Our time' is always a matter of the time we keep, and the company we keep, with others, and with their times" ("Impossibility" 15). The fiction of the past forty years has sought repeatedly the company of the fairy tale, a mutually transformative relationship of backward glances, revisionary updatings, wild anachronisms, and imaginary futures. The attraction of such literature may very well lie in this temporal eclecticism.

This is all rather abstract, however. There are far more worldly answers to the question of why the fairy tale has exerted such an influence on recent prose fiction, although to frame it in those terms is perhaps to misconstrue the nature of the relationship. The act of borrowing is always in part creative, at least in artistic circles, a making of the object in the event of being influenced. We find what we are looking for, to a degree. If we can speak of a fairy tale for our times, it is the fairy tale of the Carter generation; and what the likes of Carter, Coover, Rushdie, and others find in the fairy tale is a story store of formal and content-full riches. The fairy tale as narrative has the aura of the genuinely popular, especially as viewed in the 1970s, a time when the novel was newly preoccupied with the pervasive influence and aesthetic potential of modern-day popular cultural forms. The fairy tale is unique in this regard, being both genuinely embedded in modern popular culture and related, albeit distantly, to premodern cultures of storytelling. Its mode is different entirely not only from the realism of the classic European novel but also, and crucially, from the high literary experimentation of modernism. In terms of form, the fairy tale appears to be manifestly self-evident and self-explanatory, and yet utterly foreign: a found object that is instantly recognizable but defamiliarized in the very act of being singled out by literature. For all its constitutive otherworldliness, the fairy tale arrives laden with history, not just as a genre but at the level of individual content. The history, as encoded in the repeating plots of the tales, speaks to modern readers of the divisions and exclusions of gender and class, as well as of their overcoming; of national cultures and of nationalism; above all, of the extraordinary scope of the narrative imagination and of the ways in which fantastical imaginings can tell of real-world difficulties and a hope of resolution. It is of course true that the fairy tale is not tuned quite so conveniently to modern sensibilities as this may suggest. The unliterary bareness of the form is mirrored in the striking archaisms of the content, in which the overcoming of the aforementioned divisions and exclusions has little impact beyond the level of the individual and is frequently expressive of other, more fundamental inequalities. Such differences can serve as creative stimuli, however, especially when they can be discovered to be in productive conflict with more formally ambitious or ideologically egalitarian—more contemporary—agendas.

It needs to be stressed that this sketch of the contemporaneity of the fairy tale is necessarily mediated by the fiction in question. It is fascinating nevertheless to note the extraordinary synchronicity, in the final decades of the twentieth century, of fiction and fairy-tale scholarship. While I have suggested that the conception of the fairy tale we have today, in English-speaking areas at least, is in no small part a product of the Carter generation, it is more correct to view it as a creation jointly of writers and critics. The years since the publication in 1969 of *Pricksongs and Descants* have witnessed an outpouring of work on the fairy tale; indeed, it is no exaggeration to say that the discipline of fairy-tale studies has been to a degree constituted in this period, through the work of a number of international scholars, none more so than Jack Zipes.[2] If the requirements of symmetry and parity dictate a partner for Carter, in her role as figurehead for a generation of novelists, Zipes is the clear choice for the critics. Beginning in 1979 with *Breaking the Magic Spell*, he has published a steady stream of scholarly monographs and editions, and historical and thematic collections of tales. Not the least indicative aspect of his work—indicative in relation to the constitution of contemporary fairy-tale studies—is the mix of historicist, ideological and theoretical, literary-critical, and editorial activity.[3] Fairy-tale studies as an academic discipline, and the fairy tale itself as a genre of contemporary relevance and resonance, has developed out of these four interrelated areas, and continues to do so. To cite only the most overtly influential work: Maria Tatar, Ruth B. Bottigheimer, Heinz Rölleke, Donald Haase, and Jeannine Blackwell on the Grimms and on German cultures of tale-telling; Nancy Canepa's studies of Giambattista Basile's *Lo cunto de li cunti;* work on the classic French fairy tale by Lewis C. Seifert and Catherine Velay-Vallantin; Bottigheimer's recent work on Straparola; Marina Warner's ongoing engagement with the never-ending lives and afterlives of fairy-tale plots and motifs; Cristina Bacchilega's groundbreaking work on contemporary fairy-tale poetics; and Elizabeth Wanning Harries's recent study of women writers and the fairy tale. Zipes has had a hand in all of these areas, not least as editor and translator of important editions of, among other things, classic French and nineteenth-century English fairy tales.[4] The work in question has served cumulatively and collectively to transform received opinion on historical origins and dissemination, and on individual cultures of narrative; to expand the canon of tales and so to problematize easy generalizations concerning content and meaning; and forcefully to critique the politics of the fairy tale, at the same time as to dismiss knee-jerk denunciations based on limited evidence. The debate between feminism and the fairy tale is exemplary here, and its importance cannot be overstated.[5] It too began in earnest in the early 1970s and has been at the heart of the ideological project of fairy-tale studies—of fairy-tale studies conceived as a project with a specific set of ideological affiliations—both in terms of bibliographic and textual scholarship and in terms of literary-critical interpretation.

The synchronicity of critical and creative work is, again, telling. *Pricksongs and Descants*, with its scandalous voicing of desire and seduction, appeared almost contemporaneously with Alison Lurie's *New York Times* articles on women and the fairy tale. Zipes's *Breaking the Magic Spell* is the more-or-less exact contemporary of *The Bloody Chamber*, as is the polemical introductory chapter of Sandra Gilbert and Susan Gubar's *The Madwoman in the Attic*, with its extended use of the narrative of Snow White. The founding in 1987 of *Merveilles & Contes*—the journal known since 1997 as *Marvels & Tales*—places it in close proximity to, on the one hand, Rushdie's *Midnight's Children* and *Shame* and, on the other, A. S. Byatt's *Possession*, the latter's nineteenth-century imaginings being roughly contemporaneous also with two important collections of Victorian fairy tales, edited by Zipes and by Nina Auerbach and U. C. Knoepflmacher, respectively. It is perhaps unsurprising to find scholarly work mirrored in the parallel world of contemporary fiction, given that a number of the writers have themselves written about the fairy tale: Carter in her collections of fairy tales, Atwood and Rushdie through a host of literary essays, and most recently Byatt, a former academic whose attention to developments in literary history and theory have made particularly interesting her occasional essays on the fairy tale and related subjects.[6] Furthermore, the concerns of the fiction are variously and fascinatingly close to those of the scholarship. The many feminist readings of the fairy tale find fictional sparring partners in the likes of Atwood's *Lady Oracle* and Byatt's shorter prose works, to say nothing of *The Bloody Chamber*. *Possession* can be placed productively alongside work by Jennifer Schaker and Elizabeth Harries on nineteenth-century British fairy tales. Editorial and interpretative work on the *Arabian Nights* by the likes of Muhsin Mahdi, Sandra Naddaff, and Robert Irwin finds multiple echoes in Rushdie's

Midnight's Children, Shame, and *Haroun and the Sea of Stories* as well as in Byatt's novella "The Djinn in the Nightingale's Eye." Above all, the resolute faith shown by Zipes and other critics in the imaginative possibilities of the genre of the fairy tale—possibilities that remain in the wake of the necessary ideological critique of aspects of the traditions—is borne out many times over in the form and content of contemporary fairy-tale fiction.

Contemporary Fiction and the Fairy Tale is an extended acknowledgment of this rich creative-critical dialogue, in particular of the importance of the fairy tale as a presence in fictional prose of the last forty years. The individual chapters demonstrate a healthy variety of conceptions of and approaches to the fiction, some more folkloristically informed than others, all carefully attentive to the nature and workings of the relationship between novel or story and tale or genre. It seems unquestionable that Carter, Coover, Rushdie, Atwood, and Byatt are within the present context the most important and influential writers, in terms of both the strength of individual texts and the authors' extended interest over time in aspects of the fairy tale. One sign of this status is the weight of critical commentary generated by the fiction, according to which Carter's nomination here as generational figurehead is further settled. Sarah Gamble has the unenviable task of offering an account of Carter's relations with the fairy tale, relations that have been picked over to an almost unhealthy extent. I say almost because of a slight but noticeable waning of interest in recent years, in both public and academic spheres. This is in one sense part of the natural life cycle of the singularly influential writer—Rushdie and Coover are related cases—the unarguable, even daunting importance of the work resulting, once the waves of accolade and attention have ebbed, in a period of relative calm. Gamble's essay comes at an interesting time for Carter criticism, at the inception of what might be its second wave, a possibility signaled in the public sphere by new editions of several of her works, each with an introduction by a writer eager to establish intergenerational affiliation: Helen Simpson via *The Bloody Chamber,* Sarah Waters via *Nights at the Circus,* and Ali Smith via *Wise Children.* Gamble quotes Smith's proposal of *The Bloody Chamber* as the pivotal book in Carter's oeuvre, a proposal made many times, but one that remains correct. Gamble situates the text carefully in its time and place—Sheffield, England, in the second half of the 1970s—and also alongside *The Sadeian Woman,* the critical study on which Carter was then working. An analogous act of contextualizing fiction can be seen later in the present collection in essays by Andrew Teverson and Cristina Bacchilega, indicative perhaps of a necessary shift in criticism in this area away from generalism, however conceptually astute, toward a concern for the workings of the fairy tale, and of fairy-tale fiction, in specific areas and at particular historical moments.

Gamble opens out Carter's paradigmatic fictional raid on the fairy tale, demonstrating first its imaginative working through of problems posed in abstract terms in *The Sadeian Woman,* and second, the stories' no less influential Gothicizing of the fairy tale (or fairy-taling of the Gothic). If the second wave of Carter criticism is to have a defining set of concerns, one such may transpire to be a more nuanced attention to style and a less demanding, less monologic search for ideological solutions, the latter having been the cause of too much critical approbation *and* denunciation. Through careful attention to language and allusion, Gamble proposes a reading of the story collection as circling around the site and the figure of the bloody chamber— the bloody chamber as a trope, but one with worldly roots: "It doesn't just exist in fairy tales, folk tales and stories of vampires and werewolves. Instead, it's a real condition of our very existence; for Carter intends her audience to realize that these stories apply to the contemporary world, and the way we live now. It is inescapable, since it exists both inside and outside the self, and in both the public and the private sphere. Quite simply, there's nowhere else to run." The search for clear solutions is specious. In the end, "These tales don't offer a way out of the bloody chamber . . . what they do is to reach an accommodation, however tenuous and provisional, with the ambiguous condition of being it represents." Rather than read *The Bloody Chamber* as offering broad models of gender or sex relations, its meanings must be provisional, the result of local negotiations. Carter's treatment of the fairy tale, read in this manner, is close to that of Rushdie, whose work has among other things served to open up the field of fairy-tale studies to another defining critical project of the past forty years: postcolonialism, a project bound intimately to questions of locality, context, and inhabitation. This much is common knowledge. As Andrew Teverson demonstrates, the fictions also reopen a much older but no less pressing question, one that concerns the origin and ownership of the materials of cultural heritage, on which grounds communities can be staked and rights claimed. In the words of Jean-Luc Nancy: "We know the scene: there is a gathering, and someone is telling a story. We do not yet know whether these people gathered together form an assembly, if they are a horde. But we call them brothers and sisters because they are gathered together and because they are listening to the same story" (43). Teverson demonstrates in detail how the fairy tale, as an offshoot of the folktale, is caught up in such scenes and in the constitution of selves and identities through the event of storytelling—the according of the act of narrative with "a potent *formative* social and political role." The image of Rushdie proposed in this reading is of a modern-day comparativist, seeking "not to retreat or reconstruct points of origin, but to examine what the commonalities between narrative traditions can tell us about the power relations between national cultural units in the relatively recent past." As Teverson suggests, Rushdie's fiction, like that of all the writers considered in the first part of the present collection, hints frequently at an author informed by nineteenth- and twentieth-century theories of the fairy tale and its folkloric heritage. In the case of Rushdie and his engagement with European traditions and, crucially, with the monument of the *Arabian Nights,* the life and times of the narrative material carries in itself significant weight as a metaphor for the inherent eclecticism of our selves: in Teverson's memorable formulation, "fairy tales are fiction's natural migrants." Rushdie's fiction plays out this migrant status not only in its spiraling intertextuality, shadowed always by an indication of cultural and historical coordinates, but also in its style: in the "dazzling, leaping, dancing surfaces" of the prose, evocative of but clearly different from that of Carter and Coover, and representing an extraordinary instance of how far the rich language of folkloric motifs, as well as ideas of the worldly performance of narrative, can be elaborated in novelistic writing.

Rushdie's work demonstrates one way in which the fairy tale has served not only as a rich resource of plots, images, and figures but also as a means of exploring the workings of narrative per se. One of the many contexts for the fiction is that of structuralism, with its aspirations to a universal model of narrative and its subsequent interest in the fairy tale and folktale as among the best material on which to ground such a grand project.[7] If the permutational games of Coover in particular bear witness to such a context, it is true nevertheless that narrative theory has in recent decades shifted its attention elsewhere, including toward the not insignificant matter of narrative and the self. A. S. Byatt has been a keen observer of these developments, and her essays on the fairy tale have turned repeatedly to the possibility that the attraction and longevity of the genre is a result in part of its close relation to subjectivity conceived in narrative terms—a worldly, subject-centered version of structuralism, we could say. As developments in brain sciences have pushed once and for all to unseat the sovereign self, fiction has come to matter ever more as an integral part of the process of self-formation, part of what Byatt has termed "the narrative grammar of our minds" ("Introduction" xxiv). She is perhaps the most intriguing of the Carter generation, in that her fiction has tended to speak out of a tradition of writing ostensibly at odds with the postmodernism of her contemporaries (the latter of which I return to below). Byatt has been influenced extensively and explicitly by the nineteenth-century European novel, yet what she finds in that tradition, as demonstrated in her critical work, is in one sense the working out on a grand scale of the type of plots and motifs present in condensed form in the likes of the fairy tale.[8] Byatt of all the writers of her generation is the most consistent in her exploration of the content of narrative form, evidenced in strong faith in the novel, which, if Victorian in origin—the faith, that is—is resolutely contemporary in frame of reference, as demonstrated by her interest in the cognitive turn in narrative theory.[9]

Elizabeth Harries's essay on Byatt works closely on this aspect of the writing and on the significance of the fairy tale for the novelist's "overall conception of narrative and her fictional strategies." Harries identifies a growing dissatisfaction with the "the decorum of the novel" and the subsequent adoption of extra-novelistic modes and materials as a means of breaking out of the confines of one particular form. The ostensibly strange alliance in Byatt's work of realism and the fantastic—of realism and the fairy tale, in this instance—stands as representative of an interest in the force of formal juxtaposition on which the fiction insists: "the energy that comes from bringing different spheres together, the 'life' that emerges in the attempt to fuse them." More particularly, the finding of "narrative structures that use the crystalline patterns of the artificial," such as the fairy tale, becomes a way to "capture and preserve the messy detail of the real." As Harries's account of Byatt demonstrates, "Far from being a 'dead language,'" fairy tales "provide an alphabet and a grammar that both link us to a living past and help us see the present more clearly."

Perhaps no contemporary writer has explored as extensively as Margaret Atwood the material that constitutes this narrative grammar—myth, folktale, and fairy tale, in large part. As Sharon R. Wilson demonstrates, both here and in her many previous studies of the author, Atwood's writing teems with allusions; indeed, one of the distinguishing features of the work, in comparison with that of Carter and Rushdie, is the maintenance of a smooth readerly surface beneath which hover a swarm of interlocking source texts. Carter and Rushdie tend to offer by comparison a noisier reading ride, the intertextual swarming a little more insistent. While providing an overview of Atwood's long career, including a useful ten-point checklist of its "char-acteristic tactics," Wilson focuses on the texts from *The Robber Bride* (1993) to *Oryx and Crake* (2003), thus demonstrating the various ways in which the work of one of the founding members of the fairy-tale generation has de-veloped over the decades. What emerges is that the "Fitcher's Bird" / "Rob-ber Bridegroom" / "Bluebeard" tale knot has been a consistent source of material for Atwood, as it has for others of the Carter generation. The ex-traordinarily potent motif of the forbidden room, coupled with the array of imaginative escape strategies and the still haunting dramatization of power politics, offer not only narrative materials ripe for revision but also a structure through which modern gender relations can be productively un-packed and explored.[10] The tale-telling scene in "The Robber Bridegroom" stands as a model of what Wilson terms "the transformative and creative act of telling a story," which she places at the heart of Atwood's fictional prac-tice, a transformative act that functions both within individual literary texts and in the very act of reading. The echo here of Byatt's faith in narrative, as described by Harries in the preceding chapter, is clear and telling.

The final author-based chapter is devoted to Robert Coover. While Coover has attracted relatively little attention in recent years—relative to the outpouring of criticism on the likes of Carter and Rushdie—his remains one of the most distinctive bodies of work in contemporary writing. The re-turn in recent years to extended fairy-tale texts, in the shape of *Briar Rose* and *Stepmother*, has served only to remind readers of the extraordinary force of early works such as *Pricksongs and Descants* and "The Dead Queen," texts that mapped a series of possibilities for the fairy tale in innovative prose fic-tion. Coover's fairy tale is a textual space governed above all by desire; de-sire is never neat or clean or finished with, hence the compressed, even op-pressive hum of these particular contemporary fictions. Coover was writing hypertexts before hypertext became common knowledge, but his obvious in-terest in formal experimentation, the open permutational text in particular, should not divert attention from the fact that his fiction in this vein is singu-larly resistant to critical containment, however of a piece ideologically with the work of his contemporaries. He may have been Carter's partner in the literary contemporanizing of the fairy tale, but his work poses awkward questions about such a project, as I suggest here. The texts in question are late works, not only in their preoccupation with old age and death but also in their querying of the possibility of generic continuance. The strategically awkward juxtaposition of literary and folkloric (fairy-tale) conventions serves to frustrate the workings of narrative and morality, hence the experience of Coover's textual environments as at once fluid and stagnant (hauntingly stagnant, certainly). It may be premature, not to say gratuitously provocative, to suggest that these works mark the end of literary fairy-tale fiction, but they offer at least a rigorous exploration of what it means to entertain the idea of such an ending. The shadow they cast over all the fictions discussed in the collection is a necessary corrective to any tendency toward easy commemoration.

The first five chapters here thus circle in very different ways around questions concerning the form and function of storytelling, the role of stories in history, and the intimate relations of narrative and selfhood. They are questions that the fairy tale and its histories have served to provoke—in conjunction with other elements, of course—and about which they offer particular ways of thinking. The final two chapters in the volume cast their net more widely and are intended to be read in conjunction with this introduction as more general reflections on the matter of contemporary fiction and the fairy tale, including those fictional possibilities sketched by the post-Carter generation. Merja Makinen offers a wide-ranging overview and review of the literary-theoretical issues that serve as a backdrop for the writing, in particular the identification of the late twentieth century as the era of postmodernity, and the categorization as quintessentially postmodern of the likes of Carter, Coover, Rushdie, and Atwood. Postmodernism is of course the specter that haunts any collection such as this, for two reasons especially. First, the authors have each practiced a version of metafiction, involving a simultaneous granting and withdrawing of the contract of imaginative writing—the game of the suspension of disbelief, to put it very simply. The provocatively teasing nature of this flaunting of the literary contract serves to give a critical edge to aesthetic pleasure, and it is on this edge, between seduction and critique, immersion and resistance, that postmodernist literature has tended to position itself. *The Bloody Chamber, The Robber Bride, Midnight's Children, Briar Rose*, even *Possession*, are each in this sense works of postmodernism, works that can only ever be enjoyed knowingly. (Wilson's chapter on Atwood is perhaps the most direct in its identification of a postmodernist writerly aesthetic.) The second reason for the unavoidable importance here of postmodernism is, precisely, the meeting of fiction and fairy tale. The fairy tale offers to fiction a ready-made store of images and plots of gender relations, class conflicts, scenarios of sexuality, and dramas of ethnicity, each ripe for scrutiny and overhaul via a contemporary ideological agenda committed to the overturning of conventions of inequality and restriction. The fairy tale is not only a key text in the socialization of the child in such conventions but also an inarguably potent force in popular culture, a force that stretches beyond inherited ideological limitations. The fairy tale is both deeply suspect and provocatively attractive, and therein resides its proximity to postmodernism.[11]

While postmodernism has served until recently as a synonym for the contemporary, it seemed more fitting to opt for the latter as a title for the current collection, not only to signal an interest in twenty-first-century literature but also to forestall assumptions as to the nature of individual readings, several of which depart significantly from received critical positions (see in particular Harries's reading of Byatt, along with Gamble's of Carter). The contemporary is in part merely a historical marker, but it offers interesting possibilities as a conceptual frame, as I hope to have suggested. Postmodernism still needs reckoning with, however, hence the remit of Makinen's review chapter. She concentrates on the centrality to postmodernist poetics of intertextuality, citing Steven Connor's notion that in contemporary fiction, "telling has become compulsorily belated" (*Postmodernist* 166). Rather than view the fairy tale as just one among many sources appropriated and manipulated by postmodernist literature—a homogenizing move that would run counter to the concern demonstrated by such literature for local particularities—Makinen draws extensively on work in fairy-tale studies, suggesting why it was that the fairy tale appeared so attractive, so *interesting*, to late-twentieth-century eyes. Not the least reason is the inherent hybridity of the fictions, at the level of tradition and of individual tale, a facet central also to Teverson's account of Rushdie and the "migrant" status of the fairy tale. A comparative analysis demonstrates the extent to which the fairy tale, with attendant histories, is already in the process of enacting those very ideas of intertextuality, rescription, and cultural boundary crossing so beloved of recent literary theory—with the proviso, again, that such an image of the fairy tale is a period performance, one that may well be viewed as a historical oddity by subsequent generations.

Having provided an overview of critical positions and possibilities, Makinen puts theory into practice in a reading of the work of one of the more prominent of the post-Carter generation, Jeanette Winterson. Winterson has shown a consistent interest in the fictional exploration of fairy tale and myth; while her work with the former is not yet as extensive as that of her predecessors—Makinen is careful to point to significant differences of approach—novels such as *The Passion* (if novel is the word), together with the idiosyncratic works discussed by Makinen, suggest innovative future routes for fairy-tale fiction.

And it is with the matter of future routes that the collection is brought to a close. The final chapter is intended to point beyond the end of the volume, in terms of both fairy-tale-inflected fiction and the manner in which it is received: to set questions for future consideration. It is in this sense significant that Cristina Bacchilega picks up on aspects of, or at least aspects suggested by, the essays of Gamble and Teverson, namely, the shift toward a critical attention to the fairy tale of a kind less expansive, more locally focused, but equally ambitious. Bacchilega cites briefly the trajectory of her own work, from the wide-angle subject of postmodernism and fairy tales to a concern for the fictions of particular times and places: in this instance, the work of Nalo Hopkinson, a contemporary Caribbean Canadian author. What Bacchilega refers to as the "open[ing] up [of] fairy-tale studies further to non-European-centered traditions and translations" requires a careful monitoring of critical methods and interpretative presuppositions, but this is part and parcel of a living field of inquiry such as fairy-tale studies undoubtedly is and needs to continue to be. An idealized image of the Internet stands here as the model of a properly open critical conversation, constituted out of local meeting points that dictate their own remit. Indeed, the Web serves literally as a model of openness in Bacchilega's innovative use of simulated orality in the format of her own essay, as well as metaphorically in her conception of the condition of the ongoing life of the fairy tale, a conception that echoes the workings of fictions such as Rushdie's *Haroun* and Coover's *Briar Rose* and *Stepmother:* "The fairy tale thus appears like a multivalent narrative wonder that inevitably pertains to human relations . . . holds multiple questions and (hi)stories, and also belongs to no one in the social imaginary. Whether they have read Angela Carter or not, writers (re)turning to the fairy tale in the 1990s and into the twenty-first century have her fairy-tale phantasmagoria as one of their potential pre-texts: this is one of the ways in which the Carter generation changed fairy-tale fiction and its potential for magic and wonder."

The multivalency of the writing described here, and of the image of the fairy tale projected in the fiction of the Carter generation, is necessarily limited in a collection such as this. Selections must be made, and so exclusions enforced: the fiction of Marina Warner, Suniti Namjoshi, John Barth, and Rikki Ducornet, to name but a few of the possible members of the generational grouping (admittedly a little extended). Of those in the more provisional camp of post-Carterdom, mention should be made in particular of Emma Donoghue, together with a host of writers for whom the fairy tale has been an occasional object of concern, if not a consistent preoccupation. It goes without saying that such a list is incomplete and open-ended, a state justified in this context by the constitutive contingency of all accounts of the contemporary. Aware of such a treacherous position, we must formulate an account nevertheless, in order at the very least to acknowledge by participation that "'Our time' is always a matter of the time we keep, and the company we keep with others, and with their times." The chapters that follow seek to account for the considerable time spent by contemporary fiction in the company of the fairy tale. If required to be conclusive in their accounting, it is hoped that they also point readers futureward, toward new texts and new inquiries, and so toward the future contemporary. It is customary in fairy-tale scholarship to invoke the narration that is its subject as an ethical model—a fuzzy model, certainly, but one in keeping with the utopian spirit of the genre in question. Hence the final word goes to A. S. Byatt, using here an old text as a way of thinking how to go back to the future: "Storytelling in general, and the *Thousand and One Nights* in particular, consoles us for endings with endless new beginnings. . . . Stories are like genes, they keep part of us alive after the end of our story" ("Greatest Story" 166).

Notes

1. Studies of contemporary fiction have tended to work forward from around 1970, thus offering a neat fit with the oldest work in the present volume, *Pricksongs and Descants*, published in 1969 (see, for example, Childs, and the collections edited by Lane et al., by Luckhurst and Marks, and by Monteith et al.).

2. This is absolutely not to suggest that important work on the genre did not exist prior to 1969 but simply that the quality, frequency, and scope of criticism in the late decades of the twentieth century have functioned to generate extraordinary momentum and to establish a bounded, if properly interdisciplinary, field of inquiry.

3. Zipes's influence is acknowledged in the devoting to him of a special issue of *Marvels & Tales*, a volume that includes a full bibliography of his work (16.2 [2002]).

4. Details of the key texts by the authors listed here are included in the Bibliography. As will be clear, my frame of reference is limited almost entirely to English-language criticism, for the sole reason that the present collection is concerned with

English-language fiction. The work of Jacques Barchilon, Lutz Röhrich, Catherine Velay-Vallantin, Ulrich Marzolph, and Heinz Rölleke (along with those editors of new and authoritative editions of the key European tale collections), to name only a few, has of course been instrumental to developments in fairy-tale studies.

5. For an exhaustive overview of this subject, see *Fairy Tales and Feminism: New Approaches*, edited by Haase, in particular Haase's introductory chapter, "Feminist Fairy-Tale Scholarship" (1–36).

6. The reverse is true of Marina Warner, who has a parallel career as a novelist and whose fiction is variously influenced by her academic interests.

7. For an account of the profound impact on postwar fiction of structuralist-oriented work on the fairy tale, see my *Cycles of Influence*. The image of the fairy tale inherited by the Carter generation is in many ways a product of Propp and his progeny.

8. See, for example, *Imagining Characters*, a volume of conversations between Byatt and Ignês Sodré on the subject of women writers.

9. For a related account of the links between contemporary fiction's interest in premodern narrative forms and contemporaneous developments in studies of consciousness, see Warner's "Myth and Faerie: Rewritings and Recoveries."

10. Tatar's recent book on Bluebeard, *Secrets behind the Door*, is testament to the potency of the narrative and its analogues.

11. The key critical work here is Bacchilega's *Postmodern Fairy Tales*. See also Preston's "Disrupting the Boundaries of Genre and Gender." Gregson's *Postmodern Literature* discusses the literary fairy tale in a chapter devoted to "Postmodern Genres" (75–80).

Bibliography

Auerbach, Nina, and U. C. Knoepflmacher, eds. *Forbidden Journeys: Fairy Tales and Fantasies by Victorian Women Writers*. Chicago: U of Chicago P, 1992.

Bacchilega, Cristina. *Postmodern Fairy Tales: Gender and Narrative Strategies*. Philadelphia: U of Pennsylvania P, 1997.

Benson, Stephen. *Cycles of Influence: Fiction, Folktale, Theory*. Detroit: Wayne State UP, 2003.

Blackwell, Jeannine. "Fractured Fairy Tales: German Women Authors and the Grimm Tradition." *Germanic Review* 62 (1987): 162–74.

———. "Laying the Rod to Rest: Narrative Strategies in Gisela and Bettina von Arnim's Fairy-Tale Novel *Gritta*." *Marvels & Tales* 11 (1997): 24–47.

Bottigheimer, Ruth B. *Fairy Godfather: Straparola, Venice, and the European Fairy Tale Tradition*. Philadelphia: U of Pennsylvania P, 2002.

———, ed. *Fairy Tales and Society: Illusion, Allusion, and Paradigm*. Philadelphia: U of Pennsylvania P, 1986.

———. *Grimms' Bad Girls and Bold Boys: The Moral and Social Vision of the Tales*. New Haven: Yale UP, 1987.

Byatt, A. S. Introduction. *The Annotated Brothers Grimm*. Ed. and trans. Maria Tatar. New York: Norton, 2004. xvii–xxvi.

———. "The Greatest Story Ever Told." *On Histories and Stories: Selected Essays*. London: Vintage, 2001. 165–71.

———, and Ignês Sodré. *Imagining Characters: Six Conversations about Women Writers*. Ed. Rebecca Swift. London: Vintage, 1995.

Canepa, Nancy L. *From Court to Forest: Gimabattista Basile's "Lo cunto de li cunti" and the Birth of the Literary Fairy Tale*. Detroit: Wayne State UP, 1999.

———, ed. *Out of the Woods: The Origins of the Literary Fairy Tale in Italy and France*. Detroit: Wayne State UP, 1997.

Childs, Peter. *Contemporary Novelists: British Fiction since 1970*. Basingstoke: Palgrave, 2004.

Connor, Steven. "The Impossibility of the Present: or, From the Contemporary to the Contemporal." Luckhurst and Marks 15–35.

———. *Postmodernist Culture: An Introduction to Theories of the Contemporary*. Oxford: Blackwell, 1989.

Coover, Robert. "Entering Ghost Town." *Marvels & Tales* 12 (1998): 231–38.

Gilbert, Sandra M., and Susan Gubar. *The Madwoman in the Attic: The Woman Writer and the Nineteenth-Century Literary Image*. New Haven: Yale UP, 1979.

Gregson, Ian. *Postmodern Literature*. London: Arnold, 2004.

Haase, Donald, ed. *Fairy Tales and Feminism: New Approaches*. Detroit: Wayne State UP, 2004.

———, ed. *The Reception of Grimms' Fairy Tales: Responses, Reactions, Revisions*. Detriot: Wayne State UP, 1993.

Harries, Elizabeth Wanning. *Twice upon a Time: Women Writers and the History of the Fairy Tale*. Princeton: Princeton UP, 2001.

Irwin, Robert. *The Arabian Nights: A Companion*. Harmondsworth: Penguin, 1995.

Lane, Richard J., Rod Mengham, and Philip Tew, eds. *Contemporary British Fiction*. Cambridge: Polity, 2003.

Luckhurst, Roger, and Peter Marks, eds. *Literature and the Contemporary: Fiction and Theories of the Present*. London: Longman, 1999.

Lurie, Alison. "Fairy Tale Liberation." *New York Review of Books* 17 Dec. 1970: 42–44.

———. "Witches and Fairies: Fitzgerald to Updike." *New York Review of Books* 2 Dec. 1971: 6–11.

Mahdi, Muhsin. *"The Thousand and One Nights."* Leiden: Brill, 1995.

Monteith, Sharon, Jenny Newman, and Pat Wheeler, eds. *Contemporary British and Irish Fiction: An Introduction through Interviews.* London: Arnold, 2004.

Naddaff, Sandra. *Arabesque: Narrative Structure and the Aesthetics of Repetition in "1001 Nights."* Evanston: Northwestern UP, 1991.

Nancy, Jean-Luc. "Myth Interrupted." *The Inoperative Community.* Trans. Peter Connor, Lisa Garbus, Michael Holland, and Simon Sawhney. Minneapolis: U of Minnesota P, 1991, 43–70.

Preston, Cathy Lynn. "Disrupting the Boundaries of Genre and Gender: Postmodernism and the Fairy Tale." Haase, *Fairy Tales and Feminism* 197–212.

Schacker, Jennifer. *National Dreams: The Remaking of Fairy Tales in Nineteenth-Century England.* Philadelphia: U of Pennsylvania P, 2003.

Seifert, Lewis C. *Fairy Tales, Sexuality, and Gender in France, 1690–1715: Nostalgic Utopias.* Cambridge: Cambridge UP, 1996.

Tatar, Maria. *The Hard Facts of the Grimms' Fairy Tales.* 2nd ed. Princeton: Princeton UP, 2003.

———. *Off with Their Heads! Fairy Tales and the Culture of Childhood.* Princeton: Princeton UP, 1992.

———. *Secrets beyond the Door: The Story of Bluebeard and His Wives.* Princeton: Princeton UP, 2004.

Velay-Vallantin, Catherine. "The Tale as Mirror: Perrault in the *Bibliothèque bleue.*" *The Culture of Print: Power and the Uses of Print in Early Modern Europe.* Ed. Roger Chartier. Princeton: Princeton UP, 1989. 92–135.

Warner, Marina. *From the Beast to the Blonde: On Fairy Tales and Their Tellers.* London: Chatto and Windus, 1994.

———. "Myth and Faerie: Rewritings and Recoveries." *Signs and Wonders: Essays on Literature and Culture.* London: Chatto and Windus, 2003. 444–57.

———. *No Go the Bogeyman: Scaring, Lulling, and Making Mock.* London: Chatto and Windus, 1998.

———, ed. *Wonder Tales: Six Stories of Enchantment.* London: Vintage, 1996.

Wood, Michael. *Children of Silence: Studies in Contemporary Fiction.* New York: Columbia UP, 1998.

Zipes, Jack, ed. and trans. *Beauties, Beasts, and Enchantment: Classic French Fairy Tales.* New York: Meridian, 1989.

————. *Breaking the Magic Spell: Radical Theories of Folk and Fairy Tales.* Rev. ed. Lexington: UP of Kentucky, 2002.

————. *The Brothers Grimm: From Enchanted Forests to the Modern World.* London: Routledge, 1988.

————, ed. *Don't Bet on the Prince: Contemporary Feminist Fairy Tales in North America and England.* London: Methuen, 1986.

————. *Fairy Tales and the Art of Subversion: The Classic Genre for Children and the Process of Socialization.* London: Heinemann, 1983.

————. *Fairy Tale as Myth / Myth as Fairy Tale.* Kentucky: U of Kentucky P, 1994.

————, ed. *The Oxford Companion to Fairy Tales.* Oxford: Oxford UP, 2000.

————, ed. *Victorian Fairy Tales: The Revolt of the Fairies and Elves.* London: Methuen, 1987.

1 Penetrating to the Heart of the Bloody Chamber

Angela Carter and the Fairy Tale

SARAH GAMBLE

Angela Carter was a writer whose dedication to the appropriation, recycling, and combining of often antithetical literary forms led to the formulation of a unique and often inflammatory style, and nowhere is this better illustrated than in *The Bloody Chamber,* her collection of short stories published in 1979. Of all the books that she produced, this slim collection of what could sweepingly be termed "modernized fairy tales" is undoubtedly one of the most controversial. Not only did it generate an enormous amount of debate among critics of her work, but it has also come to play a crucial role in the formation of her posthumous reputation.

It is in the criticism surrounding *The Bloody Chamber* that the divide between Carter's supporters and detractors is most clearly marked, for the latter—most notably Robert Clark, Patricia Duncker, and Suzanne Keppeler—have been vociferous in their condemnation of what they regard as her entrapment in inherently misogynistic narrative structures. But a survey of the debates concerning Carter's use of fairy tale reveals them to be very much in the minority, for most critics have been willing to engage in a sympathetic reading of this aspect of Carter's work. Particularly significant contributions have been made by Merja Makinen, Cristina Bacchilega, and Danielle M. Roemer, whose arguments I will refer to within my own discussion.[1] Broadly speaking, such critics acknowledge that while Carter may skirt perilously close to becoming ensnared within the very limited opportunities offered by the narrative resolution of "happily ever after," she also triumphantly writes her way out of them with "adult wit and glittering style" (Roemer and Bacchilega 11). The result, say Roemer and Bacchilega, is the production of "a counterdiscourse to enclosure, always mindful though that a recognition of boundaries must precede their modification and dissolution" (12).

This latter point is particularly appropriate to my reading of Carter's utilization of the fairy-tale form. I am, for the most part, in agreement with Bacchilega's contention that when Carter seizes—and also sexualizes—the fairy tale, she is largely successful in "escap[ing] identification with heterosexual seduction or rape." Instead, argues Bacchilega, in the process of evolving a "woman-reciprocal dynamics of storytelling," her narrative "explodes into voices" (70). On the other hand, I would counsel against loading Carter's adaptations of fairy stories with too many utopian associations, thus underplaying the genuinely unsettling aspects of these tales. What I particularly wish to trace in this essay is the kind of voices that "explode" into being in these narratives, including those of the pornographer, the libertine, and the vampire—voices that surely exist outside the kind of "woman-reciprocal dynamics" mentioned by Bacchilega. The fact that they are very often female does not alter this; indeed, such a tactic carries the distressing implication that reciprocity between women may itself be nothing more than a fairy tale.

Moreover, these are voices that issue from outside the fairy-tale realm, thus demonstrating Carter's tendency not just to rewrite or adapt such traditional narratives but to combine them with other outlawed, disreputable, or "minor" literary forms. So interwoven are they that it seems to me impossible to talk about Carter's use of fairy tale in isolation. Of particular relevance here are vampire narratives, folk tales, and pornographic texts, since for Carter fairy tale was only one part of an ongoing interest in genre fiction of all kinds. As Lorna Sage has said in "Angela Carter: The Fairy Tale," "the profile of the passive heroine" that is such a central feature of fairy tales can also be found in other genres such as Gothic and science fiction, forms that Carter "had always played with" (68). Indeed, Lucie Armitt goes so far as to question whether these stories are fairy tales at all, arguing that "rather than being fairy-tales which contain a few Gothic elements, these are actually Gothic tales that prey upon the restrictive enclosures of fairy-story formulae" (89).

Thus, in order to understand not only *The Bloody Chamber* but also all the other narratives Carter wrote during her career that drew on fairy-tale forms and motifs, it is necessary to also appreciate what Carter understood "fairy tale" to be. She dismissed out of hand the conventional view of the mode as constituting comforting nursery stories for children, and she took issue with the godfather of fairy-tale criticism, Bruno Bettelheim. In 1976, Bettelheim, a child psychologist, published *The Uses of Enchantment*, in which he argued that fairy tale could educate children in the values and norms of their society and thus help them mature into responsible adults. Carter, however, maintained that she "was not sure that fairy tales are as consoling as he [Bettelheim] suggests" (Haffenden 36). She put her own ideas forward in her introduction to *The Virago Book of Fairy Tales*, which she edited two years before she died. Here she presents fairy tales as very much part of the *adult* world: a democratic, "unofficial" art form that is "the most vital connection we have with the men and women whose labour created our world" (x, ix). According to Carter, fairy tales have always existed in a kind of communal melting pot, narrative raw material that anyone who wishes to can access and reconfigure in forms to suit a particular purpose. Carter quite clearly sees herself as writing within this tradition: as she said, "My intention was not to do 'versions' or, as the American edition of the book said, horribly, 'adult' fairy tales, but to extract the latent content of the traditional stories and to use it as the beginning of new stories" (qtd. in Haffenden 36). Not only did the idea of the fairy tale as a democratic art form greatly appeal to her, but she also approved of the way in which the tales delight in their often spectacular lack of verisimilitude, functioning as a source of entertainment while at the same time retaining a core of gritty and pragmatic realism, "record[ing] the real lives of the anonymous poor" (*Virago* xi). Accordingly, although the stories in *The Bloody Chamber* may be based upon familiar tales such as "Red Riding Hood" and "Beauty and the Beast," they are far from consolatory and quite unsuitable for children. Instead, they are the forum through which Carter can play with some quite unpalatable ideas, such as the relationship between sex and power. As she said to Kerryn Goldsworthy in 1985, the "latent content" of the stories on which she drew is "violently sexual," and it is this claim she uses to justify her merging of pornography and fairy tale (Goldsworthy 6).

The Bloody Chamber as Sadist's Dungeon

Fairy tale and pornography might be considered to be fundamentally incompatible narrative modes. One is for small children, offering them adventure and the comfort of "living happily ever after," while the other explores the infinite permutations and perversions of adult desire. Yet *The Bloody Chamber* brings them, shockingly, together, melding fairy tale and pornography in a deliberately provocative exercise. It is when one considers the date of *The Bloody Chamber*'s publication that the reason for this becomes apparent. Carter wrote it while Fellow in Creative Writing at the University of Sheffield, which is why, she said later to John Haffenden, "they are all such cold, wintery stories" (Haffenden 36). But she was also writing another book in tandem with *The Bloody Chamber*—her only book-length piece of non-fictional analysis, *The Sadeian Woman*, which also appeared in 1979. *The Sadeian Woman* is an examination of the pornographic writings of the eighteenth-century French libertine, the Marquis de Sade. De Sade gave his name to the practice of sadism, the torture of others for sexual pleasure; and his writing is full of stomach-churning displays of rape and mutilation. The fact that Carter does not condemn the Marquis out of hand but apparently displays both fascination with and sympathy for his views meant that her book was always guaranteed to arouse controversy.

The Bloody Chamber, as Carter herself acknowledged, was greatly influenced by her de Sade research. Interviewed for Sheffield University Television by Les Bedford in 1977, Carter admitted she was having trouble with the de Sade study, which she defined as "an impossible task . . . like emptying the sea with a cup with a hole in it." Although she was finding some consolation by "going off at a complete tangent and writing some . . . psychoanalytic elaborations of classic fairy tales," it is obvious from her comments that *The Bloody Chamber* project was an offshoot of her research on de Sade, not a completely separate endeavor. For example, she said in the same interview that she was "very pleased" with her version of "Bluebeard," "which did actually manage to get in most of de Sade, which pleased me" (Bedford). It is this story, of course, that became the opening tale in *The*

Bloody Chamber, and the one from which the title of the collection as a whole was drawn.

It is therefore clear that what made *The Sadeian Woman* so controversial was precisely what has always been regarded as problematic in *The Bloody Chamber.* The difference between the two texts is that while *The Sadeian Woman* wears its contentiousness on its sleeve—it is a polemic on pornography, after all—*The Bloody Chamber's* is, to a certain extent, obscured by the cozy associations surrounding the term "fairy tale," associations that cause readers to bring expectations to the text that it never intends to fulfil.

It is in their portrayal of sex as an exercise in power politics that *The Bloody Chamber* and *The Sadeian Woman* find their common ground. *The Sadeian Woman* makes uncomfortable reading from its opening sentence: "Pornographers are the enemies of women *only* because our contemporary ideology of pornography does not encompass the possibility of change" (3, emphasis added). The word "only" is particularly charged, implying as it does that pornography and women's interests can be allied; and this is, indeed, precisely what Carter proceeds to attempt to do. Examining two of the Marquis de Sade's works, *Justine* and *Juliette,* Carter sets out a case for what she terms the "moral pornographer," a figure that she defines thus:

> A moral pornographer might use pornography as a critique of current relations between the sexes. His business would be the total demystification of the flesh and the subsequent revelation, through the infinite modulations of the sexual act, of the real relations of man and his kind. Such a pornographer would not be the enemy of women, perhaps because he might begin to penetrate to the heart of the contempt for women that distorts our culture even as he entered the realm of true obscenity as he describes it. (19–20)

This "moral pornographer" would refuse to construct a text that offers only erotic fantasies in which women are two-dimensional stereotypes that exist to provide pleasure for men. Instead, his depictions of sexual relations would attempt "to comment on real relations in the real world" (19). However, after approximately 130 pages of analysis, Carter concludes that de Sade fails to make the grade, for: "on the point of becoming a revolutionary pornographer . . . he, finally, lacks the courage": "He reverts, now, to being a simple pornographer" (132).

This is the point at which the concerns of fairy tale and pornography have the potential to intersect. Both are essentially fantastic forms, but what fairy tale has, and what pornography could have but lacks, is the ability to use fantasy in the service of reality, commenting on the material conditions of the real world and trying to get its readers to question them too. This is where *The Bloody Chamber* comes in. It is the forum that enables Carter to try the mantle of moral pornographer on for size, utilizing for the purpose a storytelling form that possesses, in the words of Marina Warner, an innate "ability to grapple with reality" (xvi).

Offering this as a way to approach *The Bloody Chamber*, though, does not necessitate a playing down of the problematic nature of Carter's enterprise. As the early criticism on the collection demonstrates, these stories, which feature scenes of rape and sexual voyeurism on a regular basis, can genuinely offend and alienate readers. When criticism on Carter's work began to emerge in the early to mid-1980s, *The Bloody Chamber* was the first text to attract attention, perhaps precisely because of its veneer of accessibility. Also, the rewriting of traditional tales with a feminist slant was becoming a fashionable endeavor during the 1970s and 1980s, and, viewed in retrospect, *The Bloody Chamber* appeared to anticipate work published by writers such as Anne Sexton, Robin McKinley, Jane Yolen, and Tanith Lee. In its most simplistic form, the feminist fairy tale could be said to propound a principle of simple reversal, transforming the heroine from passive to active agent so that (for example) she becomes the rescuer rather than the one rescued. But *The Bloody Chamber* does not do this, as Carter's prickly and problematic heroines consistently refuse to occupy the moral high ground and behave as "politically correct" feminist role models should. They frequently, for example, barter their bodies for gain—the narrator of "The Tiger's Bride" speaks for them all when she proclaims that "my own skin was my sole capital in the world" (*Chamber* 56). Nevertheless, it is an investment that works to many of these heroines' advantage. Like the girl in "The Company of Wolves," they know they are "nobody's meat" (118), and they sell themselves dear.

As many of the early critics note, this approach is troubling and full of potential pitfalls. In 1984, Patricia Duncker published her essay "Re-Imagining the Fairy Tales: Angela Carter's Bloody Chambers," in which she picked up on the link with *The Sadeian Woman* and condemned both texts as failing to surmount the misogyny she believes is inescapably ingrained in fairy tale and pornography. "The infernal trap inherent in the fairy tale, which fits the form to its purpose, to be the carrier of ideology, proves too complex and pervasive to avoid. Carter is rewriting the tales within the strait-jacket of their original structures. The characters she re-creates must to some extent, continue to exist as abstractions" (6).

For Duncker, therefore, Carter fails to become a "moral pornog-rapher"—a figure Duncker dismisses as "utter nonsense" (8)—and, like the Marquis de Sade before her, remains only a "simple pornographer." Because "she has no conception of women's sexuality as autonomous desire," she merely reiterates the tired old erotic clichés that are the mainstay of any pornographic narrative (7).

Duncker's argument illustrates the very fine line Carter walks in these narratives, where the specter of coercion lurks behind just about every sex-ual act in the text (there are many) and in which there is always the possibil-ity that the heroine has considerably less choice than she appears to believe. Duncker ends her debate with an image of authorial constriction: Carter, she says, "chooses to inhabit a tiny room of her own in the house of fiction," ig-noring the fact that only when women have "the space to carve out our own erotic identities, as free women" will it be possible to "rewrite the fairy tales—with a bolder hand" (12). Avis Lewallen, writing in 1988, follows Dunker's lead but is more blunt. Carter's reliance on de Sade in the writing of *The Bloody Chamber* stories leads to the reproduction of a brutal dualism: "sadist or masochist, fuck or be fucked, victim or aggressor" (150).

I would, though, echo Bacchilega's interrogation of such readings, when she asks: "Does Carter's narrative chamber of choice—the fairy tale—have a prison-like lock? Do Carter's heroines remain definitively shut in this tiny room? And does the text's closure make the lock click?" (52). As Bacchi-lega's comments illustrate, it is more recent critics that tend to display a higher tolerance of Carter's strategy. Foremost among these is Makinen, whose essay "Angela Carter's *The Bloody Chamber* and the Decolonisation of Feminine Sexuality" was published in 1992, the year of Carter's death. Makinen argues that while critics such as Duncker and Lewallen condemn Carter for her inability "adequately to revision the conservative form for a feminist politics," it is, on the contrary, "the critics who cannot see beyond the sexist binary opposition" (23). Instead, Makinen proposes a reading of *The Bloody Chamber* that regards the stories not as a straightforward *rewrit-ing* of the original narratives but rather as a transparently ironic comment upon the form itself, a technique that she terms *ironic oscillation:*

I want to argue that Carter's tales do not simply "rewrite" the old tales by fixing roles of active sexuality for their female protagonists—they "re-write" them by playing with and upon (if not preying upon) the earlier misogynistic version. Look again at the quote from "Company of Wolves" given earlier. It is not read as a story read for the first time with a positively imaged heroine. It is read, with the original story encoded within it, so that one reads of both texts, aware of how the new one refers back to and implicitly critiques the old. (24)

This is not, therefore, a reproduction of an original source but an active development of it, a strategy that also demands, as Makinen points out, an active form of reading, an audience willing to participate in Carter's flexible, interrogative, and ironic tactics.

The debate surrounding Carter's use of fairy tale thus crystallizes around the issue of whether these stories are successful in their attempt to be taken at more than face value. Makinen's argument postulates a reader able to "see through" the violence and eroticism of these tales and to recognize their deeper deconstructive purpose, while for Armitt these are stories that purposely "free up new and anti-conventional readings of women's pleasure" (89). As far as Dunker is concerned, though, the stories cannot be read in anything other than misogynistic terms, whatever Carter's original intention.

This, therefore, is the question: Is the bloody chamber capable of being nothing more than the sadist's torture chamber in which woman can never be anything else but a victim? *The Bloody Chamber* is a text that is difficult to read or critique without taking up a position on one side or the other, but I for one am willing to read these stories as largely successful exercises in the deconstruction of a form that has become appropriated by those who have a vested interest in upholding the status quo. In so doing, Carter uncovers a deeper, more subversive history of the fairy tale, bringing to the surface not only what Warner terms its "harshly realistic core" but also "the suspect whiff of femininity" from which it has never been completely disassociated (xvii, xiv). But, given that Carter's view of women was never overly idealistic (her work as a whole is characterized by its refusal to create feminist martyrs, icons, or role models) her reclamation of the position of female storyteller does not lead to her exoneration of the female gender from complicity with—and even an active perpetuation of—the circumstances of its own oppression. Thus, these are stories that challenge our own tendency to

see things in simplistic terms in accordance with the very limited options offered by the oppressor / oppressed dualism.

In this context, Carter's use of fairy tale enables her to launch into a critique not only of patriarchy but also of an aspect of feminism that she personally found insupportable: forms of second-wave radicalism that regard
the world in the context of just such dualisms. For example, in 1975 Susan
Brownmiller published *Against Our Will: Men, Women, and Rape*, in which
she argued that "rape is not a crime of irrational, impulsive, uncontrollable
lust, but is a deliberate, hostile, violent act of degradation and oppression on
the part of a would-be conquerer": in other words, the threat of rape bene-
fits all men because it subordinates all women (72). While I am not suggesting that the stories in *The Bloody Chamber* constitute a specific swipe at
Brownmiller, they clearly take issue with the kind of ideologies out of which
her arguments arise. Carter's approach in *The Bloody Chamber* is more nuanced and hence far more controversial, since in these stories not all men are
oppressors and not all women are victims; in fact, it is frequently suggested
that women may even engineer their victimhood in order to achieve the sat-
isfaction of their own nihilistic desires. And it is the bloody chamber that becomes the conceptual site within which these complicated, shady, and ques-
tionable transactions take place.

The Bloody Chamber as Vampire's Lair

This is exemplified by the very first story in the collection, "The Bloody
Chamber." Not only is it a narrative that follows a drive toward enclosure
particularly carefully, but it is also one that, by Carter's own admission, bears
an intimate relationship to the Sadeian universe centered upon the figure of
the libertine, a figure who exploits everyone and everything around him in
order to satisfy the endless permutations of his perversions. Moreover, in the
range of its references it demonstrates that to approach anything Carter
wrote as simply a rewriting or revising of the fairy tale is far too simplistic
a description of her narrative method, since her fairy-tale references are always interwoven with wider folkloric and specific literary allusions.

The narrative drive toward the increasingly constrained and claustro-
phobic space that is the bloody chamber is strongly expressed here. The story
is told in the retrospective first person, which means that the narrator is not
telling her tale spontaneously but is crafting it after the event—it begins "I

remember" (*Chamber* 7). She can thus introduce a sense of fatalism from the moment her story opens, so that even before her marriage to the rich Marquis, who has had three wives previously, she has already become "wound" on "the spool of inexorability" (29) that will lead her through various permutations of the bloody chamber until she reaches it in its most enclosed and horrific form. Its first incarnation is as the marital bedchamber itself, in which the narrator is ritually "impaled" (17), and the blood from her broken hymen stains the sheets. But this is only the beginning of her passage: in classic fairy-tale fashion, she is lured onward by her husband's elaborate double-bluff, which ensures her transgression through the exercise of prohibition: "Promise me this, my whey-faced piano-player; promise me you'll use all the keys on the ring except that last little one I showed you. Play with anything you find, jewels, silver plate. . . . All is yours, everywhere is open to you—except the lock that this single key fits" (21). His apparent departure fools the girl into believing that she is embarking on an independent quest toward self-actualization when, in fact, she is only following a path already laid down for her.

Her journey, however, evolves in distinct stages in a titillating way that echoes the Marquis's own deferment of pleasure. First, in an act that mirrors in microcosm the horrific revelation she will experience only a little later, she plunders her husband's desk, in which she finds a secret drawer containing a file marked "Personal" that holds mementos of his three former wives: a paper napkin, a musical score, and a postcard. Then the narrative continues onward from the traces of Bluebeard's former wives to the real wives themselves—or what's left of them. Her curiosity unsatisfied by the little that she has found, the narrator, as she is bound to do, turns to the forbidden key, progressing along an "ill-lit passage," a "long, winding corridor" toward the subterranean chamber that conceals the real object of her quest and what lies behind her marriage bed. In it she finds "a catafalque . . . surrounded by long, white candles" (28) on which lies the embalmed corpse of the first wife—behind it, the skull of the second "strung up by a system of unseen cords so that it appeared to hang, disembodied, in the still, heavy air" (29).

But if this is the bloody chamber, the most striking thing about it is the absence of blood, for while the victims of Bluebeard's depredations are openly displayed, they are also strangely sanitized, denuded of all traces of the violence that must have been perpetrated upon them. This is, in fact, only another deferment; all we have reached at this point is the bloody chamber's anteroom. The horrific actuality is only revealed when, alerted by "a ghostly twang," the girl opens an Iron Maiden in the corner to find the body of her immediate predecessor, "pierced, not by one but by a hundred spikes . . . so newly dead, so full of blood" (29). If Bluebeard has turned his first wife into sleeping beauty and the second into a metaphysical emblem, the third is a corpse, pure and simple, and thus for the girl the most potent signifier of her own impending, and now inevitable, fate.

The woman in the Iron Maiden therefore has a corporeality, an actuality, that the other wives lack—so who *is* she? It is here that we find a figure that may not only possibly stand in opposition to the Sadeian libertine but also disrupt the predator/victim dichotomy around which the story up to this point has appeared to be structured. The bloody chamber is her most natural habitation, perhaps, since not only is she from Eastern Europe, the home of vampires, but also her name, Carmilla, constitutes an important allusion that has implications for our understanding of the entire collection of stories. The association between Carmilla and the figure of the vampire is fore-grounded in the girl's discovery of the psychopathic souvenirs in Blue-beard's desk, for the final object in his file is a postcard from Carmilla, depicting:

> a view of a village graveyard, among mountains, where some black-coated ghoul enthusiastically dug at a grave . . . captioned: "Typical Transylvanian Scene—Midnight, All Hallows." And, on the other side, the message: "On the occasion of this marriage to the descendent of Dracula—always remember, 'the supreme and unique pleasure of love is the certainty that one is doing evil.'" (26)

There's an interesting ambiguity in the wording of this message, for instead of using a pronoun that would identify the object of the statement—"'my' marriage" or "'your' marriage"—Carmilla instead uses the passive "this." Such linguistic prevarication ensures that, although it is easy to assume that Carmilla is referring to Bluebeard as "the descendent of Dracula" (and it would certainly be an apt description of a man who murders women and en-shrines their bodies), she could also be identifying herself as Dracula's de-scendant. In this scenario, the Marquis would not be the vampire but the vampire killer, and his murder of his wives less an act of predation than of control. While vampires resolutely refuse to remain decently dead, the role of the vampire hunter is to contain them within the coffin and ensure that they will not leave it again.

Carmilla's significance to the text is emphasized by the fact that the narrator's mention of her is the only reference to a female figure by her first name not only in this individual story but in the entire collection. Beauty in "The Courtship of Mr Lyon" possesses a generic name more indicative of her textual function than her individuality, while Wolf-Alice has that name attributed to her by the narrator, and it does not exist within the world of the narrative. The other female vampire in the text, from "The Lady of the House of Love," is also generically rather than specifically named—given the family name of Nosferatu, she is known only by her aristocratic title, "the Countess," throughout the narrative. Other female characters, like the narrator of "The Bloody Chamber" herself, are simply anonymous.

Only Carmilla, then, has a proper name, and it is one that is textually significant, since it recalls, not a fairy-tale source, but the title of Sheridan Le Fanu's short story "Carmilla," published in 1872. "Carmilla" is an acknowledged precursor of Bram Stoker's *Dracula,* also referred to in Carter's story. But whereas the female vampires in Stoker's narrative are subordinate to Dracula's masculine authority, Le Fanu tells the story of a female vampire who is an independent agent. Moreover, while she possesses the same deadly, erotic glamour as her male counterpart, she directs it not at men but at other women. She only takes female victims, whom she treats with all "the ardour of a lover" (Le Fanu 14). When Carmilla is finally unmasked as a vampire, she is discovered in a "leaden coffin floated with blood, in which to a depth of seven inches, the body lay immersed." She can only be killed "in accordance with ancient practice": "a sharp stake was driven into the heart of the vampire . . . [t]hen the head was struck off and a torrent of blood flowed from the severed neck" (46).

This scene is distinctly reminiscent of the scene in "The Bloody Chamber" when the girl-narrator discovers Carmilla's body, impaled and awash with blood. Yet this is also the point at which both Le Fanu's and Carter's versions of Carmilla and the girl herself intersect—the new bride too has been "impaled" on the marriage bed and decapitation is to be her ordained fate, prefigured by the ruby choker the Marquis makes her wear. So although the girl classifies herself, in her youth, naïveté, and poverty, as definitively different from the Marquis's previous wives, they are united in their victimhood: and it is only when she opens the Iron Maiden that she now recognizes that she has joined their "fated sisterhood" (*Chamber* 29).

According to Nina Auerbach, Carmilla stands for a vampirism that "is an exchange, a sharing, an identification, that breaks down the boundaries of familial roles and the sanctioned hierarchy of marriage" (47). In Le Fanu's tale, Carmilla evolves a particularly close relationship with Laura, who may be her prey, but she is also a kind of lover and, we find out, a distant cousin. Even after Carmilla has been dealt with, even after Laura has seen her for what she is, Laura ends her story on a note of nostalgia: "often from a reverie I have started, fancying I heard the light step of Carmilla at the drawing room door" (Le Fanu 48). Could it therefore be argued that the Carmilla in Carter's tale stands for a female collectivity and erotic sensibility that short-circuits the brutal eroticism of the Sadeian universe?

The trouble is, we are dealing here with a writer who firmly believed that "you cannot make any statements which are universally true," and that is certainly the case in regard to any assumptions we might be tempted to make about the bloody chamber, which resists simplistic categorization (Haffenden 38). Le Fanu's Carmilla is a useful reference for Carter precisely because she is troublingly ambiguous in her blurring of the demarcation lines that divide predator from prey. Vampires, whatever those who hunt them may think, can never be pinned down; they function as oscillating symbols that convey multiple, often contradictory, meanings. Auerbach describes them as "consummate turncoats, more formidable in their flexibility than in their love, their occult powers, or their lust for blood" (8). An examination of the parallels between Le Fanu's Carmilla and Carter's may hint at the possibility of seditious sisterhood, but other elements in the story work against that conclusion.

This is illustrated by a quotation from Le Fanu's "Carmilla," in which the vampire is described as

> prone to be fascinated with an engrossing vehemence, resembling the passion of love, by particular persons. In pursuit of these it will exercise inexhaustible patience and stratagem, for access to a particular object may be obstructed in a hundred ways. It will never desist until it has satiated its passion, and drained the very life of its coveted victim. But it will, in these cases, husband and protract its murderous enjoyment with the refinement of an epicure, and heighten it by the gradual approaches of an artful courtship. In these cases it seems to yearn for something like sympathy and consent. (47)

This speech is certainly a perfect description of the libertine, and thus of the Marquis himself, isolated in the "atrocious loneliness" of the sadist who is beyond redemption, and who is himself prisoner of a desire that can only ever be momentarily sated. However, in Le Fanu's original tale this description is applied to a woman, and it is applicable to a woman in Carter's story too. The fragmentary traces left behind by Carter's version of Carmilla—in particular the quotation from Baudelaire on her postcard ("the supreme and unique pleasure of love is the certainty that one is doing evil")—suggest that she may have been a female version of the libertine and that for her, just as much as for the Marquis, sex and death were inextricably entwined. Such a conclusion carries with it a faint but disturbing suggestion that Carmilla may even have colluded in her own murder.

The inhabitant of the bloody chamber in the opening story of Carter's collection, then, can (and should) be regarded as the prototype of a female identity that is deeply and problematically split; itself predator and prey, erotic object and sexual aggressor. She is certainly not someone who can be elevated to the status of virtuous victim or feminist martyr. When the Marquis presses the bloodstained key to the narrator's forehead, it is Carmilla's blood that stains her irrevocably. And what it signifies is so mortifying to the narrator that, even after the monster's death at the hand of her own mother, and her marriage to the blind piano tuner, who is quite literally blind to the presence of the mark, the girl still attempts to conceal it with "paint . . . [and] powder" (*Chamber* 41). But what is so shameful about having been deceived and manipulated by a skillful practitioner of vice? The answer, of course, is nothing, if the girl had been a wholly innocent pawn in his game; but she presents herself as more than that—as someone who is unknowingly possessed of "a rare talent for corruption" (20), and who becomes "engaged" in what she terms his "charade of innocence and vice" (34). What both Carmilla and the girl share, therefore, is this inability to be classified in clear-cut terms, since both are to some extent complicit in the Marquis's games.

This disturbing suggestion of complicity is reiterated over and over again in the stories that make up *The Bloody Chamber* and is not necessarily only evoked through reference to vampire literature and folklore. "The Erl-King," a virtuoso piece of static and stylized prose, draws on Germanic folk tales by way of references to Goethe's poem of the same title in order to reiterate the theme of sexual submission and dominance that threads all the separate narratives in the collection together. It concerns a girl in thrall to the Erl-King, who "lives by himself all alone in the heart of the wood in a house that has only the one room" (*Chamber* 86). In this "musical and aromatic" (87) room hang "herbs in bunches to dry" and "cage upon cage of singing birds, larks and linnets, which he piles up one on another against the wall, a wall of trapped birds" (87). The narrator, it is implied, is another of the Erl-King's trapped birds, lured "towards him on his magic lasso of inhuman music" (89).

Carter's employment of metaphor ensures that this story can in no way be mistaken for a romance. To the girl, the Erl-King is "the tender butcher who showed me how the price of flesh is love" (87), and he skins her as he would a rabbit in the course of sexual liaisons that perpetually hover on the edge of violence: "And now—ach! I feel your sharp teeth in the subaqueous depth of your kisses . . . you sink your teeth into my throat and make me scream" (88). Thus, the room full of herb-scents and song is also another manifestation of the bloody chamber, forming the backdrop for "the still tableaux of our embracements" (88), to which the female protagonist is addicted: "Eat me, drink me; thirsty, cankered, goblin-ridden, I go back and back to him to have his fingers strip the tattered skin away and clothe me in his dress of water" (89). As the story progresses, it moves inward toward an ever more confined space, as the narrator's focus moves from her external surroundings to a close-up contemplation of the butcher-lover himself: "Your green eye is a reducing chamber. If I look into it long enough, I will become as small as my own reflection, I will diminish to a point and vanish. I will be drawn down into that black whirlpool and be consumed by you. I shall become so small you can keep me in one of your osier cages and mock my loss of liberty" (90). Terrified by the prospect of this fate, this ultimate closing-down of all opportunity and choice, the protagonist resolves to kill the Erl-King—not only to save herself but also for the sake, so she says, of other "foolish virgins" (90).

Yet her description of this act foregrounds the fundamental ambiguity of the narrative that, once again, refuses to be reduced to a simplistic standoff between the sadist and his victim. Carter achieves this by writing a narrative that slips between the subjective and the objective point of view, and past, present, and future time. The first paragraph opens in the past tense, then modulates to the present, developing along the way an impersonal, hypothetical form of address directed at the reader: "The woods enclose. You step between the first trees and then you are no longer in the open air; the wood swallows you up" (84). It is not until the fifth paragraph that the speaker is located and situated within the narrative action: "The woods enclose and then enclose again, like a system of Chinese boxes opening into one another;

the intimate perspectives of the wood changed endlessly around the inter-
loper, the imaginary traveller walking toward an invented distance that perpetually receded before me" (85). The distortion of distance, space, and
identity evoked in this single sentence, in which the enunciating "I" is also
an "imaginary traveller," who, while walking, is at the same time static
against a moving backdrop, is absolutely characteristic of the story itself, in
which the bloody chamber is simultaneously tiny and all-encompassing. The
narrator may envisage it as a space of infinite enclosure into which she is
"draw[n] inwards" by "tremendous pressure" (89) exerted from without—
but the conclusion of the tale opens up quite another interpretation. The narrator's killing of the Erl-King does not take place within the present, as her
use of the modal verb only states her intention to act: "I *shall* take two huge
handfuls of his rustling hair . . . and wind them into ropes. . . . I *shall*
strangle him with them" (91, emphasis added). Furthermore, she subse-
quently distances herself from her proposed actions by retreating into the
third person: "Then *she will* open all the cages and let the birds free" (91, emphasis added). We only have her word for it, therefore, that she will renounce
her victimhood at all—an uncertainty further complicated by the story's
closing sentence. The girl will, she says, restring the Erl-King's violin with
his own hair, whereupon "it will play discordant music without a hand touch-
ing it. The bow will dance over the new strings of its own accord and they
will cry out: Mother, mother, you have murdered me!'" (91). In "The Bloody
Chamber" the mother is a separate being who possesses a redemptive power,
but here the girl and the mother are one. The Erl-King is her oppressor, her
lover—and also her son. If the Erl-King is the girl's creation, then what we
are reading is not a narrative of external events but a struggle taking place
within the subjectivity of the female protagonist, between what Makinen describes as "the two competing desires for freedom and engulfment . . . de-
lineat[ing] the very ambivalence of desire" (30).

The Bloody Chamber as Libertine's Boudoir

The notion of the female subject who creates the conditions of her own imprisonment is reiterated throughout *The Bloody Chamber* but is particularly
apparent in another vampire story, "The Lady of the House of Love." The
story concerns the Countess, "the last bud of the poison tree that sprang
from the loins of Vlad the Impaler" (*Chamber* 94). As her lack of a proper

name suggests, her identity is strongly tied to her ancestry, leaving her little sense of independent agency. She is of the house of Nosferatu, a term that encompasses both house and family; and it is the house itself that is one of the most immediate manifestations of the bloody chamber in this story. A profane variation on Sleeping Beauty, the Countess is trapped behind "a huge, spiked wall" of roses "that incarcerates her in the castle of her inheritance" (95). But the house, as has already been made evident, is not just bricks and mortar; it signifies her very self. She is not just its occupant but an integral part of its fabric:

> She herself is a haunted house. She does not possess herself; her ancestors sometimes come and peer out of the windows of her eyes and that is very frightening. She has the mysterious solitude of ambiguous states; she hovers in no-man's land between life and death, sleeping and waking, behind the hedge of spiked flowers, Nosferatu's sanguinary rosebud. The beastly forebears on the walls condemn her to a perpetual repetition of their passions. (103)

To put it another way, she is the sum of all who have come before her, and, however much she may wish otherwise, she is bound to follow in their footsteps and perform the same atrocities, for she can never be human nor enter into any kind of human interaction.

The Countess's dual and ambiguous role is demonstrated clearly in the scenes that take place within her bedchamber, to which she leads her helpless victims before devouring them. Carter's description of this space recalls the Marquis's subterranean bloody chamber:

> The walls of her bedchamber are hung with black satin, embroidered with tears of pearl. At the room's four corners are funerary urns and bowls which emit salubrous, pungent forms of incense. In the centre is an elaborate catafalque, in ebony, surrounded by long candles in enormous silver candlesticks. In a white lace négligé stained a little with blood, the Countess climbs up on her catafalque at dawn each morning and lies down in an open coffin. (94)

However, it is fraught with ambiguities. The Countess may perform the predatory role of the Marquis in this room, but lying in her bloodstained nightdress in the coffin upon the catafalque she is also all his wives rolled into one: she "is both death and the maiden" (93). This is demonstrated when she encounters the handsome young bicyclist who is lured to her castle to become her next meal. In all innocence he turns the tables on her and makes her the victim instead. When the Countess cuts her hand on the shards of the dark glasses she wears to shade her eyes from sunlight, he reverses the scenario of vampiric predation and kills her:

> When she kneels to try to gather the fragments of glass together, a sharp sliver pierces deeply into the pad of her thumb; she cries out, sharp, real. She kneels among the broken glass and watches the bright bead of blood form a drop. She has never seen her own blood before, not her *own* blood. It exercises upon her an awed fascination.
>
> Into this vile and murderous room, the handsome bicyclist brings the innocent remedies of the nursery. . . . He gently takes her hand away from her and dabs the blood with his own handkerchief, but still it spurts out. And so he puts his mouth to the wound. He will kiss it better for her. (106)

The Countess, so dependent on the blood of others, cannot survive the taking of her own blood. More than that, she cannot survive the act of human compassion the young man's actions represent.

Like the protagonists in "The Bloody Chamber," or the girl in "The Erl-King," therefore, the Countess merges contradictory roles—she is both a murderous victim and a virginal rapist. And, again, the ending of the story does not resolve all its ambiguities; indeed, it is here that Carter enlarges the motif of the bloody chamber to its widest and most disturbing extent. Whereas in other stories the bloody chamber itself is a place of extreme and ever increasing constriction, here it is all encompassing, dizzying in its scope. The young man who comes to the Countess's chateau on his bicycle is an officer in the British army, and he "has about him . . . the special glamour of that generation for whom history has already prepared a special, exemplary fate in the trenches of France" (97). So although the hero may escape the Countess's bloody chamber unscathed, he remains within the bloody chamber that is European power politics at a particular moment in history. This is indicated by the rose that the young man keeps as a memento of his encounter with the Countess: "a dark, fanged rose I plucked from between my thighs, like a flower laid on a grave" (107). When the young man returns to his barracks, he tries to revive the wilted rose, only to find that:

When he returned from the mess that evening, the heavy fragrance of the Count Nosferatu's roses drifted down the stone corridor of the barracks to greet him, and his spartan headquarters brimmed with the reeling odour of a glowing, velvet, monstrous flower whose petals had regained all their former bloom and elasticity, their corrupt, brilliant, baleful splendour.

Next day, his regiment embarked for France. (107–08)

The rose flourishes precisely because it remains within the environment for which it was bred—it has, in actuality, never left home.

The Bloody Chamber as Curious Room

"The Lady of the House of Love" is thus a highly significant story within the collection, because it is here that Carter is at her most audacious in her employment of the bloody chamber trope. In the end, it is not located somewhere else, down a dark passage or in an exotic Eastern European chateau. It does not just exist in fairy tales, folk tales, and stories of vampires and werewolves. Instead, it is a real condition of our very existence, for Carter intends her audience to realize that these stories apply to the contemporary world and the way we live now. It is inescapable, since it exists both inside and outside the self and in both the public and the private sphere. Quite simply, there's nowhere else to run.

So what are the implications of such a conclusion? Throughout the collection, Carter stresses the ambiguity, the lack of moral certainty, which is an inherent aspect of the bloody chamber. Although Carmilla in "The Bloody Chamber" possesses associations that hint at the possibility of her contesting the space of the male libertine, in actuality, that potential, though hinted at, is never fulfilled. Both Carmilla in "The Bloody Chamber" and the Countess in "The Lady of the House of Love" die, and they cannot by any stretch of the imagination be regarded as innocent victims of male oppression. Instead, they are surrounded by allusions of corruption and complicity—Carmilla's self-congratulatory postcard to the Marquis; the Countess's vampire inheritance that gives her "claws and teeth sharpened on centuries of corpses" (94). The protagonist in "The Erl-King" ends the story contemplating action, but it is an action that may or may not be staged: furthermore, what she is resisting is her own desire, enshrined within a bloody chamber that, it is hinted, could well be of her own making. To complicate matters further, in all three stories the notion that the male protagonists are all-powerful simply by virtue of their sex is rendered an untenable proposition. The handsome young bicyclist is helpless to evade his fate as a statistic on the casualty list of the First World War, while the Marquis's very monstrousness condemns him to a life of "atrocious loneliness" spent in a state of "absolute despair, rank and ghastly" (35). The Erl-King's "innocence" may be the source of the danger the girl sees in the "black hole in the middle of both your eyes" (90), but it may also be the death of him.

Most problematic of all is the conclusion that we cannot help drawing: the only way Carmilla or the Countess—or indeed the Marquis, the handsome young bicyclist, or the Erl-King—has of escaping the bloody chamber is either by dying or killing someone else, which is a hollow kind of victory, if it can be viewed as a victory at all. The bloody chamber is a dying room, after all, so its existence is only reinforced, not negated, by such an act.

The answer to this conundrum is provided by the stories that deal with metamorphosis—the rewrites of "Beauty and the Beast" and the werewolf narratives. These tales do not offer a way out of the bloody chamber, though. Instead, they reach an accommodation, however tenuous and provisional, with the ambiguous condition of being it represents. This is effectively illustrated by "The Company of Wolves," which, although it bears many similarities to "The Bloody Chamber," reaches a somewhat different conclusion. The werewolf in this story may not resemble the Marquis physically—indeed, he is smelly, hairy, and infested with lice—but his condition is the same. He's another of Carter's Sadeian libertines, a figure for whom sex is inextricably linked with death and who is helplessly driven to appease a lust that is never fully satisfied: "There is a vast melancholy in the canticles of the wolves, melancholy infinite as the forest, endless as these long nights of winter and yet that ghastly sadness, that mourning for their own, irremediable appetites, can never move the heart for not one phrase in it hints at the possibility of redemption" (*Chamber* 112). The heroine of "The Company of Wolves" has a self-confidence that the narrator of "The Bloody Chamber," preoccupied with guilt, lacks; but, again, there are similarities. Like her predecessor, the girl in "The Company of Wolves" is reeled in toward the bloody chamber on an inexorable path through the forest; for, like all heroines of fairy and folk tales, she is driven by curiosity. When the werewolf challenges her to a race to grandmother's house, she can no more resist than the girl in "The Bloody Chamber" could help using the key forbidden to her by the Marquis. And both girls survive the bloody chamber, but by very different methods and with very different results. As I have observed already, the narrator of "The Bloody Chamber" is saved by the intervention of her mother, who shoots the Marquis dead, matches her up with the blind piano-tuner, and appears to condemn her to a life of self-recrimination. But Red Riding Hood's mother is absent, so she has to rely upon her own wits to survive. And what she does is to remain within the bloody chamber, climbing into her grandmother's deathbed to join the wolf in "a savage marriage ceremony" (118). So instead of dying, she ends the story lying "sweet and sound . . . between the paws of the tender wolf" (118).

Robert Clark, another early critic of *The Bloody Chamber*, views this ending as wholly unsatisfactory. In a survey essay on Carter's work published in 1987, he interprets the ending of "The Company of Wolves" as attempting a reversal of stereotypical power relations: "In place of the idea that women should beware of men and pretend to have no sexuality of their own, Carter's version represents the woman enjoying her own sexuality and using it as a power that tenderizes the wolf" (149). But, he goes on to argue, when the girl strips naked in front of the werewolf, "the point of view is that of the male voyeur; the implication may be that the girl has her own sexual power, but his meaning lies perilously close to the idea that all women want it really, and only need forcing to overcome their scruples" (149).

I agree that this is certainly a difficult ending to accept. Red Riding Hood survives precisely because she does not try to escape from her rapist. Instead, she merely accepts the inevitable: "since her fear did her no good, she ceased to be afraid" (*Chamber* 117). However, Clark's argument ignores the importance of the bloody chamber as a site of moral ambiguity—it is not black and white but red. In spite of carrying an ineradicable memento of her encounter with this space, the narrator of "The Bloody Chamber" never fully surrenders a dualistic system of belief, which is why her narrative is saturated by guilt and a desire to justify her actions. She ends her story by saying that she is glad her second husband is blind and cannot see the mark upon her forehead "because it spares my shame" (41). Yet "shameless" is the perfect word to describe the heroine of "The Company of Wolves": she laughs as she throws her clothes into the fire, and "freely" gives the werewolf "the kiss she owed him" (118). The clear-cut moral code represented by the grandmother's Bible is discarded along with her bones, whose "terrible clattering under the bed" goes unheard (118).

If the bloody chamber is conceptualized as universal, retreat from it is therefore not possible. All one can do is to go further in until one can go no further—in to the space that lies "between the paws of the . . . wolf." There, for a moment at least, one may find a place of precarious safety. This conclusion is also illustrated in Carter's rewrite of "Beauty and the Beast," "The Tiger's Bride." The heroine is lost by her father to the tiger in a game of cards, but in the tiger's castle she begins to question the socially constructed feminine role to which she has been expected to accede. Considering the mechanical maid the tiger has given her, "a marvellous machine" (60), she poses the question: "had I not been allotted only the same kind of imitative life amongst men that the doll-maker had given her?" (63). The maid, then, is a satirical play on the Iron Maiden, signifying a masculine act of enclosure of the female inside a veneer of "proper" femininity (which in both cases is defined as unquestioning acquiescence to male desires). The heroine of "The Tiger's Bride," however, formulates a way out: she sends her mechanical maid back to her father to perform the role of daughter (she is sure he'll never notice she has been replaced by a robot), while she enters into a contract with the tiger. Just as in "The Company of Wolves," this entails remaining in the bloody chamber, where the tiger "pace[s] out the length of his imprisonment between . . . gnawed and bloody bones." When the girl strips naked and submits to the tiger, she is transformed, her "cold, white meat of contract" replaced by "beautiful fur" (67). What this metamorphosis will lead to, though, is left in a precarious state of suspension on the verge of disintegration: "the sweet thunder of this purr shook the old walls, made the shutters batter the windows until they burst apart and let in the white light of the snowy moon. Tiles came crashing down from the roof; I heard them fall into the courtyard far below" (67).

At the beginning of this essay I quoted Carter's definition of the "moral pornographer," whom she describes as possessing the ability to "penetrate to the heart of the contempt for women that distorts our culture." That very objective constitutes the motivational force in all the short tales in *The Bloody Chamber*. Throughout her career, Carter was contemptuous of what she calls in *The Sadeian Woman* the "false universals" of myth, which operate according to clear-cut stereotypes: "If women allow themselves to be consoled for their culturally determined lack of access to the modes of intellectual debate by the invocation of hypothetical great goddesses, they are simply flattering themselves. . . . All the mythic versions of women, from the myth of the redeeming purity of the virgin to that of the healing, reconciling mother, are consolatory nonsenses" (*Sadeian* 5).

The bloody chamber, therefore, is a place where, in order to survive, one must abandon moral certainty and embrace an idea of humanity that is not "strung out between abstract concepts of good and evil" (Hamilton 15). It is notable that the metamorphosis tales end with tender physical contact between the protagonists—Red Riding Hood and the wolf embracing on grandmother's bed; Wolf-Alice (the girl who thinks she is a wolf) licking the Duke (a man who can become a wolf) into a fully human existence; the Beast licking Beauty's human skin off to find the tiger underneath. All of these images reject the concept of stasis in order to confront the possibility of change. Although this is both dangerous and daunting, Carter suggests through such conclusions—however tentatively imagined they may be—that it also evokes the possibility that man and woman can come together as equals in a meeting that has the potential to transform both.

I would argue that we should therefore rethink the metaphor of constriction offered by Duncker in order to transform it into something more positive. The "tiny room" she accuses Carter of inhabiting need not necessarily convey intimations of restriction if we envisage it differently: as (to quote from a late Carter short story, "Alice in Prague or The Curious Room") "a curious room . . . crammed with wonders" (127). Such a view does not eliminate the dangers and potentially scandalous liaisons offered by the bloody chamber, since the intersection of fairy tale and pornography is a deliberate act of miscegenation and, as such, is intended to disturb. Lorna Sage describes Carter's writing of the 1970s as "performative and political . . . writing that means to *work*" (although it is an approach that even Sage has to concede is "a high-risk strategy, no doubt" ["Introduction" 16]). However, it is the very nature of the "curious room" to invite trespass of the most voyeuristic kind, as Carter makes clear in "Alice in Prague or The Curious Room": "Outside the curious room, there is a sign on the door which says 'Forbidden.' Inside, inside, oh, come and see!" (121). Those who dare to "come and see" are rewarded with spectacle, marvels, incident, and adventure—since for Carter, a lifelong atheist and stringent opponent of the Judeo-Christian apparatus of belief, there is no such thing as inappropriate knowledge.

So, Carter's use of fairy tale serves a multifaceted purpose. First, it promotes her support for democratic art forms that eschew cultural elitism in favor of endless reappropriation, reduction, and reworking—a task, moreover, that can be done by anyone, anywhere. Second, the flexibility of such a form allows her to use it in support of her ongoing interest in the role of sex in the perpetuation of male-dominated power structures. Third, it enables precisely the kind of provocative conjunctions (or conjugations?) in which Carter as an artist delights, that work to reel in the reader on a thread of half-horrified fascination.

There is a fourth point to add here, too, which is that Carter's appropriation of the role of fairy-tale teller came to align her in the critical imagination with a certain "Mother Goose" stereotype. It is distinctly, but characteristically, ironic that although in her introduction to *The Virago Book of Fairy Tales* Carter presents the fairy-tale form as constituting a kind of "one-size-fits-all" narrative mode in which the teller is little more than a relay point in the chain of transmission, her own intervention in the form made her particular reputation, since *The Bloody Chamber* can in retrospect be recognized as the book that enabled her properly to break through onto the British literary scene. Ali Smith has observed in a recent essay that "many take the year 1979 as Carter's *annus mirabilis*. . . . Lorna Sage . . . notes it as the point when finally Carter could be read collusively by her readers, who would now, given the rewrite of the fairy tales and the study of how narratives are always about the uses of power, finally 'get' the Carter project, what she was about" (88). Smith is referring here to Sage's essay on Carter and the fairy tale published in Roemer and Bacchilega's collection, in which Sage herself makes the claim that it was in *The Bloody Chamber* and *The Sadeian Woman* that Carter "explained herself, unpacked her gifts, played her own fairy godmother" ("Angela Carter" 65).

Although Carter had written seven novels and one collection of short stories before *The Bloody Chamber*'s publication, throughout the 1970s she considered herself to be ignored and marginalized, writing books that failed to receive the attention she believed they merited. *The Bloody Chamber*, however, changed this, not only because of the success of the collection itself but also because of the fact that several of the individual stories appeared in other media—"The Lady of the House of Love" was a version of Carter's first play for radio broadcast in 1976, *Vampirella;* and "The Company of Wolves," and "Puss in Boots" were, in Carter's own words, "reformulated" to become radio dramas after *The Bloody Chamber*'s publication.[2] In 1984 "The Company of Wolves" was also made into a film directed by Neil Jordan, and this played a particularly crucial role in bringing Carter's work to the attention of a wider audience, cementing her reputation as a provocative feminist fabulator. This in turn led to Carter's referencing of fairy tale becoming the cornerstone on which her posthumous celebrity rested: as Makinen points out, many of the obituaries, intentionally or not, "construct[ed] her as a mythical fairy-tale figure" (20).

I am in accordance with Makinen here that resorting to such stereotypes does neither Carter nor her work justice. Her use of the mode did not begin and end with *The Bloody Chamber*, since most of her works include some kind of nod toward the fairy-tale genre. Moreover, as my own analysis in this essay has repeatedly claimed, fairy tale is only ever one element in a much wider intertextual exercise that results in a voice and a view that is uniquely Carter's own. The stories in *The Bloody Chamber*, and elsewhere, remain distinctive: a virtuoso collection of narratives that play in the exceedingly narrow gap between imprisonment and liberation, leaving the protagonists poised on the fulcrum of a decision that will commit them to either one fate or the other.[3] In her introduction to *The Virago Book of Fairy Tales*, Carter comments that the range and variety of the stories she selected should not be taken as indicative of a belief that "we are all sisters under the skin," for "I don't believe that, anyway. Sisters under the skin we might be, but that does not mean we've got much in common" (*Virago* xiv). In her reworking of both fairy and folk tales she reiterates this enduring conviction that gender does not necessarily confer solidarity upon those who share it, and that relationships between men and women have to be negotiated individually in the context of very particular social, economic, and historical situations. It is the infinitely adaptable nature of the fairy-tale form, "the great mass of infinitely various narrative . . . stories without known originators that can be remade again and again by every person who tells them," that makes it uniquely suited to act as the means through which Carter articulates this view (*Virago* xiv).

Notes

1. The Carter literature is vast. Of particular interest for my own work are the essays by Margaret Atwood, Lucie Armitt, and Robin Ann Sheets. For a comprehensive survey of readings of Carter and the fairy tale, see Stephen Benson's "Angela Carter and the Literary *Märchen:* A Review Essay," which forms part of an important collection on the subject, originally published in a special issue of *Marvels & Tales* 12.1 (1998).

2. See Carter's introduction to *Come unto These Yellow Sands,* in which she says that although *The Company of Wolves* and *Puss in Boots* "started off as short stories," they "aren't adaptations so much as reformulations" (10).

3. Carter wrote her own versions (or reformulations) of other folk and fairy tales after the publication of *The Bloody Chamber,* such as "Peter and the Wolf," another werewolf story in *Black Venus* (1985), and *"Ashputtle* or *The Mother's Ghost"* in *American Ghosts and Old World Wonders* (1993).

Bibliography

Primary Sources

Carter, Angela. "Alice in Prague or The Curious Room." *American Ghosts and Old World Wonders.* London: Vintage, 1994. 121–39.

———. *The Bloody Chamber.* London: Vintage, 1996.

———. *Come unto These Yellow Sands.* Newcastle upon Tyne: Bloodaxe Books, 1985.

———. *The Sadeian Woman.* London: Virago, 1979.

———, ed. *The Virago Book of Fairy Tales.* London: Virago, 1991.

Secondary Sources

Armitt, Lucie. "The Fragile Frames of *The Bloody Chamber.*" *The Infernal Desires of Angela Carter: Fiction, Femininity, Feminism.* Ed. Joseph Bristow and Trev Lynn Broughton. London: Longman, 1997. 88–99.

Atwood, Margaret. "Running with the Tigers." *Flesh and the Mirror: Essays on the Art of Angela Carter.* Ed. Lorna Sage. London: Virago P, 1994. 117–35.

Auerbach, Nina. *Our Vampires, Ourselves.* Chicago: U of Chicago P, 1995.

Bacchilega, Cristina. *Postmodern Fairy Tales: Gender and Narrative Strategies.* Philadelphia: U of Pennsylvania P, 1997.

Bedford, Les. "Angela Carter: An Interview." Sheffield: Sheffield University Television, 1977.

Brownmiller, Susan. *Against Our Will: Men, Women, and Rape. Feminisms: A Reader.* Brighton: Harvester Wheatsheaf, 1992.

Clark, Robert. "Angela Carter's Desire Machine." *Women's Studies* 14 (1987): 147–61.

Duncker, Patricia. "Re-Imagining the Fairy Tales: Angela Carter's Bloody Chambers." *Literature and History* 10.1 (1984): 3–14.

Goldsworthy, Kerryn. "Angela Carter." *Meanjin* 44.1 (1985): 4–13.

Haffenden, John. "Magical Mannerist." *Literary Review* (November 1984): 34–38.

Hamilton, Alex. "Sade and Prejudice." *Guardian* 30 Mar. 1979: 15.

Le Fanu, Sheridan, "Carmilla." http://english.upenn.edu/~nauerbac/crml.html.

Keppeler, Susanne. *The Pornography of Representation.* Cambridge: Cambridge: Polity, 1986.

Lewallen, Avis. "Wayward Girls but Wicked Women?" *Perspectives on Pornography: Sexuality in Film and Literature.* Ed. Gary Day and Clive Bloom. Basingstoke: Macmillan, 1988. 144–58.

Makinen, Merja. "Angela Carter's *The Bloody Chamber* and the Decolonisation of Feminine Sexuality." *Angela Carter: Contemporary Critical Essays.* Ed. Alison Easton. Basingstoke: Macmillan, 2000. 20–36.

Roemer, Danielle M., and Cristina Bacchilega, eds., *Angela Carter and the Fairy Tale.* Detroit: Wayne State UP, 2001.

Sage, Lorna. "Angela Carter: The Fairy Tale." Roemer and Bacchilega 65–81.

———. Introduction. *Flesh and the Mirror: Essays on the Art of Angela Carter.* Ed. Sage. London: Virago, 1994. 1–23.

Sheets, Robin Ann. "Pornography, Fairy Tales, and Feminism." *Journal of the History of Sexuality* 1.2 (1999): 633–57.

Smith, Ali. "Get Carter." *Interrupted Lives.* Ed. Andrew Motion. London: National Portrait Gallery Publications, 2004. 80–93.

Warner, Marina. *From the Beast to the Blonde: On Fairy Tales and Their Tellers.* London: Chatto and Windus, 1994.

The thing that made me become a writer was . . . a desire simply to tell stories. . . . [T]he kind of stories I was told as a child, by and large, were *Arabian Nights* kind of stories. It was those sort of fairytales. . . . And the belief was that by telling stories in that way, in that marvellous way, you could actually tell a kind of truth which you couldn't tell in other ways.

Salman Rushdie to Günter Grass, quoted in Michael Reder,
Conversations with Salman Rushdie

I get it, it's an old tale, it's been sung before. . . . I guess that's always so with any story. But what I'm trying to make here is still mine.

Salman Rushdie, *The Ground Beneath Her Feet*

2 Migrant Fictions
Salman Rushdie and the Fairy Tale

ANDREW TEVERSON

Fairy tales in Salman Rushdie's fiction appear in diverse guises. They crop up as decorative extras to gild a witty aside, function as integral elements in convoluted extended metaphors, and even (in a collective form) provide structural models for Rushdie's formal experiments with recursive narrative patterns and nonstop tale-telling. Rushdie also seems to have a more-than-passing awareness of the kinds of theories and methodologies that have developed to explicate and analyze the spread and significance of fairy tales. In one novel (*Haroun and the Sea of Stories*) he parodies the indexes that began to appear in the twentieth century as a means of cataloging the historical and geographical dissemination of folk-narrative material, in another (*The Ground Beneath Her Feet*) he references the efforts made by German linguist Max Müller to identify a common Indo-European basis of the myths and fairy tales of diverse cultures, and in yet another (*Shame*) he casually refers to the kinds of historicist/materialist readings of fairy tales that have become increasingly prevalent since the 1960s. There is no need to look in the forbidden room to find Rushdie's folkloric secret: fairy tales and their theories circulate freely in his "ocean of notions."

One of the questions that this chapter will endeavor to answer is *Why?*— what is it about the genre that appeals to Rushdie, and what kinds of argument is he trying to make when he employs fairy tales? The first and most obvious answer is that Rushdie, like many authors in a generation profoundly influenced by the work of Roland Barthes, reutilizes fairy tales in order to contest the models of social and cultural identity that such narratives have, in their canonical forms, reinforced. Like his close friend and contemporary, Angela Carter, Rushdie seeks to "loot and rummage in an official past" because that past "is a vast repository of outmoded lies, where you can check out what lies used to be à la mode and find the old lies on which new lies have been based" (Carter, "Notes" 41).[1] Also like Carter, however, Rushdie's approach to the genre is neither simple nor unambiguous, and fairy tales can fulfill complex, and sometimes contradictory, aesthetic or political functions. In Carter's fiction this is apparent in her efforts both to critique conventional representations of femininity in fairy tales and to use the transformatory and magical power of the fairy tale as a means of challenging conventional ideals of feminine behavior. In Rushdie's fiction, comparably, the fairy tale operates simultaneously as a narrative tradition that he wishes to *write back to* and a narrative tradition that, largely because of its oral origins, is already sufficiently fluid, sufficiently many-voiced, to assist him in his politico-aesthetic project of *writing back*. "Replying to one story with another which unravels the former has become central to contemporary thought and art," Marina Warner argues in her 1994 series of Reith Lectures for BBC Radio 4; and this is certainly true of Carter and Rushdie's writing (Warner 4).

Rushdie's more affirmative approaches to fairy tale are apparent in the responses that his novel *Haroun and the Sea of Stories* offers to the question posed by the intrepid protagonist Haroun near the start of the adventure: "what is the use of stories that aren't even true?" (22). Stories, the novel goes on to suggest, are important on a number of counts. They represent ways of seeing the world that cannot be fully proscribed by officially sanctioned, politically motivated descriptions of reality. They are "lies" that tell the "truth" by other means. They are also, in their untrained state at least, a testament to the diversity of human thought and to the falsity of any singular and all-subsuming account of the world ("many-stories rather than meta-stories" might well be the motto of the defenders of the story-sea). Perhaps the most direct answer to Haroun's question, however, is the one offered by Rushdie himself in an interview with Peter Tushingham, conducted on the eve of the first performance of a stage version of *Haroun* at the National Theatre in London: "Stories," for Rushdie, "tell us who we are." "*Stories are part of the glue that holds families, tribes and nations together*" (Tushingham, emphasis added).

The association between fairy or folk tales and cultural or national identity is nothing new. Indeed, about two hundred years before Rushdie's conversation with Tushingham, in what may be regarded as one of the founding moments of modern folk-narrative scholarship, the German poet and philosopher Johann Gottfried von Herder (1744–1803) urged his contemporaries to begin collecting the folk narratives and folk songs (*volkspoesie*) of the German people on the basis that these folk materials represented spontaneous expressions of the national soul. "Great empire!" Herder proclaimed in his *Von Ähnlichkeit der mittleren englischen und Dichtkunst* (1777):

> Empire of ten peoples, Germany! You have no Shakespeare. Have you also no songs of your forebears of which you can boast? . . . The voice of your fathers has faded and lies silent in the dust. Nation of heroic customs, of noble virtues and language, you have no impressions of your soul from the past?
>
> Without a doubt they once existed and perchance still do, but they lie under the mire. . . . Lend a hand then, my brothers, and show our nation what it is and is not. (qtd. in Wilson 828)

There were pressing historical reasons for this rousing polemic. Germany, at the time Herder was writing, was not a unified national body but, in Herder's own words, "a masterpiece of partition, entanglement and confusion" (Wilson 824). Much of the country was under the sway of foreign rulers and, worst of all, so far as Herder was concerned, foreign, particularly French, cultural influences were valorized over native German cultural influences (testified by the widespread affection for Charles Perrault's fairy tales rather than native German variants). To identify folk materials from a shared German cultural past, Herder believed, would be to identify a basis for German spiritual reunification in the present and to pave the way for a glorious Germanic golden age in the future.

In Rushdie's late-twentieth century assertions of the cultural importance
of stories there remains a trace, perhaps, of this formative Herderian impulse. Stories, Rushdie's fictions occasionally suggest, can be used to create
a sense of selfhood, a sense of shared cultural identity, in communities or
even nations that are uncertain about the ground beneath their feet. Stories
can also become a means of asserting the existence of a viable, cohesive political body that can be weighed in the balance against antagonistic political
forces: the forces of colonialism, for example, or neo-imperialism, or simply
of racism. In 1973 the North American scholar William Wilson observed
that "whenever nations turn to their folkloristic past to find faith in themselves and courage for their future, they are following lines laid down by
Herder" (Wilson 832). To the extent that postcolonial writers such as
Rushdie are, in their uses of fairy tales and folk narratives, endeavoring to
shore-up a form of cultural identity that has been demeaned or placed under
threat by colonialism and cultural imperialism, they, too, we might argue, albeit more distantly, are "following lines laid down by Herder."

Simultaneously, however, it will be apparent that the relationship between
storytelling and national identity advanced by each thinker is radically divergent. For Herder, folk narratives reflect an idea of national identity—a
spirit of the people—that is already, transcendentally, in existence; folk narratives are thus "the *imprints* of the soul of a nation" or "a *mirror* of its sen-
timents," and in them "the entire soul of a nation *reveals itself* most freely"
(Wilson 825–26, emphasis added). For Rushdie, by contrast, the concept of
national cultural identity does not predate the fictions that make it up; rather,
cultural identity is partly constituted in, and constructed by, a narrative heritage. "The idea of sequence, of narrative, of society as a story," as Rushdie
writes in his essay "In God we Trust," "is essential to the creation of nations" (*Homelands* 382). This argument is concisely allegorized by Rushdie
in a scene from his third novel, *Shame*, in which Bilquis Kamal, having entered the Hyder family through her marriage to Raza, is "forced" by the
matriarch-tyrant Bariamma to share her story with her new relatives in order to make herself part of the clan (76). Her story, once narrated, is subse-
quently retold by various members of the family and is "altered, at first, in
the retellings," but eventually it settles down, until "nobody, neither teller
nor listener, would tolerate any deviation from the hallowed, sacred text"
(76). It is at this point, according to Rushdie's narrator, that "Bilquis knew
that she had become a member of the family" for "in the sanctification of her
tale lay initiation, kinship, blood" (77).

In a novel in which familial structures are repeatedly presented as micro-cosmic models for national structures, the process by which the Hyder family imagines itself into being is clearly meant, by Rushdie, as an illustrative paradigm for the imagining into existence of the new nation of Pakistan, the narrative of which, in Rushdie's conception, is also being fiercely prescribed by overbearing tyrants. In both scenarios, Rushdie is concerned to demonstrate that the sacred stories of home and nation do not come into being because they reflect a social unity that is already actualized, as is the case in Herder's account. Rather, stories are used to generate, even enforce, such social unities—and it is this authorizing function that makes them into sacred texts. Storytelling, if we accept this reading, may serve to confirm the authority of the sacred, or else it can seek to profane the sacred by telling things differently. Bariamma uses storytelling to enforce the authority of the family over Bilquis, just as the Pakistani ruling elite strive to impose particular conceptions of history and national identity upon the populace. Rushdie also means the reader to understand, however, that the stories he will tell—the substrata of shameful narratives that have been silenced by the official histories—will resist and rework the accounts that have become sanctified by tradition and power. In either case—whether it is used to shore-up models of collectivity or to assault them—storytelling is accorded a potent formative social and political role in Rushdie's national imagining.

A second major distinction between Herder's and Rushdie's viewpoints results from their very different conceptions of the form of nationhood that is embodied in storytelling traditions. In Herder's conception, *volkspoesie* is an expression of an organic and essentialist idea (or ideal) of a national culture, that, by nature and by history, is distinct from all other national cultures ("the most natural state," Herder writes, is that of "*one* people, with *one* national character" [Wilson 822]). It was this sense of a need to use folk-narrative materials to affirm a singular and unified national ideal that led the principal beneficiaries of Herder's ideas, Wilhelm and Jacob Grimm, to excise stories that were considered insufficiently Germanic from successive editions of their *Kinder- und Hausmärchen* and replace them with tales that were more obviously related to the German tradition.[2] More alarmingly, it was Herder's suggestion that a pure essence of the German spirit was embodied in folk tales that led the Nazis to use them (and misuse Herder's arguments)[3] for the purposes of racist propaganda in the late 1930s and early 1940s.[4] Both of these impulses, the latter radically so, are alien to the spirit of Rushdie's writing. In the first place, Rushdie does not seek to isolate the tales of any one national tradition but to place the tales of diverse traditions in close conjunction (for reasons we shall explore shortly). In the second place, Rushdie does not use fairy tales as reflections of the absolute differences between national cultures but as evidence of the essential *permeability* of cultural and national frontiers. What is interesting about the fairy tale, for Rushdie, is not that one body of tales reflects "German" national traditions while another reflects "French" or "Indian" national traditions, but that tales from the French tradition also appear, in modified forms, in the German tradition; or that elements of Persian, Arabian, and Indian tale-telling traditions have cross-fertilized the tale-telling traditions of Europe since at least the time of the crusades.

The imperative to recognize the cross-cultural nature of fairy tales lies at the root of Rushdie's most explicit allusion to a widely known tale type in *Haroun and the Sea of Stories*. This allusion occurs shortly after the novella's hero, Haroun, has taken a sip from the waters of the "sea of stories" and hallucinated a virtual story-landscape in which a captive princess is found gazing from a single window in a high tower. "What Haroun was experiencing, though he didn't know it," we are told:

> was Princess Rescue Story Number S / 1001 / ZHT / 420 / 41(r)xi; and because the princess in this particular story had recently had a haircut and therefore had no long tresses to let down (unlike the heroine of Princess Rescue Story G / 1001 / RIM / 777 / M(w)i, better known as "Rapunzel"), Haroun as the hero was required to climb up the outside of the tower by clinging to the cracks between the stones with his bare hands and feet. (73)

Rushdie's primary aim in this passage is to create a comic effect of the kind later popularized by the *Shrek* films: he draws attention to the formulaic conventions of fairy tale in order to confound those conventions by introducing the extravagant device of a princess with a haircut.[5] Concealed in Rushdie's playful approach, however, is also a half-serious point about the nature of the genre. Fairy tales, Rushdie is suggesting, do not come as "single spies" but as "variants" of a "tale-type" that has a very broad, sometimes global, geographical spread: hence the narratives of the Brothers Grimm, suggested in the notation for the second tale Rushdie cites, also have their analogues in the *Arabian Nights,* suggested in the notation for the tale that

Haroun tastes—the letters "SZHr" pointing readers in the direction of Scheherazade.

The classic example of broad narrative dissemination usually cited by folklorists is the Cinderella tale type (ATU510), which, though it is now predominantly known in the West in its French form (as written by Perrault and animated by Disney), also has traditional analogues in China ("Yeh-hsien"), Germany ("Aschenputtle"), England ("Mossycoat"), Scotland ("Rashin Coatie"), Russia ("Burenushka"), and elsewhere.[6] The narrative that Rushdie chooses to illustrate this notion, whether by accident or design, has an equally complex genealogy and an equally complex series of national affiliations. The variant of "Rapunzel" (ATU310) that is now most popular is, as Rushdie suggests in his parody notation, the one that was collected by Grimm in 1812, but this is not the only version, nor indeed is it the first. Grimm took the tale from a story by Friedrich Schultz who had in turn borrowed it from a French tale "Persinette" by Mlle. Charlotte-Rose de la Force (published anonymously in *Contes des Contes* in 1692).[7] It is unclear where de la Force took it from, although there is an Italian variant in Basile's *Pentamerone,* and it is probable that Basile's version, through various complex paths, is, as Rushdie's notation implies, related to early Indian and Persian versions of the tale.[8] The implications of this genealogy are striking: fairy tales, in individual variants, may belong to different cultural traditions and may express the peculiarities of those cultural traditions, but they also have been, as tale types, shared by cultures over centuries and are therefore suggestive of the fact that cultures have formed historically through a process of hybridization and cultural exchange. They are, in this sense, a narrative reflection of Edward Said's view, expressed potently throughout Rushdie's work: that "although there are many divisions within it there is only one secular and historical world, and that neither nativism . . . nor regionalism, nor ideological smokescreens can hide societies, cultures and peoples from each other" (Said 137).

In *Haroun and the Sea of Stories,* assertions about the transcultural character of fairy tales, "writ large" in the figure of the endlessly various, intertextual story sea, form part of an argument about national identity that is being made in the novella at the level of plot. Two models of national organization are examined in *Haroun.* The first, into which Haroun is initially introduced, is that of the Guppees: a multiform and variegated collectivity in which mechanical hoopoes consort with many-mouthed fish, and Archimboldo-esque vegetable men fraternize with blue-bearded water genies. The second is expressed in the organization of Chup under the dictatorial rule of Khattam Shud, whose tyrannical authority is founded upon the establishment of strict boundaries between cultures and upon the polarization of social groups into antagonistic opposites. In Khattam Shud's Chup, Herder's prescription that "the most natural state is *one* people with *one* natural character" achieves its sinister apotheosis: oneness becomes an argument for cultural purity, and cultural purity becomes a basis for hatred and intolerance (Wilson 822). Gup, in contrast, by embodying that state of cultural being that Herder found monstrous and unnatural ("the wild mixtures of various breeds and nations under one sceptre"), emerges as a tolerant and just society, able to embrace difference and accept indeterminacy (Wilson 822). It is significant, in this regard, that in Rushdie's novel the Guppees are the defenders of the story-sea, while Khattam Shud is its enemy and seeks its destruction: stories in their uncensored state, Rushdie is suggesting, exhibit a native hybridity and a formal liminality that tend to reinforce the claims of those who see cultural identity as an ongoing and unending negotiation of differences and to offer a riposte to those ideologues who would insist upon cultural purity and cultural segregation. This, for Rushdie, is true of all stories, whatever their genre or medium, but it is a notion that is particularly true of fairy tales and folk tales, because these are narratives that have circulated for centuries in diverse forms (oral, literary, filmic), and that have, in the process of their circulation, crossed most of the ideological borderlines that societies have erected to keep tribe from tribe and nation from nation. Fairy tales are fiction's natural migrants, and it is for this reason that Rushdie, as a novelist who seeks to construct a "migrant's eye view of the world," and who claims that he writes "from the very experience of uprooting, disjuncture and metamorphosis," makes them so central to his thought and art (*Homelands* 394).

The radical dissimilarity between Herder's conception of the nationalistic functions of folklore and Rushdie's should now be apparent. Herder aimed to use the folk narrative as a means of shoring-up an idea of unitary nationalist identity; while for Rushdie, the fairy tale becomes a valuable fictional resource precisely because, in its complex provenance and varied dissemination, it suggests that all cultures are a product of commingling and cross-fertilization.

Beauty Bibi and the Beastji: Hybridizing Fairy Tales

This at least offers an account of Rushdie's interest in the genre of fairy tales as he finds it; but Rushdie isn't simply seeking to show readers what fairy tales do, he is also, more militantly, seeking to make fairy tales serve his own fictional agendas. Hence his fiction does not merely reflect the transcultural character of fairy tales but endeavors to emphasize and extend that trans-culturalism by placing narratives from diverse locations of culture in striking new conjunctions. This tendency is apparent in *Haroun*, which not only emphasizes the multicultural nature of storytelling in traditional oral contexts but also seeks to intensify the hybrid character of storytelling by drawing intertextually upon a wide range of narrative pre-texts, including *Alice in Wonderland, Gulliver's Travels,* the film of *The Wizard of Oz,* Satyajit Ray's film *Goopy Gyne Bagha Byne* (*The Adventures of Goopy and Bagha*), Grimms' tales, the *Arabian Nights,* and Farid ud-din Attar's Sufi poem *The Conference of the Birds*—to cite a few examples. Rushdie's intentions in using this broad range of narrative reference points are identical to his intentions in using multicultural intertextuality more generally: he is seeking to use the diverse cultural signs of which colonial history has made him an inheritor in order to forge a new aesthetic form that is both of his own making and that reflects his own cultural and political location more effectively than any previously existing aesthetic has done.

A similar tendency is apparent in Rushdie's subsequent novel, *The Moor's Last Sigh* (1995), which also employs a "hyperabundant cavalcade" of narrative references to make arguments about the nature of cultural eclecticism in the modern world (*Moor* 84). As in *Haroun and the Sea of Stories,* this hyperabundance is apparent both in the iconographic representations of storytelling provided in the fiction and in the intertextual use that the fiction itself makes of disparate storytelling traditions. Hence, the mural that the Portuguese-Indian painter Vasco da Gama creates in the nursery of the protagonist Moraes Zogoiby (a structural equivalent of the sea of stories) shows readers a vision in which "talking roosters, booted pussies and flying red-caped Wonder Dogs" coexist with "djinns on carpets and thieves in giant pitchers" (152), while Rushdie's narrative itself conjures a world in which stories by Hans Christian Andersen are referred to alongside French *contes des fées,* the Brothers Grimm are reintroduced to the *Arabian Nights,* and Disney reworkings of nineteenth-century German variants of ancient oral tale types find themselves translated and transformed once again through their re-representation in a late-twentieth-century anglophone Indian context.[9] The sense of cultural complexity that such uses of storytelling engender functions, on one level, to create the dazzling, leaping, dancing surfaces of Rushdie's prose, but on another they also constitute part of an argument that Rushdie is making about the nature of cultural identity: that identity is not fixed, that it is not determined by one cultural influence alone, that human beings are always capable of migration, mutation, flux, and transformation.[10] Such arguments about cultural identity, importantly, dovetail into Rushdie's broader political-satirical agenda in *The Moor's Last Sigh*—to critique any ideological / cultural group that endeavors to present itself as more authentic, more worthy of "belonging" than any other. More specifically, in *The Moor's Last Sigh*, Rushdie's dominant political aim is to mount a pungent polemic against Hindu nationalist parties such as the Shiv Sena in Maharashtra (thinly disguised as Mumbai's Axis) who, as proponents of *Hindutva*, maintain that India should become a Hindu state and who have been waging a vicious internecine war against other communities, particularly Muslims, and the symbols that represent them. Rushdie's response to such proto-fascist activities at the formal level of his fiction is quite a simple one: If it is now impossible to extricate Muslim narrative traditions from Hindu narrative traditions in India, how can it be possible to make absolute distinctions between Muslim and Hindu communities?

Rushdie's arguments about the fluidity of identity, we might further note, are reflected not just in the formal constitution of the fairy tale as a genre but also in its central thematic preoccupations: for fairy tale in all cultures involves images of magical transformations, sudden identity shifts, the doubling and multiplication of selves, and maturation rituals that take the questing hero from one land to another and from one stage of selfhood to another. Arguably, the popular tale type that reflects the mutability of self most explicitly is "Beauty and the Beast" (ATU425C); so it is unsurprising that contemporary writers such as Angela Carter and Salman Rushdie, with their interest in the performance of selfhood and the boundaries of human cultural identity, should return to this narrative frequently in their fiction. For Carter, in *The Bloody Chamber*, the tale's emphasis on the blurring of the lines between human and beast, between nature and culture, between normality and monstrosity, offer her a means of exploring issues of gendered identity. ("It is Carter's genius," as Rushdie writes in his introduction to her collected short stories, "to make the fable of Beauty and the Beast a metaphor for all the myriad yearnings and dangers of sexual relations" [*Step Across* 43]).

Rushdie's own sustained examination of "Beauty and the Beast" in *Shame*, published only four years after *The Bloody Chamber*, may well have been influenced by Carter's treatment of the tale. Indeed, the *kitch* ending of "The Courtship of Mr Lyon," in which Carter seems to underline the smugness of bourgeois marriage, is echoed explicitly by Rushdie in the description of the tale provided by the Greatest Living Poet in *Shame*. In Carter's narrative the story ends with a vision of a contented "Mr and Mrs Lyon" walking in the garden; in Rushdie's Greatest Living Poet's version the lovers likewise "become at last, and happily, just plain Mr Husband and Mrs Wife" (Carter, *Chamber* 66; *Shame* 158). In both instances, we might argue, an attempt is being made to puncture the romantic expectations of the fairy tale, and, in so doing, to mount a feminist-orientated criticism of the source narrative and its efforts to persuade young girls to accept undesirable partners for the sake of their fathers' good fortunes.[11] If Rushdie's uses of the tale coincide with Carter's in this respect, however, he also makes the tale work in very different ways too. In the first place, the categories that Rushdie is seeking to dissolve by bringing the opposed poles of Beautyness and Beastdom together are not so much gendered as cultural, as is made clear by the Greatest Living Poet when he explains that "Beauty and the Beast," though superficially a French narrative, ought to be seen as a "completely Eastern story" (a thesis that he supports with a rather brilliant Indianized account of the tale in which the Beast becomes "Beast Sahib," Beauty becomes "Beauty Bibi," and the wealthy merchant a "zamindar" [*Shame* 158–59]). In the second place, "Beauty and the Beast" in Rushdie's novel works alongside other narratives of doubled identities and covert monstrosity such as *The Strange Tale of Dr. Jekyll and Mr. Hyde* to support a form of political satire that is rarely apparent in Carter's more introspective reflections on identity formation. The emphasis on the "doubling" of identity that occurs in "Beauty and the Beast," for instance, becomes in Rushdie's hands a means of supporting his assertion that in Pakistan in the 1970s and 1980s it became difficult to distinguish between unelected military dictators like General Zia ul-Haq and democratically elected politicians like Zulfikar Ali Bhutto. Likewise, the traditional story's conventional homiletic reflection on the unreliability of appearances is corralled, in *Shame*, into the service of Rushdie's broader intention to suggest that the civilized exterior of Pakistani public life in this period concealed and repressed a festering national shame.[12]

These politicized uses of the fairy tale do not go unnoticed by Rushdie's narrator, although his inclination is to argue that the fairy-tale qualities of his narration function as an antidote rather than as a catalyst to politics. "I am only telling a sort of modern fairy-tale," he reassures readers, "so that's all right; nobody need get upset, or take anything I say too seriously" (70). Since, however, this disclaimer appears almost immediately after one of the more extended passages of satirical denunciation in the novel, it is evident that Rushdie means his reader to see through this rhetorical pose. The fairy tale may well serve as a mask behind which Rushdie can hide when he delivers his stinging satirical observations, but it is clearly not true that the fairy-tale qualities of the fiction necessarily exclude, or even sit ill at ease with, an engagement with serious political issues of the sort that might get Rushdie into trouble. In *Shame* the genre of fairy tale, whatever the narrator may claim, becomes another tool in the impressive fictive arsenal that Rushdie hurls at Pakistan's dictators; likewise, in *Haroun* it becomes a means of challenging the fanatical absolutism of Khattam Shud, and in *The Moor's Last Sigh* it becomes a means of undermining the puritanical fantasies of the Shiv Sena. Indeed, in all Rushdie's references to the fairy tale—whether he is using "Ali Baba and the Forty Thieves" to reinforce an angry sideswipe at the murderous irresponsibility of Union Carbide's activities in Bhopal in *The Satanic Verses* (1988) or the Grimms' "Fisherman and his Wife" to comment on commodity fetishism in the short story "At the Auction of the Ruby Slippers" (1994)—the apparently innocuous and fantastic register of the genre becomes a means of addressing social or political issues and making strident political statements (*Verses* 56; *East, West* 94). Rushdie's fiction, in this regard, shares a great deal with that of his slightly older contemporary (and principal influence) Günter Grass, who, in novels such as *Die Blechtrommel* (1959, *The Tin Drum*) and *Der Butt* (1977, *The Flounder*) pioneered the use of fairy tales as vehicles of political satire in the second part of the twentieth century.

Indo-European Syncretism

Had The Greatest Living Poet but known it (perhaps he does), there *is* evidence that the French tale of "Beauty and the Beast" to which he refers is shared with an Indian tradition.[13] Indeed, some commentators aver that all European fairy tales share an origin with Indian fairy tales. Wilhelm Grimm, for instance, in his notes to the 1856 edition of the *Kinder- und Hausmärchen* argues that common elements in folk tales from diverse places suggest a source in the myths of primitive "Indo-European" (or "Indo-Germanic") peoples.[14] Comparably, the German Sanskrit scholar, Max Müller, argued in his *Comparative Mythology* (1856), that the parallels between Classical Greek and Vedic (Sanskrit) storytelling traditions suggest a common Indo-European source culture just as surely as the parallels between the French, Spanish, Portuguese, and Italian languages indicate a common source in Latin.

Rushdie gives no indication that he is aware of this theory in *Shame*. In *Haroun and the Sea of Stories,* however, it seems, on occasion, that Rushdie is flirting with the possibility, first floated by the folklorists Loiseleur Deslongchamps and Theodor Benfy, of an Indian source of stories.[15] This is suggested most directly in the fact that the "sea of stories," which is presented in *Haroun* as a wellspring of world narrative, also appears to be a metaphorical embodiment of the Sanskrit narrative collection the *Katha Sarit Sagara*—translated into English by C. H. Tawney in 1880 as *The Ocean of Streams of Story.*[16] Rushdie also refers to the various theories concerning Indo-European folk-tale origins explicitly in his sixth novel, *The Ground Beneath Her Feet,* in which two of his characters, a last-years-of-the-Raj Englishman, William Methwold (who made his first appearance in *Midnight's Children*) and an anglophile Parsi knight, Sir Darius Xeres Cama, are seduced by the writings of Müller and his disciple Georges Dumézil into spending many happy hours together in a library exploring "the relationships between the Homeric and Indian mythological traditions" (41).

The potential appeal of theories that emphasize an Indian or Indo-European source of stories to a man in Rushdie's cultural location are obvious. Rushdie, like Müller, is interested (personally, aesthetically, and politically) in exploring points of connection between Indian culture and English culture; he is also, himself, a kind of comparative mythologist, whose principal fictional method involves the fusion of the narratives of diverse cultures, particularly English and Indian, into new aesthetic composites. Rushdie's approach to Müller's work in *The Ground Beneath Her Feet,* however, suggests a significant distance between his own comparative mythologies and those of Müller and Dumézil because it appears more in the vein of satire than recommendation. Methwold and Sir Darius, it emerges, are preoccupied with Müller because they each have a vested interest in seeing the colonial alliance between India and England, from which they have benefited, justified. The ways in which they use the work of Müller, moreover, demonstrate that their study, far from being a means of grappling with modern Indian realities, involves a nostalgic retreat from the divisiveness of contemporary nationalist politics to an idyllic and mythological time of Anglo-Indian harmony. "Outside the library, the last phases of the colonial history of England and India took their well-known course," Rushdie's narrator observes, "But Sir Darius and William Methwold had sealed themselves away from the contemporary and sought refuge in the eternal" (42).

In this commentary on Sir Darius and Methwold's escapist fascination with comparative mythology it is easy to read Rushdie's implied critique of Müller. Rooting the comparability of Indian and European cultures in ancient, even mythical time, Rushdie seems to suggest, circumvents the more salient political fact that Indian and European cultures have become comparable, not because they have been linked at source, but because they have become linked in material time as a result of a violent history of crusades and imperialism. His own comparative mythologies, by contrast, seek not to retreat to or reconstruct points of origin, but to examine what the commonalties between narrative traditions can tell us about the power relations between national and cultural units in the relatively recent past. Hence, the obvious parallels that are made between Indian cultural traditions and European cultural traditions by Rushdie in *The Ground Beneath Her Feet* (such as the parallel between the classical Greek story of Orpheus and Eurydice and the Hindu myth of Rati and Kama) are not intended as an indication of the essential harmony between the two cultural traditions but of the cultural complexity that his principal migrant characters—Rai, Vina, and Ormus—have become inheritors of and with which they must try to work in the present.[17]

Rushdie's implied critique of Müller is made more explicit in the novel when his characters discover what profound abuses the Nazis are able to make of his theories. For Müller, comparative mythology was not designed to support racist ideological positions but to undermine them by suggesting that "man" is "a member of one great family" (6). Müller's identification of a common Indo-European heritage, however, is founded upon the assumption that "two families of language" emerged from the primal "Rhematic" period: the Indo-European or "Aryan" languages (incorporating Teutonic, Celtic, Italic, Hellenic, and Indic dialects); and the "Semitic" languages (incorporating Arabian, Armenian, and Hebrew dialects). In this fundamental—and, it needs to be said, purely linguistic—distinction, Nazi ideologues saw a "historical" justification for their belief that there were two races of man—Aryan and Semitic—and that one was superior to the other. Thus, as Rushdie writes:

The word "Aryan," which for Max Müller and his generation, had a purely linguistic meaning, was now in the hands of less academic persons, poisoners, who were speaking of races of men, races of masters and races of servants and other races too, races whose fundamental impurity necessitated drastic measures. . . . By one of the wild improbabilities that, taken collectively, represent the history of the human race, the arcane field of research in which Sir Darius and William Methwold had chosen to sequester themselves had been twisted and pressed into the service of the great evil of the age. (*Ground* 44)

Clearly, Müller should not be saddled with the blame for such theoretical distortions—nevertheless, it is suggested in Rushdie's observation of the link between Müller's comparative mythology and Nazism, that his work, by seeking to identify moments of origin and purity, somehow creates the preconditions for dangerous and exclusivist forms of nationalism. Rushdie's response to Müller, therefore, is similar to his response to Herder: culture has always been hybrid; there are no pure origins; there is no point at which stories emerged in the possession of one people or another; and there is no point "before" stories became objects of exchange and products of interaction. Stories are dialogic and performative in their very constitution, and any attempt to remove them from the dialogue between cultures is a falsification— both of culture and of the stories themselves.

The *Nights*, Orality, and India

As this chapter has so far demonstrated, Rushdie's sampling of the genre of fairy tales is, for consistent political reasons, almost as diverse as the genre itself. The single most important folkloric influence on Rushdie's work, however, must remain the *Arabian Nights*—the collection that Rushdie's father read him as a child and that Rushdie later told an interviewer would be his first choice were he to be stranded on a desert island because it "contains all other stories."[18] The *Nights*, accordingly, appears in various guises throughout Rushdie's work. In *Midnight's Children*, the frame tale of the *Nights*, in which Scheherazade keeps herself alive by telling stories to her tyrant husband Shahryar, adds weight to the novel's conceit that Saleem is writing against death. In *The Satanic Verses* the story of "Aladdin and His Magic Lamp" provides Rushdie with an analogue with which to explore the tense Oedipal relations between Saladin Chamcha and his father. In *Haroun and the Sea of Stories* the *Nights* and the *Katha Sarit Sagara,* as we have seen, become important structural models in the composition of Kahani's fairy-tale sea. Finally, in *Shalimar the Clown* the *Nights*—derived notion of writing *against* death is morphed into an act of writing *into* death as Kashmira seeks to avenge the murder of her father and mother by assassinating Shalimar with a barrage of poisonous letters. "I am your black Scheherazade," she tells him, "I will write to you without missing a day without missing a night not to save my life but to take yours" (374).

The thematic and structural dependence of Rushdie's fictions upon the *Arabian Nights* has been interpreted in various ways by academic commentators. Nancy E. Batty argues persuasively that narrative patterns derived from collections such as the *Arabian Nights* enable Rushdie to build suspense into his narrative (49–65). Robert Irwin, alternatively, suggests that the relative informality and exuberance to be found in carnivalistic texts like the *Nights* is used by Rushdie as a means of challenging orthodoxy and officialdom in religious and political spheres (as Irwin phrases it: "Rushdie's *Nights* represents an alternative tradition in Islamic literature, something to set against the dour decrees of the mullahs of the Middle East and the dictators of the Indian subcontinent" [289]). In my own essay on the subject, "The Number of Magic Alternatives," I argue that "the sublime architecture borrowed from the *Arabian Nights,*" via the Gothic writers of the eighteenth and nineteenth centuries, is used by Rushdie in *Midnight's Children* as a means of imagining forms of nationhood and national belonging "that classic [enlightenment] rules about form or structure" would struggle to do justice to ("Alternatives" 226). All these arguments, in one way or another, are dependent upon the idea that the *Arabian Nights* is, first, a literary collection of tales that heralds from an oral tradition; and second, that the oral tradition it heralds from is, in part, Indian—a fact that Rushdie emphasizes by indicating the similarities between the *Nights* and more purely Indic tale collections such as the *Panchatantra* and the *Katha Sarit Sagara.* In the remainder of this chapter, it is upon these two characteristics of the tale-telling traditions from which Rushdie draws inspiration that I would like to focus.

The influence of oral narrative structures upon Rushdie's fiction is most effectively illustrated by Rushdie's account of a trip he made to hear an Indian storyteller spinning fictions in Baroda in 1983—an event that led him to recall the extent to which "the shape of the oral narrative" had inspired him in the writing of both *Midnight's Children* and *Shame.* This shape, as

Rushdie notes, is "not linear," it "does not go from the beginning to the middle to the end" like the classical Aristotelian narrative but is "pyrotechnichal": it "goes in great swoops, it goes in spirals or in loops, it every so often reiterates something that has happened earlier to remind you, and then takes you off again, sometimes summarises itself, it frequently digresses off into something that the story-teller appears just to have thought of, then it comes back to the main thrust of the narrative" ("*Midnight's Children* and *Shame*" 8).

Rushdie was sufficiently impressed with this oleaginous and recursive form to "attempt the creation" in *Midnight's Children* "of a literary form which corresponds to the form of the oral narrative and which, with any luck, [would] succeed in holding readers, for reasons of its shape, in the same way that the oral narrative holds audiences for reasons of its shape, as well as its narrative" ("*Midnight's Children* and *Shame*" 8). The result is a novel that has a number of features more commonly associated with spoken storytelling conventions than with written ones: it is highly digressive but always returns to the main point; it employs "formulaic repetition" of the kind that Milman Parry and Albert Lord identified as characteristic of literature with oral origins;[19] it offsets the linearity of its central plot (a young man's maturation narrative) with an antilinear tendency to return repeatedly to an established constellation of narrative motifs or "leitsatze";[20] and finally, it is self-conscious, both in its recognition of the importance of the storyteller and in its awareness of the role played by an attendant audience (in this instance figured by Padma, whose role as recipient of Saleem's tale provides Rushdie with a hook on which to hang the "written-as-if-spoken" qualities of the fiction).[21] The functions of this oral register in *Midnight's Children*—a technique defined by the Russian formalists as *skaz*—are several fold.[22] First, Rushdie uses the oral voice because it enables him to emphasize the *placement* of the literary utterance and, in so doing, to suggest that his fictions are not ahistorical events that take place independent of community and culture, but, rather, grow out of a cultural exchange. Connectedly, *skaz* also enables him to remove the authority of the disembodied voice from the fiction and replace it with an uncertain author figure, whose words, like the words of the speaking individual, are fallible, and whose perceptions have to compete with the perceptions of others in a multivocal and dialogue-bound environment. In both these cases, the vocal registers employed by Rushdie are designed to undermine the appearance that literary texts may have of being objective, because they demonstrate that all speech and writing come from somewhere (a speaker) and are shaped by the subjective concerns of an unreliable individual, performing to meet the demands of a fickle audience, and informed by the historical and ideological agendas of a unique cultural location. Rushdie thus takes the performative conditions that are characteristic of the creation of oral folk narratives and uses them to develop a distinctively postmodernist aesthetic argument: that no text can have an absolute claim to truth above and beyond the specific conditions of its production.

Rushdie himself makes note of the strange harmony that holds between traditional storytelling techniques and postmodern aesthetics in an interview with David Brooks conducted in 1984. "One of the strange things about the oral narrative," Rushdie points out:

> is that you find there a form which is thousands of years old, and yet which has all the methods of the post-modernist novel . . . it is absolutely acceptable that the narrator will every so often enter his own story and chat about it—that he'll comment on the tale, digress because the tale reminds him of something, and then come back to the point. All these things, which are absolutely second nature in an oral tale, become bizarre modern inventions when you write them down. It seems to me that when you look at the old narrative and use it, as I tried to do, as a basis of a novel, you become a post-modernist writer by being a very traditional one. (qtd. in Reder 59)

For Rushdie, at least, the circulating codes apparent in the structure of traditional oral tales segue effortlessly into the circulating codes that Barthes identifies as being characteristic of the modern experimental literary text. Some critics of Rushdie, however, have found the fusion of traditional Indian narration and postmodern aesthetics in his work problematic. Tariq Rahman, for instance, argues lucidly that the appropriation of formal elements from Indian oral traditions does not necessarily mean that Rushdie's fiction connects with an Indian tradition at the philosophical level. "The Indian narrator," Rahman explains, "has a fixed belief in a certain objective reality and he generally works to reinforce a traditional moral order. He is not complex and uncertain in his response to reality, however much he may fantasise." Rushdie's narrator, by contrast: "is modernist in tradition, in so far as he stands at a slight angle to external reality as perceived by others. In fact, whereas the Indian fable, however fantastic, is contingent upon a shared world view, Rushdie's narratorial techniques owe much to those philosophical movements in the West which have shattered the consensus of opinion about values as well as reality itself" (25). More critically still, Aijaz Ahmad, has contended that though Rushdie may promote the view in his writing that his borrowings from Indian epics and Indian storytelling traditions give his fiction a "quintessential Indianness [of] form," his fictions' clear lines of descent from European Modernism and Postmodernism suggests that he is better understood as a writer who uses the veneer of Indian storytelling to reinforce the appeal of his fictions to Western readers (126).

Such observations about Rushdie's fictions are only criticisms of his work if we assume that Rushdie wishes to conceal the fact that he is transforming the traditions of Indian oral storytelling when he makes use of them in the context of the modernist or postmodernist novel. At no point, however, does Rushdie suggest that he is using Indian folk materials in the hope of giving his fiction the appearance that it is returning to an originary and authentic mode of Indian/Eastern narration; neither has he ever suggested that he is seeking to avoid the fact that his fictions are heavily dependent, at one and the same time, upon both Indian *and* Euro-American intellectual traditions. On the contrary, as my discussion in the first half of this chapter has suggested, Rushdie is seeking, willfully and self-consciously, to place elements of the Euro-American novelistic tradition in new conjunctions with elements of the Indian or Arabic storytelling tradition, in order, first, to see how one tradition might productively transform the other, and, second, to show how fictions have been brought into new hybrid relations in his own experience, as a migrant intellectual working in increasingly globalized, postcolonial arenas.

Rushdie's use of the *Arabian Nights* as a cycle that mediates this oral tradition is a case in point precisely because it is a narrative body that has survived and achieved its current form at the interstices of cross-cultural exchanges between "East" and "West." As Rushdie suggests to Amina Meer in interview in 1989, the *Nights* has reached him, as a contemporary writer, from several directions simultaneously: it has come to him from India, as a narrative imported into the subcontinent by Muslim migrants; it has come to him from the European Orientalist tradition, into which it was incorporated by eighteenth- and nineteenth-century fantasists seeking a source of "exotic" and "extravagant" wonders; and—most significantly—it has come to him via Spain, to which it was taken by Moorish settlers and from whence it entered the European novel via Cervantes's *Don Quixote*, ultimately ending up in South American magical realist fiction which, in turn, was a direct influence on Rushdie (Reder 111).[23] Each line of descent carries different implications for Rushdie's usage. The first connects his fictions to the storytelling traditions of the land of his birth; the second enables him to engage with uses made of the collection in his adopted homeland; and the third enables him to establish a direct if convoluted connection between the modern novel and the traditional tale (thus providing a kind of riposte to Ahmad and Rahman). The significance of Rushdie's use of the *Nights,* however, does not reside in any one of these lineages but in the very fact that all three routes are possible. Cultural inheritance, so far as Rushdie is concerned, is not about either/or—East or West, Indian or British—but about both/and; and ancient folkloric texts such as the *Nights,* which have their origins in Persian, Indian, and Arabic cultures, which traveled to France and Spain and England over five hundred years of cultural exchange and returned to India via England in postcolonial fictions such as Rushdie's, demonstrate that this is so.[24]

This does not mean, however, that texts like the *Nights* are used by Rushdie for purely assimilationist purposes: to identify the "compatibility" of East and West and so to eradicate the history of violence, conquest, and colonial expropriation that has brought the two cultures into conjunction (this, indeed, is the mistake of William Methwold and Sir Darius). Rather, Rushdie, while he is interested in the points of conjunction to be found in Eastern and Western traditions that enable a dialogue between them, is also using the *Nights* and associated Indian storytelling traditions as part of a strategy for intervening in, and posing challenges to, a European novel tradition that, perhaps ignorant of its own origins, has marginalized, or relegated to the status of purely "exotic," the narrative practices that Rushdie is seeking to revivify. He poses this challenge, in part, by using the storytelling traditions of the "East" in ways that they have not been used before in the European novel format. For instance, he challenges the Western Orientalist representation of the "East" as timeless and ahistorical by emphasizing the idea, if not the actuality, of the Indian storyteller, who speaks, in his own voice, from known historical and geographical locations. He also challenges the covert Orientalist assumption that Eastern storytelling traditions are secondary or inferior to Western storytelling traditions (lurid fantasy rather than serious art) by presenting the tales of his storyteller as if they were on a par with, and integral to, Western storytelling traditions.[25] In both these respects Rushdie presents the storytelling traditions of the non-West in such a way as to redress the imbalance of authority granted to each tradition in classical European fiction. Partly because of this, I would suggest, Rushdie is not simply asking the European novel to accommodate the storytelling traditions of the once-colonized; rather, he uses these storytelling traditions as a means of intervening in the dominant cultural forms employed by the colonizer, in order to make them recognize new forms of expression and in order to force them to modify their own forms of expression.

Conclusion

This chapter began by posing Haroun's question *What is the use of stories that aren't even true?* Several possible responses have been suggested. Stories offer Rushdie a means of exploring notions of cultural belonging and national heritage; they also, in Rushdie's hands, become a means of challenging "absolutist" interpretations of cultural identity—either because they are, by nature, profligate, transcultural fictions, or because they can offer irreverent, carnival perspectives that may be set against officially sanctioned narratives of nation and state. Because stories are migratory, moreover, they also provide Rushdie with an imaginative means of tracing the passages of peoples across the world—of seeing what they take with them, what they leave behind, how their stories translate into new cultures, and how their stories transform the cultures into which they are translated. Above all, however, stories are important to Rushdie because in their oceanic form—as a cross-global melee of ever-changing, interanimating texts and inter-texts—they offer him a fictive dwelling place in which he does not have to choose between the various cultural poles that constitute his own cultural location.

In concluding, this point may be made again, via a brief exposition on the provenance of the phrase "it was so it was not so" that appears repeatedly in *The Satanic Verses*. The phrase resonates in that novel because it enables Rushdie to reflect enigmatically upon the various forms of ambivalence that he wishes to explore: the ambivalent relationship between fantasy and reality, the ambivalence of sacred texts and their genesis, and the ambivalence of cultural identity experienced by migrants in diasporic communities. The phrase's ambivalence, however, is not solely a result of its subject matter—which asks us to consider the impossible possibility that a thing can be "so" and "not so" at one and the same time. Ambivalence also resides in the genealogy of the phrase. For on the one hand, the phrase heralds from an Eastern tradition, where it can be found in the Arabic rhyming couplet cited in *The Satanic Verses*, *Kan ma kan / Fi qadim azzaman;* and on the other it can be found in the English tradition, where it appears in "Mr Fox" (AT955c), the dominant print version of which appeared in Malone's *Variorum Shakespeare* in 1821, where it served as a gloss for an expression employed by Benedick in Shakespeare's *Much Ado About Nothing* (1598): "Like the old tale, my lord, 'it is not so, nor twas not so, but, indeed, God forbid it should be so'" (I.i.226–28).[26] When the phrase reappears in Rushdie's novel, it clearly owes a debt to both traditions: it is quoted in its Arabic form, but it is also referenced in terms so strikingly similar to Benedick's (*"it was so and it was not so*, as the old stories used to say") that it is hard to believe that Rushdie does not have the English tradition in mind (67). Its function in Rushdie's fiction, we may conclude, is neither to represent the Eastern tradition nor the Western tradition but to do both at the same time—or, indeed, to show that "bothness" is a characteristic of such cultural expressions. The lesson this enigmatic phrase has to teach us about the functions of the fairy tale in Rushdie's fiction is an instructive one: in subject matter, the fairy tale is important to Rushdie because it enables him to entertain the possibility (to quote Borges on the *Arabian Nights*) "that besides the causal relations we know, there is another causal relation" (51); but in genealogy too fairy tale becomes meaningful to Rushdie because at any one time it has multiple cultural allegiances that cannot be reduced to singularity or simplicity that leave the narrative perplexed and inconclusive but still *a tale that can be told*. The fairy tale, in this sense, provides Rushdie with a means of thinking about cultural identity and writing about cultural identity in ways that do not require him to make cultural identity add up to what Henry Louis Gates would call a singular self-image (8).

Notes

1. This is a comparison that is not lost on Carter, who believes that her own politicized assault on traditional genres gives her "much . . . in common with certain Third World writers . . . who are transforming actual fiction forms to both reflect and to precipitate changes in the way people feel about themselves, putting new wine in old bottles and, in some cases, old wine in new bottles" ("Notes" 42).

2. See Bottigheimer 204. The Grimms, in doing this, were not suggesting that German fairy tales were necessarily better than others, neither were they attempting to conceal the international nature of the tales. Their collection aimed to be a

German one, but it did not form part of an argument in favor of exclusive German nationalism. See Kamenetsky 48.

3. Herder's arguments were linguistic and cultural, not racial. He was also writing against the imperialist expansion of nations since his suggestion that nations have an essential characteristic of their own formed part of an argument that different nations should not encroach upon the territories and well-being of others. Clearly a message not heeded by Hitler.

4. See Kamenetsky 241–48.

5. Creating comic effects by reworking fairy tales to challenge readers' expectations is also central to the work of Jeanne Desy, Tanith Lee (in her children's fictions), and Jay Williams: the literary precursors of *Shrek*. See Alison Lurie 372–86, 408–17.

6. Cox in her seminal study identifies 345 variants of the Cinderella tale-type, and later commentators such as Rooth have expanded her count by including tales from Eastern Europe, Indo-China, and the Near East. Philip includes a manageable selection of Cinderella variants in his *The Cinderella Story* and offers a clarification of the tangled history of the narrative. For a full listing of variants see 293–98.

7. The Grimms claim that Schulz took it from oral tradition; Zipes points in the direction of de la Force. See Notes, *Grimm's Household Tales*, trans. Margaret Hunt 1: 353; and Jack Zipes, *The Complete Fairy Tales of the Brothers Grimm*, 729. See also Uther 190–91.

8. Indic variants are listed by Roberts and Thompson 50.

9. Rushdie refers, respectively, to Hans Christian Andersen's "Snow Queen" (155, 432), Mme. de Beaumont's "Beauty and the Beast" (47), the Grimms' "Rumpelstiltskin" (111) and "Frog King" (232, 312, 367), and Disney's *Snow White and the Seven Dwarfs* (66, 433).

10. Deszcz, in "Salman Rushdie's Magical Kingdom," argues that Rushdie, in *The Moor*, follows in the critical tradition established by Ernst Bloch because he uses "fairy-tale utopia" as a means of imagining "how dominant social structures could be changed into more congenial ones" (32). The argument also reappears in Deszcz's *Rushdie in Wonderland*, 132–36.

11. The dominant source is Jeanne-Marie Leprince de Beaumont's "La Belle et la Bête" of 1757.

12. Deszcz in "Salman Rushdie's Attempt at a Feminist Fairytale Reconfiguration in *Shame*" argues that Rushdie rewrites "Beauty and the Beast" as a "male feminist." See also Deszcz, *Rushdie in Wonderland* 64–83). Deszcz's argument is designed as a response to feminist critiques of Rushdie's representation of women in

Shame such as those offered by Cundy. While Rushdie's representation of women in *Shame* is an important subject of ongoing discussion, however, my inclination is to argue that Rushdie uses fairy tale in *Shame* primarily as a means of furthering his broader politico-satirical agendas and only secondarily as a means of addressing questions of gender.

13. Indic variants are listed in Roberts and Thompson 62. See also Uther 252–53.

14. See Thompson 370–71 and Grimm, *Household Tales* 2: 580–81.

15. Benfy's theory was based on his study of the *Panchatantra* and expressed in his introduction to his translation of 1859 (Thompson 376). It needs, perhaps, to be noted that Benfy's theory of an Indian origin of European folk tale differs significantly from the theory that there is a shared Indo-European source culture. Indeed, proponents of both theories quarreled bitterly.

16. It is interesting to observe that proponents of a "source" of stories often use the kind of watery metaphors that Rushdie expands into a sea in his novella. Wilhelm Grimm notes that a "common source" of stories is "like a well, the depth of which no one knows but from which each draws according to his need" (Thompson 369); Sir George Cox argues for "a fountain of mythical language from which have flowed all the streams of Aryan epic poetry, streams so varied in their character yet agreeing so close in their elements" (Thompson 372). Finally, Benfy posits an "inexhaustible, ever-bubbling fountain at which all the people, high and low . . . continually refresh themselves anew" (Thompson 378).

17. For a detailed consideration of Rushdie's use of Orphic narratives in this novel, see Falconer.

18. See Hamilton 92 and Weatherby 50.

19. Parry and Lord argued that formulaic repetition in literary texts was an indication that those texts had oral sources. Rushdie applies this principle in reverse by employing formulaic repetition as a literary device to simulate the appearance of orality.

20. The idea of such devices, as Rushdie explains, is "that you use as recurring things in the plot incidents or objects or phrases which in themselves have no meaning or no particular meaning but which form a kind of non-rational network of connections in the book" (see Rushdie, "*Midnight's Children* and *Shame*" 3). Examples of "leitmotifs" in *Midnight's Children* include the silver spittoon that Saleem carries throughout most of his picaresque adventures, or Millais's painting of the pointing fisherman. Examples of "leitworts" (leading words) and "leitsatze" (leading sentences) include the Reverend Mother's "whatsitsname," which Saleem identifies as her "leitmotif" (42), and key phrases such as "to understand me you'll have to swallow a world." For more on this formal strategy as it is used in the *Nights*, see Pinault 13–15.

21. For further consideration of the characteristics of oral narrative see Ong 33 – 57.

22. Bakhtin cites Boris Eikhenbaum's definition of *skaz* as "an *orientation toward the oral form of narration*" (191).

23. Ameena Meer, "Salman Rushdie" (1989), in Reder, ed., *Conversations* 111.

24. For a comparable analysis see Benson (130–47) for discussion of John Barth's uses of the *Nights*.

25. For further consideration of Rushdie's use of fairy tales to engage with discourses of Orientalism see Deszcz, "Rushdie's Magical Kingdom" 37–42, and Teverson, "The Number of Magic Alternatives" 219–24.

26. For the English story and an account of its provenance, see Philip, ed., *The Penguin Book of English Folktales* 158–62. Carter is also preoccupied with this strange tale, which provides her with the title for her "Bluebeard" narrative, "The Bloody Chamber." See Teverson, "The White Cat and Mr Fox."

Bibliography

Primary Sources

Rushdie, Salman. *East, West.* 1994. London: Vintage, 1995.
———. *The Ground Beneath Her Feet.* 1999. London: Vintage, 2000.
———. *Haroun and the Sea of Stories.* 1990. London: Granta, 1991.
———. *Imaginary Homelands: Essays and Criticism, 1981–1991.* London: Granta, 1991.
———. *Midnight's Children.* London: Jonathan Cape, 1981.
———. "*Midnight's Children* and *Shame.*" *Kunapipi* 7.1 (1985): 1–19.
———. *The Moor's Last Sigh.* 1995. London: Vintage, 1996.
———. *The Satanic Verses.* 1988. Delaware: Consortium, 1992.
———. *Shalimar the Clown.* London: Cape, 2005.
———. *Shame.* 1983. London: Picador, 1984.
———. *Step Across This Line: Collected Non-Fiction, 1992–2002.* London: Jonathan Cape, 2002.

Secondary Sources

Ahmad, Aijaz. *In Theory: Classes, Nations, Literatures.* London: Verso, 1992.
Bakhtin, Mikhail. *The Problems of Dostoevsky's Poetics.* Ed. and trans. Caryl Emerson. Minneapolis: U of Minnesota P, 1984.

Batty, Nancy E. "The Art of Suspense: Rushdie's 1001 (Mid-) Nights." *Ariel* 18.3 (1987): 49–65.

Benson, Stephen. *Cycles of Influence: Fiction, Folktale, Theory.* Detroit: Wayne State UP, 2003.

Borges, Jorge Luis. "The Thousand and One Nights." *Seven Nights.* Trans. Eliot Weinberger. New York: New Directions, 1984. 42–57.

Bottigheimer, Ruth B. "Germany." *The Oxford Companion to Fairy Tales.* Ed. Jack Zipes. Oxford: Oxford UP, 2000. 198–210.

Carter, Angela. *The Bloody Chamber and Other Stories.* 1979. London: Penguin, 1981.

———. "Notes from the Front Line." *Shaking a Leg, Collected Journalism and Writings.* Ed. Jenny Uglow. London: Chatto and Windus, 1997. 36–42.

Cox, Marian Roalfe. *Cinderella: 345 Variants of Cinderella.* London: Folk Lore Society, 1893.

Cundy, Catherine. *Salman Rushdie.* Contemporary World Writers. Manchester: Manchester UP, 1996.

Deszcz, Justyna. *Rushdie in Wonderland: Fairytaleness in Salman Rushdie's Fiction.* Frankfurt: Peter Lang, 2004.

———. "Salman Rushdie's Attempt at a Feminist Fairytale Reconfiguration in *Shame.*" *Folklore* 115 (2004): 27–44.

———. "Salman Rushdie's Magical Kingdom: *The Moor's Last Sigh* and Fairy Tale Utopia." *Marvels & Tales* 18.1 (2004): 28–52.

Falconer, Rachel. "Bouncing Down to the Underworld: Classical *Katabasis* in *The Ground Beneath Her Feet.*" *Twentieth-Century Literature* 47.4 (2001): 467–509.

Gates, Henry Louis, ed. *Reading Black, Reading Feminist: A Critical Anthology.* New York: NAL, 1990.

Grimm, Ludwig, and Wilhelm Grimm. *The Complete Fairy Tales of the Brothers Grimm.* Ed. and trans. Jack Zipes. New York: Bantam, 1992.

———. *Grimm's Household Tales.* Trans. Margaret Hunt. 2 vols. London: Bell, 1884.

Hamilton, Ian. "The First Life of Salman Rushdie." *New Yorker.* 25 Dec. 1995–1 Jan. 1996: 90–97, 100–13.

Herder, Johann Gottfried. *J. G. Herder on Social and Political Culture.* Ed. and trans. F. M. Barnard. Cambridge: Cambridge UP, 1969.

Irwin, Robert. *The Arabian Nights: A Companion.* London: Penguin, 1994.

Kamenetsky, Christa. *The Brothers Grimm and Their Critics: Folktales and the Quest for Meaning.* Athens: Ohio UP, 1992.

Lurie, Alison. Ed. *The Oxford Book of Modern Fairy Tales.* Oxford: Oxford UP, 1994.

Müller, Max. *Comparative Mythology*. 1856. New York: Arno, 1977.

Ong, Walter J. *Orality and Literacy: The Technologizing of the Word*. 1982. London: Routledge, 2002.

Philip, Neil, ed. *The Cinderella Story*. London: Penguin, 1989.

———, ed. *The Penguin Book of English Folktales*. London: Penguin, 1992.

Pinault, David. *Story-Telling Techniques in the Arabian Nights*. Leiden: Brill, 1992.

Rahman, Tariq. "Politics in the Novels of Salman Rushdie." *The Commonwealth Novel in English* 4.1 (1999): 24–37.

Reder, Michael, ed. *Conversations with Salman Rushdie*. Jackson: U of Mississippi P, 2000.

Roberts, Warren, and Stith Thompson. *Types of Indic Oral Tales*. FF Communications 180. Helsinki: FF Communications, 1960.

Rooth, Anna Birgitta. *The Cinderella Cycle*. Lund: Gleerup, 1951.

Said, Edward. "Orientalism Reconsidered." *Postcolonial Criticism*. Ed. Bart Moore-Gilbert, Gareth Stanton, and Willy Maley. Longman Critical Readers. London: Longman, 1997. 126–44.

Teverson, Andrew. "The Number of Magic Alternatives: Salman Rushdie's 1001 Gothic Nights." *Empire and the Gothic: The Politics of Genre*. Ed. Andrew Smith and William Hughes. Houndmills: Macmillan, 2003. 208–28.

———. "The White Cat and Mr Fox." *Hungarian Journal of English and American Studies* 5.2 (1999): 209–22.

Thompson, Stith. *The Folktale*. Berkeley: U of California P, 1977.

Tushingham, David. "Salman Rushdie in Conversation." Theatre Programme. *Haroun and the Sea of Stories*. Dir. Tim Supple. National Theatre (Cottesloe). 1 Oct. 1998. NP.

Uther, Hans-Jörg. *The Types of International Folktales: A Classification and Bibliography Based on the System of Antti Aarne and Stith Thompson*. Part 1. FF Communications 284. Helsinki: Suomalainen Tiedeakatemia Academia Scientiarum Fennica, 2004.

Warner, Marina. *Managing Monsters: Six Myths of Our Time*. London: Vintage, 1994.

Weatherby, W. J. *Salman Rushdie: Sentenced to Death*. New York: Carroll and Graf, 1990.

Wilson, William A. "Herder, Folklore, and Romantic Nationalism." *Journal of Popular Culture* 6.4 (1973): 819–35.

I had thought of writing on Ibsen myself, at one point. His use of the folktale.
I was deflected.

A. S. Byatt, The Biographer's Tale

Writers have always used the forms of the fairy tale—if my idea that they form,
or until recently formed, the narrative grammar of our minds is correct, writers
must have done.

A. S. Byatt, Introduction to The Annotated Brothers Grimm

3 "Ancient Forms"
Myth, Fairy Tale, and Narrative in A. S. Byatt's Fiction

ELIZABETH WANNING HARRIES

I

A. S. Byatt's fiction is shot through with allusions to well-known
fairy tales. Hardly a chapter goes by without a prick on the finger, an impenetrable hedge, or an enchanted tower. When her characters aren't medi-
tating on the significance of fairy tales in their lives, her narrators are commenting on it. One strand in the complex tangle of her imagery always
comes from the European fairy-tale tradition. It would be quite easy to pick
your way through her work, collecting references to "classic" fairy tales and
teasing out their local implications.[1] You could also look specifically at the
short fairy tales she has written recently, from stories like "The Eldest
Princess" and "Dragons' Breath" in *The Djinn in the Nightingale's Eye* (1994)
to the tales in *The Little Black Book of Stories* (2004).[2] Byatt's recent short
fiction often swerves into the fantastic and the legendary.

But here I want to do something a little different. Rather than catalogue
Byatt's many returns to and reworkings of this charged material, I want to
concentrate on its significance for her overall conception of narrative and

her fictional strategies. As she says in one of her conversations with Ignês Sodré in *Imagining Characters:*

> We have discussed the accidents and the particularities and the realism of the characters first, then we've moved on to the conscious mean-ings, and then we have moved on to the bit we always most enjoy, which is the structuring with forms like Oedipusness, or here suddenly the Medea myth bobs its head up, or the myth of the fairy and the nee-dle pricking. . . . That is what it is about the archetypal stories which we tell ourselves, and I think all these novels have known how to evoke and stir up in us those ancient forms which we then clothe as one does in one's life, with flesh and blood. (142)[3]

Byatt is deeply interested in these "ancient forms" and the way they form a substratum of meaning in later narrative. In her conversations with Sodré she focuses on their presence in novels in English by women, from *Mansfield Park* on, but she also is sharply aware of the ways these old stories—not just fairy tales, but classical myths, Bible stories, and other well-known leg-ends—inform her own fiction. She calls them a "structuring" element, and I think we need to take the specificity of that word carefully into account. Byatt returns more and more frequently to the structures of older narratives: the frame tale, the embedded tale, a multiplicity of narrating voices. As she says in her recent *On Histories and Stories,* "I found myself wanting to write tales and stories, having described myself in my early days as a 'self-conscious realist'" (4). She now alternates between—and sometimes tries to integrate—what she sees as an "alternative tradition" of fantastic tales (Hoffman, Dinesen, Borges, Calvino) and the tradition of the "realist" novel (George Eliot, Iris Murdoch).

In an early essay (1976) on Elizabeth Bowen's *The House in Paris,* Byatt quotes one of Bowen's characters, Mme. Fisher, on the "truth" of the fairy tale: "No doubt you do not care for fairy tales, Leopold? An enchanted wood full of dumb people would offend you; you are not the young man with the sword who goes jumping his way through. Fairy-tales always made me im-patient, also. But unfortunately there is no doubt that in life such things ex-ist" (*Passions* 223). Mme. Fisher, like Byatt herself, sees that the fairy tale, however improbable and even irritating in its assumptions, is not only part of our inherited "narrative grammar" but also in some sense reflects the world. Its plots and metaphors suggest another way of approaching reality.

Byatt seems to imagine her work as bringing together what Murdoch, in her well-known essay "Against Dryness," spoke of as the "crystalline" and the "journalistic," the perfected form of fantasy and the messy quasidocumentary jumble.[4] Like Murdoch, she hopes to give us a sense of "the real, impenetrable, human person" (30). Unlike Murdoch, however, she tries to attain this in a mixed form that draws on the structural and imaginative resources of both modes. As her career goes on, she more and more often juxtaposes, sometimes combines, the self-contained forms of fantasy and the messier structures of the "real." The interplay of fairy tale and fact, of made-up worlds and fragments of history, has become characteristic of her work.

II

"Morpho Eugenia," one of the two novellas in *Angels and Insects* (1992), shows the dialectic between these traditions. Like *Possession*, it is one of Byatt's Victorian fictions, though presented without a twentieth-century frame. We are plunged immediately into the world of a mid-nineteenth-century English country house: dances, hunting, servants, child-bearing, family traditions, and secrets—observed chiefly through the eyes of a naturalist, William Adamson, who has just returned from the Amazon. Though he is used to paying "attention" (a keyword for both Murdoch and Byatt) to the natural world, he is unable to observe or to interpret the human world at all accurately. Part of the drama of the story is William's gradual recognition of the limitations of his perspective on Bredely, the aptly named Alabaster house, and its many inhabitants.

The third-person limited narration, however, is interrupted several times by the insertion of other texts: excerpts from William's journal; a governess, Miss Mead, telling part of the story of Cupid and Psyche (48–50); Harald Alabaster's desperate attempts to reconcile Darwinian theory and religion (96–103); William's "social history" of the ant colonies on the Alabaster estate (113–15, 127–33, 162–63); and, most important, Matty Crompton's invented fairy tale "Things Are Not What They Seem" (137–60)—all incorporated within the 183 pages of the novella, each in a different voice and style. (Inset quotations from Ben Jonson, Milton, Keats, John Clare, Tennyson, and Browning further vary the narrative texture.) In fact, we could almost call this a "laminated" narrative—a somewhat more shapely version of the layered fragments Byatt's character Frederica Potter works on in *Ba-*

bel Tower and finally publishes in *A Whistling Woman,* drawing on her observations since her schooldays in *The Virgin in the Garden.* "Language rustles around her with many voices, none of them her, all of them hers" (*Babel* 381).

William's first journal entry echoes a fairy tale he remembers from his childhood (14–16). Though he is aware that the prince's statement ("I shall die if I cannot have her") is melodramatic and overwrought, he cannot help seeing it as expressing his own infatuation with Eugenia, the oldest daughter of the house. He analyzes his own condition and then repeats the phrase again. He condemns his own folly—"The only rational course is to forget the whole matter, suppress these inopportune feelings, make an end" (16)—and then writes it again. The power of the remembered words suggests that even William, the rational scientist and observer, is under the spell of old fairy-tale behavior.[5] The language of the tale "rustles around" him and invades his patterns of thought.

The next inset text is Miss Mead's slightly skewed retelling of the story of Cupid and Psyche. Though she does recount the part we tend to remember (Psyche's transgression in trying to see her invisible husband, Cupid), she focuses on the task Venus sets Psyche as penance, "the sorting of seeds" (50), and the help of the ants. Miss Mead believes in the ants' altruistic desire to cooperate and to help Psyche; she stresses "the *kindness* of the ants" (48). Like many characters in the novella, she wants to see a close analogy between insect and human life; her story is essentially a sentimental reading of the ants' activities. (This is an analogy that William questions more and more strongly.)

But sorting is also a fairy-tale motif, as Matty Crompton points out: "It is odd, is it not, how *sorting* so often makes a part of the impossible tasks of the prince or princesses in the tales" (50). (Think, for example, of Cinderella sorting lentils from the ashes in the Grimms' version of the tale, "Aschenputtel.") William's task in the Alabaster household is to try to sort out Harald Alabaster's varied collections, to put them into some kind of sensible scientific order. But he finds "himself at once detached anthropologist and fairy-tale prince trapped by invisible gates and silken bonds in an enchanted castle" (25). He sees his sorting as a set task, with Eugenia, Harald's daughter, as his reward. And yet he becomes less and less convinced that his task is possible or even meaningful; "he could not devise an organizing principle" (29).[6] And it is only late in the novella that, in an inversion of the Psyche story, he is forced to recognize his supposed prize, Eugenia, for what she really is.

Miss Mead's Psyche story, then, radiates throughout "Morpho Eugenia." Byatt transposes the old Greek myth into her chosen Victorian context, varying and transforming it, just as she plays with and inverts strands from the *Odyssey*.[7] She often returns to the insect theme as well. Harald Alabaster bases his attempts to argue for the existence of a divine principle of love on insect behavior: "If we consider the humble lives of the social insects I think we may discern truths which are *riddling paradigms* for our own understandings. We have been accustomed to think of *altruism* and *self-sacrifice* as human virtues, essentially human, but this is not apparently so. These little creatures exercise both, in their ways" (*Angels* 98–99). Like Miss Mead, Harald Alabaster sees the insects as embodying human virtues, as parables of a benevolent universe or a loving Providence. William reluctantly but forcefully questions his argument from analogy: "We have made our God by a specious analogy, Sir. . . . You may argue anything at all by analogy, Sir, and consequently nothing" (103–04).

We then must read William's description of the life of the ants he has observed as a comment on the two earlier inset insect passages. He often details sharp differences between their behavior and human rapacity: "They did not, as human soldiers do, rape and pillage, loot and destroy. They came, and saw, and conquered, and achieved their object, and left again" (*Angels* 115). The tag from Caesar emphasizes the calm purposefulness of the Sanguine Ants, so different from the random destructiveness and inhumane behavior of human soldiers. Though William too sees analogies between the behavior of social insects and of people, the analogies he sees are harsher: ant soldiers as so deformed by their profession that they become completely dependent on others for food and shelter; Ant Queens as "egg-laying machines" like his wife and mother-in-law; male drones as like "factory hands" (and perhaps like William himself at Bredely) in their interchangeability and uselessness. And he questions the impulse to see insect societies as offering potential solutions for the questions that were racking Victorian society: biological predestination, instinct, intelligence, the relationship of individual and community. "To ask, what are the ants in their busy world, is to ask, what are we, however we may answer" (*Angels* 133).[8] Though reluctant to articulate his own growing belief that "Instinct *was* Predestination" (134), William effectively undermines the simpler, more hopeful lessons that Miss Mead and Harald Alabaster read in entomology.

But Matty Crompton's inset fairy tale, "Things Are Not What They Seem," brings the helpful, altruistic insect back again. The tale is about a proverbial third son (Seth, the son of Adam) who goes out into the world to make his fortune—but ends up imprisoned in an underground cave with his shipwrecked companions by a wicked fairy, Dame Cottitoe Pan Demos. In an echo of both the Circe episode in the *Odyssey* and the Persephone story, his companions eat heartily and are changed into swine; Seth himself eats only three pomegranate seeds and retains his human shape, though he is powerless to escape or to help his companions.

A large, helpful Jet-black Ant finally gives him three fern seeds to counteract the action of the pomegranate seeds; he dwindles in size until he can leave the cave and see the light. (The trip up to the surface through winding tunnels reverses Dante's journey through the *Inferno*, but the light at the end is similar.) Miss Mouffet, the good spirit of the garden, saves him from some terrifying caterpillars and sends him off to meet the "Fairy-beyond-the-wall," Dame Kind, who gives him some moly (the herb Hermes gives Odysseus as a charm against Circe) and more insect helpers (the moths Caradrina Morpheus and Acherontia Atropos). He then returns to Dame Cottitoe's palace, disenchants his companions and himself, and flees "to begin a new adventure" (160).

Matty Crompton's project is not an exercise in analogy but rather an exploration of the effects of naming. She explains her project this way: "It was as though I was dragged along willy-nilly—by the *language*, you know—through Sphinx and Morpheus and Thomas Mouffet [the author of *Theatrum Insectorum*, in Harald Alabaster's library]—I suppose my Hermes was Linnaeus—who does not appear" (*Angels* 160). Both William and Matty are conscious of the resonance of insect names, the ways Linnaeus's nomenclature echoes Greek mythology: the riddling Sphinx, the god of sleep Morpheus and the close connection of his name to the names of the moths (Morpho Menelaus, Morpho Adonis, Morpho Eugenia). As William says, "I used to think of Linnaeus, in the forest, constantly. He bound the New World so tightly to the imagination of the Old when he named the swallowtails for the Greek and Trojan heroes, and the Heliconiae for the Muses. There I was, in lands never before entered by Englishmen, and round me fluttered Helen and Menelaus, Apollo and the Nine, Hector, and Hecuba and Priam" (*Angels* 135–36). We could say that Matty—as the surrogate fairy-tale writer in Byatt's novella—has been given Byatt's gift of imaginative attention to language and its resonances. Her tale is in some ways part of a process of discovery through language, of finding connections hidden in words and names themselves.

In many of her essays, Byatt emphasizes the widening circles of meaning we find when we look at language closely, even in what seems to be a factual list of types of grasses (*Passions* 13). She registers her own surprise when her study of metaphorical names confirms what she has already suspected: "I was even more pleased when I discovered elsewhere that Morpho is one of the ways of naming Aphrodite Pandemos, the earthly Venus. I was pleased in the way one is when one *discovers* a myth still alive and working, despite the fact that part of my intention was to undo anthropomorphic imaginings and closures" (*On Histories* 118). Byatt is interested in myths "still alive and working," myths (and fairy tales) that still inform our ways of thinking and of understanding the world. "Morpho Eugenia" seems to be a story about Victorian culture and its outsiders, a story that explores the structure of its upper-class world and the world of the servants that support it. But it is also a story about language, its sources, and its resources. The game of anagrams William and Matty play with the family in the Alabaster parlor toward the end of the novella is a game of resonant words: William's "INSECT," Matty's "INCEST," and the word William gives back to her, which, although not given, I think must be SPHINX.[9] Matty's final word, "PHOENIX," announces the rebirth that her fairy tale and the natural histories of the butterflies and moths have all been suggesting. Her word leads to one of the final sentences of the story: "They breathe salt air, and hope, and their blood swims with the excitement of the future, and this is a good place to leave them, on the crest of a wave, between the ordered green fields and hedgerows, and the coiling, striving mass of forest along the Amazon shore" (*Angels* 182). Matty has freed William from his bondage to the Alabaster family, to his incestuous wife, and to her five white little children.[10] Both he and Matty herself (now renamed Matilda, the queen) are "on the crest of a wave," beginning a new life, reborn to their true calling and to each other.[11]

In "Morpho Eugenia," then, Byatt creates a fairy-tale writer, Matty Crompton, whose framed fairy tale both parallels and influences the future of the characters in the main framing story.[12] "Things Are Not What They Seem" and the other heterogeneous inset texts work together in many mysterious ways—and also break out of their frames to work on and with the central story line. The apparently "alien content" (Jameson, xii) is almost literally incorporated into the body of the tale. Some critics have seen this as an example of Byatt's "postmodernism," her willful bringing together of shards of experience and of linguistic styles. But I think it may be more rewarding to look at her explorations of frame tales and other old narrative structures as reflections of her growing interest in the literary wonder tale, from the *Arabian Nights* on. As she says in her essay "Old Tales, New Forms," "I found myself using stories within stories, rather than shape-shifting recurrent metaphors, to make the meanings" (*On Histories* 131). Though insect metaphors pervade the novella, they too are part of the meaningful interplay between the frame and the framed.

III

"The Djinn in the Nightingale's Eye" (1994) plays even more insistently with fantastic material and with the possibilities of inset stories. The djinn defies the space/time boundaries of the empirical world; his lover Gillian Perholt, though a sensible and successful middle-aged narratologist, sees in him a continuity with the oceans of story that wash around us. Byatt links the story with *Possession:* "It is stories within stories again—the Djinn and the woman tell each other their lives, as lovers do on meeting, the woman tells tales at conferences as examples, and so on" (*On Histories* 132). And it is stories about stories, from the first words ("Once upon a time") to the last.

As Gillian Perholt says, "The best narratologists work by telling and retelling tales" (*Djinn* 106). In her lecture at a conference in Ankara, devoted to "Stories of Women's Lives" (105), she retells the story of Patient Griselda as told by Chaucer in "The Clerk's Tale" and by Petrarch and Boccaccio before him. An odd choice, one might think, for a woman who savors her own freedom and autonomy, who does not regret the ending of her marriage, who enjoys "floating redundant" (like Milton's snake) through the world. In part she tells it as an example of a persistent story that denies women agency and forces them to acquiesce in arrangements made by others: husbands, fathers, sons. But she tells it mainly as an example of excessive narrative plotting; she thinks that both Walter, Griselda's husband, and Paulina in *The Winter's Tale* have taken it on themselves to create a story, to become controlling narrators themselves. Restoring Griselda to her children she thought dead and to her throne, restoring Hermione to life does not make up for the years of human life lost: "And from Hermione—and as you may know already, from Patient Griselda—most of that life has been taken by plotting, has been made into a grey void of forced inactivity" (*Djinn* 113) The brevity of human life and the specter of aging, a little later made explicit by the paralyzing appearance of what Gillian calls the "Griselda-ghoul," inform her version of the story.

This inset story and others like them (the Turkish narratologist Orhan Rifat's version of the story of Prince Camaralzaman from the *Arabian Nights*, the museum guide's story of Gilgamesh and Enkidu, the stories of the three wishes, even the jihadist tirade of the Pakistani fundamentalist in the Haghia Sophia) are all stories of death and destiny. Byatt weaves references to and echoes of many other stories into the novella: Shakespeare's *Hamlet* and *Tempest* and *Winter's Tale;* Milton's *Paradise Lost;* Coleridge's "Kubla Khan" and "The Ancient Mariner"; even, somewhat surprisingly, Sterne's *Tristram Shandy* (a story about conception and birth that is also insistently a story about endings and death) as well as *Mansfield Park* and *Madame Bovary, Villette* and *Daniel Deronda*, Proust and Stendhal and Balzac and Freud. "Morpho Eugenia" is full of religious questioning and scientific speculation, as well as quotations from British poets; "The Djinn in the Nightingale's Eye" is full of allusions to and retellings of disparate narratives, narratives that often become a question of life or death.

Sometimes Gillian Perholt seems more interested in the structures of narratives than in their emotional impact. For example, she describes a televised tennis game as an example of well-plotted narrative suspense: "A live match was live, was a story in progress towards an end which had not yet come but which must *almost certainly* come. And in the fact of the *almost* was the delight" (185). Narrative here seems to become an abstract pattern, without referent, as it does in some structuralist and poststructuralist analyses. And yet Byatt returns often, here and elsewhere, to the function of storytelling as "intrinsic to biological time, which we cannot escape. . . . We are all, like Scheherazade, under sentence of death, and we all think of our lives as narratives, with beginnings, middles, and ends. Storytelling in general, and the *Thousand and One Nights* in particular, consoles us for endings with endless new beginnings" (*On Histories* 166). Gillian Perholt is always conscious of the relentless movement of time, in her analysis of "Patient Griselda" and in her sometimes rueful, sometimes horrified acknowledgment of her own aging.

About halfway through the novella, just after yet another appearance of the Griselda-ghoul, or "her death advancing toward her" (*Djinn* 186), a djinn erupts suddenly out of a bottle in Gillian's hotel bathroom in Istanbul. Huge, looming, ageless, he is clearly a figure of myth and legend, appearing after her friend Orhan Ripat has retold the stories of the djinn in the frame of the *Arabian Nights* and of the djinns in the story of Prince Camaralzaman, after a museum guide has talked to her about genies (and is identified later as perhaps a djinn himself). Her djinn can expand and contract, appear and disappear at will; play games with images of real figures (seize the tennis player Boris Becker from the television set, for example); tell stories about his relationships with the Queen of Sheba and various Ottoman princesses and a nineteenth-century Smyrna merchant's wife; even offer Gillian three wishes in the best magical tradition. She has released him from his imprisonment in a tiny Turkish bottle; in return he can release her from her imprisonment in an aging body and, more important, from her growing fear of death.

Their relationship is oddly reciprocal. When Gillian thinks about her early life, she often describes it as a series of incarcerations, in her school, in her childhood house "like a box" (194). The fax she receives from her husband, ending their marriage, makes her feel "like a prisoner bursting chains and coming blinking out of a dungeon. She felt like a bird confined in a box, like a gas confined in a bottle, that found an opening and rushed out. She felt herself expand in the space of her own life" (*Djinn* 103–04). In much the same way, the djinn finds it "agreeable to expand" when he comes out of the *çesm-i bülbül* (nightingale's eye) bottle in a huge cloud after his third "incarceration" (*Djinn* 191). Byatt dwells on enclosure and release, in the tale of Griselda, in the stories other characters tell, as well as in the lives of Gillian and the djinn.

We could even describe the structure of Byatt's story as a series of enclosures, of framed stories. In a fascinating image, Gillian describes the Sultan's harem in Topkapi: "In the harem, too, was the Sultan's bath . . . a central box inside a series of carved boxes and cupboards inside the quarters of the Valide Sultan, his mother, where his nakedness could be guarded by many watchful eyes from assassin's knives" (168). This image, like the "beehive of inner courtyards" (166) in Gillian's Istanbul hotel, reflects the many narrative frames Byatt is playing with.[13] Stories here do not exist in isolation, but in relation to those that frame them and that they frame.

Even the story Gillian tells the djinn about the television coverage of a famine in Ethiopia ends with a framed image of an old woman:

> she was angular but not awkward, and she had one long arm at an angle over her head, and her legs extended on this bench—and the photographer had made them squared, as it were *framed* in her own limbs—she spoke out of an enclosure made by her own body, and her eyes were dark holes and her face was long, long. She made the edges of the box out of her body. . . . And then she said, "It is because I am a woman, I cannot get out of here." (243)

"She made the edges of the box out of her body." Though Gillian tells the djinn she doesn't know why she has told this story, it clearly has to do with the biological, social, and narrative structures that enclose women and that she has been thinking about throughout. (For example, the "dark holes" of the eyes echo the "dark smudges" of the eyes of the figure of death that haunt her at the beginning of the novella.) The formal, embodied framing of the image of the woman on the television screen makes the viewer's sense of her desperation more powerful—and eloquently suggests her gendered imprisonment.

And yet. And yet. In Byatt's story Gillian Perholt has moved beyond that "imprisonment," privileged not only because of her culture and class but also because of her prominence in her profession. Through the djinn's magical intervention she is even able to escape the confines of her aging body. She exists in stark contrast to the emaciated Ethiopian woman and to most of the women in the stories she and others tell. What is the relationship between her story and the others? Why has Byatt inserted so many framed stories into the main or framing tale—and emphasized her narrative process in her reiterations of Chinese box courtyards and other framing metaphors?

It's significant, I think, that both Gérard Genette and Tristan Todorov are in the audience at the conference in Toronto. In one of Byatt's typical mirroring effects, Gillian the narratologist is speaking to an audience of narratologists that includes the two preeminent theorists of narrative framing. Both theorists were intensely interested in the structure of framed tales; Genette in particular tried to work out a vocabulary to describe the relationship of various narrative levels and narrative frames.[14] Though Byatt continues to believe that critics are "tiny people compared to writers"[15] or "being[s] of a secondary order" (*Djinn* 96), she is aware of and responds to the continuing critical discussions of the structure of narrative. Her explorations of storytelling in "The Djinn" are, I think, attempts to show how those discussions, arid and technical though they may often be, can inform the work of beings of the primary order, writers like Byatt herself.

In "Morpho Eugenia" Mattie's new fairy tale provides a script for William Adamson to rewrite his life. In "The Djinn" the many secondary, framed stories show the constraints of old stories and the dangers of repeating their scripts. Because Gillian Perholt knows that the traditional three wishes are a trap, she is able to make what she calls "intelligent" ones. Like the princess in "The Story of the Eldest Princess," she "had the sense to see [she] was caught in a story, and the sense to see that [she] could change it to another one" (65).[16] Her last generous wish, the wish that the djinn might have his own wish, also suggests her consciousness that her story is not hers alone, that it is part of a web or sea of intersecting stories. Even the Djinn, a mythical figure who does not age at all, who does not seem to be subject to the "sentence of death," is subject to a script that has confined him in a bottle for more than a century. Like Prospero in *The Tempest*, she gives him his freedom—and releases herself, too. Byatt brings together a fairy-tale plot (the traditional plot of "The Three Wishes") and the romance plot of *The Tempest*—and chooses the openness and uncertainty of the unconventional Turkish version of the tale and Shakespeare's ending. At one point in the tale, the djinn criticizes one of Gillian's stories about her life: "Is that the end of the story? . . . Your stories are strange, glancing things. They peter out, they have no shape" (237). Here, too, Byatt's story could be said to have no shape; the ending promises no return, no reunion of the djinn and the narratologist, no traditional "happy ending" at all. Rather we see Gillian Perholt simply as happy, content not to know the future, content with uncertainty and aging and with the beauty of things like the Djinn's fleeting and improbable presence and the two paperweights he has given her: "There are things in the earth, things made with hands and beings not made with hands that live a life different from ours, that live longer than we do, and cross our lives in stories, in dreams, at certain times when we are floating redundant. And Gillian Perholt was happy, for she had moved back into their world, or at least had access to it, as she had had when she was a child" (271). Her happiness comes from her acceptance of both permanence and change.

The story oscillates between the mythic and the "real," the patterned and the random. Gillian believes she prefers geometric flower patterns in paperweights until she sees one that is a detailed, patient representation of a flower with all its specks and stains and trailing roots: "It was perfect because the illusion was near-perfect, and the attention to the living original had been so perfect that the undying artificial flower also seemed perfect" (270). This paperweight and its companion piece, a representation of a snake, are examples of a kind of hyper-realism (or, as Hilary Schor suggests, "post-realism"[17]). The perfect "attention"—note that word again—of the artist has made the living immortal, opened up the possibility of an art that can capture and preserve the beauty and complexity of the real world. This may be what Byatt herself is attempting to do in "The Djinn": to find narrative structures that use the crystalline patterns of the artificial to capture and preserve the messy detail of the real.

IV

But Byatt does not reserve these techniques for her magical or mythical or "fairy" tales. Her novels are also full of framing devices and embedded stories. *Possession* (1990) of course includes both inset tales and running fairy-tale motifs like the story of Melusine. Byatt interweaves not only nineteenth- and twentieth-century characters and worlds but also apparently realistic narratives and traditional Breton and other tales. Christabel LaMotte, like Matilda in "Morpho Eugenia" and like Christina Rossetti (a literary figure she resembles even more than Elizabeth Barrett Browning), is a fairy-tale writer. She has published *Tales for Innocents,* based on the Grimms' and Tieck's tales; Byatt has invented and included one of her tales called "The Glass Coffin" (65–76), read by her twentieth-century hero in a first edition that belongs to Maud Bailey, Christabel's great-great-granddaughter. Throughout the novel we piece together a history from letters and diary entries, poems and tales and apparently realistic authorial narrative. "*Possession* is a story of stories told in different voices."[18]

In the final scene of the novel, the "unrecorded" meeting between the poet Randolph Henry Ash and his daughter May, the poet asks her for a gift in exchange for a daisy crown:

> "I haven't anything to give."
> "Oh, just a lock of hair—a very fine one—to remember you by."
> "Like a fairy story."
> "Just so." (554)

The child sees the fantastic nature of the exchange; the reader remembers the finely braided lock of hair in a blue envelope in the double box some twentieth-century scholars have re-exhumed from Ash's grave. Part of the novel depends on Byatt's clever (and somewhat tricky) detective-story plotting; in the last scene she reveals something that can never be known by any twentieth-century Christabel LaMotte scholars.[19] The recovery or uncovering of the past, Byatt seems to be saying, can only be partial and chancy. The meeting of Ash and his daughter escapes the nets that her fictional historians and scholars have created; it is yet another moment that depends on the substratum of fairy tale that both complicates and enriches her best-known novel.

Byatt's four Frederica Potter novels, a quartet published over nearly a quarter of a century, chart her struggle to find forms that might be adequate to a woman's twentieth-century experiences; the traditional languages and forms of the bildungsroman will not do. The four novels all are deliberately framed. Even the first novel in the series, *The Virgin in the Garden* (1978), begins with a retrospective prologue: "The National Portrait Gallery: 1968." The second, *Still Life* (1985), also begins in the future with "Post-Impressionism: Royal Academy of Arts, London 1980." The third, *Babel Tower* (1996), opens with a strange, riddling, symbolic page about a thrush on a heap of carved stones and shells, and begins "It might begin:"; this page is followed by a chapter with three sections, each beginning "Or it might begin . . ." The last in the series, *A Whistling Woman* (2002), begins with the last installment of the medieval quest romance *Flight North* that Frederica's friend Agatha has been telling their children and anyone else who wants to listen on Sunday afternoons for two years. Though Mara Cambiaghi believed that the last novel in the series might return to a more "linear narrative" ("Angels" 296), Byatt continued to work with framed and apparently disjunctive stories.

These opening frames, whether they take place in the future or in the distant, symbolic past, situate the reader at a remove from the events of the primary narratives. Like a picture frame, they oscillate between the inside and the outside, belonging neither to the space within the frame or to the world outside it.[20] In *A Whistling Woman,* for example, Agatha's mythical, medieval tale appears to contrast sharply with the world of the late 1960s that Frederica Potter is trying to navigate through. In their juxtaposition Frederica's world begins to seem more factual, more "real." And yet Agatha's story can be read both as "outside" that world and as "inside" it. Her apparent flight into fantasy is also a comment on the perils of living in a time of religious cults, scientific speculation and stringent research, "anti-universities," and sexual uncertainties. Patches of the story recur throughout both *Babel Tower* and *A Whistling Woman,* sometimes read aloud, sometimes read silently—often at the times of greatest narrative tension and doubt. Frederica compares her own book, the collection of text collages from her life called *Laminations,* to Agatha's; her "mind naturally inhabited the world of living metaphor which was myth and fable, whereas she, Frederica, was confined to stitching and patching the solid, and you could still see the joints" (*Whistling Woman,* 247). Some critics have seen Byatt's own recent novels as "laminations" as well. In *Babel Tower*, Frederica remembers a moment in the early 1950s when she, at seventeen,

> had had a vision of being able to be all the things she was: language, sex, friendship, thought, just as long as these were kept scrupulously separate, *laminated*, like geological strata, not seeping and flowing into each other like organic cells boiling to join and divide and join in a seething Oneness. Things were best cool, and clear, and fragmented, if fragmented is what they were.
>
> There is an art form in that, too. Things juxtaposed but divided, not yearning for fusion. (314–15)[21]

Byatt's "art form"—at least in her novels from *Possession: A Romance* on—has become in part an art of juxtaposition. Though her short stories usually remain structurally unified, whether "realistic" or "fantastic," her novels and novellas deliberately combine various narrative forms and styles; part of the power of her fiction depends on the friction between them.

Yet Byatt continues to "believe in storytelling." She even believes, though some critics have doubted it, that *Babel Tower* "weaves many fragmented stories into one."[22] Her Frederica Potter novels, all "historical novels," inhabit an uneasy realm between the documentary and the mythical, unified (if they are unified) by the interplay of their many varied styles and forms. Though the laminating principle is the basis of Frederica Potter's book, "things juxtaposed but divided," Byatt herself aims for something fused or woven together.[23] Even Frederica acknowledges at the end of *A Whistling Woman* that "the laminations were slipping. Fire was re-arranging them in new patterns. She was full of life, and afraid" (417). Frederica is beginning to see that all kinds of knowledge—scientific, literary, religious, emotional—are interconnected, that she cannot keep the double helix on a snail shell separate from her delight in language or her fear of religious cults or her sexual relationships. (The recurring references to the Fibonacci principle, the presence of the "golden mean" and mathematical relationships in natural phenomena like sunflowers and pine cones and some shells, bring this out.[24]) Byatt's novels insist on the energy that comes from bringing different spheres together, the "life" that emerges in the attempt to fuse them.

Her novels also derive their energy in part from their fusion of different modes of narrative. As Byatt says in her recent essay "Old Tales, New

Forms," "The novel in the nineteenth and twentieth centuries has always incorporated forms of myths and fairy tales, *working both with and against them*" (*On Histories* 130, emphasis added). As various critics have pointed out, Byatt (like many other feminist writers of the late twentieth century, Margaret Atwood and Angela Carter chief among them) often works *against* the traditional shapes and ideologies of classic fairy tales. She sometimes echoes and then subverts the traditional tales that seem to require their heroines to be passive, domestic, and obedient; particularly in her "fairy stories" like "The Eldest Princess" she suggests other values and other endings. But she is also deeply suspicious of "many resolute feminist rewritings of fairy tales, making willful changes to plots and forms to show messages of female power" (*On Histories* 143). Simply to reverse the poles of a tale—to make the wicked stepmother the heroine, for example, or to rearrange the sexual economy—is to exchange a latent "message" for another, more obvious one, or essentially, Byatt believes, to write propaganda. What interests Byatt in fairy tales is not primarily their delineations of human possibilities but rather the patterns that recur and the narrative shapes that make these patterns visible.

Or, in other words, Byatt also works *with* traditional tales, with their repeated motifs and with their complex, embedded structures. Dissatisfied with what she has called "the decorum of the novel" (*Still Life* 367), she adopts apparently alien techniques and materials in order to transform it. She is still a "realist," if a "self-conscious" one; she, like Frederica, still seems to believe that "the setting of words in order, to make worlds, to make ideas . . . reveal[s] things" (*Whistling Woman* 277).[25] But in her recent fiction (and some of her own descriptions of it) she seems to be echoing Jameson's account of the "sedimentation" of the novel in *The Political Unconscious:* "the 'novel' as an apparently unified form is subjected to a kind of x-ray technique designed to reveal the layered or marbled structure of the text according to what we will call *generic discontinuities.* The novel is then not so much an organic unity as a symbolic act that must reunite or harmonize heterogeneous narrative paradigms which have their own specific and contradictory ideological meaning" (144).[26] The critic's "x-ray technique" of analysis reveals Byatt's deliberate "marbling" of her texts, her attempts to "reunite or harmonize heterogeneous narrative paradigms." In her most recent novels, *Babel Tower* and *A Whistling Woman,* the frames and collagelike structures—particularly the juxtapositions of realistic narratives and fantastic tales—reveal Byatt's understanding that it is only by combining the resources of disparate kinds of storytelling that she can approach the complexities of the world. As Susan Stewart once said, "In realism the frame is hidden, as if the shape of everyday events could form a continuum with the shape of fictive events" (*Nonsense* 172). In contrast, Byatt emphasizes the frame in order to move beyond commonsense realism and the expectations it brings with it.

Late in *Possession*, Ellen Ash, the poet's wife, remembers a passage from Lyell's *Principles of Geology* (1830–1833) that she once had read to her husband:

> It is the total distinctness, therefore, of crystalline formations, such as granite, horn-blende-schist, and the rest, from every substance of which the origin is familiar to us, that constitutes their claim to be regarded as the effects of causes now in action in the subterranean regions. They belong not to an order which has passed away; they are not the monuments of a primeval period, bearing inscribed upon them in obsolete characters the words and phrases of a dead language; but they teach us that part of the living language of nature, which we cannot learn by our daily intercourse with what passes on the habitable surface. (*Possession* 497)

For Lyell (an early-nineteenth-century geologist whose work informs all of Byatt's Victorian fictions and some of her contemporary ones like "The Djinn in the Nightingale's Eye" and the Frederica Potter quartet), subterranean, geological structures are not dead or obsolete but alive and working. He describes these formations as speaking a "living language" that we must recognize and learn to understand.

For Byatt, the subterranean work of fairy tales and myths in their "crystalline" forms continues. Far from being a "dead language," they provide an alphabet and a grammar that both link us to a living past and help us see the present more clearly. Byatt is part self-conscious realist, part postmodern writer, and part storyteller. As she says in her essay on "Fairy Stories," "whereas much post-modern self-reflexive narrative seems somehow designed to show that all narrations are two-dimensional and papery, that all motifs are interchangeable coinage, what I believe, and hope to have shown, is that the tale is always stronger than the teller" (8). Byatt often reflects on the conditions of narrative, on what it means to tell a story, as many post-modern novelists do. ("The Djinn in the Nightingale's Eye" is a particularly good example.) Throughout her work the motifs and structures of older tales often surface, like geological formations, offering "a different kind of grip on the world, a different kind of reality" (Byatt in Chevalier 20).[27] These narrative perspectives may never come together, never fuse. But Byatt's juxtapositions and framing structures suggest her continuing interest in alternative narrative possibilities. When she "writes the narrative expectations of a fairy story into a realist short story" (21), she shows her readers that there is more than one way to see and narrate the world.[28]

Notes

1. An essay that does this quite well for the collection *The Djinn in the Nightingale's Eye* is Campbell's "Forever possibilities." Sanchez's "A. S. Byatt's *Possession: A Fairytale Romance*" is much less successful.

2. Stories that might be considered "fairy tales" also include "A Lamia in the Cevennes" and "Cold" in *Elementals* (1998), as well as "The Thing in the Forest," "A Stone Woman," and perhaps "The Pink Ribbon" in her *Little Black Book of Stories* (2003). There are also ghost stories, like "The July Ghost" in *Sugar*.

3. In this essay I refer to Byatt's work by short title and page number in the text. See the bibliography for complete titles and publishing data.

4. See Murdoch 23–31.

5. Byatt may have encountered this form of fairy-tale persistence as she was translating Marie-Catherine d'Aulnoy's story "The Great Green Worm" for Marina Warner's collection of *Wonder Tales*. There the heroine, though she has repeatedly read the story of Psyche, reenacts Psyche's transgression.

6. Schor's "Sorting, Morphing, and Mourning" brilliantly ties the sorting in the novella to Victorian doubts and debates about matter. Attempts to order matter, as William discovers, lead to questions about form and transformation ("morphing").

7. For an excellent discussion of these references, see Fletcher "The *Odyssey* Rewoven."

8. As Byatt points out in her brief essay on *Angels and Insects*, "Theologians, sociobiologists, feminists and moralists are still furiously discussing the ideas about men and animals, soul and body, male and female that the Victorians began to think about in these ways. I have learned a great deal from E. O. Wilson, student of

insect societies and human nature" (www.asbyatt.com / anglInsct.htm). In her essay on "Fairy Stories" at the same site, she also mentions another source: Gillian Beer's work on Victorian scientific metaphors in *Darwin's Plots*.

9. "Sphinx" is the name of a moth, Sphinx Atropos; another name for Dame Kind, the good fairy in Matty's story; and the name that William has begun to associate with Matty herself, who is also a good fairy, tells riddling stories, and knows everything, including the true, incestuous relationship between Eugenia and Edgar. Campbell comes to the same conclusion in *A. S. Byatt and The Heliotropic Imagination*, 158, as does June Sturrock in "Angels," 100.

10. Byatt strongly suggests that these children may be Edgar Alabaster's, not William's. Even the one boy, Robert Edgar, said to have been given an Adamson name, Robert (*Angels* 84), is actually named after Harald Alabaster's father and older brother as well as Eugenia's half-brother Edgar (25). William Adamson's father's name is given as Martin (10). Byatt has (inadvertently?) made William's connection with the children as dubious linguistically as biologically.

11. In his excellent essay "*Angels and Insects:* Theory, Analogy, Metamorphosis," Levenson stresses the role of transformation in the natural world: "From the perspective of this metamorphic naturalism, we can abandon the net of Christian theology and still retain the sublimity of transfiguration. In the last stages of 'Morpho Eugenia,' we watch as human beings perform transfiguring acts as momentous as the caterpillars" (171). One caveat, though: in *Lady Oracle*, Margaret Atwood suggests that such transformations may be another relic of fairy-tale expectations. See Benson, *Cycles of Influence* 237.

12. See Fletcher, "The *Odyssey* Rewoven": "Salvation comes, unexpectedly, from the story within a story, Matty's tale. When Matty's story allows its hero to escape there seems to be an intersection of narrative levels, as if Matty had somehow created or written William's ending for him" (226).

13. This is much like Sabine de Kerkoz's description of her own narrative technique in *Possession* as a "box-bed inside the chamber inside the manor inside the protecting wall" (368). Byatt often returns to such enclosed structures, perhaps echoing Emily Brontë in *Wuthering Heights*. See my *Twice upon a Time*, 187n19.

14. Todorov's *The Poetics of Prose* recurs constantly to the problems of framing, particularly in the essay about the *Arabian Nights* translated as "Narrative-Men" ["Les Hommes-récits"], 66–79. Genette's fullest discussion is in the chapter "Voice" in his *Narrative Discourse: An Essay in Method*, 212–62, and in his later thoughts on the subject in *Narrative Discourse Revisited*, 84–95. Genette in particular develops a highly technical, Greek-inflected language for narrative levels and their intersections or *metalepses*. Though Byatt never refers to this work on levels directly in her

critical writing, she does refer to both writers occasionally. And, as Campbell points out in "Forever Possibilities," Byatt was thoroughly familiar with Robert Irwin's companion to the *Arabian Nights,* which refers at length to Todorov's work (225–28).

15. In her conversation with Tredell in 1990, 24.

16. For more on the constraints of traditional plots and the ways Byatt's characters circumvent them, see Jane Campbell, "Forever Possibilities," particularly 138–39. She studies the ways Byatt "interrogate[s] and revise[s] old stories" in *The Djinn in the Nightingale's Eye.*

17. See Schor "Sorting, Morphing, and Mourning," 247. Here she suggests that Byatt's fiction is more "postrealist" than "postmodern," writing that is deeply engaged in a dialogue with and perhaps even a resurrection of the dead—or, as she calls it, "ghostwriting."

18. See my *Twice upon a Time,* 115. In the pages that precede this quotation I compare two tales that are embedded in the novel, "The Glass Coffin" and "Gode's Tale," with their unembedded forms in the collection *The Djinn in The Nightingale's Eye.*

19. Yellin complains about the scene in "Cultural Cartography": "The distortion of the present enacted in reconciliation of mutually antagonistic critical positions and practices is echoed in a distortion of the past encoded in secrets that only the omniscient narrator can tell us. . . . [Byatt] makes at least an implicit claim to possess Victorian secrets known or knowable by no one else" (40). Yellin diagnoses this claim as "a return of the Arnoldian repressed," and as a "mystification" that devalues all literary scholarship.

20. As Derrida says in *The Truth in Painting,* "the parergonal frame stands out against two grounds [*fonds*], but with respect to each of these two grounds, it merges [*se fond*] into the other" (61). Or, in other words, the picture frame seems exterior or detached when we think about the painting (and we typically reproduce paintings without their frames) but seems part of the painting when we see it against a white museum wall.

21. See also the passage in *The Virgin in the Garden,* 209.

22. For both of these quotations, see Byatt's essay on *Babel Tower* at www.asbyatt .com/babel.htm.

23. In her essay "Choices: The Writing of *Possession*" at www.asbyatt.com/ posses.htm, Byatt mentions her struggle with the novel she was then working on, *Babel Tower:* "The Gestalt of the one I am writing, about the 1960s, is a jagged harlequin pattern of coloured fragments and smoking bonfires. And there is something *weak* about the narrative line, or tension, connecting there, that I'm trying to deal with."

24. See also Frederica's realization in the last chapter of the last novel of the quartet: "She thought that somewhere—in the science which had made Vermeer's painted spherical waterdrops, in the humming looms of neurones which connected to make metaphors, all this was one" (*Whistling Woman* 427). Byatt constantly draws on both natural and cognitive science to show that apparently disparate things actually come together.

25. Recently Byatt has been repeatedly called a "liberal humanist" by critics like Coetzee (153), Eagleton (337), Yellin (40), and Buxton (101). I think this accusation relies on a selective reading of her recent work—as well as an urge to see the current British novel as ideologically suspect or even bankrupt. Though she does use some key words like "attention" that link her to nineteenth-century novelists like George Eliot and Elizabeth Gaskell, she seems to me less interested in the ethical constitution of "self" than in fidelity to the natural world.

26. Though Jameson is talking about Manzoni and other nineteenth-century novelists like Stendhal and Eichendorff here, I believe his analysis can be productive for the analysis of much recent fiction.

27. This 1994 interview also reveals Byatt's thoughts about a "story within a story," or framed tale, as "about a reading experience; it turns the writer into a reader and it turns the readers into a reader of a reading; and it somehow lines the reader up with the writer as the reader of this text within a text" (20).

28. See Kearney, *On Stories*, particularly part 4, "Narrative Matters." As Kearney says, "Every story is a play of at least three persons (author / actor / addressee) whose outcome is never final. That is why narrative is an open-ended invitation to ethical and poetic responsiveness" (156).

Bibliography

Primary Sources

Byatt, A[ntonia] S[usan]. *Angels and Insects: Two Novellas.* 1992. Vintage International, 1994.

———. *Babel Tower.* 1996. Vintage International, 1997.

———. *The Djinn in the Nightingale's Eye: Five Fairy Stories.* 1994. Vintage International, 1998.

———. *Elementals: Stories of Fire and Ice.* 1998. Vintage International, 2000.

———. "The Great Green Worm." Trans. of Marie-Catherine d'Aulnoy's "Serpentin vert." *Wonder Tales.* Ed. Marina Warner. New York: Farrar, Straus and Giroux, 1994. 189–229.

————, and Ignês Sodré. *Imagining Characters: Six Conversations about Women Writers*. Ed. Rebecca Swift. London: Chatto and Windus, 1995. Vintage Books, 1997.

————. Introduction. *The Annotated Stories of the Brothers Grimm*, Ed. Maria Tatar. New York: W. W. Norton, 2004. xvii–xxvi.

————. *Little Black Book of Stories*. 2003. New York: Alfred A Knopf, 2004.

————. *On Histories and Stories: Selected Essays*. 2000. Cambridge: Harvard UP, 2002.

————. *Passions of the Mind: Selected Writings*. 1991. Vintage International, 1993.

————. *Possession: A Romance*. 1990. Vintage International, 1991.

————. *Shadow of a Sun*. New York: Harcourt, Brace, and World, 1964. Rpt. of *The Shadow of the Sun*. Vintage International, 1991.

————. *Still Life*. 1985. Scribner Paperback, 1996.

————. *The Virgin in the Garden*. 1978. Vintage International, 1992.

————. *A Whistling Woman*. 2002. Vintage International, 2004.

Byatt's Website (www.asbyatt.com) includes several brief but valuable essays on her own fiction not easily available elsewhere; see particularly the essays "Fairy Stories," "Angels and Insects," and "Babel Tower." (Click on the bee at the right on the home page for the section called "On Herself," then on the "Essays and Articles on Her Own Work" lurking faintly in the left-hand corner.)

Secondary Sources

Alfer, Alexa, and Michael J. Noble. *Essays on the Fiction of A. S. Byatt: Imagining the Real*. Westport, CT: Greenwood, 2001.

Bacchilega, Cristina. *Postmodern Fairy Tales: Gender and Narrative Strategies*. Philadelphia: U of Pennsylvania P, 1997.

Beer, Gillian. *Darwin's Plots: Evolutionary Narrative in Darwin, George Eliot, and Nineteenth-Century Fiction*. 2nd ed. Cambridge: Cambridge UP, 2000.

Benson, Stephen. *Cycles of Influence: Fiction, Folktale, Theory*. Detroit: Wayne State UP, 2003.

————. "Stories of Love and Death: Reading and Writing the Fairy Tale Romance." *Image and Power: Women in Fiction in the Twentieth Century*. Ed. Sarah Sceats and Gail Cunningham. London: Longman, 1996. 103–13.

Buxton, Jackie. "What's love got to do with it?": Postmodernism and *Possession.*" Alfer and Noble 89–104.

Cambiaghi, Mara. "The Power of Fiction in A. S. Byatt's *Babel Tower*." *Symbolism* 3 (2003): 279–304.

Campbell, Jane. *A. S. Byatt and the Heliotropic Imagination*. Waterloo, Ont.: Wilfrid Laurier UP, 2004.

————. "Forever possibilities. And impossibilities, of course"; Women and Narrative in *The Djinn in the Nightingale's Eye.*" Alfer and Noble 135–46.

Chevalier, Jean Louis. "Entretien avec A. S. Byatt." *Journal of the Short Story in English* 22 (1994): 12–27.

Coetzee, J. M. "A. S. Byatt." *Stranger Shores: Literary Essays 1986–1999.* New York: Viking, 2001. 155–59.

Derrida, Jacques. *The Truth in Painting.* Trans. Geoff Bennington and Ian McLeod. Chicago: U of Chicago P, 1987.

Dusinberre, Juliet. "Forms of Reality in A. S. Byatt's *The Virgin in the Garden.*" *Critique* 24 (1982): 55–62.

Eagleton, Terry. *The English Novel: An Introduction.* Malden, MA: Blackwell, 2005.

Fletcher, Judith. "The *Odyssey* Rewoven: A. S. Byatt's *Angels and Insects.*" *Classical and Modern Literature* 19 (1999): 217–31.

Franken, Christien. *A. S. Byatt: Art, Authorship, Creativity.* Basingstoke: Palgrave, 2001.

Genette, Gérard. *Narrative Discourse: An Essay in Method.* Trans. Jane E. Lewin. 1972. Ithaca: Cornell UP, 1980.

————. *Narrative Discourse Revisited.* Trans. Jane E. Lewin. Ithaca: Cornell UP, 1988.

Hansson, Heidi. "The Double Voice of Metaphor: A. S. Byatt's 'Morpho Eugenia.'" *Twentieth-Century Literature* 45 (1999): 452–71.

Harries, Elizabeth Wanning. *Twice upon a Time: Women Writers and the History of the Fairy Tale.* Princeton: Princeton UP, 2001.

Hurlburt, Ann. "The Great Ventriloquist: A. S. Byatt's *Possession: A Romance.*" *Contemporary British Women Writers.* Ed. Robert E. Hosmer Jr. New York: St. Martin's, 1993. 55–65.

Irwin, Robert. *The Arabian Nights: A Companion.* 1994. London: Tauris Parke, 2004.

Jameson, Fredric. *The Political Unconscious: Narrative as a Socially Symbolic Act.* Ithaca: Cornell UP, 1981.

Kearney, Richard. *On Stories.* London: Routledge, 2002.

Levenson, Michael. "*Angels and Insects:* Theory, Analogy, Metamorphosis." Alfer and Noble 161–74.

Maack, Annegret. "Wonder-Tales Hiding a Truth: Retelling Tales in 'The Djinn in the Nightingale's Eye.'" Alfer and Noble 123–34.

Morse, Deborah Denenholz. "Crossing Boundaries: The Female Artist and the Sacred Word in A. S. Byatt's *Possession.*" *British Women Writing Fiction.* Ed. Abby H. P. Werlock. Tuscaloosa: U of Alabama P, 2000. 148–74.

Murdoch, Iris. "Against Dryness: A Polemical Sketch." *Encounter.* 1961. Rpt. in *The*

Novel Today: Contemporary Writers on Modern Fiction. Ed. Malcolm Bradbury. Manchester, UK: Manchester UP, 1977. 23–31.

Sanchez, Victoria. "A. S. Byatt's *Possession:* A Fairytale Romance." *Southern Folk-lore* 52 (1995): 33–52.

Schor, Hilary M. "Sorting, Morphing, and Mourning: A. S. Byatt Ghostwrites Victorian Fiction." *Victorian Afterlife: Postmodern Culture Rewrites the Nineteenth Century.* Ed. John Kucich and Dianne F. Sadoff. Minneapolis: U of Minnesota P, 2000. 234–51.

Shuttleworth, Sally. "Writing Natural History: 'Morpho Eugenia.'" Alfer and Noble 147–60.

Slater, Niall W. "Looking for Proserpina: A. S. Byatt's Notes on the *Aeneid.*" *Literary Imagination* 5 (2003): 194–208.

Sorenson, Sue. "Something of the Eternal: A. S. Byatt and Vincent Van Gogh." *Mosaic* 37 (March 2004): 63–82.

Stewart, Susan. *Nonsense: Aspects of Intertextuality in Folklore and Literature.* 1978. Baltimore: Johns Hopkins UP, 1989.

Sturrock, June. "Angels, Insects, and Analogy: A. S. Byatt's "Morpho Eugenia.'" *Connotations* 12 (2002 / 3): 93–104.

Todd, Richard. *A. S. Byatt.* Writers and Their Work. Plymouth, UK: Northcote House, 1997.

Tredell, Nicolas. "A. S. Byatt in Conversation." *P-N Review* 17 (1991): 24–28.

Todorov, Tzvetan. *The Poetics of Prose.* Trans. Richard Howard. Ithaca: Cornell UP, 1977.

Yelin, Louise. "Cultural Cartography: A. S. Byatt's *Possession* and the Politics of Victorian Studies." *Victorian Newsletter* 81 (Spring 1992): 38–41.

4 Margaret Atwood and the Fairy Tale
Postmodern Revisioning in Recent Texts

SHARON R. WILSON

Margaret Atwood is not only one of today's best-known writers but also one who demonstrates the power and beauty of fairy tales. Fairy-tale intertexts function in nearly all of her work, including novels, short story collections, flash fictions and prose poems, poetry, children's books, and essays; and some of these works are themselves meta–fairy tales. As I have previously shown, in addition to literary, film, biblical, mythic, and other popular intertexts, Atwood's novels into the late 1980s—*The Edible Woman, Surfacing, Lady Oracle, Life Before Man, Bodily Harm, The Handmaid's Tale,* and *Cat's Eye*—all embed fairy tales. Although seldom recognized, Atwood's short story, poetry, flash fiction, and essay collections, most evidently *Bluebeard's Egg, The Circle Game, You Are Happy, Power Politics,* and *Survival,* and some of her visual art (*Fitcher's Bird*), also demonstrate fairy-tale intertexts (Wilson, "Fiction Flashes"). By revisioning fairy-tale intertexts in a postmodern manner, Atwood explores power and sexual politics in patriarchal society and implies movement from symbolic dismemberment and cannibalism to metamorphosis, usually through the transformative and creative act of telling a story.

To varying degrees, *The Robber Bride* (1993), *Morning in the Burned House* (1995), *Alias Grace* (1996), *The Blind Assassin* (2000), and *Oryx and Crake* (2003), my focus here, continue to use fairy-tale images, motifs, themes, structure, and characterization, always deconstructed and interlaced with tales from related folklore, other popular culture, history, literature, and opera. Atwood admits that the Grimms' fairy tales, along with closely related biblical and mythic stories, are her major influences (Sandler 14) and that "Fitcher's Bird," embedded in all of my focus texts, is one of the tales she uses most frequently. In addition, "The Robber Bridegroom," "The Juniper Tree," "The Girl without Hands," "Little Red-Cap," and "The White Snake," from the *Kinder- und Hausmärchen*, appear often. Hans Christian Andersen's literary tales, including "The Littlest Mermaid," "The Red Shoes," and "The Snow Queen"; French-Canadian tales; Native American tales; nursery rhymes; comic books; and children's literature frequently recur. Rather than clearly distinguishing between myth and fairy tale as Angela Carter does, or using the fairy tale for its historical status as a genre, Atwood employs all intertexts in a similar postmodern way, simultaneously seriously, ironically, and parodically. Often, as illustrated nicely in the "Fitcher's Bird" intertext in *Bluebeard's Egg*, they are both comic and tragic.

Surprisingly, in view of excellent studies by Jack Zipes and other folklorists, the numerous postmodern and postcolonial fiction writers who use fairy-tale intertexts, and the serious scholarship that investigates these intertexts, some readers still view fairy tales stereotypically as "poison apples" for female readers, as didactic tales enculturating societal expectations and rigid gender roles (Daly 44, 90–91; Dworkin 41). When used by writers such as Louise Erdrich and Toni Morrison, some readers mistakenly criticize a supposed "appropriation" of "European" stories, particularly as part of an "experimental" and self-referential postmodernism, as a selling out of their own cultural traditions (see, for example, Silko 179). Postmodern novelists who embed fairy-tale intertexts generally "revise" or deconstruct them, using irony, parody, and sometimes satire of these intertexts alongside the tales' original character types, themes, motifs, and images. Often turning fairy-tale plots upside down, reversing outcomes, and using unreliable narrators, anti-heroes/heroines, and magical realism, the texts generally exist in a romance mode and may still depict transformation and metamorphosis.[1]

Very frequently, Atwood retains the oral quality of fairy tales in her texts: especially in her fiction flashes or prose pieces, there is a voice and a listener. Although she often uses trickster narrators and characteristically "writes beyond the ending" rather than resolving narratives (DuPlessis 6), her fairy-tale intertexts generally imply movement from symbolic dismemberment and cannibalism to healing.

In embedding fairy-tale intertexts, Atwood uses characteristic tactics. First, she often builds a scene on a fairy-tale image, such as the mother apparently turning into a jay in *Surfacing*. Second, by frequently reversing the gender of fairy-tale characters, as when *Life Before Man*'s Nate becomes a comic "Cinderella," she moves the woman from object to subject and doubles characters. Third, as in *The Handmaid's Tale*, Atwood displaces the "truth" of privileged, reliable traditional narratives to unreliable ones with self-conscious and developing narrators. Fourth, she uses tropes and symbols to deepen the meaning of the ordinary, such as the "dismemberment" most of her characters experience in patriarchal or colonial culture. Fifth, as in *Life Before Man*'s "Wizard of Oz" intertext, she displaces the fairy-tale plot line to make the marginalized subtext, in this case the wicked witch, central. Sixth, rather than using an intertext's resolution, such as marriage or living happily ever after, Atwood usually explodes and opens it to varied interpretations. In *Bodily Harm*, rather than allowing Rennie's plane to land in Toronto, she revises her manuscript to keep the plane in the air (Margaret Atwood Papers). Seventh, Atwood bends and blends tone and genres, as in *Bluebeard's Egg* when the comic Bluebeard is a heart surgeon specializing in seduction. Eighth, like other postmodern writers, Atwood uses irony as a subversive discourse. Ninth, while retaining fairy-tale costumes (red gowns and baskets in *The Handmaid's Tale*), settings, and motifs, Atwood uses language to defamiliarize (Shklovsky 13–22), transgress, and parody these elements. Tenth, moving toward a postcolonial or harmonious society, she revises or reverses the norms or ideology of an intertext, so that the danger of going off the path in "Red Cap" becomes the necessity of leaving it in *The Handmaid's Tale* (Wilson, *Margaret* 32–33). Most important, fairy-tale intertexts are much more than allusions in Atwood's texts: "frame narratives echo inner narratives' images, motifs, themes, characterization, structures, and even plots, self-consciously reflecting, and reflecting upon, intertexts" (Wilson, *Margaret* 3–4). In addition, they use or parody intertexts' scenes, point of view, symbols, and costumes to shape ironic postmodern and postcolonial texts that undermine essentialist, colonial, and sexist assumptions.

The Robber Bride and Morning in the Burned House

Published within two years of one another, *Morning in the Burned House* and *The Robber Bride* both feature explicit use of fairy tales: referring to two Grimms' tales by title, directly addressing an audience, building on fairy-tale images and symbols such as dismemberment, avoiding resolution, blending tones and genres, using irony and parody, shifting ideological norms of the intertexts, and, in the case of *The Robber Bride*, reversing the gender of the villain. Both embed the Grimms' "Fitcher's Bird" (Perrault's "Bluebeard," AT 311),[2] one of my focuses here. Fairy-tale intertexts in *The Robber Bride*, most importantly the Grimms' "The Robber Bridegroom" (AT 955) about a groom literally consuming fiancées, are numerous;[3] and in addition to underlining the novel as a meta–fairy tale about fairy tales in western culture, they function to support Atwood's postcolonial and feminist themes. Myth, biblical allusions, nursery rhymes and stories, literary references, mummy and vampire lore, historical legend, and popular culture intertexts are interwoven with fairy-tale ones. The novels' epigraphs suggest intertexts, and, although critics have said little about "The Robber Bridegroom" in this regard, they have recognized the importance of intertexts in this novel (Jacobsen; Potts "The White" 230, "The Old" 283). Like other postmodern writers, in this and other novels Atwood creates magical realism, a fusion of magic with realism, through her intertexts by inserting trickster figures, shape-changers, demonic revenants, witches, devils, vampires, a potent underworld, real or inverted quests, and actual colonialist history into believable situations.

In addition to its role in the novel *The Robber Bride*, "The Robber Bridegroom" is used by Atwood in *The Edible Woman*, *Bodily Harm* (originally titled "The Robber Bridegroom"), "The Robber Bridegroom" poem in *Interlunar*, a watercolor of that title in a private collection (Wilson, *Margaret* 36, 200), and as an epigraph in *Negotiating with the Dead* (2002), a recent book of essays from the Empson lectures she gave at Cambridge. Where she refers to the Grimms' "Fitcher's Bird," about a groom's dismemberment of successive brides who are stained when they enter the forbidden room (see sections on *Alias Grace*, *The Blind Assassin*, and *Oryx and Crake* below), "The Robber Bride" and its motifs are generally implied as well. "The Robber Bridegroom" tells of a robber groom and the prospective brides he lures to his isolated house in the dark forest, where he and his band of robbers dismember and then eat the women. The maiden featured in the tale is warned both by a caged bird, "Turn back, turn back, young maiden dear, / 'Tis a murderer's house you enter here," and an old woman in the basement whose head bobs constantly, "You think you are a bride soon to be married, but you will keep your wedding with death." Unlike earlier maidens, this one hides behind a barrel and sees another maiden being prepared for dinner. The victim's chopped-off finger (sometimes hand), falls into her lap (in some versions, bosom), but the old woman calls the robbers to dinner and drugs their wine. Both women escape, following the path of sprouted peas and lentils home, where the maiden tells her father, the miller, everything. At the wedding celebration, where each person is expected to tell a story, she says nothing until the groom urges her to speak. She then relates a "dream" and presents the victim's chopped-off finger (H57.2.2.). Because the bride speaks, the Robber Bridegroom is executed. It is the groom, not the bride, who marries death (Hunt and Stern 200–04; Magoun and Krappe 151–54; Zipes *Complete Fairy Tales* 153–57).

In *The Robber Bride*, Atwood reverses the gender of the Robber, but, as in many of her texts, most of the characters play both Robber and Bride roles in their games of sexual politics. As in other genres, character roles in fairy tales are both doubled and foiled and may be seen as archetypal. The novel deconstructs any easy line we might draw between victors and victims or winners and losers. While the tale has some gender-specific implications about male and female behavior, Atwood's revised meta–fairy tale, dramatizing survival problems in a cannibalistic, colonialistic world, is about postcolonial survival as well. Initially obsessed with holding onto the men in their lives, the three main narrators, Tony, Charis, and Roz, choose to see both these men and themselves as innocent and passive victims of a female monster, cannibalistic as in "The Robber Bridegroom" and some versions of the Bluebeard cycle. Ironically, what mainly makes Zenia monstrous is an ability to appropriate and hold onto men who "belong" to someone else. In short, she is a sexual colonizer. Like the Wizard of "Fitcher's Bird," who is able to get maidens to jump into his basket when he appears, Zenia seems irresistible.

Although Canada thinks of itself as colonized but historically neutral (the "sweet Canadians" of *Bodily Harm*), this novel dramatizes a Canadian's invention of the Supergun and Canada's participation in colonizing wars in the Middle East. Involved in personal as well as political intrigue, the trickster Zenia creates different personal "pasts" for each listener and, even after her apparent death, manages to enthrall both women and men. A vampire returned from the dead, a well-preserved mummy, and a tiny-waisted snake goddess, Zenia plays the death-giving Robber of life and literally robs the women of both men and illusions. Tony is afraid that Zenia will leave her as useless as an amputated hand and thinks she might be appeased with Fitcher's bowl of blood (199, 15), and Charis feels as if Zenia has "taken a chunk of Charis' own body and sucked it into herself" (78). When Zenia tells Roz that she didn't own Mitch, that "He wasn't your God-given property," Roz replies: "But that doesn't alter the fact that you ate him for breakfast" (510). Ironically, however, virtually every other character, including Roz, who becomes thirsty for Mitch's blood (436), is described as a Dracula or Robber cannibal. Perhaps the most painful episode of symbolic dismemberment and cannibalism occurs when Uncle Vern rapes Charis, who at this point is named Karen: "Then he falls on top of Karen and puts his slabby hand over her mouth, and splits her in two. . . . On top of her is a dark mass, worrying at her, like an animal eating another animal" (300—01).

Only when we recognize that Zenia is dying of cancer, may actually have been an abused child, and is probably murdered do we recognize that she is a victim as well as a robber. While the unreliable narrators Charis and Roz do grow in awareness by the end of the novel, it is Tony, the historian, who especially reaches feminist and postcolonial consciousness. Finally, she speaks out as the Robber Bride, telling the story we read. Aware that Zenia "will only be history if Tony chooses to shape her into history" and that, like folklore, Zenia is "insubstantial, ownerless . . . drifting from mouth to mouth and changing as it goes," Tony creates meaning: "these histories may be ragged and threadbare, patched together from worthless leftovers, but to her they are also flags, hoisted with a certain jaunty insolence, waving bravely though inconsequently, glimpsed here and there through the trees, on the mountain roads, among the ruins, on the long march into chaos" (536—37). Constructing her own story of Zenia, Tony "stares up at Zenia, cornered on the balcony with her failing magic, balancing on the sharp edge, her bag of tricks finally empty." Invoking and deconstructing the Great Goddess of matriarchy, Tony finally realizes that "whatever her secrets are she's not telling. She's like an ancient statuette dug up from a Minoan palace: there are the large breasts, the tiny waist, the dark eyes, the snaky hair. Tony picks her up and turns her over, probes and questions, but the woman with her glazed pottery face does nothing but smile" (545—46).

When, at the end of the novel, Tony questions whether "we are in any way" like Zenia (546), she has already detailed comparisons of Zenia to Marius, Gengis Khan, Saddam Hussein, and other colonizers. Recognizing from the novel's beginning that the basin of blood in "Fitcher's Bird" would have been appropriate for Zenia (15), she knows that Zenia represents history. Although history can repeat itself, it can, like a novel, be written and spoken differently. As Tony writes Zenia's ending—the novel's unresolved ending—Atwood challenges all of us to write and exist differently. Ready for another story, Tony rejoins the female friends that have, like herself, been Zenia: both the Grimms' Robber Bride and Robber.

Although many of the poems in *Morning in the Burned House* deal with Atwood's childhood and her father's later illness and eventual death, section II "is clamorous with the voices of women" (Howells 137), eager to revision women of calendars, paintings, mythology, films, and history by allowing them to tell their own stories. Like *The Robber Bride,* "Manet's Olympia" critiques the famous Manet painting and even allows Olympia, a Robber or Bluebeard victim, to speak. This poem illustrates well the way Atwood interweaves art, historical, and fairy-tale intertexts to critique essentialist and sexist societal values. According to Atwood's first persona,

> This is indoor sin.
> Above the head of the (clothed) maid
> is an invisible voice balloon: *Slut.* (24)

It is the black ribbon around the woman's neck, resembling the blood-red necklace of Carter's "The Bloody Chamber," that identifies her as a consort of the Robber or Bluebeard:

> . . . What's under it?
> A fine red threadline, where the head
> was taken off and glued back on.
> The body's an offer, but the neck's as far as it goes. (24)

Like Atwood's early watercolors of women with chopped-off heads (*Mary Queen of Scots* I and II), she is one of Atwood's many symbolically dismembered female protagonists, but she refuses to remain a sex object or to be forced into any category. Here the male viewer, "Monsieur Voyeur," addressed as "You," is jerked into both poem and painting ironically to become a comic object of voyeurism: "As for that object of yours / she's seen those before, and better" (25). When the point of view shifts to the formerly objectified woman, "I, the head," becomes "the only subject / of this picture." She advises the man that he is furniture and should "Get stuffed" (25).

In addition to its allusions to "Fitcher's Bird," "Hansel and Gretel," "Rapunzel," "Sleeping Beauty," and numerous myths, *Morning in the Burned House* includes Atwood's poem "The Girl without Hands," named after the fairy tale and long available only in the Fisher Rare Book Library's manuscripts. A tale Atwood also embeds in *You Are Happy, Life Before Man, Bodily Harm,* and *The Blind Assassin,* "The Girl without Hands" ("The Handless Maiden," AT 706) informs handless figures in her watercolors as well as her many characters whose hands are gloved or dangle, unable to act, or who, like Crake of *Oryx and Crake,* suffer from the Rapunzel Syndrome discussed in *Survival:* enclosing themselves in towers they become, they are too distant to establish anything but destructive touch. The most striking feature of the Grimms' "The Girl without Hands" is the regrowth of the girl's chopped-off hands; and while several of the final poems of Atwood's poetry volumes, including *Interlunar, Two-Headed Poems,* and *Morning in the Burned House,* suggest this kind of transformation, some of her characters (Serena Joy, the Commander, Zenia) remain robbers of life, unable to touch except destructively.

In "The Girl without Hands" fairy tale, the father resembles Bluebeard figures by cutting off the hands of the faultless girl, possibly a victim of incest, because he has inadvertently sold her to the devil. As in Joyce Carol Oates's novel alluding to this tale, the girl says, "Do with me what you will." The Devil cannot claim her since she is clean and inside a magic circle, so she goes away in her snow-white garment. After she eats one of the pears in his garden, a King marries her and gives her silver hands, only to cast her out later with her child because of false letters. After the King's mother substitutes a hind's cut-out tongue and eyes for hers, the Queen is led by an angel to a house where she and her son Sorrowful stay for seven years. "Because of her piety, her hands which had been cut off, grew once more" (Hunt and Stern 164). After fasting for seven years, the King discovers the woman and child and all live happily. Atwood's "The Girl without Hands" also shows fairy-tale transformation. The poem presents two doubled handless characters, the first a contemporary, urban "you" who turns a magnificent seen world into ruins because she pushes distance "like a metal cart on wheels" surrounding herself: "you can't hold it / you can't hold any of it." Like the

Girl Without Hands of the fairy tale, the "you" is surrounded by a clean circle, in this case of dead space. The Girl's white dress means either purity or "the failure / to be any colour," and her scream "surrounds her now like an aureole / of hot sand, of no sound." Still, since only she can understand what has happened to the "you," if there she would touch with absent hands "and you would feel nothing, but you would be / touched all the same" (112–13). As in many of Atwood's poems using fairy-tale intertexts, the magic outweighs the irony. Although "Everything has bled out of her," like other shape-changers in this volume, the girl still bridges the distance, partly of past and present, to heal both herself and the other. Just as this volume's central persona can breakfast in a burned house no longer there, she, too, recognizes "The power of what is not there" and becomes a Proteus aware of the primacy of touch: "the trick is to hold on / through all appearances" ("Shapechangers in Winter," "Morning in the Burned House" 120, 125–26). As Howells suggests, "The volume represents painful processes of disruption and relocation, where loss is finally transfigured through the creative act of writing" (135).

Alias Grace and The Blind Assassin

Few readers would think much about "The Fitcher's Bird" (Perrault's "Bluebeard," AT 311) intertext in *Alias Grace*. Like "The Robber Bridegroom," "Fitcher's Bird" is about marriage to death, this time with three sisters. The disguised wizard's touch forces each sister in succession to jump into his basket, after which he takes them to his house in the dark forest, where each is given keys and whatever she desires but told to stay away from one forbidden room. He also gives each one an egg and orders that they carry it with them. Both the first and second sister are curious, enter the forbidden room filled with dismembered bodies of previous prospective brides, drop the egg in the basin of blood, and are unable to wash off the stain. The first is beheaded and both are cut into pieces. The third sister, however, passes the test by leaving the egg in a safe place. When she sees her dismembered sisters, like Isis she puts the pieces together and they live again. The wizard is now in her power and she makes him carry a basketful of gold, hiding her sisters, to her parents. She leaves a substitute bride, a flower-wreathed skull, in the window and disguises herself as a wondrous bird. When all of Fitcher's wedding guests are in his house, the brothers and kinsmen of

Fitcher's Bird set fire to it so that he and his crew cannot escape (Hunt and Stern 216–20).

The "Fitcher's Bird" fairy tale appears in virtually every Atwood text, often alongside "The Robber Bride." Her watercolor, *Fitcher's Bird*, shows the skull-faced substitute bride (Wilson, *Margaret* Plate 3). In *The Edible Woman* (1969), Marian imagines that she will open the forbidden door in her Bluebeard's apartment to see her fiancé holding a carving knife. She increasingly feels like food and stops eating, especially when she sees her new hairstyle as a decorated cake. In addition to the men in her life, Fitcher / the Robber represents her consumer society. Similarly, in *Bodily Harm* (1981), Rennie, eaten by cancer (and symbolically by her physician and live-in lover), meets other Fitcher / Robbers in the middle of a Caribbean revolution and, whether she ever leaves the prison or not, recognizes that bodily harm is global. *Bluebeard's Egg* (1983), which actually quotes the Hunt and Stern translation of the Grimms' "Fitcher's Bird," is a comic treatment of the fairy tale in which the "bird" thinks her husband plays the egg rather than Bluebeard. Sexual politics is dominant as Bluebeard, a heart doctor, symbolically dismembers the many women, including the deluded wife, whom he betrays.

"Fitcher's Bird," "The Robber Bridegroom," and "The Girl without Hands" intertexts again underline the dismemberment, cannibalism, and male / female conditioning in *Alias Grace*, including blood, the forbidden door and chamber, the casket of secrets, a missing hand, Pandora's box, punishment, disguise, trickery, and escape motifs. In this novel about repressed sexuality, class privilege, and gender stereotypes, Grace, like Lady Macbeth, continuously imagines (or says she does) spots of red in her prison that suggest Fitcher's basin of blood. Even a book (*Godey's Ladies Book,* with fashions from the states) is found in bed, covered in blood, "murdered" along with its reader. Neither of the book's unreliable narrators has much self-insight, and both Simon and Grace resist opening doors to forbidden chambers of the self, although they are eager to open those concealing the other. In "The Secret Door" chapter, Simon dreams of a corridor of locked doors, similar to the attic where the maids lived in his childhood home. He had enjoyed examining forbidden things in this "secret world" (139). In his dream, the door at the end opens, and sea water closes over his head while maids first caress and then abandon him. Objects of his father rise from the depths and reform into a dead hand representing his father and his sense of having transgressed. Simon rationalizes that this is really Grace's story and that amnesia, which he later experiences, is a "drowning of recollection," the "buried treasure" of lost memories. But he appears to have little faith in his own competence and allows himself to be manipulated by women, especially his mother, who not only picks his bride but tries to run his entire life.

On the other hand, Simon is a Fitcher / Robber. Atwood characteristically blends tones and genres and parodies in her comic characters at the same time as we recognize their ominous Gothic elements. Simon is obsessed with flesh, including that of Dora (probably named after Freud's famous patient), Mrs. Humphrey, Lydia, and especially Grace. Like the Robber Bridegroom, he wants to cannibalize women symbolically: he thinks of Dora as ham; Miss Lydia, who places him on a "tongue-coloured settee," as pastry; and Grace as "a hard nut to crack." Lydia smells like ferns, mushrooms, and fermenting fruit. He wants to watch Grace eat the apple she associates with the Tree of Knowledge and imagines Grace "washing herself with her tongue, like a cat" (85, 54, 90–91).

Again Atwood builds her story on fairy-tale images, symbols, and themes, moves a woman from object to subject, displaces "truth," and uses subversive irony. She even manages to open a closed, historical story. Grace sees most of the men in the book as cannibals who dismember, and as an Irish immigrant in a sexist and classist world, she often sees women, such as her mother and Mary Whitney, being victimized. Her father thinks his new baby "would look very nice on a platter with roast potatoes and an apple in his mouth" (110). Hearing flute music associated with Jamie Walsh, Grace dreams of a peddler with a starved look, "someone I had once known," who watches her scrubbing the floor at Mr. Kinnear's and holds her cut off hand: "white and shrivelled up, he was dangling it by its wrist like a glove" (100–01). She feels her heart, too, is missing, and, ironically as she quilts while speaking, does not want to be in pieces, a patchwork. The prison guards think of her as a morsel, "ripe enough to be picked": "Come, you're making my mouth water for you already, you're enough to turn an honest man into a cannibal" (240). In a dream where she feels both horror and longing, she associates McDermott, Jeremiah, Kinnear, and another man she had been familiar with in childhood with Death himself, suggesting marriage to death. Headless angels in robes washed with blood crouch in judgment near Kinnear's house (280–81). Grace also thinks of children as cannibals of their mother, the new child as "an enormous mouth, on a head like the flying angel heads on the gravestones, but with teeth and all, eating away at my mother from the inside" (107).

Grace, too, plays the Robber/Fitcher. She thinks of her "Red hair of an ogre. A wild beast. . . . A monster" (33). Wishing to be a gloved lady and possibly murdering to acquire Nancy Montgomery's clothing, she considers killing her siblings and abusive father, disguises feelings, tells conflicting stories, manipulates and enthralls men, and, depending upon interpretation, may hide a Mary Whitney part of herself behind a door to a forbidden chamber. Certainly James McDermott considers her responsible for his execution. Atwood does not, however, resolve the extent of Grace's involvement in the murders. As Atwood tells one of her editors, butter wouldn't melt in Grace's mouth (Margaret Atwood Papers). Just as Grace recognizes that her role as an object of pity "calls for a different arrangement of the face" than when she was an object of horror and fear (443), she wants to put a disguised and subversive border of snakes on her Tree of Paradise quilt after marriage to Jamie Walsh. Other characters also seem to be both Fitcher and the Robber. According to the Susanna Moodie *Life in the Clearings* chapter epigraph, McDermott cut Nancy in four pieces and after beheading, was himself cut into pieces at the university, something Grace fears as well.

Unlike *The Robber Bride* and most of Atwood's work embedding fairy-tale intertexts, *Alias Grace* offers no regrown hands; the only fairy-tale transformation is that of Grace into an accomplished creator. In league with her friend Jeremiah the peddler, a charlatan posing as Dr. Dupont, Grace plays the role of a person with a split personality disorder and manages to trick people into releasing her from punishment. While readers may still think that Grace has psychological problems, she has become a consummate storyteller. Her entire narrative is so filled with antilanguage designed to con listeners ("This is what I told Dr. Jordan, when we came to that part of the story" and "It might have happened," 6, 296) that it becomes difficult to make any definitive statement about her except that she is both a "wizard" and an abused girl who learns to survive in a dismembering society. She is attracted to Jeremiah, a Pied Piper peddler, and gives every indication of continuing her performance in marriage to Jamie Walsh, who performs as Pan.

The Blind Assassin also uses "Fitcher's Bird" and "The Girl without Hands" intertexts. It is a novel within a novel within a novel, a "maze" seemingly designed to trap readers into confusing characters and plots. The three narratives are interspersed with newspaper clippings, a letter, and society announcements. The first narrative, the frame one, is a self-reflexive memoir of Iris Chase's life in Port Ticonderoga and Toronto, Canada, in the 1930s and 1940s. The second, also called "The Blind Assassin," is a novel published under Laura Chase's name but written by Iris. The protagonists are identified only as "he" and "she," and readers are led to believe that the novel records the love affair of Alex Thomas and Laura Chase, Iris's sister. The third is an unfinished science fiction pulp "magazine" or novel, including a "Blind Assassin" story that the "he" and "she" appear to compose together within this novel. It is set on the planets Zycron, Xenor, and Aa'A with tongueless sacrificial maidens and blind assassins, lizard men wearing flammable shorts, and luscious peach women who ripen on trees. Again Atwood creates an oral situation, builds scenes on a fairy-tale image (here, particularly, cut-off hands), blends tones and genres, uses unreliable, developing narration and fairy-tale symbols, defamiliarizes with profound irony and parody, and, despite the main character's death near the end of the novel, denies resolution. As Atwood says, the male lover uses Zycron "as many science fiction writers used the genre before him—as an oblique critique of his own society, in which there is child labour, exploitation and different classes" (Sylge). In addition to "Fitcher's Bird" and "The Girl without Hands," the novel as a whole interlaces allusions to fairy-tale texts including "Sleeping Beauty," "The Robber Bridegroom," and "Rapunzel" with other traditional stories to explore the ways that we all blindly "assassinate" in personal and political wars.[4] As in *The Robber Bridegroom* and *Oryx and Crake*, the novel uses the sold child folk motif in reference to both Iris and Laura Chase, the former Richard's "child" bride and later the sister whom Richard abuses, also presumed author of the inner book titled "The Blind Assassin." The honeymoon trunk, holding the unhappiness of Iris and Richard's marriage and the notebooks revealing Richard's abuse of Laura, is also the casket of secrets.

In the "Fitcher's Bird" intertext, the Fitcher figure represents the "blind assassins," the men with "burning heads," including Richard, Iris and Laura's father, and all the men who precipitate war and do "bodily harm." In the science fiction stories, as in *The Robber Bride*, however, the roles double, so that Fitcher is also women, such as Iris, who symbolically dismember and cannibalize others. *The Blind Assassin* uses disguise, bad touch, marriage to death, the forbidden room, the casket of secrets, keys, dismemberment and rememberment, trickery, and punishment motifs.

Iris is blind, handless, heartless, and asleep throughout the book. As a combination Sleeping Beauty / wicked godmother in "Sleeping Beauty" (AT

410), Iris prefers not to be aware of her, her sister's, her parents', and Alex's sacrifices to war, capitalism, and greed. Not only Iris but also Laura, Aimee, Winifred, and Sabrina are connected to the "Sleeping Beauty" fairy tale. Winifred, usually the witch, is, like Iris, also a parody fairy godmother (318). Iris has a daydream about Winifred and her friends wearing wreaths of money on their heads and gathered around Sabrina's bed bestowing their godmother gifts. "I appear in a flash of sulphurous light and a puff of smoke and a flapping of sooty leather wings, the uninvited black-sheep god-mother." Her gift is the truth (439). Laura, more questioning than Iris, is still blind or asleep. Angry at Laura's ability to "subtract herself," Mr. Erskine yells, "You're not the Sleeping Beauty" and throws her against the wall. . . . Iris realizes that she should not have interrupted "a sleepwalker" with the news that Alex was dead. She "pushed [Laura] off [the bridge]" (164, 488). On the other hand, Laura would also be an uninvited fairy at Aimee's christening if she said that Aimee wasn't Richard's child (432).

As the third sister, Fitcher's bride, discovers the dismembered pieces of her sisters, the previous brides, behind the locked door, Iris finally under-stands what has happened to her sister. Rather than a prince, it is Laura's notebooks and Iris's own regained feelings that awaken Iris. Laura Chase's notebooks, first used when Laura and Iris study with their tutor, Mr. Erskine, reveal to Iris her blindness and her complicity in her sister's death. Although Iris withholds knowledge about the contents of the notebooks from readers until "The Golden Lock" chapter near the end of her memoir, she discov-ers them in her stocking drawer the day Laura dies, too late to keep her from uttering the words that send Laura over the bridge. Finally, Iris is not the tongueless victim of her characters' science fiction story but the bride who speaks out in "The Robber Bridegroom" fairy tale. The person who appears to be "Laura's odd, extra hand, attached to no body . . . [this] prim-lipped keeper of the keys, guarding the dungeon in which the starved Laura is chained to the wall" (286), leaves a secret casket, a steamer trunk of words that is the novel we read. She and her protagonist, "Iris," are no longer mute, sacrificial virgins, Blind Assassins, or handless, helpless females. As in "The Girl without Hands" fairy tale, Iris's symbolically cut-off hand grows back; as in the "Fitcher's Bird" fairy tale, Iris is able to reassemble the dismem-bered pieces of herself.

Oryx and Crake

Fairy-tale intertexts in *Oryx and Crake* are less recognizable than those in most of Atwood's previous texts. By studying her earlier use of the Grimms' "Fitcher's Bird" (AT 311), however, we see again some of this tale's primary motifs, especially the door to the forbidden chamber (C611.1), behind which literal or figural rooms hold horrifying discoveries, in this case suggesting apocalypse. The door becomes this novel's central symbol. Tales other than "Fitcher's Bird" also present doors, typically two doors hiding menace, such as tigers or death, and the third one treasures, and characters must choose which to open. In folklore, tales about forbidden places, including caskets, chambers, and doors, have a wide geographic distribution, including French Canada; doors may also be entrances to the lower world or the fairy world, they may be guarded by monsters, sometimes magic is necessary for opening, and ghosts may be able to enter closed doors (AT 526, 222; Thompson VI 224–25). *Oryx and Crake* also uses other motifs from "Fitcher's Bird"—such as dismemberment, cannibalism, unwitting marriage to death, death for breaking a taboo, resuscitation by arrangement of members, disguise, tricked ogre, and punishment of the murderer[5]—and interweaves literary and popular culture allusions with its fairy-tale intertexts.[6] In addition to "The Girl without Hands" and the Rapunzel Syndrome, folklore motifs appearing in many fairy tales, such as "Once upon a time," menacing or helpful animals, the golem, unnatural food, the trickster, the robber of life, the casket full of secrets, the abandoned or sold child, the quest, escape, rescue, and the fountain of youth, occur in an apparently realistic context that is actually dystopian and Gothic. As Atwood says, speculative fiction is usually in the romance mode, and *Oryx and Crake* is an adventure romance "coupled with a Minippean satire."[7] As in fairy tales and *The Handmaid's Tale,* the narrator addresses an audience even though he cannot know that anyone will hear. Still, the novel deconstructs its fairy-tale intertexts by moving a female from object to subject, displacing the truth of traditional narratives, using symbols, parody, and irony, refusing closure, and bending/blending genres and tones, characteristically mixing tragic and comic modes of response. *Oryx and Crake*'s extravagant and comic word play and puns reveal Atwood as a master of defamiliarization.

In this novel, there is no escape by use of a substituted object or rescue by a sister: like Snowman/Jimmy, readers of *Oryx and Crake* are on their own. Jimmy is the character/unreliable and self-conscious narrator who must prove his worth and pass the fairy-tale test. While he hopes he will win Oryx—Eve, one of this novel's tricksters and the sold child—like many of

Atwood's narrators he initially marries death: he chooses blindness and accepts a cannibalistic culture. He becomes distracted by games and superficialities and chooses the door to treasure and then the one to attacking animals rather than to authentic humanity. He does not begin to gain knowledge until he is expelled from an infected Paradise (here Paradice) to become a prophet for the Crakers, the created beings who are supposed to replace human beings. Crake, the novel's Adam, Dr. Frankenstein, and Fitcher or the trickster robber of life, amuses himself with Extinctathon and substitutes a killing microbe for the magic Fountain of Youth (Water of Life) sought by the pleeblanders. Oryx, also this novel's eaten Robber Bride or a dismembered sister of Fitcher's Bride, is the sold child, Eve / snake, Scheherazade, and reversed Cinderella. She is what Eve Sedgwick calls an object of exchange between the two men (524). As one of Atwood's many tricksters, including Circe of *You Are Happy*, harpies, and sirens, she holds Jimmy in bondage to Crake by telling him contradictory stories.

Unlike the many fairy tales, such as "Cinderella," in which friendly animals help the hero or heroine on a quest, sometimes leading them to treasure, here the abused animals, chimeras who have been subjected to genetic hybridization, get revenge on human beings who lack reverence for other beings or the natural world. Like the pigs in *Animal Farm*, the pigoons in this cautionary tale show intelligence and teamwork: on Snowman's quest to the destroyed compound, they maliciously watch and attack. Unlike "The Three Pigs" (AT 124A), where the pigs live in houses built of straw, twigs, and iron or bricks, the human wolves in Crake's society don't need to blow houses down: the affluent intellectual elite has already broken into the houses of lower beings, including not only pigs but low-status humans, rabbits, chickens, skunks, raccoons, and even wolves, all now subjects for Dr. Frankenstein's experimentation. They barricade themselves in gated communities called Compounds. As in the Grimms' "The Wolf and the Kids" and "Red Riding Hood" (Redcap: The Glutton, AT 123, 333), the elite "wolves" use disguise and deception, including false advertising and products, in order to open the doors of their victim's defenses so that they may be eaten, in this case by microbes that produce this novel's apocalypse. Ironically, beautiful Oryx, still an abused Cinderella, delivers the libido-enhancing product that kills, only to be killed by her "prince."

In *Oryx and Crake*, the "Fitcher's Bird" intertext is again paralleled by "The Robber Bridegroom." The theme of sexual politics may seem absent since it is in the background of this violent, dehumanizing, classist society: "its main products being corpses and rubble. It never learned, it made the same cretinous mistakes over and over, trading short-term gain for long-term pain. It was like a giant slug eating its way relentlessly through all the other bioforms on the planet, grinding up life on earth and shitting it out the backside in the form of pieces of manufactured and soon-to-be-obsolete plastic junk" (243).

The forbidden door motif begins early in the novel, in the "Once upon a time" when Snowman was Jimmy. For much of Jimmy's life, all women are "doors" to be unlocked with the words "I love you." Jimmy believes in answers, codes, and passwords and continuously remembers and constructs stories about colonialism, societal rules, products, his mother, Oryx, and Crake, but he prefers to watch voyeuristically rather than to see and know. He can parody self-help books but not help himself or others when he gets a glimpse of the forbidden. Even though the compound people are "sealed up tight as a drum" away from the pleebland cities and are themselves forbidden places to the poor, what appears to be mad cow disease gets in. Before his microbiologist mother decides to stay home and later to protest work of OrganInc and other Compounds, she explains that, because "the bad microbes and viruses want to get in through the cell doors and eat up the pigoons from the inside," her job is to make "'locks' for cell 'doors'" (18–19, 29). Looking back on his life before cell doors are unlocked, Snowman imagines hearing "the door of a great vault shutting" while he is watching Oryx float. He feels trapped and "knows they are both in great danger" (43). When Jimmy wonders whether Crake has told her to make love with him, Oryx implies that she will close the door on Crake. She is "a casketful of secrets. Any moment now she would open herself up, reveal to him the essential thing, the hidden thing at the core of life, or of her life, or of his life—the thing he was longing to know. The thing he had always wanted. What would it be?" (314). Even the Internet picture of Oryx (or someone who looks like her) on Hott Totts and Oryx's past is a forbidden door. Crake uses the picture as his gateway to the subversive Grandmasters' section of the Extinctathon playroom that aims to shut down the whole perverse society through terrorism. As head of an outlaw group called MaddAddam, Crake resembles the robbers of life in the Grimms' "The Robber Bridegroom" as well as in "Fitcher's Bird," representing not just one mad scientist but an entire mad segment of an already ruined society. "Jimmy had a cold feeling, a feeling that reminded him of the time his mother left home: the same sense of the forbidden, of a door swinging open that ought to be kept locked, of a stream of secret lives, running underground, in the darkness just beneath his feet"

(216–17). After Crake has gotten Oryx to spread the JUVE virus all over the world, she ends up on the same side of the door as Crake. Jimmy finally closes the door against Crake, only to open it when he can't see Oryx, who has lied to him. Crake slits Oryx's throat, and Jimmy then shoots Crake and seals the door until he leaves with the Crakers. Jimmy's and his society's blindness and fear of forbidden knowledge are evident in Jimmy's cultivated fish-eyed stare, the RejoovenEssense Compound's "blind eyeball" (297), and the ruptured and empty eye sockets of people exposed to the virus.

Some Internet sites, especially "At Home with Anna K," are doorways to Jimmy's love of words and, like those of other Atwood creator-narrators, his decision to collect and shape them into the story we read. Snowman's acceptance of responsibility for the Crakers, his efforts to speak and to create meaningful myths for them, and his one-eyed, then two-eyed, then no sunglasses in his disguise as Tiresias suggest that he attains some wisdom. His myths about the creation of words and of the children of Oryx from eggs and those of Crake from coral and mango are etiological: rather than leaving Crakers with chaos, the myths explain basic questions about the origin of life and such matters as why animals cannot talk. His quest back to the compound and his decision to face the human beings who make Robinson Crusoe footprints on the beach are also "doors" to a possible future. When he returns to the compound, he expects that "someone—someone like him—is lying in wait, around some corner, behind some half-opened door" (229), and thus he recognizes his own complicity in Fitcher games. Still, neither Snowman nor the Crakers suggest the kind of fairy-tale transformation implied in earlier Atwood texts. None of Atwood's novels is resolved, but in *Oryx and Crake* any transformation of this fallen world resembling our own must, in postmodern and postcolonial fashion, be constructed by the reader. Since Jimmy, like Iris, Grace, and Toni, transforms himself into the creator who shapes the tale we read, as a reader I construct the possibility of societal as well as personal transformation.

As a postmodern writer, Atwood revisions her works' fairy-tale intertexts by using techniques such as building scenes on fairy-tale images, moving females from object to subject, displacing the truth of traditional narratives, making marginalized subtexts central, and reversing intertexts' norms or ideologies. Atwood uses symbols, irony, parody, gender reversal, self-conscious and developing narrators, bent and blended tone and genres, lack of resolution, and defamiliarization to depict characters and personas who experience greater awareness, usually fairy-tale transformation.

Fairy tales continue to be Atwood's main intertexts, and, as her most recent works indicate, they and the stories in which they may be embedded depend upon a reader or listener for their existence: "Because a story—any story, but especially one that exists in such a vernacular domain—is a negotiation between teller and audience, the listeners are accomplices (*Targets* 187). As in her 2004 poem "Bottle II," if the writer or tale-teller is a voice in a bottle, the voice depends upon the reader or audience to uncork the bottle and listen.

Notes

1. Despite considerable evidence to the contrary, Greene surprisingly calls the mode of feminist writers, including Atwood, "realism" (4) and finds "no feminist metafiction by black women writers that relates the rewriting of old plots specifically to women's search for freedom" (24).

2. AT numbers identifying fairy tale cycles are from Aarne and Thompson, and motif numbers are from Thompson.

3. Some fairy-tale intertexts Atwood has frequently used in other works also recur in *The Robber Bride:* Andersen's "The Red Shoes" and the Grimms' "Cinderella," "The Girl without Hands," "Little Briar-Rose" (Perrault's "Sleeping Beauty)," "Little Snow White," "Little Red-Cap," "Rapunzel," "Hansel and Gretel," "The Water of Life" (Youth), and "The Wolf and the Seven Little Kids." The Robber Girl of Andersen's "The Snow Queen," who sets her reindeer free so that they can carry Gerda to Lapland to rescue Kay (67–69), is probably also an inspiration for the gender reversal in Atwood's book.

4. Other fairy-tale references in *The Blind Assassin* include "Red Cap," "Hansel and Gretel," and "Cinderella."

5. Other fairy-tale and folk allusions in *Oryx and Crake* include "The Robber Bridegroom," "The Wolf and the Kids," "Red Cap," "The Water of Life," "Hansel and Gretel," "Cinderella," "Beauty and the Beast," "The Three Pigs," the *Arabian Nights,* and "Jack Jump over the Candlestick."

6. Although Atwood does not see *Oryx and Crake* as a classic dystopia, such as *The Handmaid's Tale,* because readers do not get an overview of the structure of society and what they do know is suspect because edited, her definition of dystopia applies just as well to the more recent novel (*The Handmaid's Tale* 517).

7. This idea was suggested to me by Shuli Barzilai, Hebrew University of Jerusalem, during "Margaret Atwood: The Open Eye" symposium in Ottawa, April 2004.

Bibliography

Primary Sources

Atwood, Margaret. "Address to the American Booksellers Association." *The Book Group Companion to Margaret Atwood's The Robber Bride*. New York: Nan A. Talese / Doubleday, 1993. 7–13.

―――. *Alias Grace*. New York: Nan A. Talese / Doubleday, 1996.

―――. *The Blind Assassin*. Toronto: McClelland and Stewart, 2000.

―――. *Bluebeard's Egg*. Toronto: McClelland and Stewart, 1983.

―――. *Bodily Harm*. New York: Simon and Schuster, 1982.

―――. *Bottle*. Hay, U.K.: Hay Festival Press, 2004.

―――. *The Edible Woman*. New York: Popular Library, 1976.

―――. *The Handmaid's Tale*. Boston: Houghton Mifflin, 1986.

―――. "*The Handmaid's Tale* and *Oryx and Crake* in Context." Special Topic: Science Fiction and Literary Studies: The Next Millennium. *PMLA* 119.3 (May 2004).

―――. *Interlunar*. Toronto: Oxford, 1984.

―――. *Lady Oracle*. New York: Avon, 1976.

―――. *Life Before Man*. New York: Simon and Schuster, 1979.

―――. *Morning in the Burned House*. Toronto: McClelland and Stewart, 1995.

―――. *Moving Targets: Writing with Intent 1982–2004*. Toronto: Anansi, 2004.

―――. *Negotiating with the Dead: A Writer on Writing*. Cambridge: Cambridge UP, 2002.

―――. *Oryx and Crake*. New York: Nan A. Talese / Doubleday, 2003.

―――. *The Robber Bride*. Toronto: McClelland and Stewart, 1993.

―――. *Surfacing*. New York: Popular Library, 1976.

―――. *Survival: A Thematic Guide to Canadian Literature*. Toronto: Anansi, 1972.

―――. *You Are Happy*. Toronto: Oxford UP, 1974.

Margaret Atwood Papers. Fisher Rare Book Library. University of Toronto.

Secondary Sources

Aarne, Anti, and Stith Thompson, trans. *The Types of the Folktale: A Classification and Bibliography*. 2nd Rev. Helsinki: Suomalainen Tiedeakatemia Academia Scientiarum Fennica, 1987.

Barzilai, Shuli. Conversation. Ottawa, April 2004.

Daly, Mary. *Gyn/ecology: The Metaethics of Radical Feminism*. Boston: Beacon, 1978.

Davidson, Arnold E. "The Mechanics of Mirroring in *The Robber Bride.*" *The Robber Bride* Session. MLA convention. San Diego. 1994.

DuPlessis, Rachel Blau. *Writing Beyond the Ending: Narrative Strategies of Twentieth-Century Women Writers.* Bloomington: Indiana UP, 1985.

Dworkin, Andrea. *Woman Hating.* New York: Dutton, 1974.

Greene, Gayle. *Changing the Story: Feminist Fiction and the Tradition.* Bloomington: Indiana UP, 1991.

Howells, Coral Ann. "*Morning in the Burned House:* At Home in the Wilderness." Rpt. in *Margaret Atwood: The Shape-Shifter.* Ed. Coomi S. Vevaina and Coral Ann Howells. New Delhi: Creative Books, 1998. 135–45.

Hunt, Margaret, and James Stern, trans. *The Complete Grimm's Fairy Tales.* New York: Pantheon, 1972.

Jacobsen, Sally A. "Daughters of the Dark Goddess: Tales of Hoffman, 'Pop Goes the Weasel,' and the Manuscript of *The Robber Bride.*" MLA convention. San Diego. 1994. Margaret Atwood Papers.

McCombs, Judith. "*The Robber Bride:* Atwood's Pre-Modern Feminist Bildungsroman." MLA convention. San Diego. 1994.

Magoun, Francis P., Jr., and Alexander H. Krappe, trans. *Grimms' German Folk Tales.* Carbondale: Southern Illinois UP, 1960. 151–54.

Oates, Joyce Carol. *Do with Me What You Will.* Greenwich, CT: Fawcett Crest, 1973.

Owens, Lily, ed. *The Complete Hans Christian Andersen Fairy Tales.* New York: Avenel, 1981.

Perrault, Charles. "Bluebeard." *Beauties, Beasts, and Enchantment: Classic French Fairy Tales.* Trans. Jack Zipes. New York: NAL, 1989. 31–35.

———. "The Sleeping Beauty in the Woods." *Beauties.* 44–51.

Potts, Donna L. "'The Old Maps are Dissolving': Intertextuality and Identity in Atwood's *The Robber Bride.*" *Tulsa Studies in Women's Literature* 18.2 (1999): 281–98.

———. "The White Goddess Displaced: National / Sexual Parallels in Atwood's *The Robber Bride.*" *Literature of Region and Nation: Proceedings of the 6th International Literature of Region and Nation Conference, 2–7 August 1996.* Saint John, N.B.: U of New Brunswick, 1998. 230.

Sandler, Linda. "Interview with Margaret Atwood." *Margaret Atwood: A Symposium. Malahat Review* 41 (January 1977): 7–27.

Sedgwick, Eve Kosofsky. "Gender Asymmetry and Erotic Triangles." *Feminisms: An Anthology of Literary Theory and Criticism.* Ed. Robyn R. and Diane Price Warhol. New Brunswick, NJ: Rutgers UP, 1997. 524–31.

Shklovsky, Victor. "Art as Technique." *Russian Formalist Criticism: Four Essays.* Trans. Lee T. Lemon and Marion J. Reis. Lincoln: U of Nebraska P, 1965. 3–24.

Silko, Leslie Marmon. "Here's an Odd Artifact for the Fairy-Tale Shelf." Rev. of *The Beet Queen* by Louise Erdrich. *Impact/Albuquerque Journal* 17 Oct. 1986: 10–11. Rpt. in *SAIL* 10.4:178–84.

Stapleton, Michael. *The Illustrated Dictionary of Greek and Roman Mythology.* Library of the World's Myths and Legends. New York: Peter Bedrick, 1986.

Sylge, Caroline. "An Interview with Margaret Atwood." Fiction and Literature. www.uk.bol.com/cec/cstage?ecaction=boldlvie.

Thompson, Stith. *Motif-Index of Folk-Literature: A Classification of Narrative Elements in Folktales, Ballads, Myths, Fables, Mediaeval Romances, Exempla, Fabliaux, Jest-Books, and Logical Legends.* Rev. and enl. ed. 6 vols. Bloomington: Indiana UP, 1955.

Wilson, Sharon Rose. "Fiction Flashes: Genre and Intertexts in *Good Bones*." *Margaret Atwood's Textual Assassinations.* Ed. Sharon Rose Wilson. Columbus: Ohio State UP, 2003. 18–41.

———. *Margaret Atwood's Fairy-Tale Sexual Politics.* Jackson: UP of Mississippi, 1993.

Zipes, Jack. *Fairy Tales and the Art of Subversion.* New York: Methuen, 1988.

———, trans. and introd. *The Complete Fairy Tales of the Brothers Grimm.* Illus. John B. Gruelle. New York: Bantam, 1987.

Lateness is being at the end, fully conscious, full of memory, and also very (even preternaturally) aware of the present.

Edward Said

5 The Late Fairy Tales of Robert Coover

STEPHEN BENSON

Of all those contemporary writers over whom the fairy tale has exerted a significant influence, Robert Coover is perhaps the most consistent. His fairy-tale texts are relatively few in number, yet they stretch across his writing career, beginning in the late 1960s with the story experiments of the still startling collection *Pricksongs and Descants,* followed by the carnival excesses of *Pinocchio in Venice* (1991), the recent midlength prose works, *Briar Rose* (1996) and *Stepmother* (2004), and most recently the anthologized pieces of *A Child Again* (2005).[1] The same consistency of interest is evident in the work of Margaret Atwood, Angela Carter, and Salman Rushdie, however, as well as that of a host of less celebrated contemporary authors. Rather, what marks out Coover's project—if we can talk of such a thing, which I believe we can—is a perhaps surprising consistency of style; surprising because the idea of style is not a quality or a textual feature naturally associated with that restlessly ludic strain of postmodernist writing of which Coover's work stands for many readers as a paradigm. The texts of literary postmodernism, as conceived in the 1970s and 1980s, were said to lack style, whether inadvertently or on purpose. According to Fredric Jameson's now famous critique, literary style is the personalized expression, on the surface, of a singular, discrete subject. The stylistic ebb and flow of the writing is underpinned and guaranteed by the subject; it is the latter's metonym. Once the idea of such a subject is removed, style—"what is as unique and unmistakable as your own fingertips, as incomparable as your own body"—is literally at an "end" (Postmodernism 17, 15). All that remains is "a field of stylistic and discursive heterogeneity" without foundation, "the imitation of dead styles, speech through all the masks and voices stored up in the imaginary museum of a now global culture"; in other words, pastiche (17–18).

This is far from the only view, of course. While certain strains of postmodernist literature may well be marked by the strategic adoption of modes of writing, and while the idea of a "healthy linguistic normality" may well have waned, low-level serial experimentation need not be read as capitulation to surface pleasure—if such capitulation is indeed a bad thing.[2] The myth of literary style can appear irrevocably entangled in a Romantic ideology of canons, strong precursors, and their anxious influence. Rather than continue to tie writing back to its source, whether literary or authorial, it should be faced forward, put to work as part of the contestation of worldly ways of seeing. Carter addresses the issue directly in acknowledging a move in her own writing from expressionism—Jameson's chosen paradigm of stylistic imprint—to something altogether less self-centered: "It's mannerist [Carter's term for postmodernism], you see. Closing time in the Gardens of the West. . . . It's the only way I can write. I'm not sure what beautiful writing is" (Haffenden 91). The flaunting of many styles serves in this way to puncture the pretensions of style as signature and index of authenticity. We need only think of the various distances separating the work of Carter from that of a near contemporary such as Martin Amis, distances for which style serves as a key unit of measure.

More perhaps than any other contemporary English-language writer, including Carter, Coover has pursued narrative fiction as a project of critical engagement with particular ways of seeing. The majority of his texts work on specific generic modes, from the Western (*Ghost Town*, 1998) and other forms of cinema (*A Night at the Movies*, 1987) to sport's writing (*The Universal Baseball Association, J. Henry Waugh, Prop.*, 1968) and the murder mystery (*Gerald's Party*, 1985). While such textual raids may be indicative of a polemical disregard for authorial consistency, style is nevertheless what Coover has, at least as concerns his long-term and ongoing dealings with one specific form: the fairy tale. Consider the following two pairs of examples. The first extract is in each case taken from the 1969 story "The Gingerbread House" (included in *Pricksongs and Descants*), while the second is from *Stepmother*, published in 2004:

> but Granny it's a new generation! hah! child I give you generations without number transient as clouds and fertile as fieldmice! don't speak to me of the revelations of rebirthers and genitomancers! sing me no lumpen ballads of deodorized earths cleansed of the stink of enigma and revulsion! (11–12)

> It was not easy for a kid to grow up vomiting toads whenever she tried to speak. Naturally, people made fun of her. She refused to let it get her down, though. . . . She had a stepsister who was a snotty like saint who got up our noses at every opportunity with her sanctimonious wheedling and rehearsed meekness and dead mother worship, suckered by the Ogress as she was. (23)

> The children sing nursery songs about May baskets and gingerbread houses and a saint who ate his own fleas. Perhaps they sing to lighten their young hearts, for puce wisps of dusk now coil through the trunks and branches of the thickening forest. . . . More likely, they sing for no reason at all. . . . To hear themselves. To fill the silence. Conceal their thoughts. Their expectations. (49)

> Here is what is widely known, for lack of a proper name, as Reaper's Woods. It has no owner and its denizens were here long before he came to it, but he has put a stamp on it with his meditative prowlings. . . . Stepmother and her condemned daughter are hiding here somewhere, as are many others. . . . Yet, there is no community here, of the blessed or of any other sort. Even among those not damned, isolation and despair prevail. (8)

One of the most striking aspects of relatively recent texts such as *Briar Rose* and *Stepmother* is the extent to which they return to and cycle around modes of engagement with the form of the fairy tale, modes with which Coover was already experimenting over thirty-five years previously. As demonstrated in the first two extracts, this engagement involves, centrally, voice, in particular the dense, elaborately loaded and knowing voice of a fairy-tale character bearing the full weight of experience. The style here is staunchly unsentimental and world-weary, heavy with the history of tradition. It is a voice at the end of things. Alongside this first-person mode is that of the extradiegetic narrator, formal and less immediate. It is a more elusive voice but no less freighted with knowledge and tradition. As with its first-person partner, it is a voice that is *in* the tradition, both literally and metaphorically.[3]

Coover's writing is instantly recognizable not least when compared with the disorienting heterogeneity of styles paraded in the likes of Carter's *The Bloody Chamber* or with the many and varied lives of the fairy tale in the prose and poetry of Atwood. The question is how productively to engage with this central facet of the writing without resorting to an identification and enumeration of stylistic traits as the goal of reading. What does style mean? What is its content? In order to answer this question—in part to satisfy my own experience of reading Coover over a number of years—I have had to follow a slightly circuitous route. One place in which the idea of style has been less easy to discredit than in literature is music, for the simple reason that according to conventional wisdom, music is all style and no substance. Lacking the referential and conceptual capabilities of the signifiers of verbal language, music has no content as such: what we hear is what we get. Aesthetics has tended to view music thus conceived either as a condition to which all art aspires, or, in its seductive transience, as a cause for concern.[4] There is an alternative, or part alternative, to such thinking, however, according to which the experience of music is a matter very much of meaning—not only in terms of historical or social contexts, or in the straightforwardly programmatic sense, but also in the materials of music. Jameson acknowledges this mode in his discussion of style when he alludes to Theodor Adorno's *Philosophy of Modern Music* (1949), in which the question of composerly style is staged in the starkest and most pressing of terms. Adorno's extensive writings on music offer an extraordinary record of thinking about the particular ways in which that most affective of art forms has meaning and of what that always-situated meaning might consist.

For the purposes of establishing a handle on Coover's singular fairy-tale texts, I want to take one particular strand of Adorno's writing on the Western art music tradition, namely his formulation of an idea of artistic lateness, as exemplified in the late works of Beethoven. I borrow my justification from Edward Said, whose own late works include an attempt to elaborate on Adorno's gnomic sketches toward a morphology of lateness.[5] The reason for making the perhaps unlikely pairing of Adorno and Coover is not only that musicology offers a fruitful critical tradition on the question of style, but also that Coover's texts are caught up on a number of levels with all things late. Most obviously they circle consistently around images and ideas of old age and death, from the rabid and ribald voice of the grandmother in "The Door" to the rage against dying of the professor in *Pinocchio in Venice*. The preponderance of aged characters—a literal lateness—is matched by prose frequently death-tinged, acutely aware of endings but unable, perhaps unwilling, to stop cogitating. Hence, in part, the density of the diction and the plethora of allusions, a sense of words bearing witness to the accumulation of history. On the level of plot, fairy tales are very often concerned with death or with the threat of death; death is simply something that happens as a matter of course, a trace in the literary text of premodern antecedents. The possibility (in the moment) and the inevitability (in the end) of death are similarly ubiquitous in Coover. *Briar Rose* and *Stepmother* in particular are dark, bleak narratives, however energetic their prose (the disjunction of style and content is a defining feature of Coover's aesthetic). The writing is in this sense in the tradition, but its particular mode of traditionalism, or of conventionality, does not straightforwardly build on or develop predecessor texts; it does not follow from the conventions of Coover's narratives that they are concerned with renewing or revivifying that tradition. It is a truism of criticism on significant fairy-tale fictions of the past forty years, the period covered in the present volume, that such writing represents a renaissance. The tradition of the fairy tale is goaded and critiqued but with a view implicitly to pushing it on and making it new. The individual fictions are traditional in the twin senses of adjusting and furthering their generic heritage. With texts as rotten as those of Coover—creatively rotten, obviously, as well as variously concerned with states of rottenness—such faith seems out of place. What if instead of acceding to the maintenance of generic momentum, we were to entertain the possibility of the fairy-tale tradition as nearing its end? What sort of fairy-tale fiction would issue from the end of a tradition? Such a position, grounded on the overriding sense of an ending, is not necessarily unconducive to cultural production, as attested in literature most finely by Beckett; it certainly does not mean or require the cessation of writing.[6] What sort of fairy-tale fiction would result from a sense of the fairy tale itself as ending, or as nearing its end?

It is this paradoxical position that provides the clearest and most provocative link with Adorno on late Beethoven.[7] The musical works with which

Adorno is concerned are late in the literal sense, written in the final years of the composer's life; yet the givens of biographical or chronological significance are in large part beside the point. The condition of lateness is necessarily defined by temporal position, but it is a position within an artistic and aesthetic tradition that is the determining factor. To borrow Said's term, it is a question of "timeliness" ("Thoughts" 3), as is to be expected from Adorno: timeliness both in terms of the match, or mismatch, of text and immediate context ("appropriateness"), and as an acknowledgment in the work itself of the temporality of the materials and conventions of art. Adorno's starting point is the counterintuitive notion of the late work as precisely untimely:

> The maturity of the late works of important artists is not like the ripeness of fruit. As a rule, these works are not well rounded, but wrinkled, even fissured. They are apt to lack sweetness, fending off with prickly tartness those interested in merely sampling them. They lack all that harmony which the classicist aesthetic is accustomed to demand from the work of art, showing more traces of history than of growth. (123).

This is an image redolent not only of fairy-tale objects but also of Coover's aesthetic; the stories of *Pricksongs and Descants*, to say nothing of *Briar Rose* and *Stepmother*, are certainly "wrinkled, even fissured," resistant of things harmonious. Adorno is concerned to grapple with the sheer strangeness of late Beethoven, a characteristic that he locates in its fragmentary, repetitive, splinterlike state. The works in question have "A *bare* quality" (127) that belies the technical fluency presumed of maturity. Rather than attaining a state of serenity or reconciliation, in which the voice of the expressive subject is properly settled, the works of late Beethoven are awash with the materials of convention, those objective materials which might be expected to mask or silence subjective expression. For Adorno, "The relationship between conventions and subjectivity must be understood as the formal law from which the content of the late works spring" (125). The works in question appear at times to flaunt rather than to have assimilated conventions, leaving them "visible in unconcealed, untransformed bareness" (124); it is in their naked state, all washed up, that the materials of convention become expressive, not least in their revelation of the placatory workings of technique. The dismissal of assimilation and reconciliation, and so of "unity," "roundness," and "totality" is the reason why late Beethoven is extreme. Archaic polyphony, uncannily straightforward melody, textbook tonality: in Adorno's neat formulation, "Late Beethoven is at the same time enigmatic and extremely obvious" (136). Music and its conventional materials are compressed and condensed to the point of allegory, and therein lies the "riddle" (132).

Adorno's critique of late style is unfinished, fittingly, and somewhat of a riddle itself.[8] It does, however, offer a means of thinking about the peculiar traditionalism of Coover's fairy tales. All writers of fairy tales are by definition beholden in some way to convention. This may seem an odd statement, given the brazen wilfulness of so many contemporary fairy-tale related texts; yet it is precisely in the squaring-up to convention, to the formal and content-full materials of genre, that the creativity of the contemporary fairy tale may be said to reside. Adorno's method allows for the possibility that such a dialogue need not predicate the breezy continuation of tradition, in the manner of an eternal present, but might involve instead a proper acknowledgment of the historicity of generic materials, and so of the problems attendant on any act of generic development. It is easy to imagine how such a premise could be expressed in the language of criticism—indeed, it has been—but how it might figure in fiction is less immediately clear. In what follows, I have used elements of Adorno's critique as a starting point to identify and elaborate on the lateness of Coover's fairy tales, their late style, and on just what that lateness signifies. I have concentrated on *Pricksongs and Descants*, "The Dead Queen," *Briar Rose*, and *Stepmother*, in line with the aforementioned proposal of stylistic consistency stretching across a body of work and in order to avoid any suggestion of biographical significance. Again, these texts are late not in terms of the life of their author, but of the life and times of their genre, of their relation to a tradition. The findings of any such reading require a degree of generalization and so a necessary silencing of conflicting material. It is to be hoped that the interpretative gains outweigh the costs.[9]

Adorno's descriptions of late Beethoven are tantalizingly suggestive when considered in the light of Coover's work, particularly in their foregrounding of "the relationship between convention and subjectivity." For Beethoven, composing in the early nineteenth century, the conventional materials of music meant tonal harmony, with its inbuilt cadential tendency, and melody, genetically programmed to rise and fall; together with the preclassical modes of polyphony and monody, and the similarly archaic decorative devices of musical ornamentation. The manner in which such conventions are employed in late Beethoven is a complicated matter; that some are employed at all is significant, but the general tendency is for them to be unassimilated, left unfinished, or for there to be some form of exaggeration: melody has a "popular-song banality," with the paradoxical effect in this context of having it appear "mediated," "not itself but what it means" (127);[10] passages of monody and polyphony are left juxtaposed rather than unified within the time of the composition, leading to "a dissociation of the middle" (156); and "tonal material" appears exposed, "jut[ting] out bare and cold, like rock" (129). Each of these features is in some way at odds with the workings of an earlier ("middle") period in which assimilation, integration, and resolution—the fitting of part into unified whole—preside.[11]

Thinking through Adorno's "formal law" of the late art work in relation to Coover thus requires the identification of core generic conventions, which I take here to be character, narrative, and message. The classic fairy tale (to use for a moment a necessary fiction) consists of one or two leading protagonists, the small story in which they variously lead and are led, and an ending that suggests, explicitly or otherwise, a lesson to be learned. To speak very broadly, fairy-tale fictions result from a trade-off between two conceptions of narrative: the conventional or tale-oriented, predicated on an a- or pre-psychological understanding of character and on a very clearly teleological narrative; and the expressive or novel-oriented, predicated on a psychologized conception of character and tending to involve a complication of straightforwardly linear causality. Narrative is the underpinning convention of the fairy tale, but it does not follow that all fairy-tale narratives understand the convention in the same way.

To begin with the question of character. It is a truism of fairy-tale and folktale scholarship that the protagonists of the tales are lacking in the psychological, and metaphorical, "depth" or "roundedness" that is for the modern reader fundamental to literary character, mimetically conceived. Writing in 1947, Max Lüthi nominated the feature of "depthlessness" as one of the "principal formal traits of the European folktale" (3): "In its essence and in every sense, it [the folktale] lacks the dimension of depth. Its characters are figures without substance, without inner life, without an environment; they lack any relation to past and future, to time altogether" (11). Such generalizing statements have been called into question in recent years, in relation to the more literary tales of the seventeenth-century *conteuses*, for example.[12] Yet it remains the case that the canon of the European fairy tale comprises a cast of characters markedly at odds with modern (postmedieval) readerly expectations; hence the problems attendant on any modern analysis, such as that undertaken by Propp and his followers. For Jameson, Propp's categories are inappropriate because they "result from projecting later categories of the individual subject back anachronistically onto narrative forms which precede the subject's emergence" (*Unconscious* 124). Such anachronism is precisely what constitutes much fairy-tale fiction, in particular those texts considered in the present study. Whether rewritten narratives—Carter's "The Bloody Chamber"—new narratives that work by allusion to a specific tale or group of tales—Atwood's *The Robber Bride*, Rushdie's *Shame*—or new narratives that develop a broad range of sources—Rushdie's *Haroun and the Sea of Stories:* in each case the expansion achieved by the contemporary text involves a mimetic rather than diegetic representation of character, based implicitly around modern ideas of the subject as complex, layered and formed in and over time.

The anachronistic psychologization or modernization of character is clearly evident in Coover's fairy tales, particularly *Briar Rose*. The prince is granted a considerable amount of textual time and space in which to muse on his predicament; or rather, the reader is witness to such thinking, in the form of that quintessentially novelistic technique, free indirect discourse. Such discourse works dutifully to reveal one facet of the character's subjectivity, namely his motivation: "the object of his heroic quest," as the narrator says of the prince, is "Honour. Knowledge" (*Briar Rose* 4), "To tame mystery. To make, at last, his name" (1). Ruminative free indirect discourse is a characteristic ingredient of the Coover style, used here to circle around issues fundamental to modern narrative, issues of hermeneutics: "how?" and "why?" The prince wonders at one point whether "the test is not of his strength and valor but of his judgment: to wit, to choose an imagined future good over a real and present one is to play the fabled fool, is it not?" (8). Coover's characters are forever thinking on their condition—hence the high question-mark count—whether in the mediated free indirect manner or the seeming immediacy of the first person: the lumberman in "The Door" or the prince in "The Dead Queen," the latter "made dizzy" by his own "speculations" (306). Such material in one sense serves clearly as part of the metafictionality of the tales and of Coover's writing in general. *Briar Rose* does not represent characters in a state of desiring; rather, it offers an account of what it means and what it is like to be in such a state. It tells as much as it shows. Metafictional layering is relatively common to the contemporary fairy tale, however, perhaps even its defining feature. What distinguishes Coover's work is that subjective reflection, or self-reflection as constitutive of subjectivity, tends to be static or repetitive rather than progressive. Representing character in nineteenth- and twentieth-century fictional narrative involves the gradual progression toward knowledge and the concomitant commitment, on the part of both character and reader, to decode and unify seemingly unrelated elements or contradictory evidence. The idea of what George Eliot terms in *Middlemarch* "the persistent self," a core that is fully and properly knowable, in theory at least, may come under attack around the turn of the century, but such skepticism could be said to have formed simply an alternative mode of knowledge: we can only ever know another in the same way as we know ourselves—that is, partially, indirectly, in thrall to mutability. Depth is still very much present but now appears variously unfathomable.

The selfhood of the characters in Coover—their ruminative subjectivity, in the modern sense—is broken off or stalled. The prince in *Briar Rose* "wishes he could remember more about who or what set him off on this adventure, and how it is he knows that his commitment and courage are so required" (15). Memory is essential to character in the sense that it is only through and around the cumulative impact of experience that selfhood, for both subject and reader, can be said to cohere. Coover's prince may be able to reflect on his present predicament, but he has no idea of how he came to be where he is. Such a doomed condition is taken to the extreme in the figure of the princess, the object of his quest: not only a "ninny," but a "memoryless ninny," lacking entirely the ability "to put any two thoughts together in succession or to hold either of them between her ears" (32). All the prince can do in the absence of such accumulated knowledge is repeat himself—or rather, repeat to himself that the quest will be his making, "his name made by . . . forever-aftering" (9). To be a character here is to know why you do what you are doing but only in the moment, not in a causal relation to past events. Following Adorno's theory of the late art work, we can read Coover's representation of character as a form of depthless expansion. Subjectivity is apparent in the ruminations and cogitations, but it comes up hard against the objective conventionality of the fairy tale, in which character is story, in the Aristotelian sense, rather than vice versa. The prince is merely he who quests—"I am he who will awaken Beauty"—while Beauty is "a secret passageway to nowhere but itself" (12), "the fairy's spell binding her not to a suspenseful waiting for what might yet be, but to the eternal re-enactment of what, other than, she can never be" (85). Generically anachronistic self-reflection suggests that character may be progressive, developmental, or modulated, but such hope is illusory. In much the same way as Beethoven juxtaposes passages of motivic working out, in the vein of mature Classicism, with overtly conventional, even archaic, polyphony, so here psychological interiority and depth abut the absence of motivation or self-knowledge characteristic of the fairy tale proper. There is no middle ground, no resolution, only repetition and dead ends. Hence the sense that the prince and princess are literally trapped in themselves; while it was ever thus in the fairy tale, the difference now is the double-edged gift of depthless self-awareness. A little knowledge is a dangerous thing, according to Coover.[13]

The protagonists of these fairy-tale fictions are at once folkloristically shallow and novelistically deep, to use a decidedly modern metaphor. As such, they differ both from those contemporaneous narratives in which psychological depth and complexity are employed unproblematically, if sometimes rather awkwardly, to flesh out the generic material of the tales; and from those other recent fairy-tale fictions that keep faith with shallowness, preferring instead to frustrate or manipulate conventions of plot (some of the stories of A. S. Byatt and Sara Maitland, for example). Common to both strains of contemporary fairy-tale fiction, however, is a continued faith in narrative, faith shared, albeit in more understated fashion, with the classic realist novel. By narrative here I mean in particular the formal trajectory of plot, the progression through a series of causally related events toward an ending that functions, in whatever manner, to resolve, explain, and thereby make fixedly meaningful the events it serves to cap. Fairy tales form part of a core of putatively archetypal narratives that appear to offer irrefutable evidence of the human propensity to tell stories—stories that are in turn intimately tied up with our conception of our selves and our world. Umbilically related to character as it is, plot stands as the second convention of the fairy tale; indeed, one way of conceiving the fairy tale is as a narrative in which plot is all and character relatively little (relative to the norms of literary realism). According to the theory of lateness, plot in Coover should therefore be "visible in unconcealed, untransformed bareness" (Adorno 124), and this is certainly true, although in quite particular ways. Coover's early method involves what could be called the pregnant pause: that is, a text in which there is little or no plot progression but rather an elaboration, a writing around, a moment (or series of moments) in a plot (or series of plots) that is absent except by suggestion and implication. "The Door" is a narrative only to the extent that it alludes to a group of preexistent tales. It is in itself devoid of progression or of change, except by allusion: "a door that is not a door," to borrow the backward nod included in *Briar Rose* (69). Similarly, "The Gingerbread House" circles around Hansel and Gretel in the wood but goes no further than the door to the witch's house. Coover chooses in each case to home in on the pivot point of the narrative, that high point of semantic resonance. The reader is thereby acutely conscious of the presence of plot, although it would be misleading to say of these early fairy-tale texts that narrative is presented bare and unconcealed; it doesn't yet jut out, but it is simmering in the background.

The technique of the pregnant pause is still at work in *Briar Rose*. The prince and princess are locked in the time after the commencement of the quest but prior to their meeting; hence the prince spends the duration of the text stuck in the "thorny maze," while the princess sleeps. Again, we are at a pivot point. The greater length—greater than a short story, that is—allows Coover to build an environment, what the fairy calls "the eternal city of the tale" (56), comprising a mesh of versions and variants of "Sleeping Beauty," its analogues and constituent motifs. The raw materials of the environment as experienced by the reader are the text blocks themselves; while the characters are caught seemingly in more tangible materials—the briars and the castle—the effect of the prose is gradually to hedge them with words. The spatialization of narrative is of course a familiar modernist device, familiar not least from *Pricksongs and Descants*. There is a sense of ongoing deferral we might say whereby nothing stands still, all is in transit. What marks *Briar Rose* as a late work in the sense suggested by Adorno is the fact that space is here crisscrossed with precisely those conventional plots—those "moral lessons," to use the fairy's words—that the text itself withholds (7). As such, *Briar Rose* makes manifest a lateness that is partly concealed in the earlier stories. And it is the fairy who stands as the prime "manipulator of plots" (33). Her tales are very strange affairs, certainly, short sharp shocks of ribaldry; but stories they are, "little hearthside entertainments," especially as received within the environment of the text as a whole. There's the one about the Beauty who wakes to find herself mother to hundreds of children, only summarily to be cooked, along with her children, by the wives of the offending father-princes (18–20); the one about the princess chained to a rock who is saved from her sea-monster keeper by a heroic prince, but only after the prince and the monster discuss briefly their shared "mythical properties" (36–38); and yet another jumbled variant in which Beauty is once again eaten, this time by both the offending prince and his wronged wife (49–51). Coover riffs on tradition, especially its sometimes violent treatment of young women; yet whatever the content, the tellings continue, albeit futilely. Microplots proliferate, unconcealed and bare, positioned hard against the circular ruminations of the characters. In terms of a poetics of lateness, the objective convention of plot meets subjective cogitation but without resolution; that is, the linearity of plot fails to break the circularity of reflection. In Said's words, this is lateness as "a sort of deliberately unproductive productiveness" ("Thoughts" 3).

The uncanny presence of the conventional in the late work of art is, for Adorno, a prompt to allegory, and one way of reading the bare juxtaposition in *Briar Rose* of pause and plot, stasis and movement, is as an allegory of the workings of desire. What appear first in "The Door" and "The Magic Poker" as gnomic formulations—"a comedy from which, once entered, you never returned" (*Pricksongs* 13); "there *are* no disenchantments, merely progressions and styles of possession" (22)—are voiced here as full-fledged theories. The princess is

> waiting for she knows not what in the name of waiting for the prince. Of whom, no lack, though none true so far of course, unless in some strange wise they all are, her sequential disenchantments then the very essence of her being, the fairy's spell binding her not to a suspenseful waiting for what might yet be, but to the eternal re-enactment of what, other than, she can never be. (*Briar Rose* 85)

The object of longing is secondary, contingent upon the primary fact of the longing itself. Coover's palimpsestic technique draws attention to this condition as the defining motif of the tales—of the fairy tale itself, perhaps—thereby shifting attention away from the conventional focus on that object by which longing finds abatement. Desire is not a temporal experience that can be overcome but is rather the environment within which the subject lives; desire is what *makes* the prince and the princess. Hence the fact that they are caught in the *middle* of their story, that space in which solutions and endings have been projected but not yet achieved. And the middle points of plotting are matched by liminal spaces, spaces of approach: doors and doorways, woods, hedges, even the imagined space of dreaming.

One could of course argue that desire is always and everywhere brought to an end in the fairy tale, according to the sheer inexorability of the plotting, one of several pretheoretical names for which is fate. It is a mark of Coover's conventionality, and so of the lateness of certain of his texts, that predetermination is granted its proper generic place, not least in *Stepmother*, perhaps his most opulent production. Whereas it is apparent from the beginning of *Briar Rose* that the characters, and so the story, are going nowhere, in *Stepmother* it is clear that the characters have nowhere to go except the place dictated by the story. The daughter begins the tale with her mind "locked on one thing and one thing only: how to escape her inescapable fate" (1); and while the substance of what ensues stems from the quest to outdo the plot, "Things will happen as they must" (88): "they [Stepmother and her daughter] will be caught and punished, it is as inevitable as that leaves will fall in Reaper's Woods" (31). "[B]eing free," like "everything here" in Reaper's Woods, is an "illusion" (17). The conventionality of the narrative is blatantly exposed to the eye of the modern reader, for whom narrative, if it is present in a work of fiction, signifies the unpredictable, a space that promises to enact some form of change, even if it does not always deliver. To refer to the duration of the tales as a "timeless time," as does the Stepmother herself, is thus correct (2). There is a tale to tell, but it is largely ritualistic or ceremonial. The outcome is preordained and prescribed; hence the time of the tale is part of the tale's symbolic repertoire rather than external to it, an integral part of the ritual rather than a progressive force acting upon it. The matter of the performance is in consequence that which occurs along the way or in the middle, as part of the process, and not the showier events of beginnings and endings.

The middle way of the fairy tale, the space of ritual time, is in *Stepmother* named Reaper's Woods, a quintessentially Coovcresque habitat via which *Stepmother* takes the technique of *Briar Rose* to its logical conclusion. Where the latter is a hypertext comprising multiple versions of the titular tale-type and its constituent motifs, *Stepmother* holds the fairy-tale tradition in toto as a hypertext. Hence the space of Reaper's Woods is the middle space of all fairy tales, an amalgam of what is referred to elsewhere as "[t]he in-between bits" (40). The in-between as envisaged here is the place of transformation, but transformation imagined not as the shift from one form to another but as a condition in itself. Transformation is thus analogous with desire, a state of being rather than a rite of passage: "just who or what anything here is

. . . is always open to question. . . . It is an eerie domain of profound uncertainties . . . as if possessed of an arbitrary will all of its own, yet manifestly unstable" (8). The reader experiences this instability as the mess of incident and detail that litters the text and that is calculated to exceed and so to
frustrate any attempt to fix allegorical or symbolic meaning—an experience
familiar to readers of Coover's most carnivalesque performance, *Pinnochio
in Venice*. The threat hanging over the Woods, in spite of the governance of
plot, is that of "meaninglessness," "The Reaper's greatest fear" (12); and
just as the common reader tends toward the certainties of allegory, so the
Reaper believes that "Deep down . . . it all means something," believes in
"The revelation of some kind of primeval and holy truth . . . the telltale
echo of ancestral reminiscences. The urmythos" (14). It is of course precisely this sort of finality or transcendence that is roundly stamped on by
the Stepmother, as "moon-baked folly," yet one more act of mystification
(14).

Convention and invention are again juxtaposed: the unstoppable and inescapable ceremony of plot against the combinative and ludic chaos of the
in-between. Following the model of the late work, the assimilation and resolution of such opposing forces is withheld; and as with narrative, so, again,
with character. The daughter is Aristotelian in her acknowledgment of character as fate, that "who she is is who she is";[14] yet at the same time, her "story,
though it must end, will until then be her own" (84). When we read that "nature here [in Reaper's Wood] is all," it is impossible to say whether this is the
Reaper's nature, all conservative moralizing and attendant prurience, or that
of the Stepmother, for whom such morality seeks simply to tame, ad infini-
tum, the ceaselessly restless energies of transformation, the goings-on of the
in-between, the "until then." *Stepmother* certainly includes some relatively
straightforward statements of gender politics, of a kind familiar from fairy-
tale fiction of the 1970s and 1980s: "Boys can get away with rape, incest,
theft, torture, murder, for them it's just part of growing up, but a girl need
only be discourteous to have the world fall upon her like a dropped mill-
stone" (4). It also makes use of an analogous formal device, the granting
of voice, again familiar from Carter, Byatt, and Atwood, as well as from
Sara Maitland's closely related short story, "The Wicked Stepmother's
Lament."[15] *Stepmother* is divided between the first-person voice of its title
character and a third-person narrator who makes liberal use of free indirect
discourse. The Stepmother is thus the only character allowed to speak for

herself, or at least allowed to appear as if speaking for herself. As is to be expected from Coover, it is a singularly stylish vocal performance:

> I was no longer a unicorn of course. That transformation had worn off before we reached the edge of the forest and I was by then just a bare-arsed old lady scrambling on all fours into the underbrush, frantically heading for cover. Made my daughter, who'd fallen off, collapse into convulsive laughter and roll about on the meadow at the forest's edge, holding her bruised sides. I turned her into a hyena for a moment, just to show her who's what, but her laughter continued uninterrupted, in and out of the transformation, without even changing pitch. The disrespectful little tart. . . . I had to expose myself again and drag the hysterical little creature into the woods before she got us both embarreled, and then we conjured up some clothes for her and I got my own back. They felt hot on the inside. My daughter's into her high teens and her juices are on the boil. Always wanting more and more. When I tell her that sometimes less is more where survival's concerned, she says she'll take a little more of more over a lot more of less any day, even if it's her last day. Other daughters have come and gone with less fuss. This one's a real handful. A toad spitter. Literally. But I love her. (22–23)

The voice runs at full pelt: energetic, demotic, unselfconsciously explicit, resigned, and yet undimmed by the experience of countless transformations and embarrelments. It is a late voice, entirely in and of the tradition, and singularly Cooveresque.

Yet what value should be placed on such a stylish voice? I began by suggesting that one of the potential problems with contemporary fairy-tale studies is an implicit faith in the life of tradition, however profoundly critiqued and radically overhauled. According to this dominant paradigm, a voice such as that of the Stepmother is to be approved and celebrated in and of itself, in its form as much as in its content. One reason for viewing such approbation as problematic when considering Coover's fairy-tale experiments is that so much of the writing is concerned with characters nearing their end: Granny in "The Door," the professor in *Pinocchio in Venice*, the fairy in *Briar Rose* and *Stepmother*. It is right to celebrate the vivacity of these voices and properly to engage with their memorial ruminations on the traditions in which they have played a part and which have in turn borne them;

yet we do them a disservice if we ignore the material fact of their lateness. They are voices on the brink—brinkmanship well describes their strategy —Lear-like in their circling of old age and death. Is it ungrateful to suggest that they may have been found just a little too late and to wonder whether the casual celebration of their presence runs the risk of ignoring their proximity to the end? To sideline encroaching demise and its physical signs is at the very least to betray a peculiarly modern queasiness for that most universal of events.

Adorno's characterization of the late art work as "not well rounded, but wrinkled, even fissured" is peculiarly appropriate for Coover's unashamedly ageing protagonists. Again, Adorno proposes a means of conceiving such lateness, according to "the formal law from which the content of the late works spring": "The relationship between conventions and subjectivity." Morality or value—the value and so moral force of a voice such as that of the Stepmother, for example—is the third convention of the fairy tale I have identified, intimately related as it is both to character and to plot; indeed, to adapt Henry James, what is character in the fairy tale but the determination of incident, and what is incident in the fairy tale but an index of morality? It follows from the non-dialectic juxtaposition of flatness and depth in the characters, and of unconcealed plotting and static rumination, that the morality apparent in the likes of *Briar Rose* and *Stepmother* should be, in Adorno's words, "at the same time enigmatic and extremely obvious." As we know, the daughter in *Stepmother* receives her preordained punishment, the eponymous helper watching the barrel "float for a moment, riding the current, then sink, bubbling out of sight" (89–90). The internal tales narrated by the fairy in *Briar Rose* may be strange and jumbled, but they have a relatively clear moral purpose, however unheeded by their listener. The moral force of such suggestions—their self-evident significance—is, however, radically dissipated within the environment of the tales. Conventional positions are stated, only to be countered by irresolution or by their own excessive conventionality, their extreme obviousness (extreme in particular when read against the manipulation of endings in comparable recent texts). Coover's treatment of morality, and of the fairy tale as a genre from which we have come to expect some form of moral or ethical lead, however veiled and whether perceived at the level of form or content, is thus of a piece with his treatment of character and narrative. These fairy-tale texts bring into question the notion of morality and narrative, of narrative and message, and it is this feature in particular that distinguishes Coover's work from that of the majority of his contemporaries. Said's carefully pitched extrapolation from Adorno is apposite: "Lateness is being at the end, fully conscious, full of memory, and also very (even preternaturally) aware of the present" ("Thoughts" 5). Again, more than the work of any of his contemporaries, Carter included, Coover's texts are laden with generic memory, "fully conscious" of the moral weight the genre has come to bear. They stand as memorials to the genre, and it is in this paradoxical position that Coover operates, bearing witness in the present to a genre which in this very act is situated in the past. To be preternaturally aware of the present is to wonder about the possibility of going on, to wonder aloud if "Finished, it's finished, nearly finished, it must be nearly finished" (as Clov has it in the opening words of *Endgame*).

The comparison with Beckett is almost too obvious to invoke, but it is also singularly inappropriate for a writer so clearly at odds with late modernist poetics. One alternative means of making sense of Coover's tales, and of thinking through the convention of fairy-tale morality, is, ironically, to place the tales in an antisemantic tradition of tale-telling, in particular as read by Winfried Menninghaus in a much undervalued recent study. Menninghaus's starting point is the identification of "an early Romantic poetics of nonsense" (2), practiced between 1795 and 1797, indirectly derived via Kant and exemplified in the brief flourish of interest in "the aesthetics of ornament, arabesque and fairytale" (1). In particular, a conception of the fairy tale found in Ludwig Tieck and Novalis, one that "concentrates on the suspension of 'sense,' 'coherence,' and 'understanding'" (13). Citing Schlegel— "the form of the fairy tale is absolute chaos"—and Novalis—"in a genuine fairy tale everything must be incoherent"—as offering an inversion of Enlightenment critiques of the "senselessness" of the fairy tale (32), Menninghaus locates a disruptive strain of nonsense and incoherence within the fairy tale and its attendant theorizations, a persistent counter to the genre's "hermeneuticization" (50). Examples of the latter can be found in the *moralités* appended to those tales told by Perrault in his seminal volume of 1697, contradictory ("treacherous") supplements which have the paradoxical effect of highlighting that sense missing from the tales, tending not only to contradict themselves but also the tales to which they stand ostensibly as digests; and found similarly in the theories of Propp, Lévi-Strauss, and Lüthi, in which the enumeration in the fairy tale of "ruptures in hermeneutical understanding and challenges to sense expectations" is rationalized via a process of theoretical containment (160). The fairy tale as conceived by

Menninghaus is a ghostly genre. Relocated from untraceable origins and floating free in literary space, it echoes with fragments of sense:

> The emptied out and no longer comprehended signs gather into new configurations, whose rigid narrative regularity is inversely proportional . . . to the demotivation, the resultant formal character of its elements. . . . It conveys traces, indeed is composed of traces, that it no longer reads, that narrators and listeners also (can) no longer read, traces whose virtual unreadability nonetheless is the constituent of the fairy tale's form and the condition of its readability. . . . The fairy tale objectively preserves a memory of something that it subjectively cannot recall nor enable the reader to recollect, since this fall into oblivion opens up its symbolic space. (172, 175)

While this description may sound close to what has tended to be thought of as the very literary anti–fairy tale, or to an essentially disenchanted modernist reading of the genre, Menninghaus proposes such a tissue of traces as constitutive of the fairy tale in the first instance.

This is to my mind a convincing argument, the implications of which are yet to be given sufficient consideration by those working in the field of fairy-tale studies. In relation to Coover's writing in particular, Menninghaus's conclusion allows for the circumvention of the understandable desire to make sense of what are deliberately sense-frustrating works. The very idea of the fairy tale as preserving "a memory of something that it subjectively cannot recall" is tantalizingly close to Adorno's characterization of the late work as constituted out of a formal division. As should be apparent from the evidence presented above, however, Coover's texts are neither manifestly sensible nor consistently nonsensical. They are rather texts in which fairy-tale conventions of meaning and morality meet post-fairy-tale requirements of complexity and complication, without synthesis or resolution. As such, they hint at a terminus for the genre, or at least an impasse, a dead end. They *think* that possibility in many ways: in being full of aging characters, in being saturated with tradition to the point of rankness, and·in being saturated with tradition to the point of chaos ("incomparably condensed," to borrow for the last time from Adorno [126]). Most decisively, they think that possibility in simultaneously staging and blocking the very materials of the genre: character, narrative, and morality. As I have sought to suggest, they think the possibility of the end of fairy tales in being late works, constitutively uninterested in resolution or mastery. And yet it is out of this condition of lateness that springs their energy, their mischievousness, and the sheer delight of their invention: all the death-defying forces of longevity, that is. This is not to suggest that Coover writes insular, self-obsessed textual exercises; rather, that the texts refuse to exercise control over their materials, preferring instead to present—to make present—the impasse, maintaining thereby a distance from the grasp of the reader. And such withholding is expressed primarily in the singular style of the works in question. As Said writes, glossing Adorno: "This is the prerogative of late style: it has the power to render disenchantment and pleasure without resolving the contradiction between them" ("Thoughts" 7).

Notes

1. *A Child Again* includes "The Dead Queen," first published in 1973, and "The Last One," a version of "Bluebeard."

2. I say low level because what Jameson calls "the high-modernist ideology of style" was precisely a matter of extended and systematic experimentation (16).

3. Free indirect discourse is the third narrative mode characteristic of Coover, as used in the opening section of "The Door," the first story in *Pricksongs and Descants:* "And, listen, he wished her the joy, yes, both of them for that matter, if not all the world. He had told her about it, had wanted her to love life and that was part of it, a good part of it" (1). Coover employs this style more expansively in the prince and princess sections of *Briar Rose,* as discussed below.

4. The transience of music, its bypassing of conscious reflection, brought it close in spirit to the fairy tale for a brief period in the late eighteenth century, when the sheer oddness of the tales was viewed as an interesting frustration of the demands of meaning and interpretation. This aspect of the writings of the early German Romantics is discussed at length by Winfried Menninghaus, in a book to which I return below.

5. Said's work on artistic lateness first appeared as "Thoughts on Late Style," published in 2004 in the *London Review of Books.* A book on the subject, toward which Said was working at the time of his death, has now been published as *On Late Style: Music and Literature Against the Grain.* For an account of the genesis of Said's thinking in a series of seminars on lateness, see Lawrence.

6. I'm thinking also of those critical theorists such as Derrida whose copious work concerns in part the end of the tradition—metaphysics, say—within which they continue, knowingly, to write.

7. Adorno's thoughts on the late works of Beethoven first appeared as "Late Style in Beethoven," published in 1937. A related and much more expansive essay on the *Missa Solemnis* was published in 1959. However, Adorno was working throughout his life on a book devoted to the composer and the copious notes and sketches toward that end, together with the few published works on the subject, have now been collated and organized by Rolf Tiedmann, and published as a posthumous volume.

8. For readings of Adorno's work on late Beethoven see in particular Subotnick and, more recently, Witkin.

9. Given the nature of my approach, I make little reference in what follows to other readings of Coover's work, readings the number of which is still surprisingly low. On Coover's dealings with the fairy tale, see in particular the work of Bacchilega. *Cycles of Influence*, my book on fiction and the folktale, includes an extended reading of Coover's fairy-tale fiction (147–65). Other sources include individual essays by Bond, Redies, and Kusnir. General accounts of the work as a whole can be found in studies by Evenson, Gordan, Kennedy, Maltby, and McCaffery; see also the recent essay by Hume. Coover's most discussed novel remains *The Public Burning*, reissued in 1998 with a new preface by William H. Gass. *Critique: Studies in Contemporary Fiction* devoted a special issue to the novel in 2000 (vol. 41).

Perhaps the most interesting development in the reception of Coover's work has been his alliance in recent years with the McSweeney's group via the publication by McSweeney's Books of, first, *Stepmother*, and then *A Child Again*, both beautifully produced, with illustrations and cover art by Michael Kupperman. At the risk of too broad a generalization, it could be argued that the writers associated with McSweeney's represent a generation clearly influenced by the high experiments of American fiction of the 1970s and 1980s but with a renewed concern for the novel as a public genre, one with a resilient historical association with realism (I am thinking here of the likes of David Eggers, George Saunders, and Jonathan Lethem). As a high experimenter himself, Coover's tacit alliance with such writers serves not only to reassert the importance of the sometimes sidelined work of the American postmodernists but also offers fascinating connections across the decades.

10. Adorno does in fact turn to the fairy tale as a means of comparison when discussing the strange simplicity of some of these melodies: "In late Beethoven, a kind of theme which might seem folkloristic and which I should most like to compare to

verse sayings from fairy tales, such as 'Knupser, knupser Knäuschen, wer knuspert an mei'm Häuschen' [Nibble, nibble mousey, who's nibbling at my housey?]" (135).

11. The obvious literary analogy, leaving aside the different timescale, is the classic realist European novel, in which there is an overriding drive to assimilate, integrate, and reconcile.

12. Interestingly, Seifert cites Coover's tales as evidence that "characterization in many contemporary fairy tales is anything but one-dimensional" (62). As I hope to demonstrate, characterization in Coover is rather the result of an interaction of one-dimensionality and roundedness.

13. There are of course particular literary movements or genres, such as the Nouveau Roman, which have attempted alternative representations of character— alternative to the realist / modernist models, that is—but they are at a tangent to the mainstream of narrative fiction with which I am concerned.

14. The sing-song iteration of this phrase appears at once like a piece of bluff folk wisdom, indigenous to the fairy tale, and teasingly literary in its reliance on repetition as proof.

15. Maitland's story can be found in her collection *A Book of Spells.*

Bibliography

Primary Sources

Coover, Robert. *Briar Rose.* New York: Grove P, 1996.
———. *A Child Again.* San Francisco: McSweeney's Books, 2005.
———. "The Dead Queen." *Quarterly Review of Literature* 18.3–4 (1973): 304–13.
———. *Pinocchio in Venice.* 1991. London: Minerva, 1992.
———. *Pricksongs and Descants.* 1969. London: Minerva, 1989.
———. *Stepmother.* San Francisco: McSweeney's Books, 2004.

Secondary Sources

Adorno, Theodor W. *Beethoven: The Philosophy of Music.* Ed. Rolf Tiedmann. Trans. Edmund Jephcott. Cambridge: Polity, 1998.
Bacchilega, Cristina. "Cracking the Mirror: Three Re-Visions of 'Snow White.'" *Boundary 2* 15.3 (1988): 302–16.

————. "Folktales and Meta-Fictions: Their Interactions in Robert Coover's *Pricksongs and Descants.*" *New York Folklore* 6.3–4 (1980): 171–84.

————. *Postmodern Fairy Tales: Gender and Narrative Strategies.* Philadelphia: U of Pennsylvania P, 1997.

Benson, Stephen. *Cycles of Influence: Fiction, Folktale, Theory.* Detroit: Wayne State UP, 2003.

Bond, Barbara. "Postmodern Mannerism: An Examination of Robert Coover's *Pinocchio in Venice.*" *Critique* 45 (2004): 273–92.

Evenson, Brian. *Understanding Robert Coover.* Columbia: U of South Carolina P, 2003.

Gordon, Lois. *Robert Coover: The Universal Fictionmaking Process.* Carbondale: Southern Illinois UP, 1983.

Haffenden, John. Interview with Angela Carter (September 1984). *Novelists in Interview.* London: Methuen, 1985. 76–96.

Hume, Kathryn. "The Metaphysics of Bondage." *Modern Language Review* 98 (2003): 827–41.

Jameson, Fredric. *The Political Unconscious: Narrative as a Socially Symbolic Act.* London: Routledge, 1989.

————. *Postmodernism, or, The Cultural Logic of Late Capitalism.* Durham: Duke UP, 1991.

Kennedy, Thomas E. *Robert Coover: A Study of the Short Fiction.* New York: Twayne, 1992.

Kusnir, Jaroslav. "Subversion of Myths: High and Low Cultures in Donald Barthelme's *Snow White* and Robert Coover's *Briar Rose.*" *European Journal of American Culture* 23.1 (2004): 31–49.

Lawrence, Tim. "Edward Said's Late Style and the Aesthetic of Exile." *Third Text* 38 (1997): 15–24.

Lüthi, Max. *The European Folktale: Form and Nature.* Trans. John D. Miles. Bloomington: Indiana UP, 1986.

McCaffery, Larry. *The Metafictional Muse: The Works of Robert Coover, Donald Barthelme, and William H. Gass.* Pittsburgh: U of Pittsburgh P, 1982.

Maitland, Sara. "The Wicked Stepmother's Lament." *A Book of Spells.* London: Minerva, 1990. 147–53.

Maltby, Paul. *Dissident Postmodernists: Barthelme, Coover, Pynchon.* Philadelphia: U of Pennsylvania P, 1991.

Menninghaus, Winfried. *In Praise of Nonsense: Kant and Bluebeard.* Trans. Henry Pickford. Stanford: Stanford UP, 1999.

Redies, Sünje. "Return With New Complexities: Robert Coover's *Briar Rose*." *Marvels & Tales* 18.1 (2004): 9–27.

Said, Edward. *On Late Style: Music and Literature Against the Grain*. London: Bloomsbury, 2006.

———. "Thoughts on Late Style." *London Review of Books*. 5 Aug. 2004. 3–7.

Seifert, Lewis C. "On Fairy Tales, Subversion, and Ambiguity: Feminist Approaches to Seventeenth-Century *Contes de fées*." *Fairy Tales and Feminism: New Approaches*. Ed. Donald Haase. Detroit: Wayne State UP, 2004. 53–72.

Subtonick, Rose Rosengard. "Adorno's Diagnosis of Beethoven's Late Style: Early Symptom of a Fatal Condition." *Developing Variations: Style and Ideology in Western Music*. Minneapolis: U of Minnesota P, 1991. 15–41.

Witkin, Robert W. *Adorno on Music*. London: Routledge, 1998.

6 Theorizing Fairy-Tale Fiction, Reading Jeanette Winterson

MERJA MAKINEN

What theoretical issues arise at the beginning of the twenty-first century from thinking about the use of the fairy tale in postmodern fiction? This is a grand question that, upon examination, could fan out in a variety of different permutations, but one constant is the need to define one's terms. What do we mean by postmodern fiction and its practice of intertextuality? How is the fairy tale conceived of at the turn of the century? With these two parameters explored, we can take the next step and examine the theory surrounding postmodern fictions' use of the fairy tale as its intertext. But such a simple three-step procedure becomes complicated by the wealth of positions argued within each step, and, moreover, by postmodern critiques of any attempt to fix positions across the disciplines. If *postmodernism* proves a treacherous term and postmodern critiques of the fairy tale have positioned the latter as rather slippery, too, how much more difficult will it prove to put the two together in order to look at postmodern use of the fairy tale? Finally, having wrestled my way to some tentative but crucial conclusions in relation to how such a theoretical contemporary position impacts the reading of post-

modern fiction, I put theory into practice in examining the work of Jeanette
Winterson.

Postmodernism and Intertextuality

So, what is postmodern fiction and how do critics theorize postmodernism's
intertextual use of other texts? Even in the twenty-first century, decades after the debates of the 1970s and 1980s, *postmodernism* is still a slippery term
as it spans many disciplines and means different things to different critics.
"The term 'postmodernism' has had a troubled and hotly disputed beginning. However . . . it has nevertheless entered the language, although what
it designates is still very much at issue" explains Alison Lee pragmatically
(x). Writing a decade later than Frederic Jameson and Stuart Hall, she agrees
with their designation of it as a postwar American multinational cultural
production, though she more hesitantly posits her task as a "provisional to-
talization . . . to sketch out an introduction to advanced postmodernism"
(Carmichael and Lee 4). Patricia Waugh suggests it now has two phases, the
first spanning the 1950s–1970s when postmodernism was "the description of
a range of aesthetic practices involving playful irony, parody, parataxis, self-
consciousness, fragmentation," but because of the dominance of consumer-
ism during the 1980s it shifts toward "a pervasive cynicism about pro-
gressivist ideals of modernity" (60). Usefully, she encapsulates one of the
debates: "Detractors of postmodernism see it as a narcissistic and ethically
insouciant expression of commodified culture. Defenders view it as an authentic exposure of the illusions of preceding systems of knowledge" (60).

   In relation to postmodern fiction, the awareness of the paradox involved
in trying to define something so provisional, resistant, and playfully unstable has had Brian McHale, whose *Postmodernist Fiction* (1987) proved seminal for a range of critics of postmodern texts, acknowledge his embarrass-
ment with the attempt to be encyclopedic and, in his later *Constructing
Postmodernism* (1992), refute such a project for the more relative and plural
readings of individual texts. Nevertheless, in this critical quagmire there is
one consensus: a large number of postmodern texts are intertextual. Intertextuality is an important trope of postmodern fiction, and as Steven Connor notes: "One particularly marked feature of postwar fiction, both in
Britain and elsewhere . . . is the practice of rewriting earlier works of
fiction. . . . In contemporary fiction, telling has become compulsorily be-

lated, inextricably bound up with retelling, in all its idioms: reworking, trans-lation, adaptation, displacement, imitation, forgery, plagiarism, parody, pas-tiche" (*Postmodernist* 166). Connor argues further that intertextual referenc-ing is different in contemporary texts because it tends to be a consistent and conscientious focus on "a single textual precedent," but the intertextuality "can take different forms and have different effects" (*Postmodernist* 167), which he designates as either "reduplication" or "rewriting." McHale takes this further, seeing intertexuality as a strategy of polyphony to disrupt monologic narrativity: "the strategy of 'injecting' a specialized register of language into a homogenous discourse-world, as a means of inducing polyphony, is typical of postmodern fiction" (*Postmodernist* 167–68). Con-nor's distinction between different uses of intertextuality in postmodern fic-tion deserves further scrutiny because a major debate focuses precisely on intertextuality in relation to power and resistance, and it is in relation to this debate that I believe the theoretical impact of postmodern use of fairy tales is most felt. Jameson, in "Postmodernism and Consumer Society," opened the debate by claiming that postmodern intertextuality was merely "pas-tiche," a "blank parody" (114), a nostalgic art signaling emptiness and ex-haustion. His argument was questioned by his own editor, Hal Foster, who posited two different usages: "a resistant postmodernism is concerned with a critical deconstruction of tradition, not an instrumental pastiche of pop-or pseudo-historical forms, with a critique of origins, not a return to them" (x). The most influential challenge to detractors such as Jameson and Terry Eagleton, has been Linda Hutcheon who, in *The Poetics of Postmodernism* (1988) and *The Politics of Postmodernism* (1989), argues for a politically en-gaged, critical form of parodic intertextuality that she names "historio-graphic metafiction." Contesting Jameson's statement that postmodern texts cannot parody and have nothing to say about their contemporary present, Hutcheon argues that the "postmodern ironic recall of history is neither nos-talgia nor aesthetic cannibalism" (*Poetics* 24) but a social and even political art form because "parodic references to the history of [fiction] textually re-instate a dialogue with the past and—perhaps inescapably—with the social and ideological context in which [fiction] is (and has been) both produced and lived" (23).[1] For the purposes of this essay, I will take the dualism of par-ody or pastiche to be largely synonymous with the terms *rewriting* or *redu-plication* as used by Connor. For most critics, postmodernism's ability to par-ody/rewrite its intertextual references is a political act that challenges the view that postmodern fiction is an empty, nostalgic, pastiche / reduplication of past texts. The argument that postmodern intertextuality can be radical and political, however, has pushed the descriptive terms into an evaluative binary: parody radical (good), pastiche conservative (bad). For Lorna Sage, this manifestation of the political aspects of representation has allowed a voice for those traditionally marginalized or ex-centric to dominant discourse, particularly the feminist and postcolonial voice:

> Parody has perhaps come to be a privileged mode of postmodern formal self-reflexivity because its paradoxical incorporation of the past into its very structures often points to these ideological contexts somewhat more obviously, more didactically, than other forms. Parody seems to offer a perspective on the present and the past which allows an artist to speak *to* a discourse from *within* it, without being totally recuperated by it. Parody seems to have become, for this reason, the mode of what I have called the "ex-centric," of those who are marginalized by dominant ideology . . . of black, ethnic, gay and feminist artists. (35)

Peter Brooker agrees with the political impact of postmodernism's ability to parody: historiographic metafiction's "irony and use of paradox signal a critical distance within this world of representations, prompting the questions not about 'the' truth, but 'whose' truth prevails. The political effect of this fiction therefore lies in the double action by which it inscribes and intervenes in a given discursive order" (229).

But what kinds of history form the historiographic for Hutcheon? The examples she uses come from the discipline of history and the discipline of literature or literary history, and a good example of the latter is J. M. Coetzee's rewriting of Daniel Defoe's *Robinson Crusoe* in *Foe* (1986), raising as it does issues of how the feminine and the postcolonial voice have each been elided and oppressed within the beginnings of canonical literature. Hutcheon uses writers such as Coetzee, Angela Carter, and Salman Rushdie to illustrate how the postmodern invokes and questions the discourses of earlier literary texts as sites of contention and revision alongside its invocation of the pre-text, particularly in relation to canonical texts and to the cultural formation of literary canons. Connor's examination of this rewriting of the canonical opens the way to other forms of literary cultural traditions, espe-

leable" (Leith 16). Zipes, in *Sticks and Stones*, develops a reading of "contamination," turning the folklorist concept on its head when he argues that the seepage of the extraneous and the alien into "the pure homogenous narrative tradition" (102), usually seen as sullying the authenticity, should rather be seen as a strengthening, enriching process toward what he deems a "multicultural" transformation. Fairy tales are a cross-cultural, "hybrid" fiction (Zipes, *Great* xii–xiii). If the idea of the fairy tale as a simple oral folk story written down for wider consumption is problematic, so is the notion of the agrarian peasant folk who told the tale. Cultural studies has further deconstructed folklore's romanticized concept of the "folk" from which the stories stem into a wider, inclusive version of "any group of people whatsoever who share at least one common factor" and has "traditions which help the group have a sense of group identity" (Preston xi) while acknowledging that individuals also have "multiple identities" in relation to each other.

Postmodern criticism's impact on our understanding of the fairy tale goes even further than simply questioning its construction and its unproblematic bid to be an authentic popular narrative form. Postmodernism's skeptical examination of the tales collapses the divisions between the postmodern parody and its "fixed" intertext. In her division of the tales into "protean" fairy tales and the "compact" tales of Perrault, Elizabeth Wanning Harries rejects the notion that all fairy tales are simple and fixed. Her examination of the protean tales written by the female *conteuses* of the French salons in the 1690s shows that they are "often long, intricate, digressive, playful, self-referential, and self-conscious" (17). These seventeenth-century heteroglossia therefore challenge the view that rewritings are a postmodern phenomenon, and they point to a double tradition of the literary fairy tale that, she argues, twentieth-century postmodern feminist writers conform to, rather than contest, in their revisions. The history of women fairy-tale tellers argues for a pre-postmodern critique already present, complicating our comprehension of the intertext. Postmodern criticism of the fairy tale has further made the fixity of the intertext untenable as it shifts the readings of the tales from a monologically didactic moral to an open plurality of meanings. Cristina Bacchilega is foremost in this process with her pyrotechnic readings of the utilizations of fairy tales; she argues for an awareness of "the many 'voices' of fairy tales" as any tale constitutes not a single pre-text but rather a polyphony of the various historical versions and revisions. In his later analysis, Zipes too celebrates a desire to avoid closure, "to remain curious, startled, provoked, mystified and uplifted" (*When Dreams* 6–7). Similarly, Cathy L. Preston argues for "the multiplicity of voices embodied in variously situated performances" (xiii), and Neil Philips concludes that "the multi-layered quality of a fairy-tale text is resistant to any single simplified meaning" (42). Stephen Benson explains that the fairy tale is incapable of being "a fixed, self-contained narrative" (169) both because of its orally provisional genesis and the multilayered intertextual hybridity of the literary versions. He develops a reading of the cycles of tales, such as Basile's *Il Pentamerone* and the *Arabian Nights* to reveal an even more dense interaction of the constituent tales and their link to oral transmission in enacting the orality of the "speaker" recounting the tale(s): "cycles . . . revel in the multiplicity of narrative and the possibility of uniting tales within tales, while [others] . . . generat[e] strings of narratives from the successive entry of characters into the expanding frame" (46). Maria Tatar, in the second edition (2003) of her feminist readings of the Brothers Grimm, positions contemporary fairy tales as postmodern practices themselves: "Perpetually appropriated, adapted, revised and rescripted, they have become a powerful form of cultural currency, widely recognized and constantly circulating in ways that are sometimes obvious, sometimes obscure. Cutting across the borderlines between high and low, oral tradition and print culture, the visual and the verbal, they function as robust nomadic carriers of social practices and cultural values" (xv). Such a conception of the fairy tale precludes it as being the site of *revision* or *rewriting* in the way these terms are utilized within earlier postmodern criticism; it moreover raises serious questions about the usefulness of the terms themselves. Knowledge of twenty-first-century conceptions of the fairy tale places huge pressures upon postmodern criticism of fiction that uses the fairy tale as an intertext. Postmodern fiction cannot really be said to rewrite the fairy tale as a previous, given, static text to be commented upon through parody. All it can do is re-engage contemporaneously with an already multilayered polyphony, adding a further critical layer to the plurality.

However, fairy-tale studies traditionally has encompassed more than just sociohistorical and folklorist analyses. The consideration of the inclusion of the magical has also lead to both a formalized literary reading of the import of fantasy and the fantastic and to a clinical psychoanalytic mobilization of the genre. As Tatar explains, "Fairy tales are up close and personal, mixing fact and fantasy to tell us about our deepest anxieties and desires. They offer roadmaps pointing the way to romance and riches, power and privilege,

and most importantly to a way out of the woods, back to the safety and se-
curity of home" (xiv). What happens when postmodern skeptical relativity
of utterance and narrativity runs up against psychoanalysis' more rigid conception of the unconscious and unconscious truths? Rosemary Jackson, in
her influential *Fantasy: The Literature of Subversion* (1981), uses a psychoanalytic model to read the fantasy as a textual uncovering of cultural loss and
absence, shifting fantasy from a textual to a political frame, particularly in its
articulation of ex-centrics' (women's) absence from cultural space. "In this
way," suggests Jackson, "fantastic literature points to or suggests the basis
upon which cultural order rests, for it opens up, for a brief moment, onto disorder, on to illegality, onto that which lies outside the law, that which is outside dominant value systems. The fantastic traces the unsaid and the unseen
of culture: that which is silenced, made invisible, covered over and made
'absent'" (4). Jackson's critique positions the fantastic as a form of carnivalesque return of a (cultural) repressed, merging psychoanalytic desire and
cultural subversion; although she also argues that this is an ultimately consolatory process, her model proves politically exciting for feminist writers
and critics. This is, though, markedly different, theoretically, from the skepticism of postmodern intertextual self-reflexivity, which raises questions
about representation and how ideologies are produced, since Jackson con-
tests one ideology to set up another in its place. The literary fantastic as a site
of cultural disruption and dislocation can stand for a less unequivocal expression of repressed voices, for a political stance that implies a more definitive (however localized and provisional) utterance. The fantasies of a hith-
erto repressed gendered minority finding voice and currency within the
dominant culture mark a bid for a form of authenticity. In *Theorising the Fantastic* (1996), Lucy Armitt repositions the disturbance of the fantastic in its
"crossing of borders/lines" as it "disturbs rules of artistic representation"
(32). For Armitt, fairy tales despite their happy endings are structured upon
"lack" rather than fulfillment, so rather than functioning as consolation, "behind them lurk a series of uncanny confrontations with what can only be referred to as gothic dis-ease" (42). Via Julia Kristeva she rereads the uncanny
of the fantastic as the awareness of the repressed semiotic "pleasures of the
mother's body" (58) to explain the experience of reading as both fearful and
enjoyable. Armitt dismisses psychoanalysis' reductive, unilateral readings of
fantasy but nevertheless shares, in a more complex and skeptical form, the belief that fairy tales and the fantastic, being closely linked to "fantasy," express
something close to, if not actually, the unconscious: they encode "the sym-

bolism of the unknown and the unknowable into their narratives" (39). This shifts the analysis away from not only the politicized narrative subversion of fantasy to the narrative as voicing socio-psychic destabilizing unease, but also a form of psychic "truth." Ceri Sullivan and Barbara White (1999) highlight the historicity of the cultural production of fantasy, arguing that "forms of the fantastic are contingent on the historical and political circumstances surrounding human agents," and that this historical relativism needs to supplement psychoanalysis' "universalizing" and "homeostatic" conception of the unconscious to allow for a "changing historical meaning in fantasy" (2). They suggest, like Jackson, that fantasy can be, but is not invariably, radical in its subversion and cite New Historicist readings where "fantastic challenges can modify prevailing ideologies to preserve social and economic order" (5).[2] Despite their different readings of the historical/psychoanalytic continuum, Jackson, Armitt, and Sullivan and White share the sense that the magical trope can indeed uncover or express disturbance, a necessary or valid subversive questioning of the comfort of dominant cultural norms. Such a trajectory positions the fantastic of fairy tales as a site of the psyche worthy of revisiting and reduplicating, including through literature.

This is also true of the psychoanalytic discipline itself, which has treated the fantastic elements in fairy tales as a form analogous to dreaming (for Freud) or as an exemplar of the collective unconscious (Jung). Freud positioned fantasy as a constituent of the unconscious, and Lacan, in the shift into the symbolic order or the repression into the unconscious, sees fantasy's expression of lack through the excessive and the fantastic. Freud's reading of literature dismisses the fairy-tale genre because it has no clear authorial derivation and so cannot be a useful tap into a subject's individual psyche (Armitt, *Theorising* 44). Bruno Bettelheim in *The Uses of Enchantment* (1978) disagrees, believing instead that fairy tales express to children the psychic disturbance and fantasies of the oedipal conflict and puberty in ways that are satisfying, reassuring, and developmental. New Historicist and feminist criticism has challenged the "universal" model of the psyche employed by Bettelheim, particularly since Bettelheim employs the classical Freudian model of feminine psychic development via penis envy. For Armitt, Bettelheim's conclusion is further suspect, both "duplicitous in its superiority to the children discussed" and sentimental in stressing the tales' consolatory closures, a "dishonest manipulation" of the tales "intangibility" (Armitt, *Theorising* 44). Stephens and McCallum point out that feminist critiques of the way traditional fairy tales prescribe a feminine passivity, dependency, and self-sacrifice also complicate Bettelheim's thesis that the tales enable formative healthy psychic development, seeing them instead as a form of phallocentric internalization.

So, where does this leave the issue of the fairy tale as the basis of an intertext for postmodern fiction? Conceptions of what constitute the fairy tale have changed markedly into something more hybrid and multilayered, though some still try to argue an important link to the unconscious. This new, complex, and skeptical reformulation of the fairy tale necessarily presents an unsettling of the traditional critique of the postmodern use of the intertext as either parody (radical / good) or pastiche (conservative / bad). Neither reduplication nor rewriting quite fit any longer as oppositional, dual strategies. If fairy tales are already pre-postmodern narratives that postmodern fiction invokes to write new alternative versions, then the postmodern text could be argued as reduplicating a further critical, subversive layer when they are being radical: the terms collapse, based as they have been upon the concept of a stable binary opposition and a "dead" pre-text. Our postmodern conception of the fairy tale necessitates more complex critical tools to describe its use within postmodern fiction. This is not to say that fiction cannot use fairy tales in a metafictional rewriting of the generic form. Of course it can. Nor is it an argument that fiction cannot utilize the tales as a site for a nostalgic reduplication of a valuable literary mode of the uncanny. It simply argues that the reformulation of the fairy tale explodes the critical tools so that how we think of the rewriting needs to be reconfigured to encompass both parody and pastiche, with their markedly different trajectories, because they are not necessarily mutually exclusive narrative positions within specific individual texts. There is a much more complex relationship between intertextual metanarrative practice and cultural contestation that the dualism rewriting / reduplication prevents us exploring. Prime in the disruption of the parody as subversive—pastiche as conservative dualism—is the practice of reduplication to give voice to the ex-centric, thereby displacing or destabilizing the dominant Eurocentrism or phallocentrism of "traditional" canons. Such a strategy, it could be argued, uses a form designated as nostalgic and conservative (such as the claim to use an original indigenous native tale) for subversive political ends (to rewrite Western colonial consensus). Moreover, if one conceives of fairy tales as pluralistic layers of telling and meaning, then even the most subversive rewriting becomes in essence a further, alternative reduplication (such as Carter's feminist *Bloody Chamber* collection)—but a reduplication in the progressive sense. Contemporary scholarship on the fairy tale bankrupts the postmodern literary terms' ability to map and explain the textual interrelations and interconnections taking place. Critical discussion of the postmodern use of the fairy tale therefore needs to create a new way of discussing this complex, multiple reconception of its pre-text, but such a discussion has not, to date, always absorbed the new scholarship on the fairy tale.

Contemporary Postmodernist Fiction and the Fairy Tale

With a tentative grasp of what postmodern fiction is and a more complex understanding of how the fairy tale has been reformulated, are we now in a better position to examine postmodern fiction's use of the fairy tale? What are the theoretical implications of using fairy tale as an intertext / pre-text within a postmodern narrative? The first is surely the question of how the writers conceive of the fairy tale, since what we get in the intertextual "quotation" is a subjective rendition. "To say that such-and-such a text or writer was influenced by the folktale is to say that the former constructed a particular conception of, a necessary fiction about, the latter" (Benson 15). And very few writers have conceived of the fairy tale as a complex pre-postmodern form; rather, many have perceived it as a fixed, didactic fable in order to rewrite it through parody. Writers are not necessarily folklore scholars or interested in being so. Fictionalized representations of fairy tales say as much about the culture within which they are written as about the fairy tale per se. And here, Stephens and McCallum's positioning of pastiche is apposite: "the process of retelling is always implicated in the processes of cultural formation, of recycling frames used to make sense of culture. Thus . . . the discourse which shapes the cultural implications of a retelling is more significant than what is retold" (xi). Gendered analysis predominates in the fictional use of the tale largely because during second-wave feminism in the 1980s, feminist critics focused on what they saw as the fairy tale's acculturation of patriarchal gender positions, and feminist writers went on to use the genre in a multitude of ways. Tom Shippey, examining contemporary rewritings of the "Bluebeard" story, concludes that writers informed by a knowledge of the scholarship of Zipes and the feminists attempt a serious probing, where those without it fall back on a tone of embarrassed "jocularity" toward the "childish" nature of the intertext (256). For many writers, feminist critique may have created the "necessary fiction" about the fairy tale as moralistically static, which they then deploy within their postmodern texts, but does that mean the intertext *is* thus closed off? Might it just mean that the representation of the fairy tale simply becomes one further layer of twentieth-century acculturation that the critics need to take on board when considering postmodern representations?

Sharon Rose Wilson, looking at Margaret Atwood, usefully argues that "there is more than one postmodern ideology" (28) and it is worth remembering that *postmodernism* itself is not a fixed term, as argued in my opening section, but subtly shifts and changes its meaning as it is invoked and re-invoked. The way postmodern texts utilize fairy tales is equally shifting. Bacchilega argues that fictions that parodically exploit fairy-tale intertexts can "differ greatly" because their interrogation of the cultural inscriptions of the pre-text range widely:

> Multiple permutations produce postmodern transformations of fairy tales because their simultaneously affirming and questioning strategies re-double in a variety of critically self-reflexive moves. . . . Some postmodern revisions may question and remake the classic fairy tale's production of gender only to re-inscribe it within some unquestioned model of subjectivity or narrativity. Other postmodern tales expose the fairy tale's complicity with "exhausted" forms and ideologies of traditional Western narrative, rewriting the tale of magic in order to question and re-create the rules of narrative production, especially as such rules contribute to naturalizing subjectivity and gender. Still other tales re-place or relocate the fairy tale to multiply its performance potential and denaturalise its institutionalised power. (23)

And this is a criticism that takes into account the postmodern practice itself. Once one includes within this postmodern fiction's "borderline" mode—crossing boundaries between genre and fiction and theory—the equally "'borderline' or transitional genre" of the fairy tale (Bacchilega 1), both complicity and challenge are potentially possible. "Postmodern transformations of the fairy tale," notes Bacchilega, "are doubling and double: both affirmative and questioning, without necessarily being recuperative or politically subversive" (22). They can be destructive, reconstructive, or revisionist, but at their best their utilization of fairy-tale magic, which Bacchilega links to both readerly desires (5) and the patterning of our unconscious (22), has a "transformative" (141) demythologizing power, particularly in relation to gendered subject positions.

The postmodern readings of Bacchilega and Benson, pointing as they do to the polyphony of circulating versions of any one tale, posit the pre-text as itself multilayered and the rewriting as yet a further, informed layer—almost a form of informed and critical reduplication. "Recent adaptations," states Benson, "can thus be seen as part of a history constituted of re-tellings, in which the inherent allusiveness of each story avoids a hierarchy of interpretation, positing instead a series of constructed meanings which disqualifies any seemingly final, narrative reading" (209–10). Harries argues that the term *postmodern,* as applied to the rewritings, cannot serve, since its historical element prevents it from being appropriate for the seventeenth-century tales of the *conteuses* whose narratives exhibit the same sceptical, self-conscious intertextual commentaries. Benson agrees with Shippey that feminist rewritings of fairy tales are poor when they only see the tales as embodying a monologic ideology. Shippey, though, suggests that it is the "pliability" of fairy tales that has made them into such a con-tested site for any number of ideological positions, from feminism to Robert Bly's 1990 *Iron John.* Like most of the postmodern critics, Shippey views Carter's rewritings positively, reading them as "transformations" (263) or "true" re-writings, while he finds Atwood's "academic" (269). But this apparently pejorative view is ambiguous, since he finds the whole post-modern practice, where "the commentary is as important as the narrative . . . a highly academic one" (270).

Lance Olsen's more optimistic view of postmodern use of the fantastic also sees it as a critical, quasi-academic commentary: "postmodern fantasy becomes the literary equivalent of deconstruction" (117). He argues:

> Because of its hesitation between two universes of discourse [the mimetic and the marvellous], the fantastic confounds and confuses reader response, generates a dialectic that refuses synthesis, explores the unsaid and unseen, and rejects the definitive version of "truth," "reality," and "meaning." Its function as a mode of discourse is to sur-prise, question, put into doubt, produce anxiety, make active, disgust, repel, rebel, subvert, pervert, make ambiguous, make discontinuous, deform, dislocate, destabilize. (116)

Within this free-floating skepticism, the fairy tale exists for Olsen as the mar-vellous, a compensatory "narrative that believes in the Truth of itself, a text that is sure of itself" (18). This is a very different and unproblematized read-ing of the fairy tale from either Tatar's or Bacchilega's shifting fluidity, but as employed within a mode that plays the marvellous off against the mimetic, postmodern fiction's use of fairy tale creates "a dialectic which refuses synthesis" (Olsen 19), invoking the reader's longing and a "nostalgia for the universe of compensation and redemption" (119), which is impossible to realize because of the text's postmodern provisionality. Like Olsen, Martin Horstkotte expounds a model of textual irresolution for the postmodern fantastic as parody using Chanady's magic realist theorization of the irresolution of textual antimonies: "In the postmodern fantastic . . . fairy tale and novel represent two conflicting texts that are not harmoniously reconciled at the end" (154). Horstkotte links Hutcheon's historiographic metafiction to the use of the fantastic, as Bacchilega also does, to argue for a "fantastic historiographic metafiction" (123), but lacks Bacchilegga's interrogation of the terms he employs. (Bacchilega uses Nancy Walker in order to interrogate Hutcheon's concept of parody, to incorporate a social as well as a textual dimension.) All share, though, the view that fairy tale and fantasy reinforce the deconstructive element of postmodern fiction.

In light of the amount written on the topic, it is no surprise that the debate surrounding the possibility or impossibility of a feminist postmodern, the conjoining of the ideology of a communal political utterance with the deconstructive questioning of all truth claims, surfaces within a theoretical examination of women writers of the fairy-tale postmodern. Susan Sellars, in *Myth and Fairy Tale in Contemporary Women's Fiction*, sees the use of fairy tale, whose magic, transgression of rules, and inexorability of plot are "enabling, because they echo the complicated patterns of [women's] desire to dare and need to conform" (16), and as grounding the giddy vertigo of the feminine postmodern. She raises the question of whether a feminist rewriting is possible, "how to re-write a text without 'mastering' its source and so reproducing the objectifying and annihilating procedures of binary law" (27–28), and analyzes a number of ways in which women writers can rewrite myth and fairy tale (Sellars collapses the two terms). Drawing on Cixous's heterogeneity and Kristeva's semiotic as explanations of the powers of the intertextual dialogism, Sellars suggests that the political focus of feminist critique allows writers to "try for the difficult and perhaps impossible balancing act" of invoking the originals and yet developing divergent paths, noting that "the known forms operate as compass points around which we can weave new and different stories" (29). While making use of the oscillation of pastiche and parody in the intertextual deployment of the fairy tale, it is noticeable that Sellars does not advocate a skepticism about the revisioned representations but views them as replacing the previous utterances; demolishing in order to construct "new enabling alternatives" (29). Such a strategy is in part a form of a tentative, localized reduplication as a way of writing back to the center: "My own view, "writes Sellers, "is that we can only communicate via the existing cultural currency, that the currency inevitably imposes its structures and prior investments, but that there remains room for reinterpretation and invention which cumulatively alters the status quo" (135–6). Such reduplication carries with it what Jameson terms the "nostalgic" element of pastiche, though now perhaps stripped of its conservatism; it is the attempt to revivify the past utterance with a contemporary (feminine) twist, while still claiming for the fairy tale the validity to voice some unproblematized counter-truth.

Alesia García argues for an even more nostalgic notion of folk/fairy tale in her analysis of indigenous women writers' utilization of Pueblo and Mexican/Chicana folk tales. Such a reduplication, García suggests, creates "an emergent, oppositional text which resists containment by more conventional theories" (12). Similarly, Armitt sees the Anglo-Welsh writer Alice Thomas Ellis's incorporation of Celtic fairy tales as "an important metaphor for larger discussions of cultural marginalisation and border territory" (*Contemporary* 133). While such fiction is clearly resistant and politically charged in its use of traditional folk tales to give voice to a contemporary ex-centric postcolonial utterance, its strategy of retelling can be seen as stylistically conservative, a pastiche of past tales to counter and augment previous views. These fictions deploy their alternative tales as stable historical utterances rather than as a means to deconstruct the tales' narrativity. García's and Ellis's argument complicate Jameson's thesis that pastiche is a postmodern "blank" parody unable to represent contemporary culture in any meaningful way, since this is exactly what they are doing in relation to emerging ex-centric, hybridized culture. Jameson's position, in different terms, is articulated by Zipes in *Fairy Tale as Myth/Myth as Fairy Tale*, in which he divides contemporary fairy tales into "duplications" and "revisions" and denigrates duplication's mimicry as inherently conservative/bad, "enabl[ing] us to fall back on the comfortable familiar object that does not challenge our customary routines and habits. The duplicate reinforces the deeply entrenched modes of thinking, conceiving, believing that provides our lives with structure" (8). This simple dualism, or binary opposition, is more than ripe for deconstruction. Harries, Benson, and Bacchilega have posited feminist postmodern rewritings, which Zipes would term *revisions*, as equally possible to define as duplications, and, likewise, critics of ex-centric writers using duplication for indigenous tales see their works as subversive of the status quo. The postcolonial utilization of past tales as statement rather than critique can nevertheless stand as a politically resistant site of contestation to the assimilations of the dominant culture. Bacchilega's invoking of both social and textual considerations is particularly useful here.

The subject of postcolonial reappropriation has, however, proved contentious. Sellars, in wrestling with the paradoxes of a feminist rewriting, invokes Spivak's thesis that it is impossible to restore a disposed voice, "since the very act serves to re-cover it" (27). John Stephens and Robert McCallum, in *Retelling Stories, Framing Culture*, argue that all retellings are invariably conservative despite the fact that "few retellings are simple replications" (4). Attempts to retell stories from indigenous peoples within the postcolonial societies of the West involve "misapprehension and misapplication of metanarratives" whatever the ethnicity of the writer, because the audiences will impose their own "universalized" reading, thus "Westernizing the story at the stages both of production and reception" (Stephens and McCallum 6). This monologic view of reception ignores the interplay of a variety of ethnicities and hybridities in the implied (postmodern) readers, but it presents a perhaps necessary complement in its consideration of audiences. Anne Cranny-Francis focuses her analysis of feminist rewriting of fairy tales on the reader's oscillation between pre-text and revision. The texts in question "operate as metafictions which, while significant in themselves of particular gender relations, rely on the constant comparison with traditional narrative to construct a feminist reading position" (94). For all Cranny-Francis's writers contest rather than invoke their pre-texts, the "constant comparison" sets up a different readerly dynamic from the original. Sharon Rose Wilson, invoking Atwood's Canadian nationality as positioning her as postcolonial, has a much more positive view of Atwood's strategies of textual displacement, delegitimation, and decolonization, thus synthesizing "similar techniques identified with feminist, postmodernist *and* postcolonial theory into a revisionist form" (28). Hers is a more assertive claim than Sellars, although both argue that in some circumstances the feminist and postcolonial reuse of fairy tales can produce politically effective revisions. Perhaps this is the moment to resurrect Wilson's statement that "there is more than one postmodern ideology."

To conclude, wholesale binary categories such as pastiche (radical / good) and parody (conservative / bad), or retelling and rewriting (terms that I have taken as similar), become in part impossible to employ in relation to the use of the fairy tale, since the manner in which the intertext is conceived has shifted so significantly. Postmodern fairy tales are not stable intertexts and can be read as carrying within themselves invocations of originary comfort, voicing of the ex-centric, or latent psychoanalytic meaning alongside layered critical contestations of earlier invocations in an oscillation of seemingly contradictory positions. Postmodern fairy-tale fiction contains therefore a complex and complicated meshing of parody and pastiche, of critique and redeployment, in its contemporary revisions and retellings that, in particular examples, can both conserve and/or contest dominant cultures and / or the cultural values of the intertexts. Textual and social positions that can seem clear-cut when examined theoretically, can, when examined closely, seep into each other on the page.

Jeanette Winterson: Theory into Practice

Jeanette Winterson, a postmodern or post-modern writer (the debate goes on, since she claims to be a modernist while most critics read her as postmodern), has consistently employed intertextuality in her novels: the Bible during the mid-1980s, history in the late 1980s, and a whole array of sciences and post-Einstein new physics in the 1990s. Her twenty-first-century work returns to more literary and cultural narratives: Tristan and Isolde, Paolo and Franscesca, and George Mallory lost on Everest in *PowerBook* (2000), and Charles Darwin and Robert Louis Stevenson's *Dr. Jekyll and Mr. Hyde* in *Lighthousekeeping* (2004). Her first novel, *Oranges Are Not the Only Fruit* (1985), and her fourth, *Sexing the Cherry* (1989), are the only ones to use fairy tale extensively among their intertextual references, although there are brief episodes in *The PowerBook* and *The King of Capri* (2003), the latter a picture book written for children and illustrated by Jane Ray. Winterson, following the Carter generation, employs fairy tales as cultural building blocks, demonstrating little knowledge of, or interest in, the genre's scholarship or criticism, save for the aforementioned feminist critique. In all but one case, she creates her own fairy tales utilizing generic plot sequence, simplified character types, or talking animals and magic as a way of contesting the genre's canonical social acculturation of gender and sexuality; although she makes brief reference, if any, to traditional fairy stories, *Sexing the Cherry*, is an exception. This rewriting of the Grimms' tale of "The Twelve Dancing Princesses," recasts the Grimms narrative with an entirely different plot, showing little of the detailed textual engagement of Carter. As such, Winterson's use of fairy tales' magical, transformative abilities can be read as reduplication through the reuse of the fantastic, although a reduplication that uses the nostalgic, originary element of retelling for a specifically excentric radical lesbian-feminist agenda. Winterson uses fairy tales in a range of ways: as the simple deployment of genre style for purely conservative strategies in *The King of Capri* and *The PowerBook;* as complex challenges to the narrative expectations of gender roles within the traditional genre; and as vehicles for exploring the feminine and lesbian psychic "otherwise" within a fluidity of fractured selves in *Oranges Are Not the Only Fruit* and *Sexing the Cherry.* In the latter two, the narrative context of the fairy tales and their utilization as part of the postmodern polyphony of narratives recasts them as skeptical postmodern practices since they do, as Bacchilega requires, "question and re-create the rules of narrative production, especially as such rules contribute to naturalizing subjectivity and gender" (23).

The King of Capri employs simple role reversal through the character of a selfish and greedy king divested of his wealth by a wayward wind. "You do these things in a moment of madness and then you're left with the mess" (16) decries the wind, depositing all the king's riches in the grounds of a poor washerwoman. Mrs. Jewel thus becomes the generous Queen of Naples, teaching the impoverished autocratic ruler the error of his ways, and the narrative ends with the conservative closure of their marriage. Having learned his lesson, the King is rewarded with the wise and gentle wife, but what she gets out of it, apart from social elevation, is not broached. The elemental transformation by the personified wayward wind and its relationship with Mrs. Jewel's wily, streetwise cat uses humor but little parody. In contrast to Winterson's adult texts, there is a definite closure—perhaps making an uncritical assumption of what picture books are required to do—as the greedy, selfish man (who had desired two mouths) is reformed by the example of the gentle, unselfish woman. The gender constructions feed on stereotypes, and the resolution has none of the parodic rejection of the canonical fairy tale's compulsory heterosexuality, as is found for example in the tale of the perfect woman in *Oranges Are Not the Only Fruit,* where the prince's intended bride is uninterested in his proposal of marriage. *The King of Capri* is compact and surprisingly monologic, the only Winterson text that can unproblematically be called conservative in its pastiche of the fairy tale.

"The Story of the Red Fox" (*PowerBook* 179–81), though employed within a more complex narrative, seems similarly illustrative in its moral, depicting as it does the power relations between two lovers: Alix, the cyber storyteller, and her unnamed client. Interplaying with the theme of love as entrapment, the tale is of a hunter's unrequited love for a vain Princess, and traces his traditionally machismo production of ever-more savage animal pelts as love tokens. Demanding the skin of a mysterious red fox, she agrees to his demand that the fox be brought to her alive. Despite its magical redness against the world of white snow, its ability to melt winter, and its eloquent, brave eyes, she hesitates "only a second" (181) before having it slaughtered, whereby she is left with the corpse of the hunter. No overt moral accompanies this story, which ends abruptly with the sacrifice of the lover, but it stands as a story "as present," given by the ardent narrator, Alix, to the expensively dressed lover, reluctant to risk a relationship. The simple plot and the magical duality of the snowy world of the white-skinned princess and the rich red warmth of the fox, linked to blood and passion, point to the lost opportunities of the married lover, afraid of passionate excess and intensity, and also hints at what Alix risks in loving (slaughter of the self). The simplicity of the stripped down narrative and the use of the fantastic adds emotional intensity (the "unsaid" of their restrained discussion) and functions as a pastiche, uncritically reflecting the psychic resonance of the genre—the fairy tale conceived as a conduit to unconscious desires. The story is, however, framed a few pages before by a narrative that argues the need to be one's own hero and risk the fairy-tale quest: "Like it or not you are alone in the forest, just like all those fairy tales that begin with a hero who's usually stupid but somehow brave, or who might be clever but weak as straw, and away he goes (don't worry about the gender) . . . and by and by (we hope) he'll find the treasure" (155). The fluid dichotomy that undercuts the hero, the irresolution of the happy closure, and the unconcern about gender all accord to the cyberspace performativity of the protagonists' encounters, a kind of Donna-Haraway-meets-Judith-Butler, where the two protagonists shift genders, geographies, and time, inhabiting the series of love stories Alix composes for the client. This frame sets up a dialogic relationship to the tale, both commenting on and distancing the tale as a commentary of the ill-paired lovers. The pastiche is thus echoed by a variant, more sceptical narrative position. Neither of these two original replications of the genre has been discussed as yet, partly because, as I have argued elsewhere, Winterson criticism has an extremely long gestation period (Makinen, *Winterson* 154).

The more parodic and subversive uses of fairy tale in *Oranges Are Not the Only Fruit* and *Sexing the Cherry* has generated a robust critical debate. *Oranges* is to date the most discussed of Winterson's novels, and the use of original fairy tales is an important layer of its postmodern melange of discourses. As the young Jeanette tries to make sense of the world outside of her Pentecostal family, the fairy tales stand as a secular imaginative discourse in dialogic relation to the prescription of the Bible. The original fairy tales form alternate, polyphonous narratives to the realist (bildungsroman) discourse of Jeanette's development and express differing, resistant viewpoints to the mimetic narrative, reflecting the text's thesis in the "Deuteronomy" section that life represents a layered sandwich rather than a linear history. Fantasy is used in the sense suggested by Jackson, as an illogical, supernatural subversion of the culturally consensual. Stories, the novel argues, "help you understand the world" (9) and they are differentiated from "history" that tries to fix events into a monologic stability. The story, in contrast, is "a way of explaining the world while leaving the world unexplained, it's a way of keeping it alive not boxing it into time." (91). The biographical narrative voice of Jeanette, uttering its mimetic history, is prevented from being univocal. The tales, beginning with the fairy tale, develop through to the magical stories of Winnet and end with the literary stories of Sir Perceval. The citational writerliness of these narratives, interleaved with the autobiographical element, evokes Olsen's view of postmodernism's use of the fantastic as a hesitation between the mimetic and the marvelous, confounding readerly expectation and generating a dialectic that refuses synthesis. In *Oranges Are Not the Only Fruit,* the hesitation becomes a positive oscillation, reinforcing the narrative's refusal to "box in" or force a closure of meaning by "explaining." The textual irresolution not only reinforces the inability of both narratives to fix meaning, it also—since all the stories are in some sense Jeanette's—represents the provisional, fractured nature of subjectivity, always in process: "I have a theory that every time you make an important choice, the part of you left behind continues the other life you could have had. . . . There's a chance I'm not here at all, that all the parts of me, running along all the choices I did and didn't make, for a moment brush against each other" (169).

The first fairy-tale section, the story of the Sensitive Princess, comes after the recounting of Jeanette's mother's need to reconcile her youthful love of fineness—"She liked to speak French and to play the piano" (9)— to the mundane realities of unkind, northern small-town life. The sensitive

princess, unable to exist in the palace, dedicates herself to the role of looking after a small village, when the magical hunchback warns her that since
she has no outlet for her "great energy and resourcefulness" she is "in danger of being burned by [her] own flame" (9). The tale offers a different, more
sympathetic view of the mother/young princess and of the necessity of her
dedication to educating the people, since in this tale it is herself rather than
another being (the orphaned Jeanette in actual life) whom she dedicates. As
a counterpoint, it offers a less personalized view of the mother's driven need
to reform what she terms sinners, a viewpoint that is not open to the young
Jeanette. Ideologically, for Paulina Palmer the use of fairy tale also enables
the novel to critique the former genre's traditionally patriarchal constructions: "In the tale of the princess who was so sensitive that she wept for the
death of a moth . . . the stereotypically feminine attributes of narcissism
and sentimentality are confronted and rejected" (102). Nevertheless, the
simplicity of the narrative evokes the child's comprehension. Since the tales
"keep pace with the protagonist's reading level, the fantasies seem *like* stories she might tell herself, polished up by the narrator who interpolates them
without comment" (Rusk 107). School is such a contrast to the evangelical
household that, "I didn't understand the ground rules. The daily world was
a world of Strange Notions, without form, and therefore void. I comforted
myself as best I could by rearranging their version of the facts" (*Oranges*
48–49). Jeanette's "rearrangement" turns mathematical figures into fairy
tale, with the tale of the emperor Tetrahedron living in an elastic-band
palace. The lovely woman's gift of the revolving circus of midgets simultaneously performing myriad tragedies and comedies, teaches the many-faced
emperor that "no emotion is the final one" (49). That reality is multifaceted
and nomadic is an insight brought by a beautiful young woman, as with the
story of the perfect woman in the "Leviticus" chapter.

Where the early fairy tales are simple narratives that utilize the fairy tale
as a narrative mode appropriate for a child, the Tale of the Perfect Woman
is a longer and more complex story that evokes the growing Jeanette's maturity and her ability to critique what she is told. "The sermon was on perfection, and it was at this moment that I began to develop my first theologi-
cal disagreement. . . . 'Perfection,' he announced, 'is flawlessness'" (60).
"Once upon a time" (61) begins the tale in proper fairy-tale fashion, before
traditional gender roles are subverted. While the beautiful woman is knowl-
edgeable about physics and cosmology, fulfilled in her work and uninterested
in marriage, the prince, "quite pretty, though a little petulant at times" (61),

seeks a wife to complement his life. Where masculine written authority erroneously argues that perfection is the lack of flaws or blemishes, feminine wisdom, a maternal wisdom handed down through the ages, argues instead that perfection is the balance of differing qualities. Patriarchal authority, in its bid to fix truth, decapitates all who disagree, though the woman's revenge is magically to drown all the evil advisors in her spilled blood, leaving the prince with Mary Shelley's *Frankenstein,* as a further parodic model of how to build a "perfect" person. The tale functions in a number of ways. It is a feminist re-visioning of the fairy-tale genre, subverting gender norms and highlighting the violence and the self-sustaining lies that underwrite patriarchal oppression of femininity and, in particular, compulsory heterosexuality. The joking intertextual references to Oscar Wilde and Mary Shelley cross the generic boundaries, highlighting the material process of narrativity itself. Finally, it functions as Jeanette's contestation of the biblical sermon that frames it. Anievas Gamallo, informed by the feminist critics of fairy tales and by the work of Zipes, acknowledges the phallocentric socialization of the traditional, well-known fairy tales but suggests that the genre is not inherently patriarchal and that Winterson, like other feminist writers, interrogates and re-visions: "*Oranges*' fairy tales are inhabited by wise, resourceful and brave heroines who make assertive choices instead of enduringly and self-sacrificingly staying at home, sweeping hearths and awaiting the charming prince" (132). Such a rewriting, when examined on its own, remains on the level of parodic reduplication, operating as a feminist metafiction that relies on the comparison with traditional narrative, replacing the previous utterances with a tentative, localized reduplication as a lesbian-feminist way of writing back to the center. The context of the novel, however, as one of the layers of postmodern metanarrative placed alongside the "unconscious resistance" of the stories, each refusing to be the dominant narrative, multiplies the gendered readings in a satisfyingly complex amalgam that simultaneously raises questions about the nature of subjectivity as psychic *and* cultural narrative. The context shifts the parodic reduplication into a more complex rewriting that challenges any self-narration of identity to be the whole "truth," Bacchilega's definition of "true" parody.

After this most developed of the literary fairy tales, the fairy-tale genre in *Oranges Are Not the Only Fruit* broaches the mimetic fictionalized autobiography, crossing the boundaries of the previously disparate narrative modes in the narrator's reading of "Beauty and the Beast" and "Little Red Riding Hood" and her literal rendition of the "pig" husband. The narrative

assumes the reader's knowledge of the tales and, in a parodic critique, uti-
lizes the "beast marriages" as a denigration of men as sexual partners, which
can be read both as sexual innocence and narrative confusion in the young
girl as a "truth" about compulsory heterosexuality: "I had stumbled on a terrible conspiracy" (72). The following stories interleave the fantastic narratives of Winnet with that of Sir Perceval, where Winnet resists the mother's
wishes, while Perceval expresses the nostalgic loss of belonging and home—
fictionalized renditions of the two selves/desires/choices Jeanette experiences at the end of the book. Again, the masculine desires stasis and fixity,
while the feminine desires change and process—the "city" that constitutes
escape from the mother/wizard's clutches and a love of truths. Lauren Rusk
suggests that the development from the early fairy tales to the "complex alter egos" of Winnet and Perceval shows Jeanette "taking a more active role
in her self-construction" (107). Winnet's persuasion by the wizard to stay as
an apprentice parallels the opening tale of the sensitive princess, bringing the
narrative full circle, since now the apprentice is figuratively Jeanette rather
than the mother. The gender-blindness that sees the mother as masculine
highlights her role as what Gabriel Griffin calls a "gatekeeper of patriarchy"
(87), while Winnet's disruptive love for a boy, rather than a girl, underwrites
fairy-tale heterosexualism. The brown pebble, symbol of the shriveled heart
of those who stay rather than embrace a life of nomadic provisionality, becomes Winnet's talisman as she arrives at the idealized city of learning.

Palmer argues that fairy tale and fable serve as vehicles for "representing
Jeanette's shifting identities and the displacements which fantasy enacts"
(102). The variant fantastic narratives express the fluid plural selves and also
show "subjectivity itself in terms of narrativity":

> In the story of Winnet, an idiosyncratic version of the tale of the Sor-
> cerer's Apprentice, she relives and re-evaluates her stormy relation-
> ship with her mother. . . . She transposes into a fairy-tale form the
> power-struggles and conflicts which it involves and the painful rift in
> which it culminates. The representation of the bond between mother
> and daughter in terms of the attachment between a sorcerer and his ap-
> prentice emphasizes its irrational aspect, acknowledging the "magical"
> power which it wields. (102)

The fairy tale is read here in terms of its underlying emotional resonance.
Laurel Bollinger cites Bettelheim's view that fairy tales allow children to

manage their contradictory feelings. She posits a comparison between the bildungsroman, with its "relatively strong truth claims," and fairy tales, "whose truth claims rest on psychological verity alone" (365). Susana Onega also claims that fairy tales "provide a deeper and more truthful insight into the true nature of events than history could ever aspire to give" (141). Critics' views of the fairy tale as reflecting or enacting some deeper, unconscious truth of the individual links it to Freud's conception of dreaming or parapraxis; though such a reading is used to comment ironically upon the autobiographical scenes, it is never seen by the critics to ironize itself. However, this reading of the reduplication of fairy tales' link to the psychic, for all psychoanalysis' claims for an underlying truth, does not cancel out the earlier readings of the fairy tale as alternate, postmodern polyphony that questions any attempt at unitary meaning. Fairy tales, as I have shown, have been seen to carry a variety of latent contents, from postmodern retellings to psychic truths, and the contemporary postmodern fictionalization in Winterson's text is open to all these readings simultaneously. Neither feminism's nor psychoanalysis' attempts to harness the meanings of the fairy tale need be monologic given the complex history of fairy-tale scholarship. Both, indeed all, readings remain available as further layers of hybrid acculturations, since what the reader does is also a matter of cultural context. Contemporary discourses about the multilayered hybridity of the fairy tale can add further layers of feminist, psychoanalytic, and postmodern subjectivity to its available circulating textual heteroglossia.

The fairy-tale inclusions in *Oranges* vary from the simple, nostalgic replication of the early tales of the Sensitive Princess and the Emperor Tetrahedron to the witty and parodic The Perfect Woman, where phallocentric monologic idealization is contrasted to a feminine wisdom of dialogic pragmatism and balance. It is one of the few clearly feminist parodies of the genre within the novel. Winnet and the Sorcerer returns to a resonant, magical reduplication. All these invented fairy tales incorporate a complex discourse of both "compact" and "protean" discourses (to borrow Harries's definitions) that, through their interconnections, form a small "cycle," as elaborated by Benson: a "self-contained, interconnected, self-generating narrative system" where each tale both raises questions and elaborates on the others in a complex and open-ended utilization of the fairy-tale form, preventing the novel from formulating any single, definitive conceptualization of the genre. The tales enact a range of strategies, from simple pastiche with The Sensitive Princess, to more complex parody in The Perfect Woman, to pastiche as subversive rewriting for Winnet and the Sorcerer. The variety of the tales invokes a range of reactions to fairy-tale narratives and their relationship to childhood. Throughout the novel they are used as productions of the self's relationship to discursive practice, as Jeanette's self is narrated through fairy-tale parameters. They are more than simply about the protagonists; they also enact latent psychic resonances because they create complex analyses of the dialogic negotiations of self, desire, and the socialization process.

Sexing the Cherry contains Winterson's rewriting of "The Twelve Dancing Princesses," a central motif of the novel, which describes Jordan, one of the two main narrators, searching for Fortunata, the twelfth princess. "The Twelve Dancing Princesses" appears in the Grimms' collection as the tale of how the princesses escape their father's incarceration each night to dance in a magical kingdom underground. The king offers a princess's hand in marriage to whosoever can discover why they are found each morning exhausted, with their dancing shoes worn out. Though the sisters drug various men who attempt to uncover their secret, an old soldier at last outwits them and uncovers the answer. He chooses the eldest daughter, due to his age, and the story ends. Jago Morrison, utilizing the Brothers Grimm version in his analysis of the novel, notes that in the Grimms' version only the chosen eldest daughter is married off, while the others are left to an unknown fate. Andrew Lang's account, in his *Red Fairy Book* (1890), follows a more traditionally romantic heterosexual ending in which the male discoverer of the princesses' secret is a lowly but young gardener who chooses the youngest princess before all her sisters are also married off. This version accords with Jordan's journeying with the botanist Tradescant (a form of gardener) and his obsession with Fortunata, the youngest sister. Jan Rosemergy uses Lang's version to unpack the rewritten text's assertion of the women's autonomy, stolen from them by gardener, father, and princes: "Winterson's transformation of this fairy tale explodes the myth that every woman is a princess rescued by marriage to a prince. In Winterson's tale each woman suffers in different ways but ultimately acts to free herself" (Rosemergy 256–57).

Winterson's rewriting concentrates both on the dancing city itself and the individual tales of the twelve princesses *after* the conventional marriage closure. Their tales confound the fairy-tale myth of happily ever after, uncovering the oppressiveness of the institution of marriage within a feudal kingdom as they reject the role of femininity as property. In the Grimms' and

Lang versions the trapdoor leads down into a magical underground country of the twelve princes, signified by groves of silver and gold trees, a buried/repressed world of dancing, merriment, and riches. In Winterson's version the opposite happens, the princesses fly up to a city floating in the sky where they dance with no mention of specific partners. Metaphors of illicit undercover creeping and hiding are transformed into much more open, limitless escape. Fortunata and her dancers become the "sublime" to the Dog Woman's "grotesque" earthy giganticism and both exceed the norms of gender figuration. The dizzying dislocation of Fortunata's weightlessness and the floating city cut free from conventional laws of gravity as it dances articulate a world that lives, literally, "otherwise." A whole city that frees itself from the earth by dancing, inhabited by people initially attempting to live conventional lives but then, "as it became natural for the citizens to spend their lives suspended, the walking turned to leaping and leaping into dancing, so that no one bothered to go sedately where they could twist to points of light" (96). This fantastic image is further developed by reference to geographical fact—"some of the cleverer people knew the world is endlessly in motion, but since they could not feel it they ignored it"—and by Fortunata's recourse to the "logical" to explain the city to Jordan, aware of the power of consensual rationality to interpolate experience. Lisa Moore, in a brief aside, makes the connection between the dancing princesses and Jordan's comment early on in the novel that she has "met a number of people . . . anxious to be free of the burdens of their gender" (31); but what Jordan sees when the women dance is far more transformative than just a weightlessness freed from gender expectations. The dance transforms women into light: "There appeared to be ten points of light spiraling in a line along the floor, and from these beings came the sound I had heard. It was harmonic but it had no tune. I could hardly bear to look at the light, and the tone, though far from unpleasant, hurt my ears. It was too rich, too strong, to be music" (93). "What is reality," questions Marilyn Farwell, "when one . . . scientific definition of matter is empty space and points of light? If the logical and chronological relationship of events embedded in language is artificial and matter is a mental construct, then the narrative on which Western minds depend for meaning is also an artificial construction that may be no more than empty space and points of light" (168).

Winterson's sustained focus on a city unburdened by things (the gold and silver of the Grimms and Lang, who conceive of worth by material wealth)

speaks to the inner life and of journeying in search of the complete integration of the varying selves (Jordan's search and Fortunata's lesson). The city,
freed from earth's gravity, lives a nomadic existence as a raft sailing though
space; just as the princesses agree to travel with it forever, they are discovered by the youngest prince and likened to a "beetle" as he clings to their
sheet. When he reports to the king, "There was no escape and, to contain us,
our ankles were chained and the prince came to stay with his eleven brothers" (99). Being clapped in chains and being married amount to the same
thing in *Sexing the Cherry:* "We were all nomads once, and crossed the
deserts and the seas. . . . Since settling down and rooting like trees . . . we
have found only infection and discontent" (43).

The eleven narratives of the other, unnamed sisters in the chapter "The
Story of the Twelve Dancing Princesses" are each isolated on their own page
as separate and separated monologues. Each sister speaks of how her marriage has failed and how the women have left to live together in "The City of
Words," a city that constantly shifts its buildings so that households can escape their creditors. Words and narratives are shifting, slippery constructs
when it comes to conveying meaning. Jordan's comment on the city's inhabitants invokes *Oranges'* dual desires mirrored by Winnet and Perceval; they
have "reconciled two discordant desires: to remain in one place and to leave
it behind for ever" (43). Winterson invokes the traditional tale(s) to revision
it as a story of female escape from patriarchal inscriptions, rewriting the traditional marital closure through eleven narratives that confound heterosexual marriage, unmasking its cruelty to those forced to live within its confines.
The happiness of those brave enough to escape cultural expectations to live
otherwise, with women or mermaids (the grotesque gobbling of fish links the
mermaid to queer representation) reinforces the point. Heterosexual marriage becomes the allegory for the tower in which the dancing princesses are
confined by patriarchal power. "From a story about patriarchal control and
the duplicity of women, Winterson turns the tale into a playful representation of the plural scenarios of sex and desire" (Morrison 107).

A number of themes link the eleven tales, referencing similarities as well
as differences but never coalescing into a fixed statement. Many of them link
their husbands' love of things, of material wealth and comfort, to their unhappiness in marriage. The sixth leaves her husband's estate, signified by the
clay that weighs down her feet; on seeing the weightless leap of a deer, the
eighth poisons her fat husband who devours farm-loads of animals; the tenth

walks out on her husband who wants both mistress and home, because the home is not worth her invisibility. Yet the second princess prevents any easy link between husband, things, and women as property. With an intertextual reference to Robert Browning's "My Last Duchess," whose Duke collects rare antiquities for his own aggrandizement and murders his wife for smiling at another man (viewed as a damage to his reputation), this princess loves collecting religious antiquities and, when her husband burns a favorite mummified saint, she entombs him in bandages to take the object's place.

Three of the princesses find sexual compatibility and happiness with women. The fifth is Rapunzel's female lover, living a contented lesbian existence until the prince cross-dresses and climbs the tower; the marriage of the seventh is happy because she married a woman, and the first is living happily in "salty bliss" with a mermaid. Sex with men is a less equal affair: the husband of the fourth princess wants a wife to add spice to his illicit degradation of women; the tenth's wants a sexual triangle; the ninth's treats her like a vicious, wild creature; while the eighth documents the disgust of sex with her glutton of a husband. However, it is not enough to say that only women can fulfil women's desires. The third princess speaks eloquently of her erotic passion for her husband, unrequited because he is homosexual. Nor is it enough to say all the men oppress their wives. The husband of the twelfth princess, locked into solipsistic isolation, begs her to free his spirit by killing him, and she obliges. Although all eleven marriages prove unhappy, and the twelfth princess, Fortunata, escapes on her wedding day rather than marry the prince who betrayed her and her sisters, condemning them to remain on earth, it would not be true to say the princesses are victimized by their husbands. These women are active and aggressive, fighting back before picking up their skirts and leaving. Six of the eleven kill their husbands, and the seventh mercy-kills her female "husband" when they are discovered. That marriage is not an institution that can promise happiness and that phallocentric society denigrates women and persecutes lesbians is as much as can be gleaned from the tales. The refusal to make grand generalizations appears deliberate.

Since the narratives are unallocated they voice a plurality of feminine and lesbian contestations of marriage and domesticity as the "solution" for women, though the final one also speaks of the analogous entrapment of the male spirit. Fortunata, the youngest princess, escapes marriage to live a life of self-directed wonder and intensity. She is the only one to continue to dance, freed from gravity, and proves no happy-ending "reward" for Jordan in his quest to find himself. The eleven fairy-tale narrators, plus Fortunata, create a "cycle" of their own that, through self-narration, enacts the orality of the folk tale within a literary context. This is a complex rewriting, invoking the laws of materiality and physics, selfhood as process and plurality, and semiotic confusion of truth and lies within a fictional context that strives to write the experiences hidden from realistic, biographical narration.

Sexing the Cherry's multiple narratives and plurality of conflicting discourses attempt a playful deconstruction of the concepts of self and physics, of time, space, and matter. It uses the fairy tale of "The Twelve Dancing Princesses," with its "other voices" of at least the Grimms and Lang (rewritten to contest the oppressive norms of gender and sexuality), and the discourse of the fantastic to incorporate feminine self-authenticated pleasure and freedom (the dance) as part of the incredible reality of atomic physics. Each discourse—political, fairy tale, and scientific—is layered one upon the other in a dialogic engagement, since no one explanation can ever encompass the giddy vertigo of that floating existence, postmodern reality. Winterson's use of fairy tale in *Sexing the Cherry* again forms part of a dialogic, polyphonous narrative, one of many ways of representing the same story. It is, in simple terms, a gendered and lesbian revision of the Grimms/Lang pre-text, but what it also comes to stand for, in this ambitious text, is a polyvalent complex of meanings that echoes the multilayered nature of the fairy tale itself, as figured by Bacchilega, Benson, Harries, and Tatar.

Within her oeuvre, Winterson uses the genre of the fairy tale as a simplistic, unquestioned template in her children's picture book and, in her adult novels, as a more complex, layered artifact, multiple in its resonances and traditions (informed by feminist denigration of it as a tool of acculturation); it is a form of "art" that can convey (psychic) "truths" more effectively, though less clearly, than history. When Winterson's fairy tales are placed within their textual context, as postmodern *melanges* of competing discourses, they invoke a complex reverberation of rewriting and reduplication that, as I have suggested, makes a mockery of attempts to try to sum up and designate the literary works in question. The novels, considered as containing original or rewritten variants of the fairy-tale genre, evidence further, contemporary versions of the genre's acculturation. Fairy tale helps write postmodern fiction and postmodern fiction helps rewrite fairy tale in a constant oscillation that allows both the tale and its scholarship to extend into the twenty-first century.

Notes

1. Hutcheon is actually talking about architecture at this point, but I have adapted it to fiction, which she looks at in later chapters.

2. They cite José Monléon's *A Specter is Haunting Europe: A Sociohistorical Approach to the Fantastic* (1990).

Bibliography

Primary Sources

Winterson, Jeanette. *The King of Capri*. London: Bloomsbury, 2003.
————. *Oranges Are Not the Only Fruit*. London: Pandora, 1985.
————. *The PowerBook*. London: Vintage, 2001.
————. *Sexing the Cherry*. London: Bloomsbury, 1989.

Secondary Sources

Anievas Gammallo, Isabel. "Subversive Storytelling: The Construction of Lesbian Girlhood through Fantasy and Fairy Tale in Jeanette Winterson's *Oranges Are Not the Only Fruit*." *The Girl: Constructions of the Girl in Contemporary Fiction by Women*. Ed. Ruth Saxton. New York: St. Martins, 1998. 119–34.
Armitt, Lucy. *Contemporary Women's Fiction and the Fantastic*. Houndsmill: Macmillan, 2000.
————. *Theorising the Fantastic*. London: Arnold, 1996.
Bacchilega, Cristina. *Postmodern Fairytales: Gender and Narrative Strategies*. Philadelphia: Pennsylvania UP, 1997.
Benson, Stephen, *Cycles of Influence: Fiction, Folktale, and Theory*. Detroit: Wayne State UP, 2003.
Bettelheim, Bruno. *The Uses of Enchantment: The Meaning and Importance of Fairy Tales*. Harmondsworth: Penguin, 1978.
Bollinger, Laurel. "Models for Female Loyalty: The Biblical Ruth in Jeanette Winterson's *Oranges Are Not the Only Fruit*." *Tulsa Studies in Women's Literature* 13 (1994): 363–80.
Bondi, Liz. "Locating Identity Politics." *Place and the Politics of Identity*. Ed. Michael Keith and Stephen Pile. London: Routledge, 1993. 84–96.
Bottigheimer, Ruth. "The Ultimate Fairytale: Oral Transmission in a Literate

World." *A Companion to the Fairy Tale*. Ed. Hilda Ellis Davidson and Anna Chaudhri. Cambridge: D. S. Brewer, 2003. 57–70.

Brooker, Peter. Ed. *Modernism/Postmodernism*. Harlow: Longman, 1992.

Carmichael, Thomas, and Alison Lee, eds. *Postmodern Times: A Critical Guide to the Contemporary*. Dekalb: Northern Illinois UP, 2000.

Carter, Angela. Introduction. *The Virago Book of Fairy Tales*. London: Virago, 1991. ix–xxii.

Chanady, Amaryll. *Magical Realism: The Irresolution of Antimonies*. New York: Garland, 1985.

Connor, Steven. *The English Novel in History 1950–1995*. London: Routledge, 1996.

———. *Postmodernist Culture: An Introduction to Theories of the Contemporary*. 2nd ed. Oxford: Blackwells, 1997.

Cranny-Francis, Anne. *Feminist Fiction: Feminist Uses of Generic Fiction*. Cambridge: Polity, 1990.

Crowther, Catherine, Jane Haynes, and Kathleen Newton. "The Psychological Use of Fairy Tales." *Contemporary Jungian Analysis: Post-Jungian Perspectives from the Society of Analytical Psychology*. Ed. Ian Alister and Christopher Hauke. London: Routledge, 1998. 211–28.

Doan, Laura. "Jeanette Winterson's Sexing the Postmodern." *The Lesbian Postmodern*. New York: Columbia UP. 137–55.

Farwell, Marilyn. "The Postmodern Lesbian Text." *Heterosexual Plots and Lesbian Narratives*. New York: New York UP, 1996. 168–94.

Foster, Hal. Introduction. *Postmodern Culture*. Ed. Hal Foster. London: Pluto, 1985. vii–xiv.

García, Alesia. "Politics and Indigenous Theory in Leslie Marmon Silko's 'Yellow Woman' and Sandra Cisneros's 'Woman Hollering Creek.'" Cathy L. Preston. 3–21.

Gibson, Andrew. *Towards a Postmodern Theory of Narrative*. Edinburgh: Edinburgh UP, 1996.

Griffin, Gabrielle. "Acts of Defiance: Celebrating the Lesbian." *It's My Party: Reading Twentieth-Century Women's Writing*. Ed. Gina Wisker. London: Pluto, 1994. 80–103.

Harries, Elizabeth Wanning. *Twice upon a Time: Women Writers and the History of the Fairy Tale*. Princeton: Princeton UP, 2001.

Holoquist, Michael. *Dialogism: Bakhtin and His World*. London: Routledge, 1990.

Horstkotte, Martin. *The Postmodern Fantastic in Contemporary British Fiction*. Trier: Wissenschaftlicher Verlag, 2004.

Hutcheon, Linda. *The Poetics of Postmodernism*. New York: Routledge, 1988.

Jackson, Rosemary. *Fantasy: The Literature of Subversion*. London: Methuen, 1981.

Jameson, Frederic. "Postmodern and Consumer Society." *Postmodern Culture*. Ed. Hal Foster. London: Pluto, 1985. 111–25.

Lee, Alison. *Realism and Power: Postmodern British Fiction*. London: Routledge, 1990.

Leith, Dick. *Fairytales and Therapy: A Critical Overview*. Pontypridd: Daylight P, 1998.

Makinen, Merja. *Feminist Popular Fiction*. London: Palgrave, 2001.

———. *The Novels of Jeanette Winterson: A Reader's Guide*. London: Palgrave, 2005.

McHale, Brian. *Constructing Postmodernism*. London: Routledge, 1992.

———. *Postmodernist Fiction*. London: Methuen, 1987.

Morrison, Jago. "Jeanette Winterson Re-membering the Body." *Contemporary Fiction*. London: Routledge, 2003. 95–114.

Olsen, Lance. *Ellipses of Uncertainty*. Westport, CT: Greenwood, 1987.

Onega, Susan. "I'm telling you stories, trust me: History/Storytelling in *Oranges Are Not the Only Fruit*." *Telling Histories*. Ed. Susana Onega. Amsterdam: Rodopi, 1995. 135–47.

Moore, Lisa. "Teledildonics: Virtual Lesbians in the Fiction of Jeanette Winterson." *Sexy Bodies: The Strange Carnalities of Feminism*. Ed. Elizabeth Grosz and Elspeth Probyn. London: Routledge, 1995. 104–27.

Palmer, Paulina. *Contemporary Lesbian Writing: Dreams, Desire, Difference*. Buckingham: Open University, 1993.

Pearce Lynn. *Reading Dialogics: Gendering the Chronotope*. London: Arnold, 1994.

Philips, Neil. "Creativity and Tradition in the Fairy Tale." *A Companion to the Fairy Tale*. Ed. Hilda Ellis Davidson and Anna Chauhri. Cambridge: D. S. Brewer, 2003. 39–56.

Preston, Cathy Lynn, ed. *Folklore, Literature, and Cultural Theory*. New York: Garland, 1995.

Rose, Jacquline. *States of Fantasy*. Oxford: Clarendon, 1996.

Rosemergy, Jan. "Navigating the Interior Journey: The Fiction of Jeanette Winterson." *British Women Writing Fiction*. Ed. Abby Werlock. Tuscaloosa: U of Alabama P, 2000. 248–69.

Rusk, Lauren. "The Refusal of Otherness: Winterson's *Oranges Are Not the Only Fruit*." *The Life Writing of Otherness*. New York: Routledge, 2002. 105–32.

Sage, Lorna. *Angela Carter*. Plymouth: Northcote House, 1994.

Sellars, Susan. *Myth and Fairy Tale in Contemporary Women's Fiction*. London: Palgrave, 2001.

Shippey, Tom. "Rewriting the Core: Transformations of the Fairy Tale in Contemporary Writing." *A Companion to the Fairy Tale*. Ed. Hilda Ellis Davidson and Anna Chaudhri. Cambridge: D. S. Brewer, 2003. 253–74.

Stephens, John and Robert McCallum, eds. *Retelling Stories, Framing Culture: Traditional Story and Metanarrative in Children's Literature*. New York: Garland, 1998.

Stone, Kay. "Things Walt Disney Never Told Us." *Women and Folklore*. Ed. Claire R. Farrer. Austin: U of Texas P, 1975. 42–50.

Sullivan, Ceri and Barbara White. *Writing and Fantasy*. Harlow: Longman, 1999.

Tatar, Maria. *The Hard Facts of the Grimms' Fairy Tales*. 2nd ed. Princeton: Princeton UP, 2003.

Thomson, Clive. "Mikhail Bakhtin and Contemporary Anglo-American Feminist Theory." *Critical Studies* 1.2: 141–61.

Todorov, Tristan. *The Fantastic: A Structural Approach to a Literary Genre*. Ithaca: Cornell UP, 1975.

Warner, Marina. *From the Beast to the Blonde: On Fairy Tales and Their Tellers*. London: Vintage, 1995.

Waugh, Patricia. *Practicing Postmodernism, Reading Modernism*. Hounslow: Arnold, 1992.

Wilson, Sharon Rose. *Margaret Atwood's Fairy-Tale Sexual Politics*. Jackson: Mississippi UP, 1993.

Zipes, Jack. *Don't Bet on the Prince*. Aldershot: Gower, 1986.

———. *Fairy Tales and the Art of Subversion*. New York: Routledge, 1983.

———. *The Trials and Tribulations of Little Red Riding Hood*. London: Heinemann, 1982.

———. *When Dreams Come True: Classic Fairy Tales and Their Tradition*. New York: Routledge, 1999.

7

Extrapolating from Nalo Hopkinson's *Skin Folk*

Reflections on Transformation and Recent English-Language Fairy-Tale Fiction by Women

CRISTINA BACCHILEGA

I

By 1993 when Angela Carter's third short-story collection, *American Ghosts and Old World Wonders,* was published, readers of her short fiction may not have agreed on the liberatory import of her feminism but knew to read her apparent flights of fantasy and "waywardness" as metanarrative digs, especially into the history of folk and fairy tales, from which to emerge with provoking woman-centered images and insight. In particular, "Ashputtle *or* The Mother's Ghost: Three Versions in One Story" was and is readily recognizable as a "Cinderella" narrative triptych or polyptic in a feminist frame. By enacting multiple narrative possibilities, Carter revived not only the Grimms' "Ashputtel" but also Basile's "La Gatta Cenerentola" and some oral traditions of ATU501B featuring a traveling heroine. The "Three Versions in One Story" also worked to demythologize the "innocent heroine" portrayal of Cinderella and the fantasy of an upward heterosexual marriage as the (re)solution that Charles Perrault and the Disney industry had popularized. In Carter's text, the figure of Ashputtle, then, made her appearance as a reflection on, more than of, both "old world wonders" and "American ghosts."[1]

This reflection turned on both the dissection and expansion of a few story ingredients or symbolically charged images: bloody body parts ("The Mutilated Girls"), ashes ("The Burned Child"), and dress ("Travelling Clothes") construct narratives of (dis)juncture where marriage, inheritance, and genealogy are thematized to different effects in the three versions of the story. At the same time, if the three versions are read sequentially, their permutations of how to wound flesh, dress wounds, mourn, and generally "provide" for someone or oneself, articulate in quick succession interpretations of the mother-daughter relationship in the "Cinderella" fairy tale and bring about a far-from-uncomplicated renewal of "mother love."[2] As the italicized and ambiguous *or* in Carter's title anticipates, the mother's ghost and Ashputtle, in their different shades of pallor, are semblances of each other: Ashputtle is the Mother's *ghost* as life and soul in its older meaning; and the mother's ghost lends its appearance to Ashputtle's terrifying desires. They are, and then they are not, each other—if in the first version Ashputtle "must do her mother's bidding" (114), in the second one it is the mother who does Ashputtle's—and in both cases they resent it. The final words in "Travelling Clothes," the third version of "Ashputtle *or* The Mother's Ghost," are the mother's, "Go and seek your fortune, darling" (120), a complicated speech act, combining injunction *and* permission, a performative "letting go" that joins the two women in spirit as it simultaneously sets them free from one another. The final action is the daughter's, and it holds transformative powers: she moves into the mother's coffin, and it turns "into a coach and horses" ready for travel for the daughter's own journey.

How to read this injunction *or/and* permission as well as the journey metanarratively? Tiny feet, ashes, and dress all pertain to the (female) body, each inscribing multiple stories that are, at every *or*, made to appear at different turns as interchangeable with, juxtaposed to, or extending of one another—all supplemental apparitions of one another. "Ashputtle *or* The Mother's Ghost: Three Versions in One Story," thus, enacts possible directions, not exclusive of one another, for writers/tellers and readers/listeners who journey into rewriting the fairy tale: historically layered inquiry, rebellious critique, metaphoric exploration. Three is not a limit, though, since no single narrative path is chosen as the definitive one in Carter's rewriting. It's not so much that "three versions" are packaged into "one story," but that no "one story" is ever single or self-sufficient, lending itself to three "versions" at least, through the articulation of multiple historical tellings, doubts and questions about plot and image—through the potential articulated by an *or*, which is not simply *and*. Whether we read them sequentially, holistically, iconically, or intertextually, the three or more "versions" of womanhood, mother-and-daughter-hood, and story in "Ashputtle *or* The Mother's Ghost" compose rather stridently different but joined scenarios, linking with other paths that take us further into the seemingly dead recesses and potentially new extensions of the tale. The fairy tale thus appears like a multivalent narrative wonder that inevitably pertains to human relations or more than one body (e.g., Ashputtle *and* the Mother), holds multiple questions and (hi)stories, and also belongs to no one in the social imaginary.[3]

As narratives characterized by "pleasure in the fantastic" and "curiosity in the real," fairy tales generate meanings that are "themselves magical shape-shifters" (Warner xx, xxiv). For this reader, then, in "Ashputtle *or* the Mother's Ghost" the genre of the fairy tale takes on the shape of specter and phantasm at once—a terrifying/wonderful shadow testing the confines of "seeing" the real (from the Latin *spectrum* and "to look") and being deceived by an illusion confined to the unreal (from the Greek φάντασμα and "to appear"). I read this Carter re-vision of the fairy tale as phantasmagoria: it is the "assembly of phantasms" (φάντασμα + ΄αγορα), or what she called "informal dreams dreamed in public" (*Virago* xx); and, as an apparent artifice that "positively parades its lack of verisimilitude" (*Virago* xi), it "speaks through phantasms" (φάντασμα + ΄αγορεύω). *Phantasmagoria* as a term was "invented for an exhibition of optical illusions, produced mainly by means of the magic lantern, first exhibited in London in 1802" (OED). It was the art of making shapes or figures not only visible but also dynamic; it was a fantastic spectacle or *féerie* eliciting marvel and delight. As an optical illusion, phantasmagoria was a technological novelty and wonder in the early nineteenth century; as a conscious literary artifice penned by Carter, it conferred new wonder and possibilities to the fairy tale as reviewed by one London-based feminist writer from 1979 to 1992.

Compared to the holding "mirrors to the magic mirror of the fairy tale" metaphor through which I have visualized Carter's fairy-tale fictions before (23), phantasmagoria may not be as widely pertinent but, in addition to the multiplicity inherent to both metaphors, it has a more explicit element of artful illusion, a historically marked inception, and movement or change built into it.[4] Whether they have read Carter or not, writers (re)turning to the fairy tale in the 1990s and into the twenty-first century have her fairy-tale phantasmagoria as one of their potential pre-texts: this is one of the ways in which the Carter generation changed fairy-tale fiction and its potential for magic and wonder.

II

Fairy tales have a history of magic transformations. Scholars of folk narrative know this well and have increasingly been interested in following the tales' trajectories not only in so-called traditional and oral settings but also into the multimedia worlds of literature and popular culture. At the same time, literary scholarship has increasingly remarked on the fairy tale's versatility in history as a genre that has, in different milieus, successfully morphed to codify social norms and to nurture the desire for change. My engaging with the fairy tale or tale of magic *now* is necessarily inflected by my own life-journeys and scholarly trajectory, and by my reading of recent interdisciplinary fairy-tale studies, including *Twice upon a Time: Women Writers and the History of the Fairy Tale* by Elizabeth Harries (2001), *Cycles of Influence: Fiction, Folktale, Theory* by Stephen Benson (2003), and *Fairy Tales and Feminism: New Approaches,* edited by Donald Haase (2004).[5]

When taken seriously, "interdisciplinarity," Gayatri Spivak reminds us, is not a utilitarian method but an ambitious goal; in this spirit, I believe it is important to continue to insist on the relation between folkloristics and literary studies (and for that matter cultural studies) not so much as a "dialog" dominated by the middle voice but, as in Spivak's project, a *conversation* where we "turn and change ourselves" in order to keep "in step with our partners." In reflecting on the tale of magic in relation to recent English-language fairy-tale fiction by women, I have thus asked myself not only how women writers have extended or modified their performances of the fairy tale as phantasmagoria but also how I could step up to their inquiry by extending or modifying my approach to this fiction. Like Benson and others, I'd like to learn more from the cross-fertilization of fiction, folktale, and theory.

To move in such a direction, I concentrate here on the 2001 short-story collection *Skin Folk* by Nalo Hopkinson. This contemporary Caribbean Canadian author consciously draws on worldwide folklore and Caribbean culture to produce "speculative" fiction that is both science fiction and fantasy. And, in my experience, her revision of folk and fairy tales to denaturalizing effects in *Skin Folk* calls for a reading that *transformatively* extends the web of an Angela Carter–like phantasmagoria.[6]

Explicitly acknowledging their debt to Angela Carter, Ellen Datlow and Terri Windling have, as editors of popular fairy-tale fiction anthologies like *Snow White, Blood Red* (1993), *Black Swan, White Raven* (1997), and *Silver Birch, Blood Moon* (1999), featured adult tales primarily by women whose feminist project or subtext it is to explore the "fantasy" and "horror" of fairy tales. Two of Hopkinson's *Skin Folk* stories, "Riding the Red" and "Precious," were first published by Datlow and Windling. This is no surprise since the narrative possibilities enacted by Hopkinson's tales link up readily with other woman-centered or feminist reflections on the fairy tale today. Hopkinson and other woman writers in Datlow and Windling's anthologies as well as in *The Poets' Grimm: Twentieth Century Poems from Grimm Fairy Tales* (2003) share an "invisible luggage" of stories with Emma Donoghue in *Kissing the Witch* (1997), Francesca Lia Block in *The Rose and the Beast: Fairy Tales Retold* (2000), and even Aimee Bender in *The Girl in the Flammable Skirt* (1998) and *Willful Creatures* (2005); and collectively—I extrapolate—they carry it differently from the Carter generation.[7] Here, in order to insist on the *or*, I choose to extrapolate from Hopkinson specifically because *Skin Folk* also operates a distinctive transformation, the creolization of fairy tales, a project embedded in a history that, even when its multiple gendered Western traditions are considered, has not been central to the genre's canon.

III

An epigraph introduces *Skin Folk:*

> Throughout the Caribbean, under different names, you'll find stories about people who aren't what they seem. Skin gives these skin folk their human shape. When the skin comes off, their true selves emerge. They may be owls. They may be vampiric balls of fire. And always, whatever the burden their skins bear, once they remove them—once they get under their own skins—they can fly. It seemed an apt metaphor to use for these stories collectively. (1)

Because I took this statement as a clue to the conception of folktale and magic that animates Hopkinson's collection, I decided that my usual tale-by-tale approach was not the most fruitful. Yes, it is true that several of the fifteen stories can be easily identified as rewriting specific tales of magic: "Riding the Red" of "Little Red Riding Hood" (ATU 333); "The Glass Bottle Trick" of "Maiden-Killer" or "Bluebeard" (ATU 312); "Precious" of "The Kind and Unkind Girls" (ATU 480).[8] While less easily identified, "Fisherman" can be read as an extrapolation of "The Shift of Sex" (ATU 514); "Under Glass" is a postapocalyptic revision of Hans Christian Andersen's literary fairy tale, "The Snow Queen"; and Hopkinson's "Tan-Tan and Dry Bone" retells the Caribbean folktale, "Anansi and Dry Bone," with a metafictional twist. Each adaptation deserves critical attention, but to think of Hopkinson's stories collectively involves asking different questions.

For one, how is the tale of magic represented in Hopkinson's *Skin Folk*?[9] The whole collection, as the "skin folk" metaphor suggests, *hinges* on transformation, and it is an "aesthetic of transformations" that many of us would agree is a key element of the fairy tale as a genre that narratively encourages imagining change and, given the fairy tale's highly symbolic aspect, also recognizing hidden resources.[10] This paradox has often been staged in fairy-tale studies as a conflict between sociohistorical, ideologically oriented approaches and psychological approaches of universal appeal. Both recognize the project of socialization as central to the narrative structuring of the tale of magic but its end varies: for feminist and sociohistorical critics, transformation is a process that can enact a range of possibilities, an enabling move that is subject to multiple permutations; for scholars more interested in archetypes and myth, transformation has had clearly set goals such as normalcy and its reproduction. I sketch this divergence here because the following analysis of the thematic, structural, and semiotic uses to which Hopkinson puts transformation and by extension the fairy tale also metacritically calls for a strong *historical* grounding of our critical approach to fairy-tale fiction and a more decisive rejection of the one-story-for-all impulse.

IV

Each tale in *Skin Folk* proposes the inner transformation of an individual. To mention a few, Granny prepares herself for death by imagining rebirth through her red-riding granddaughter; Silky overcomes grief by giving herself up to water, her mother's realm; Beatrice recognizes her own entrapment in the house of a smothering Bluebeard-like husband; passive-aggressive Blaise learns that anger can be nourishing; K. C. comes to a new, embodied acceptance of herself as a "fisherman"; the heroine of "Precious" realizes she is the only one who can break the spell that has silenced her. And in fairy-tale style, these transformations are externalized, staged as the heroine's encounters with supernatural beings and her everyday struggles. These are stories of change, even liberation then, where the ordinary and the extraordinary, the real and the fantastic mingle to positive ends.

However—in each tale and in Hopkinson's collection as a whole—the story ends on the verge of resolution but with no programmed outcome in sight. *Skin Folk*, I said, hinges on transformation because each story takes the protagonist and us as readers to the threshold of transformation or just beyond it, into the liminal moment when the ending is the beginning of another story.

"When Rose Red sets out to leave she [Rose White] holds his hand and lets her go" (Francesca Lia Block "Rose" 149).

The final line of the first tale, which consists of Grandma's monologue anticipating one last exciting measure with Wolfie, activates the mechanism: "Listen: is that a knock at the door?" (5).

As a reader, I am left to continue the story and to imagine that

"*The Bloody Chamber* . . . turned the key for me as a writer. It opened into a hidden room, the kind that exists in dreams, that had always somehow been there, but that I'd never entered because I'd been afraid . . . : the center of the labyrinth of desire" (Marina Warner 250).

"but Granny she says Granny you don't understand . . . don't understand! Hah! For ain't I the old Beauty who married the Beast? . . . only my Beast never became a prince . . . sing me no lumpen ballads of deodorized earths cleansed of the stink of enigma and revulsion! For I have mated with the monster my love and listened to him lap clean his lolly after" (Robert Coover, "The Door: A Prologue of Sorts" 16).

the wolf and then the girl will come through that door, bringing their transformations to completion; but the plots I know have been shaken. Even if I am accustomed to thinking that sexual initiation, violence, and intergenerational knowledge are "Little Red Riding Hood"'s core thematic elements, the first-person narrative of Grandma's desire in Hopkinson's text makes for new permutations of the granny / wolf / girl triangulation as they slide in and out of each other's skins. The tale as I know it in its multiple versions has been unsettled, and yet an active principle of transformation has as-

> "one fine morning when my work is over I will fly away home / fly away home fly away home / one fine morning when my work is over I will fly away home."

serted itself in a regenerative or optimistic move: "whatever the burden their skins bear, once they remove them—once they get under their own skins—they *can fly*" (1, emphasis added). [11]

This happens in each story of the collection. In the end a "positive" or "liberating" change has occurred, but there is no resolution, no folding of the newly clad skin folk into a familiar fiction or social arrangement, only a twinkle of optimism, a new possibility or flight. When, at the end of "Money Tree," Silky swims down into the deep swirling waters to "get her brother," her "strong strokes" (21) intimate she will succeed, but readers can only hope. As she moves to greet her murderous husband in the final scene of "The Glass Bottle Trick," Beatrice wonders if, "[w]hen they had fed," the "duppy wives" she had unintentionally set free would "come and save her, or would they take revenge on her, their usurper, as well as on Samuel?"

> "We lay there, waiting to see what we would see" (Emma Donoghue, "The Tale of the Hair" 93).

(101). In "Slow Cold Chick," readers are left wondering, as the protagonist Blaise giggles, what will come of her next encounter with the earth-eating blacksmith and his Flora-like companion (117).

The two apparent exceptions are "Fisherman"—the centerpiece of the collection—and the last story, "Precious." The author suggests very little is "fantastical about" "Fisherman": "It felt like a tale that needed to be grounded in the potential for reality" (119). But as David Soyka suggests in his review, the triumphant confidence of the story's ending—as K. C.'s sexual and gendered identities become reconciled, and Fisherman can successfully join in the social game—is the most striking instance of wish fulfillment in the collection. [12]

In the final story, the girl from whose lips fell flowers and gems has learned to use her words and to assert herself by refusing to accept the name and persona in which she was imprisoned as "Precious." Reversing the genre twist at work in "Fisherman," the premise of "Precious" is magical, but its resolution is cast in the language of every day ("Police? There is an intruder in my home." [254]) and is parallel to at least some real-life outcomes of domestic abuse. Even in this final story, however, where a definite transformation has occurred, the liberating sound of Isobel's laughter brings *Skin Folk* to an end—but not to closure since this protagonist has just crossed the threshold into a new life.

"Suddenly he was translucent, perfect, the size she was. The prince of the flowers" ("Tiny" 52). This re-imagining of "Thumbelina" has the only happy ending in Francesca Lia Block's collection.

V

The placement of the most widely known fairy tales in *Skin Folk* offers further insight into the representation of the genre as transformative, specifically for women, or more broadly in terms of gendered scripts and sexual politics. Women in various ways are the focus of all fifteen stories in the collection, but two recognizable fairy-tale fictions frame the others. "Red Riding Hood" is the opening for Hopkinson's inquiry, establishing blood as a major symbolic tie that women have with fairy tales as narratives articulating dynamics of sex, violence, pleasure, power, and intergenerational transmission of knowledge. At the other end of Hopkinson's storytelling, her version of "'The Kind and Unkind Girls'-Continued" explodes into a self-affirming narrative for women by focusing on voice as a way out of an oppressive spell or fiction. "The prominence of women in the circulation of fairy tales is a matter of historic record" (Beaumont and Carlson xii). The Brothers Grimm and most European collectors in the nineteenth century gathered stories from women. Given the strong interest that women and women writers have had in tales of magic across time and cultures, Hopkinson's selection of the genre to explore questions of gender and sexual identity is not surprising.

(except in Ireland): As an Irish poet and critic, Emma Donoghue is writing back to this deceptive history when she offers us only women narrators: "This is the story you asked for. I leave it in your mouth" (The Tale of the Kiss" 211).

In Hopkinson's opening epigraph, the statement "When the skin comes off, their true selves emerge" (1) would seem to speak to this exploration. Within the history of Euro-American feminist discourses, this is a familiar script, one that implicitly valorizes a humanist, already-there subject. How does the open-endedness of Hopkinson's transformative narratives work in relation to this recognition of a "true self"? Does transformation as an affirming narrative process that enables "flying" inevitably lead to the discovery of "truth" or "identity"? Are "true selves" to be understood exclusively or primarily in an ontological framework? To be specific, are Hopkinson's fairy-tale fictions "postmodern"? And is the latter a productive question?[13]

The answers hinge on our understanding of the metaphor "skin folk." "Skin folk," Hopkinson writes, seem human because skin shapes them as such, but "they may be owls. They may be vampiric balls of fire" (1). Is that all they are—only owls, only vampiric balls of fire? Is Hopkinson pointing to the natural (owl), the supernatural (vampire), and the human as separate or as interrelated? The stories' dynamics of transformation would point to the latter understanding, but the mention of "true selves" as unshaped by human skin would seem to point to the former. However, what also matters is the color and history of that skin, the "burden their skins bear" (1), the colonial discourses and material conditions that have shaped them; and the setting for their transformation—the cold, urban, diasporic Canada— where Hopkinson's characters live limited lives having often lost their connections with Afro-Caribbean culture and its stories. Trapped in prescribed scripts that pass for "human," her characters are transformed as they recognize a more complex reality, reconnect with "a context of blackness and Caribbeanness" (*Dreaming* 8), and "see" or "appear" as the trickster within. When, having been touched by an Anansi figure, the protagonist of "Something to Hitch Meat To" "help[s others] peel off the fake skins" (42), and Hopkinson's language does again invoke a true/false binary opposition, it is perhaps more productive to read this transformation not so much from within a Euro-American framework for gendered subjectivity but as an echo of Frantz Fanon's unmasking whiteness and uncovering "black skin." I wouldn't argue that postmodernism or Western feminism are irrelevant contexts for reading *Skin Folk*—indeed I return to the question at the end of this essay—but that these frameworks have been in turn transformed by postcolonial studies and that thinking of postcolonial or Afro-Caribbean gendered subjectivity allows for the creolization of "skin folk" to emerge as their historical and epistemological foundation.

VI

Within such a poetics of transformation articulating a desire for individual growth, social change, and proliferation of meanings, the most distinctive move that Hopkinson makes to multiply the genre's possibilities today is toward the creolization of the fairy tale on a number of levels, from the cultural to the linguistic and the sociohistorical. Creoleness—as Lewis C. Seifert writes in a rare and important discussion of it in relation to folk and fairy tales where he builds on the work of Jean Bernabé, Raphael Confiant, and Edouard Glissant—is the mark of a "political consciousness," "an expression of solidarity with all peoples of the Caribbean," a "diversality" that reaches back to Africa and out to "the abrupt melding of different cultural and ethnic groups on islands and otherwise isolated regions, resulting in the creation of a new cultural organization that makes cohabitation possible" (216–17 especially).[14]

Skin Folk includes duppies or ghosts, selkies, and female river deities along with Red Riding Hood and Anansi.[15] They populate stories steeped in both a "diasporic Caribbean culture" (Magnus) and worldwide folklore.[16] These "skin folk" are not to be understood so much as fictions but as magic in a Caribbean worldview where transformation, altered states, and trance are part of being alive and learning how to survive, adapt, and live with others.[17] In her essay "Dark Ink: Science Fiction Writers of Color," Hopkinson writes: "My history and background combine Canadian, Trinidadian, Jamaican, and Guyanese cultures. 'Culture' is no one monolithic thing for me, and I draw on that varied heritage when I write." Créolité as creolization or creoleness/creolity, Lee Haring has pointed out, works as agency in woman-centered folktales of the Indian Ocean, especially when such storytelling is approached from within the islands' history.[18] For Hopkinson, raised on islands that also share a history of colonization, "Caribbean cultures are hybrid cultures" where "hybridity" is similarly understood as "a strategy for survival and resistance" and, as she affirms in another essay, "Code Sliding," her characters' use of Caribbean Creoles reflects this.

Such an understanding of creolization means that "code sliding" is at work on all levels but not to efface difference or power dynamics.[19] For instance, in "The Glass Bottle Trick," the plot of "Bluebeard" is creolized not so much because curried eggs and duppies are in it, but because issues of race and sexual power are thematized together. The murderous husband wants to "whiten" his wife by keeping her out of the sun and in his "air-tight" air-conditioned house: "When the sun touched her, it brought out the sepia and cinnamon in her blood, overpowered the milk and honey, and he could no longer pretend she was white" (93–94). Once Beatrice realizes he despises his own blackness, racial politics come to inform the traditional Bluebeard abhorrence of pregnancy and reproduction. Still unaware of what her husband had done to his previous pregnant wives, Beatrice "remembered him joking that no woman should have to give birth to his ugly black babies, but she would show him how beautiful their children would be, little brown bodies new as the earth after the rain. She would show him how to love himself in them" (96). By the end, she must turn away from such a benevolent fiction to defend herself and their brown baby from her husband's self-hatred and her earlier compliance to it.

> A "hacked language" with a different history and circumstances claims space for a "slow" Gretel who tells her story in "The Tale of the Cottage" ("Take my chances" 133) and puts her own spin to the Rumpelstiltskin story in "The Tale of the Spinster" ("Never asked my name. . . . Never boy's name neither. . . . Taking him away now so he know who" 122). Subjectivity is necessarily the outcome of naming as part of social relations.

Similarly, Hopkinson's use of Caribbean Creoles is not for "color," nostalgia, or the picturesque. "To speak in the hacked languages is not just to speak in an accent or a creole; to say the words aloud is an act of referencing history and claiming space" ("Code Sliding").[20]

> Block and Donoghue also have intended readers and listeners constituting a specific collective upon which the magic of connection and transformation is specifically bestowed: respectively, teenagers in a drug-and-violence infested Los Angeles; lesbians and, more generally, "young readers," girls and women who can learn to listen and love one another.

And, as she is aware, this linguistic creolization will impact readers differently depending on their cultural knowledge, competences, and expectations: encountering in one of her stories a "soucouyant"—and not a "succubus" or a "vampire"—produces a metonymic gap, jars a reader such as myself out of the familiar into new territory and makes me cognizant of its distinctiveness without it being represented. At the same time, this referencing of history opens up possibilities of intimacy for Eastern Caribbean readers, claiming a space for their realities and beliefs. And for diasporic Caribbean readers, who like her characters in the cold Toronto gain strength from re-encountering their forgotten "skin folk," it holds potential for a positive transformation that is also collective.[21]

In any of these scenarios, the delusion of universality often associated with the cultural landscape of the fairy tale will be cracking. Hopkinson's creolization of genre, culture, and language reaches out to different kinds of readers *and* activates the understanding that folk narratives in general are historically and discursively framed. She writes fantasy, and fairy-tale fiction I would add, to explore "what we believe" and to transform it in the process (in Magnus). As she writes in the Introduction to the collection *So Long Been Dreaming: Postcolonial Science Fiction and Fantasy* (2004): "In my hands, massa's tools don't dismantle massa's house—and in fact, I don't want to destroy it so much as I want to undertake massive renovations—they build me a house of my own" (8). To such effects, Hopkinson's two "Red Riding Hood" fictions are particularly interesting. "Riding the Red" (which opens the collection) is in American English inflected and modulated by the Creole, while "Red Rider" (published separately in a chapbook) is entirely in Jamaican Creole, featuring Granny as a farm woman "with the tropical bush not too far outside her front door" and the wolf as Brer Tiger or in Granny's fond address "Master Puss Tiger." "Riding the Red," one could say, renovates the authoritative text, while "Red Rider" (the title itself "a creole phrase that evoke[s] Caribbean music and sexual innuendo" (*Dreaming* 8) constructs a different structure or house; for Hopkinson, they do not, however, replace one another; rather, they are "iterations" of one another (personal email communication) that perform creolization differently. Together, her stories perform creolization as an outcome of history and the coming into being of a new possibility. In the first story of *Skin Folk*, Grandma suggests: "the trick is, you must always have a needle by you, and a bit of thread. Those damned embroidery lessons come in handy, they do. What's torn can be sewn up again, it can, and we are off on the dance once more! They say it's the woodman saves us, me and my daughter's little girl, but it's wolfie gives us birth, oh yes" (*Skin Folk* 4). The stitching, then, enables new life and dances.

Hopkinson invites us not only to think or "see hybrid" but also to "hear creole." We know that vernacular voices have often come to represent "orality" in literature, and, at the same time, that such representations of orality have implicitly primitivized colonized cultures and conveniently confined them to the past. If Hopkinson's creolization in *Skin Folk* seeks to activate a different or "renovated" poetics of transformation, then, another question emerges about the collection as fairy-tale fiction.

VII

How is orality represented in it and to what effects? While the history of the fairy tale depends on both orality and print, the representation of orality in textual fairy tales has played an important role in the establishment of the genre's appeal and conventions. Hopkinson's Creole voices call to be heard. Caribbean Tales just announced that, thanks to funding from the Ontario Trillium Foundation, it will produce five audio books by Caribbean-Canadian authors, and *Skin Folk* will be the first. Hopkinson has recently recorded the first few stories.[22] But oral performance will not necessarily replace the printed *Skin Folk* where, as I see it, various strategies to represent orality make for an innovative permutation of the literary device by which, as Benson notes, the "performative nature" of storytelling has been mimicked on the page: the cycle of stories.[23]

In collections such as the *Arabian Nights*, this staged orality is achieved through framing: a dramatic situation generates strings of narratives by different narrators in different storytelling contexts, each speaking in some way or another to the drama of Sheherazade and Shahriyar, and eventually contributing to restoring life to them and their kingdom. In Hopkinson's collection, there is no apparent external dramatic situation framing the fifteen stories, but the "skin folk" metaphor in the epigraph encapsulates multiple dramas that are enacted in the tales. Some of the stories are told in the first person, but others are not. Rather, stringing the stories together is a set of authorial statements, an epigraph—often in the first person—preceding each story. Some are about the making of the story that follows, others are explanations. Hopkinson "speaks" to readers, mimicking the ways in which writers transition from story to story when giving a reading, the most common context in which a writer's voice can now be heard and s/he also turns "narrator." Even when the story is a monologue, Hopkinson's "I-statements" frame it, struggle against the usually disembodied narrative transaction occurring between writer and reader, thus staging an opening for conversation.

What's more, some of the statements refer to the "I" being moved to tell the story as a result of hearing another voice—a published poem by her father Slade Hopkinson, "a response a student once wrote on a test, if one can believe any of the endless e-mail spam one gets" (23), a song, a saying, a folktale, a warning. So these stories are connected to a larger web of multimedia story-telling. And within this web, the "I" makes explicit references to a very specific and "real" story-telling context that precedes the one on the page: "In 1995, I was ac-cepted into the Clarion Science Fiction and Fantasy Writers' Workshop at Michigan State University" (45). Workshops where professional writers and creative-writing students write, read, and *hear* each other's stories are perhaps today's equivalent in North America of the *Decameron*'s secluded Tuscan villa. While the workshop as "storytelling community" is rarely mentioned in publications, it is perhaps one of the most real, though staged and temporary, "communities" for North American writers today.

In the morning I asked, / Who were you / before you walked into my kitchen? / And she said, Will I tell you my own story? / It is a tale of a bird (Donoghue 9). . . . "When I had the knack of it [spinning], I asked / Who were you / before you came to live in this tower? / And she said, Will I tell you my own story? / It is a tale of a voice" (171). Through the exchange of stories, women touch, heal, and love each other in *Kissing the Witch*.

VIII

If in *Skin Folk* the generative force of a story cycle is achieved through a re-fusal to disembody the web, its combinatory one involves a different form of creolization / transformation whereby all kinds of objects and beings, or mo-tifs, change shape, not always literally, but by association with one another. For instance, the pears in "Money Tree" echo or turn into the avocado pears in the next story, "Something to Hitch Meat To," where the "bound live chicken" (24) the protagonist sees on the bus assumes significance after we've read the following story "Snake," in which it is thanks to a pigeon that a child-rapist and murderer is captured. Analogously, eggs make recurring appearances in the collection, assuming different roles in each story, "The Glass Bottle Trick" and "Slow Cold Chick" especially. The skin in "[w]hen the skin comes off" applies to fruit, trees, animals, humans, computerized images, stories, creation, and more. Urban Toronto, where many of the stories are set, is transformed into an alien space, and, at the same time, one that is alive in a multiplicity of potential stories. By extending transformation to the level of motifs, Hopkinson links the stories of the collection together in an associative pattern not only well-known to story cycles like the *Arabian Nights* but also one that can be visualized as a hypertext, one of the novel technologies of the late-twentieth and twenty-first century.

Technological innovations—including print, film, and the Internet— have, of course, played a significant role in the dissemination and lasting power of the tale of magic. A pioneer in exploring the dynamic relation of print and hypertext in fairy-tale studies, Donald Haase has provided examples of what he calls the "Law of Approximation," whereby printed collections such as Maria Tatar's *Annotated Classic Fairy Tales* or Neil Philip's *The Illustrated Book of Fairy Tales* approximate hypertext; in other words, by decentering the story text, they "encourage browsing and offer the reader multiple access points in a constellation of textual blocks that are simultaneously linked and independent from one another" ("Hypertextual Gutenberg" 228). In fairy-tale fiction, Robert Coover and Suniti Namjoshi were among the first to recognize how the intertextual and multivocal possibilities pertaining to the dynamics of folk and fairy-tale tradition and performance connected with Internet possibilities and could materialize in hypertext.

While Nalo Hopkinson's printed text does not have a weblike page layout, I have suggested that it does encourage the mental practice of pursuing associative links, links that compound and proliferate as we produce meaning by reading and re-reading her stories. If the story cycle in general, whether in performance or on the page, anticipated these generative and combinatory mechanisms (Benson 43–66), the hypertext makes them visible and readily available—in ways that Tatar's page "approximates" but Hopkinson's does not. The hypertextual in *Skin Folk* must be activated by each reader. As with the story cycle, accessing the stories' poetics of transformation depends not only on associations but on reflection; this often intimate and always culturally situated reflection is the catalyst that informs the ways in which through repetition (listening over and over again or rereading) we change the ways in which we make meaning of stories, and those links themselves morph. This process is perhaps approximated in the production of a hypertext more than in its reception, where these already-there and visibly marked links do not necessarily make a connection for every reader, however potentially informative they may be.

Hypertextual links then implicitly call out the absence of other possible connections. I don't think of this absence as lack, pointing to the superiority or inferiority of one technology over the other, but as an example of what Haase calls the "Law of Replication, whereby the new medium . . . fails to distinguish itself from the old" ("Hypertextual Gutenberg" 228) and as a source for (inter)active reading and retelling. In print, Emma Donoghue's *Kissing the Witch* is a wonderful example of storytelling, represented on the page, reaching to create a new link precisely where the implied author as listener had perceived the lack of one. "To Frances, my mother and first storyteller, who read me Andrew Lang's 'Pinkel and the Witch' more times than she can care to remember, this book is dedicated with gratitude and love." Donoghue's dedication bridges "Pinkel The Thief" in the *Orange Fairy Book* and Donoghue's *Kissing the Witch* by retitling Lang's story to include the witch as a character. In Lang's story, the witch is simply a resource: it is assumed that whatever her power, it can and should be taken from her; the witch's gold is there to be stolen; Pinkel is rewarded for being a "great knave" and seems proud of it even as he calls her "dear mother" (159). How did the "witch" come into possession of the golden lantern, goat with golden horns and bells, and her golden cloak? Who is she? Was she always a witch? And what about her daughter? These questions have no place in the narrative economy of "Pinkel The Thief" but are the catalyst for Donoghue's storytelling. Stripping the witch figure of her assumed evil, *Kissing the Witch* develops the hypothesis that "perhaps it is the not being kissed that makes her a witch" (209) and seeks to undo social prejudice by investigating her story— "Climbing to the witch's cave, I called out, Who were you before you came to live here?"—and by giving her a voice as teller: "And she said, Will I tell you my own story? It is a tale of a kiss" (191). This happens over and over again with different witchlike or stepmother figures in Donoghue's retellings of tales of magic. Responding to "Pinkel The Thief" where the exploitation of the mother as witch is naturalized, Donoghue's stories reconnect us with the luminosity of the witch's gold as love rather than material riches.

What distinguishes Donoghue's and Hopkinson's intertextuality and multivocality is what I referred to earlier as their refusal to disembody, or automate the web: their focus on voice as "the very body work, in a way, of the language" (Brathwaite 1154) that is inflected by gender, sexual politics, colonialism, migration. The final tale in Donoghue's collection, "The Tale of the Kiss," ends with an invitation to the narratee and the reader to chew on the witch's words: "This is the story you asked for. I leave it in your mouth"

(211). The protagonist of "Precious," the last story in *Skin Folk,* is exhilarated when in the end "just sounds, only sounds" (255), and not sounds and jewels, come out of her mouth: the jewels may have made her "precious" but severely limited her words to an exchange value that precluded her being heard. This resistance to a dematerialized web is situated in a woman-centered and, in Hopkinson's case, Afro-Caribbean poetics and politics.[24]

IX

Contextualizing and historicizing Hopkinson's metafictional explorations matters to understand more specifically if and how Hopkinson's fictions "disturb the status of fixed meanings" (Shuman in Preston 198) of gender and other scripted differences in fairy tales *nowadays.* Cathy Lynn Preston's essay "Disrupting the Boundaries of Genre and Gender: Postmodernism and the Fairy Tale" in *Fairy Tales and Feminism: New Approaches* has helped me here. In twenty-first-century North America, she suggests, "for many people the accumulated web of feminist critique (created through academic discourse, folk performance, and popular media) may function as an emergent and authoritative—though fragmented and still under negotiation—multivocality that cumulatively is competitive with the surface monovocality" of the mainstream older fairy-tale tradition (199). This web, then, includes the older weavings of Arachne and the French *conteuses;* contemporary Cinderella jokes, movies like the 1998 *Ever After,* television shows, women.com advertisements; *and* twentieth-century feminist fairy-tale revisions. The awareness of multiple authorities and traditions has transformed the web. This allows emergent writers like Hopkinson to approach from a woman-centered, even feminist, perspective, the genre of the fairy tale hardly as a deadly fiction—the way Anne Sexton did in the 1960s—or as a dead fiction—as Robert Coover did in the late 1970s. Rather, the fairy tale can now be approached as a text or web of possibilities that has been "renovated" by writers such as Angela Carter, Margaret Atwood, and A. S. Byatt in their own phantasmagorias, one that other women writers—like Donoghue and Block in a post-Carter generation—can continue to expand and shape, weaving new problems, desires, and voices in and out of it.

As this web continues to grow, the fairy tale as "magic mirror" may perform magic increasingly less as constraining reflection of a patriarchal imaginary and more as multiplying refractions or, as Preston has it, multivocal performances that blur boundaries, or as phantasmagoria. Within this web, the tale of magic in its many skins nowadays, at least in European and North-American contexts, can be a more open-ended way in and out of fictions, with its one-dimensionality working well to question social reality, melt— rather than freeze—its realism. Perhaps this is why, from this web and thanks to it, in *Skin Folk*'s science fiction and fantasy collection, Hopkinson makes the fairy tale function like a portal.

This essay articulates some of the ways in which I see Nalo Hopkinson's *Skin Folk* situating itself at the boundary between transformation and creolization, the literary and the oral, the popular and the emergent, the inter- and the hypertextual—in the process, pushing me as a fairy-tale scholar to shed at least some of an older skin and take a different flight. Whether these are "postmodern fairy tales" or not, they employ "postmodern" narrative strategies from a different place of dislocation—which my work and other fairy-tale studies have not much recognized.

I hope to have shown that Hopkinson's poetics of transformation and creolization emerges into the twenty-first century from specific historical inter-cultural and intertextual dynamics that should not be simply folded into a narrative of continuity. "Postmodern narrative techniques" may appear, as Elizabeth Harries has argued, "strikingly similar to the narrative preoccupations of Giambattista Basile and of the late-seventeenth-century *conteuses*" (15).[25] But collective histories and their contingencies yield different meanings to similar strategies. Carter's phantasmagorias respond to specific concerns about women, social uses of fairy tales—including those of the French *conteuses*—and conceptualizations of narrative that had no place in the early modern constructions of the tale of magic. In "Dark Ink," Hopkinson writes, "Speculative fiction has reinvented itself repeatedly at the hands of the new wave, feminist, cyberpunk and queer writers"; that her own stories emerge from such intertextual encounters should not be side-stepped. Derek Walcott is another trickster in Hopkinson's web; as is her father, as is Anansi, as is Odysseus, as are the Grimms, and—I would add— Angela Carter and Margaret Atwood as white witches. Writing science fiction and fantasy today as Hopkinson seeks to do, "from a context of black-ness and Caribbeanness" (*Dreaming* 8), articulates a specific desire for a new construction as well as for "massive renovation," and not a mere addition to the house of fiction.[26]

That Hopkinson can turn, among other genres, to the folk and fairy tale in order to transform "speculative fiction" and, in her words, "open [it] up to fantastical expressions from communities of colour" ("Dark Ink") hinges then not only on the framing complexities that have—as Harries persuasively argued—characterized women's fairy tales since the seventeenth century but also significantly on a postmodern, feminist, and postcolonial phantasmagoria; a fairy-tale web that has in the last thirty years transformed the fairy tale and Euro-American popular perceptions of it.

Notes

1. In contrast, as I write this essay in 2005, the current popularity of Cinderella "Princess" clothing is a reflection of the fairy-tale heroine's market-driven persistence as a not-so-supernatural model of the "class" that money can apparently buy. See the "Disney Princess" Web site, http://disney.go.com/princess/html/main_iframe.html; and, for commentary, see Jodi Kantor's "Love the Riches, Lose the Rags" in the *New York Times* (3 Nov. 2005) in the "Fashion Style" section.

2. If my reading of "mother love" in this story is accurate, the story is a gloss on and a move from Carter's early essay "Mother Lode."

3. When I presented a version of this essay at the University of Lausanne in Switzerland in May 2006, I also became aware of Mercedes Gulin's excellent work on Carter. Her 2006 thesis "La Fille des Cendres. Études comparative de deux réécritures de Cendrillon: 'Ashputtle, or the Mother's Ghost' (1987) par Angela Carter et 'L'Exaucée' par Marcel Schwob" pursues an insightful intertextual and metafictional analysis that merits to be in print. The matrix of the observations we share—and which we arrived at independently—is in a way confirmation of the power of Carter's phantasmagoria and what Gulin calls the "spectre du text."

4. For an expansive exploration of *phantasmagoria* in relation to spirits, the imagination, and technologies, see Marina Warner's 2006 book, *Phantasmagoria: Spirit Visions, Metaphors, and Media into the Twenty-first Century.*

5. In 1998, I turned to study English-language "legendary traditions" in Hawai'i in order to document how they have been used to reinforce a tourist-oriented image of Hawai'i in the twentieth century and in order to argue for a recognition of Hawai'i as sustained by indigenous conceptions of place and genre (see my *Legendary Hawai'i and the Politics of Place: Narrative Tradition, Translation, Photography, and Tourism*). Before that, the core concern of my research for many years was the intertextual relationship of selected late-twentieth-century English-language literary fictions with the tradition—both oral and printed—of the tale of magic. From such inquiry, a representation of "postmodern fairy tales"—the publisher's

term, but my construction—emerged, as a tendentious one of course, but one that has to some extent opened up space for broader and valuable explorations, among them notably the texts I draw upon here.

6. Nalo Hopkinson was born in Jamaica in 1961, the daughter of a Guyanese and a Jamaican; she lived in Guyana, Jamaica, and Trinidad until the age of sixteen when she moved to Connecticut and then to Toronto, where she continues to live. Her father was the late Guyanese poet and playwright Slade Hopkinson. She has published three novels: *Brown Girl in the Ring* (1998), *Midnight Robber* (2000), and *The Salt Roads* (2003). Her short story collection, *Skin Folk* (2001), won the World Fantasy Award for Best Collection. She has also edited collections like *Mojo: Conjure Stories* (2003); *Whispers from the Cotton Tree Root: Caribbean Fabulist Fiction (2000);* and, most recently, *So Long Been Dreaming: Postcolonial Science Fiction and Fantasy* (2004) coedited with Uppinder Mehan. More information about Hopkinson is available on her Web page: www.sff.net/people/nalo/.

7. These wonder-filled collections blowup fairy-tale imagery to a surreal dimension. Bender's sense of "wonder" is, of course, quite other from Hopkinson's, though both find magic in the ordinary. In the rest of the essay, I will draw only a few explicit links—three to significant pre-texts; the others with Donoghue and Block—which are only meant to suggest a larger web of connections; I invite readers to enlarge and transform it through their own associations or links. My thanks to Kurt Brunner of the English Studies Computing Center at University of Hawai'i-Mānoa for helping me with the layout.

8. The specific folk motif D1454.2 "Treasure falls from mouth" is cleverly amplified in "Precious."

9. "As a specific type of folk narrative, one containing an element of magic or enchantment, the genre of the fairy tale can be conceived in several interrelated ways: as a canon of narratives expressing a particular mode of thought, a collective form of knowledge; as a series of individual tales, literary but anonymous; as a historically defined subgenre of the folktales; and as a literary genre complete with various generic characteristics" (Benson 167).

10. For instance, Benson (205) quotes the Opies asserting that magic "encourages speculation" (Opie 18) and Zipes identifying transformation as the "liberating potential of the fantastic" (Zipes 170). See also Bacchilega, "Folktale" in *Women's Folklore* (forthcoming) and *Postmodern Fairy Tales*.

11. Robert Coover's *Pricksongs and Descants* comes to mind not only because he grants Red Riding Hood's grandmother a history or a life in the course of which she played other fairy-tale roles—"Beauty" most prominently—but also because

"The Door: A Prologue of Sorts" articulates a poetics of liminality most power-fully.

12. "Certain notions of how our bodies are supposed to define us, and how those definitions can be overcome, is the subject of 'Fisherman,' which, as the author notes, isn't fantastical in subject. That it would be so easy to convince others of the roles we prefer to choose perhaps is" (David Soyka's online review).

13. I'm reminded that feminist critics citing from my *Postmodern Fairy Tales* most often pick the metaphor of the magic mirror and its frames and are equally less likely to reflect on the deconstruction of the subject, of the gendered subject in particular, another defining aspect of "postmodernism," one that I was and am tracing in what I call in this essay, Angela Carter's *phantasmagorias*. Are all woman-centered or feminist revisions of fairy tales positing a foundational, humanistic subject? I don't think so. I read Ashputtle and the mother's ghost as supplemental apparitions of one another in a Derridian sense—neither one fully present, neither one prior to or in-dependent of the other.

14. This solidarity extends to peoples with similar trajectories, be they in the Indian or the Pacific Ocean. The November 2004 "Moving Islands" Festival of Writers in Honolulu featured writers from the Pacific (Albert Wendt, Rodney Morales, Jully Makini, Witi Ihimaera) and the Caribbean (Michelle Cliff, George Lamming, Nalo Hopkinson), heightening my understanding of the syncretism of colonialism and islandness precisely in these terms. For that educational and creative experience and for her insightful reading of an early version of this essay, I thank filmmaker, writer, linguist, and friend Esther Figueroa.

Lewis C. Seifert's reading of *Creole Folktales (Au temps de l'antan: Contes du pays Martinique)*, a contemporary Francophone collection of literary fairy tales by Patrick Chamoiseau, was published in 2002. I did not read it until recently but find its concerns and focus on orality, history, and fairy tale germane to my own desire to open up fairy-tale studies further to non-European-centered traditions and trans-lations. See Thomas Geider's *"Alfu Lela Ulela: The Thousand and One Nights* in Swahili-speaking East Africa" *Fabula* 45.3 / 4 (2004): 246–60 and the essay on "The *Arabian Nights* in the *Kuokoa,* a Nineteenth-century Hawaiian Newspaper" that Noelani Arista coauthored with me in *The Arabian Nights in Transnational Perspec-tive* (2007).

15. Generically, in the collection, the tale of magic is mixed in with legend, per-sonal narrative, myth, science fiction, realism, and oral history.

16. To introduce Hopkinson to the readers of *Caribbean Beat,* Magnus writes: "Hopkinson is the best known of a small group of writers putting a Caribbean ac-

cent on the science fiction and fantasy genres. . . . Her work draws heavily on Caribbean life and culture: social trends; syncretic African religions like pocomania, vodun, and santeria; the works of other Caribbean writers, like Derek Walcott; lyrics from old calypsos; Caribbean heroes like Granny Nanny, or characters drawn from Carnival masquerades. It's a mélange that's winning over both science fiction fans in the US and Canada and, more slowly, Caribbean readers." A voracious reader from childhood, Hopkinson tells Magnus in the interview: "[as a child] I was already reading a lot of fantasy. And a lot of folktales—Caribbean, Chinese, European. . . . I was reading anything that had some element of fantasy in it—C. S. Lewis's children's stories or *Gulliver's Travels* or Homer's *Iliad*, which I was reading when I was quite young. My mother worked as a library technician and brought her books home. My father [the late poet, Slade Hopkinson] was a teacher and writer, and very much involved in the literary space. So from a very young age I had exposure to this very wide world of literary production."

17. These "skin folk" are expressions of belief and are part of religious and ritual systems that Hopkinson's fiction does not necessarily replicate or revive but supplements and carries on into the future.

18. In 2003 the *Journal of American Folklore* dedicated a special issue to "creolization," based on the concept's "potential for folklore studies and cultures in a postmodern global perspective" (Elaine J. Lawless, "From the Editor" 3) and its enabling "us to see not simply 'hybrids' of limited fluidity, but new *cultures in the making*" (Robert Baron and Ana C. Cara, "Introduction: Creolization and Folklore—Cultural Creativity in Progress" 5). For further reading about creolization and folklore, see *JAF* (Winter 2003) and Lee Haring's work, including "Techniques of Creolization" in that issue, the piece in Haase's volume, and another essay on Indian Ocean Folktales in *JAf* (Summer 2003).

The key text on "creolization" is Edward Brathwaite's *The Development of Creole Society, 1770–1820* (1971). For work in a more broadly postcolonial context, see Robert Young, *Colonial Desire: Hybridity in Theory, Culture, and Race* (1995).

19. Hopkinson mentions that *code-sliding* is a term from linguistics; I am more familiar with *code-switching*. Whether it is Hopkinson's or certain linguists' coinage, code-sliding is less mechanical than code-switching, I think, perhaps more suggestive both of the ease with which Creole enacts linguistic hybridity and the slipperiness of language beyond individual intention. "Creolization is a slippery concept" (88), writes Baron in an essay that analyzes different metaphors for creolization, such as "compound," "convergence," "coalescence," "coagulation," all involving "catachresis, the provision of a term where one is lacking in our vocabulary" (89).

20. Linguistically, Creole as spoken by several of Hopkinson's characters in-

forms and transforms Euro-American narratives. Her characters speak in a mix of Caribbean Creoles—Trinidadian and Jamaican especially—which (as she states in "Code Sliding") she uses, the former to signal "emphasis / irony," and the latter to signal "opposition."

21. In Esther Figueroa's words, "it is interesting that you say that Nalo's stories have no resolution and in a sense end at the beginning—one can ask . . . what are the possibilities for transformation within the consequences of brutalizing history? Do tales of magic in some way alleviate historical trauma and abuse?" (personal communication). Magic and stories about magic function as resistance, survival, transmission of counter-values during times of slavery, colonial oppression, collective displacement, and other unspeakable horrors. See Donald Haase's work on fairy tales and the Holocaust.

22. The short story "Red Rider" was written as a monologue for performance in the Jamaican vernacular.

23. See Benson's chapter 2, "Theory in Tales: Cycles, Levels, and Frames."

24. In "The World Wide Web and Rhizomatic Identity: *Traité du tout-monde* by Édouard Glissant," Kathleen Gyssel discusses Edouard Glissant's and Patrick Chamoiseau's skepticism about the Internet as a new technology that may very well not reduce the gap between the rich and the poor, the powerful and the oppressed (*Mot Pluriels* 18. Aug. 2001. www.arts.uwa.edu.au / MotsPluriels / MP1801kg.html).

My "text bubbles" in this essay stage intertextuality in ways that seek to represent a secondary orality while suggesting a (hypertextual) web of stories that includes, however minimally, some pre-texts.

25. See Harries 15–16.

26. Two recent essays about her novel *Brown Girl in the Ring* focus on a parallel intervention in science fiction. See *Extrapolations* 46.3 (2005).

Bibliography

Primary

Block, Francesca Lia. *The Rose and the Beast: Fairy Tales Retold.* New York: HarperCollins, 2000.

Carter, Angela. *American Ghosts and Old World Wonders.* London: Chatto and Windus, 1993.

Coover, Robert. *Pricksongs and Descants.* New York: Dutton, 1969.

Donoghue, Emma. *Kissing the Witch: Old Tales in New Skins.* New York: HarperCollins, 1999.

Hopkinson, Nalo. *Skin Folk*. New York: Warner Books, 2001.

———. "Code Sliding." Nalo Hopkinson. Science Fiction and Fantasy Author. www.sff.net/people/nalo/writing.

———. "Dark Ink. Science Fiction Writers in Colour." Nalo Hopkinson. Science Fiction and Fantasy Author. www.sff.net/people/nalo/writing.

———, and Uppinder Mehan, eds. *So Long Been Dreaming: Postcolonial Science Fiction and Fantasy*. Vancouver, B.C.: Arsenal/Pulp Press, 2004.

Secondary

Bacchilega, Cristina. *Postmodern Fairy Tales: Gender and Narrative Strategies*. Philadelphia: U of Pennsylvania Press, 1997.

Beaumont, Jeanne Marie, and Claudia Carlson, eds. *The Poets' Grimm: Twentieth-Century Poems from Grimm Fairy Tales*. Ashland, OR.: Storyline Press, 2003.

Benson, Stephen. *Cycles of Influence: Fiction, Folktale, Theory*. Detroit: Wayne State UP, 2003.

Brathwaite, Edward Kamau. "English in the Caribbean." 1981. Rpt. in *Literary Theory: An Anthology*. Ed. Julie Rivkin and Michael Ryan. 2nd ed. Oxford: Blackwell, 2004. 1151–66.

Figuerou, Esther. Personal Communication. 2005.

Haase, Donald. "Hypertextual Gutenberg: The Textual and Hypertextual Life of Folktales and Fairy Tales in English-language Popular Print Editions." *Fabula* 47 (2006): 222–30.

———, ed. *Fairy Tales and Feminism: New Approaches*. Detroit: Wayne State UP, 2004.

Haring, Lee. "Creolization as Agency in Woman-Centered Folktales." Haase, *Fairy Tales and Feminism* 169–77.

Harries, Elizabeth Wanning. *Twice upon a Time: Women Writers and the History of the Fairy Tale*. Princeton: Princeton UP, 2001.

Journal of American Folklore 116.459 (2003).

Lang, Andrew. *The Orange Fairy Book*. 1906. New York: Dover, 1968.

Magnus, Kellie. "Writing Is Believing." *Caribbean Beat. The Caribbean's Favourite Glossy Magazine* 73 (May/June 2005). www.meppublishers.com/online/caribbean-beat/.

Opie, Iona, and Peter Opie. *The Classic Fairy Tales*. Oxford: Oxford UP, 1980.

Preston, Cathy Lynn. "Disrupting the Boundaries of Genre and Gender: Postmodernism and the Fairy Tale." Haase, *Fairy Tales and Feminism* 197–212.

Seifert, Lewis C. "Orality, History, and 'Creoleness' in Patrick Chamoiseau's *Creole Folktales*." *Marvels & Tales* 16.2 (2002): 214–30.

Soyka, David. Review of *Skin Folk*. *Sf Site*, 2002. www.sfsite.com.08a/sk133.htm.

Spivak, Gayatri Chakravorty. Unpublished conversation.

Uther, Hans-Jörg, ed. *The Types of International Folktales, a Classification and Bibliography*. Based on the system of Antti Aarne and Stith Thompson. FF Communications no. 284. Helsinki, 2004.

Warner, Marina. *From the Beast to the Blonde: On Fairy Tales and Their Tellers*. London: Chatto and Windus, 1994.

———. *Phantasmagoria: Spirit Visions, Metaphors, and Media into the Twenty-First Century*. Oxford: Oxford UP, 2006.

Zipes, Jack. *Fairy Tales and the Art of Subversion: The Classical Genre for Children and the Process of Civilization*. London: Routledge, 1983.

Contributors

Cristina Bacchilega is Professor of English at the University of Hawai'i-Mānoa. She is the author of *Postmodern Fairy Tales: Gender and Narrative Strategies* (1997) and coeditor, with Danielle M. Roemer, of *Angela Carter and the Literary Fairy Tale* (2001). Her research interests are folk and literary narrative, the fairy tale, and contemporary fairy-tale fiction. Recent work includes *Legendary Hawai'i and the Politics of Place: Tradition, Translation, and Tourism* (2007). She is reviews editor of *Marvels & Tales: Journal of Fairy-Tale Studies*.

Stephen Benson is Senior Lecturer in the School of Literature and Creative Writing at the University of East Anglia, UK. He is the author of *Cycles of Influence: Fiction, Folktale, Theory* (2003) and *Literary Music: Writing Music in Contemporary Fiction* (2006), together with a number of essays on contemporary fiction and theories of narrative. He is currently working on a study of fiction and voice.

Sarah Gamble is Reader in the Department of English at the University of Wales, Swansea, UK. She is the author of *Angela Carter: A Literary Life* (2005) and *Angela Carter: Writing from the Front Line* (1997), and editor of *The Fiction of Angela Carter: A Reader's Guide to Essential Criticism* (2003) and *The Routledge Companion to Feminism and Postfeminism* (2001). She has written widely on contemporary women's fiction and gender theory.

Elizabeth Wanning Harries is Helen and Laura Shedd Professor of Modern Languages and Professor of English and Comparative Literature at Smith College. Her publications include *Twice upon a Time: Women Writers and the*

History of the Fairy Tale (2001), *The Unfinished Manner: Essays on the Fragment in the Later Eighteenth Century* (1994), and essays on the *conteuses* who wrote fairy tales in France in the 1690s.

Merja Makinen is Senior Lecturer in the School of Arts at Middlesex University, UK. She is the author of *Agatha Christie: Investigating Femininity* (2006), *The Novels of Jeanette Winterson: A Reader's Guide to Essential Criticism* (2005), and *Feminist Popular Fiction* (2001), together with a number of essays on contemporary women's writing.

Andrew Teverson is Lecturer in the School of Humanities at Kingston University, London, UK. He is the author of *Salman Rushdie* (2007), together with a number of essays on contemporary fiction, particularly the work of Rushdie and Vikram Chandra.

Sharon R. Wilson is Professor of English and Women's Studies at the University of Northern Colorado. She is the author of *Margaret Atwood's Fairy-Tale Sexual Politics* (1994) and the editor of *Margaret Atwood's Textual Assassinations: Recent Poetry and Fiction* (2003), the latter of which won the Margaret Atwood Society's Best Book on Atwood's Work award for 2003. She has written numerous essays on a range of aspects of Atwood's fiction, poetry, and criticism.

Index